T0149357

Also by Doug Zipes

Nonfiction
Into Africa
Taking Ban on Ephedra
I Was a Target of the KGB

Fiction
Stolen Hearts (short story with Joan Zipes)
The Black Widows (a novel)
Ripples in Opperman's Pond (a novel)
Not Just a Game (a novel)

Memoir
Damn the Naysayers

Medical Textbooks (coeditor, coauthor)
Comprehensive Cardiac Care (seven editions)
The Slow Inward Current and Cardiac Arrhythmias
Cardiac Electrophysiology and Arrhythmias
Nonpharmacologic Therapy of Tachyarrhythmias
Treatment of Heart Diseases
Catheter Ablation of Cardiac Arrhythmias
Antiarrhythmic Therapy: A Pathophysiologic Approach
Arrhythmias and Sudden Death in Athletes
Electrophysiology of the Thoracic Veins
Sudden Death: A Handbook for Clinical Practice
Heart Disease: A Textbook of Cardiovascular Medicine (seven editions)
Cardiac Electrophysiology: From Cell to Bedside (seven editions)
Clinical Arrhythmology and Electrophysiology (three editions)
Electrocardiography of Arrhythmias (two editions)
Case Studies in Electrophysiology (two editions)

Medical Articles
Almost nine hundred authored/coauthored

BEAR'S PROMISE

DOUG ZIPES

iUniverse®

BEAR'S PROMISE

iUniverse books may be ordered through booksellers or by contacting:

iUniverse
1663 Liberty Drive
Bloomington, IN 47403
www.iuniverse.com
1-800-Authors (1-800-288-4677)

Because of the dynamic nature of the internet, any web addresses or links contained in this book may have changed since publication and may no longer be valid. The views expressed in this work are solely those of the author and do not necessarily reflect the views of the publisher, and the publisher hereby disclaims any responsibility for them.

Any people depicted in stock imagery provided by Getty Images are models, and such images are being used for illustrative purposes only. Certain stock imagery © Getty Images.

ISBN: 978-1-5320-7970-2 (sc)
ISBN: 978-1-5320-7972-6 (hc)
ISBN: 978-1-5320-7971-9 (e)

Library of Congress Control Number: 2019916167

Print information available on the last page.

iUniverse rev. date: 10/21/2019

At his best, man is the noblest of all animals;
separated from law and justice, he is the worst.

—Aristotle

CONTENTS

ACKNOWLEDGMENTS

I am indebted to the following, who read drafts, uncovered errors, and made great suggestions: Clair Lamb; Michael Rosen; Marilyn Wallace; and my children, Debra, Jeffrey, and David. Debra brought psychological and emotional expertise; Jeffrey, legal advice (the court scenes reflect his guidance, except where I deviated because of story flow or personal experiences); and David, a medical perspective. As always, my wife, Joan, did the heavy lifting, at home and for the novel. Her suggestions paved many of the trails I followed. Finally, I thank brave law enforcement men and women who put their lives at risk every day to try and keep us safe.

CHAPTER ONE

As Melanie watched helplessly, Jared, his gaze unfocused and brow wrinkled in confusion, lurched in front of the television set in the small living room. He looked fierce with a broad forehead and thick dark eyebrows and a face sooty with stubble from an unshaved beard. The red-striped golf shirt and jeans were wrinkled as if he'd slept in them. His wide stance blocked the children's view of *Sesame Street*, and they began to whimper. Their soft snivels escalated as their eyes followed his hulking figure staggering about.

Jared's knees bumped their tiny chairs, and his huge shoulders brushed finger paintings masking-taped to the wall. The papers fluttered to the floor like large colorful snowflakes.

He pitched into a wooden bookshelf standing in a corner, sending Dr. Seuss's *The Cat in the Hat, Green Eggs and Ham,* and *One Fish Two Fish Red Fish Blue Fish* tumbling, along with a midmorning snack of milk and chocolate chip cookies.

The four-year-olds ran for Melanie, their cries intensifying. They hugged her legs and buried teary faces in her yellow cotton apron as she dried drippy eyes and gave reassuring squeezes.

She knelt down on the rug to be with the children but kept her eyes fixed on him, worrying what he might do next, where he might walk, what he might bump into and knock over.

Small fingers entwined her hair, which was pulled into a keep-out-of-the-way ponytail. Gray roots had begun to replace the russet tint, like weeds reclaiming a garden. The Clairol bottle of hair coloring was dry, and so was the cash box.

"It'll be okay, children. I'm here." Melanie spread her arms to embrace them. Her eyes darted about the living room as she decided her next move. "I won't let Jared hurt you. He's just a little confused right now. Why don't you go color a pretty picture for me while I help him?"

But they were too frightened to leave her side and whimpered and trembled like lost kittens. She needed to call their mothers to come and get them, but she was afraid to leave them alone. Jared wouldn't harm them intentionally, but he could stumble over their little frames.

Jared returned to the television set and stared at the whimsical *Sesame Street* characters. The portable was perched on a rickety metal cart almost begging for destruction. Melanie had bought the Sony with a donation from a grateful single mom. The mom had switched to a higher-paying job after Melanie had made room in the day care center for her twin four-year-olds. She promised Melanie a microwave next paycheck. Melanie wished she had more angels like her. The day care center needed so many things.

Jared's thick fingers thrummed on the bridge table in the middle of the room, brimming with Lego pieces. The children had spent many hours arranging them into a colorful community of houses, a school, a grocery store, and a school bus full of children.

Melanie wondered if he might take a swing at her. He'd never hit her before—hardly even raised his voice—but in his present confused state, there was no telling. She had to chance it for the children.

She tugged on his arm. "Jared, please leave this room," she said. "You're scaring the children. Let me take you back to bed."

He wrenched free and shoved her away, her 130 pounds no match for his 220. His mouth opened, and his tongue protruded, but no words followed.

"At least let me wipe your face," she said. She stood on her tiptoes and used a paper napkin to mop the rancid white foam trickling from his nose and mouth. It had a foul smell, like vinegar left overnight on the kitchen counter.

He slapped her hand away and stared at her with clouded eyes. "Who're you?" he asked, the words slurred together. "Get outta my way."

"It's me. Your wife, Melanie. Remember?" she said.

No recognition showed on his face.

The morning's three grand mal seizures—one after the other, until he fell unconscious—had robbed him of the ability to think, to remember, to reason, as it had once before, right after they were married. That first time, the postseizure psychotic state had lasted two days and had so frightened him that he'd not missed a single medication dose in the twenty-two years since.

Until two weeks earlier.

That's when he got fired—downsized, the building contractor had told him. Their medical insurance stopped, and they could no longer afford the medication. The forty-five-dollar copays every ninety days had been bad enough, but without the insurance package, there was no way they'd come close to covering the drug cost.

She was now the sole breadwinner, and income from the day care center had to cover all their expenses. She'd pleaded with the pharmacist for more clonazepam, but he would give her only a two-day free sample—six two-milligram tablets that Jared had consumed more than a week ago.

She'd seen one of those pharma ads on TV that said, "If you cannot afford to buy our drug, we're here to help." What a load of garbage. She'd contacted the drug company, but they never responded.

Jared gaped at her, brows creased together in concentration. Then he shrugged and shook his head with a blank look. He elbowed her aside, his momentum making him sway and almost fall. He righted himself and stumbled toward the front door.

She ran after him and grabbed at a sleeve. Bed was the safest place for him, for all of them, until the psychosis wore off. She tried to block his steps, but he pushed her aside and went out.

A late-fall storm raged, and cool westerly September winds drove slanting spray into the room. She had to lean hard against the door to close it. The downpour mixed with hail sounded like muted gunshots on the window. Lightning flashed overhead, followed by a horrific rumbling that sent her scurrying from the door.

Through the window, she watched Jared pause on the porch, then shuffle out into the storm.

With the children safe inside, her fear shifted to Jared. Their small house in Hopperville, just outside Indianapolis, was a stone's throw from a busy four-lane highway where cars raced by, oblivious to the torrents obscuring visibility.

What if he wandered into traffic? He could be killed. She had to stop him.

She dialed 911.

"Ma, who you calling?" Ryan asked, rubbing his eyes as he walked into the room. He was a high school senior, six feet tall, broad shouldered like his dad and muscular from the football team's weight lifting program. Purdue, Notre Dame, and Indiana had offered him football scholarships, and he was in the middle of deciding. The football concussion that had caused his father's seizures didn't dissuade Ryan a bit.

"Helmets are a lot better now," he'd said. "And they have concussion rules."

BEAR'S PROMISE

As an eighteen-year-old, he figured he'd live forever. She remembered the feeling. Life was so simple then. Going to school, going to parties, having parents and an older brother to protect her. Life now seemed so … so heavy, so complicated. She had no idea how she'd deal with Jared's illness. How she'd pay for the medicine he needed to prevent a recurrence.

"I thought you were sleeping," Melanie said. "An upset stomach, you told me. Isn't that why you stayed home from school? Or was it really the physics exam?"

"I'm feeling better. Where's Dad?" Ryan asked.

"Walked outside."

"In this storm? That's crazy."

"The seizures came back," she said. "He's not thinking clearly."

"Want me to go get him?" Ryan asked, heading toward the door.

"No," she said, holding up her hand. "I called the police. They should be here any minute. Go check on the kids. They're upset. Your dad frightened them."

CHAPTER TWO

BEAR'S PROMISE

Shorty took the 911 call and raced to the Simpsons' home with lights flashing and siren screeching. By the time he arrived, the rain had slackened, winds from the west driving away the dark, heavy rain clouds. Lightning was just an impotent sparkle in the east, followed by a muted grumble, and the sun was filtering between feathery white clouds.

He parked in the Simpsons' driveway and stepped out of the patrol car. He inhaled a deep breath. The air hung heavy from the storm but had a rich, earthy fragrance.

The house sat in the middle of a block of cookie-cutter houses. Come home drunk one night, and you could easily wander into your neighbor's bedroom.

Shorty watched the house for any movement. Hopperville cops were well trained in the potential dangers of home calls and domestic disputes. One of their guys took two 9 mm slugs in his chest three years ago blundering into the middle of a family argument. Shorty adjusted his Kevlar vest and radioed his position to the base station.

"Approaching the Simpsons' house. All seems quiet, but better alert backup, just in case."

Shorty was a great believer in "just in case" preparations. He was often the butt of practical jokes and detested his nickname. He spent lots of bucks buying drinks at the Blue Goose for the big, tough guys in the squad, like Sparafucile. They became his just-in-case buddies to return pranks other guys played on him. The squad enjoyed his impotent rage—until a pal like Sparafucile evened the score. No one messed with Chilli—his squad's nickname—unless they wanted a busted jaw.

The house was small, maybe three bedrooms, not much bigger than 1,800 square feet. White stucco with green trim, nicely kept up. Mowed lawn and manicured bushes. A basketball backboard at the end of the driveway was a good sign. But even with kids around, danger was possible.

Mud puddles pooled in the gaps and cracks of the asphalt driveway. Shorty sought dry ground to avoid dirtying his black boots. He'd spent twenty minutes shining them that morning: Kiwi black polish, followed by neutral, and then a spit shine to enhance the luster. He still wasn't used to the thick heels. They made his ankles

7

wobble and his calves ache. He marveled at how women walked about in high heels.

He figured the $300 was well spent if the boots made him look five four instead of five three. He hated being short and was self-conscious about his large head topping such an undersized body. He'd once read a novel about some rich guy his height who said he felt ten feet tall when he stood on his wallet. Shorty's wallet was thinner than a bulimic's ass, so that didn't work for him. What did work was each morning when he put on his Hopperville police uniform. Then he felt ten feet tall. Hell, he *was* ten feet tall.

Hopperville police had a well-earned reputation for being tough. A reporter for the *Hopperville Daily* thought they were too tough and once wrote an article about the Hopper*vile* police.

A couple of weeks later, his house caught fire from a gas leak. Burned right to the ground because the Hopperville Fire Department got lost en route, took a wrong turn, and arrived too late to save it. The reporter never again left out the second *l* in a Hopperville news article.

As Shorty neared the front door, a figure to his left walked toward him across a neighbor's yard. He took his Smith and Wesson baton from its holster in his belt and shook it to its full twenty-one-inch length. This was a neat weapon. It folded nice and tiny but grew to over a foot and a half of tough metal protection when he needed it—Shorty's just-in-case friend.

The guy was dripping wet, hair plastered down, the red-striped golf shirt in tatters, and his jeans mud blotched. His face had a weird expression.

He was barefoot and slogged through murky puddles and spongy grime, eyes wandering, not focused on where he was going. Mud squished between his toes and ran over the tops of his feet as he walked. Shorty wiggled his toes stuffed into his boots, thinking how that must feel.

The front door opened. A woman stepped out, followed by a young boy. She was short and chubby, with a round face, and the kid towered over her. The lady held out her hand, while the boy just stood there.

"I'm so glad you're here, Officer. Thank you for coming. I'm Melanie Simpson, and this is my son, Ryan. That's my husband,

Jared." She pointed at Jared. Shorty turned to look at him. "He's a good man, but he's out of his head after his seizures. I called 911 because I'm afraid he might hurt himself. He won't listen to me. Can you help him?" Melanie held trembling hands prayer-like in front of her face.

She spoke in rapid bursts, Shorty noted, like she was trying to set the stage before the Jared guy reached him.

The guy was a big dude, his size alone intimidating. And that weird look—mouth open, drooling, eyes wandering.

"He needs to go to the hospital emergency room," she said, "so they can give him his seizure medicine. Will you take him there?" Her eyes shifted to Jared as he approached. "I tried to bring him, but he wouldn't get into the car."

"What happened to him?" Shorty asked. His breathing quickened as Jared drew near. He debated drawing his Electric Gun but held off.

"Hey, you. I need you to stop, stay where you are," Shorty said.

Jared kept walking.

"Drugs?" he asked Melanie. Shorty's free hand rested on the handle of his Electric Gun. The other hand gripped the baton.

"Yes, but not that kind. Not street drugs. You see, he ran out of—"

Jared got to Shorty before she finished. He stopped, stood next to Shorty, and looked down. *Must be at least six foot four or five,* Shorty thought. His arms were thick, muscles ropey, but were at his sides, and he made no threatening moves. Still, Shorty's hand tightened around the baton handle.

"Who're you?" Jared asked, his voice calm, questioning.

"Police Officer Chester Devine," Shorty said, squaring his shoulders and standing tall in his new boots. He adjusted the police cap to sit lightly on his head, adding to his height.

"This lady says you need to go to the hospital."

Shorty tapped Jared on the shoulder with the baton as he spoke. That move always established his role as the alpha male. "She wants me to take you there."

"Not going anywhere with you," Jared said. He brushed the tip of the baton off his shoulder, clenched his jaw, and shook his head. Staring at Shorty, he said, "Don't do that again."

"Jared, please listen to the officer," Melanie said. "I asked him to take you to the hospital, so you could get clonazepam. You need that for your seizures."

"Dad, let him take you," the boy added, nodding.

Jared looked at the boy with a quizzical expression that showed a glimmer of recognition. He turned back to Shorty. "Not going anywhere," he repeated.

A dog barked from across the lawn. Jared turned toward the noise. "Sounds like my dog," he said. "Hey, Fresco!" he shouted. "Come here."

"Look, you," Shorty said, "I'm talking to you." He didn't like being ignored, even by somebody a foot taller.

Jared continued to gaze at a distant target.

A blurred movement behind some bushes caught Shorty's eye.

Jared pointed at the spot. "I need to go get him." He started to walk away.

Shorty was getting angry. After all, he was a Hopperville police officer. The guy needed to listen and show some respect if he wanted his help.

"Hey, you," Shorty said. He hit Jared's shoulder twice with the metal baton—not too hard but hard enough to get his attention.

Jared spun on him, yanked the baton from his hand, and smacked him across the face with it.

"I told you not to do that again!" Jared shouted.

Shorty collapsed, screaming, hands holding his bleeding nose. The searing pain blocked rational thought, and tears blurred his vision. On his knees in the wet grass, he groped for the speaker microphone clipped to his shirt.

"Officer down," he radioed. "Repeat. Officer down. Active assailant on premises. Request immediate assistance."

When Shorty's vision cleared, he saw Jared had let the baton fall from his hand and had wandered off in the direction of the dog's bark. The kid ran after his father. Melanie brought ice for Shorty's nose and then chased after her son and husband.

Within minutes, sirens disrupted the quiet neighborhood. Two black Crown Victoria police interceptors screeched to a stop in front of the Simpsons' house. Two cops from each car barreled out and ran toward Shorty, who was sitting on the grass applying ice to his nose, now swollen almost balloon size.

"That big black bastard assaulted me," Shorty yelled, pointing at the neighbor's yard. "For no reason. Name's Jared. Grabbed my baton and hit me with it. Maybe broke my nose." Shorty ran a light finger over his swollen nose. "Then he ran off." In the distance, Shorty could see Jared had collared a black-and-brown dog and was walking back, Melanie tugging one arm, and the kid the other.

"That's him. Over there with his wife, Melanie, and the son, Ryan. Get the bastard and teach him a lesson about attacking a Hopperville police officer."

"We will, Shorty. First, though, are you okay?" Sparafucile asked, bending over Shorty and checking his nose. "You need me to call a doctor?"

"I'll be fine, Chilli. Thanks. Just get that guy."

Sparafucile and two other cops ran after Jared. One stayed with Shorty, took the ice from his hand, and pressed it against his nose.

CHAPTER THREE

BEAR'S PROMISE

"**H**ey, you," Sparafucile shouted at Jared. "I'm Lieutenant Vincenzo Sparafucile, Hopperville police. Put your hands behind your head and get down on your knees." Sparafucile felt the surge of adrenalin that always hit when he faced a potential takedown. He hoped the guy resisted arrest. That made it more fun. His heart began to race, and his breathing quickened as he prepared for a fight.

Sparafucile beckoned to Jose Diaz, one of the patrol officers who had answered the call, and Jim Bennett, a newbie on the force, to block off any escape route.

Bennett, a slim redhead with a crew cut and freckles, looked like a kid, almost as young as Ryan. Diaz—his buddies called him Fisheye—was mostly blind in his left eye from a knife fight as a boy. He always cocked his head left, and it was sometimes hard to know who he was looking at. His left eyelid draped over the pupil as if it were ashamed how it appeared and tried to hide it. Fisheye wore a long ponytail to distract people from looking at his eye. That was against police regulations, but Sparafucile let it go, along with his gold earring.

Jared stopped walking and gawked at Sparafucile and the other two cops. The dog, a Doberman-Rottweiler mix, growled and yanked at its collar, struggling to break free. Sparafucile liked dogs, usually more than people. But if that mutt broke loose and came at him, he swore he'd strangle him with his bare hands.

Sparafucile studied Jared. Chilli was big, though not quite as tall as Jared. His size made him the squad's enforcer. Sparafucile's muscular chest threatened to pop his shirt buttons, and his large neck required an open collar and loosely knotted necktie. Chestnut-brown hair and squinty hazel eyes along with a bearded stubble created a perpetual dark scowl that intimidated those who disagreed with him. *You either agree with me or you don't understand* was Chilli's mantra, and he was more than happy to enlighten you. If fact, he *liked* clearing up any confusion a person might have.

"Now, goddammit!" Sparafucile yelled, pointing his Electric Gun at Jared. The laser dot from the gun bounced off Jared's chest.

Jared wrinkled his brow and tried to brush the dot away, like a bug on his chest. Then he struggled to pick it up between his thumb and forefinger. When that failed, he eyed the cops surrounding him. Jared's dripping, dark eyebrows looked like wet, hairy caterpillars crawling across his forehead. They arched, his eyes opened wide, and he looked confused. Or crazy. Sparafucile couldn't tell which. Jared's hands, black hairs sprouting from the backs of his fingers, opened and closed into fists.

"Who're you? Leave me alone," Jared said in an unsteady voice. He loosened his hold on the dog's collar. The dog jerked its head and broke free, then barked once and ran off, tail between its legs.

"Lady, and you, kid, step away from him," Sparafucile ordered, waving his gun at the pair flanking Jared, each holding onto an arm. "You might get electrocuted."

Melanie moved from Jared's side to stand in front of him, her jaw set. She leaned back against his chest, her head just beneath his chin. Her shaking hands gripped the sides of his pants, steadying herself. The laser beam bounced off her breasts.

"Please," she said. "He's hasn't done anything wrong. He just needs his medicine—for his seizures. Leave him alone. I'm sorry I called you."

"Nothing wrong? Are you crazy, lady?" Sparafucile shouted. "He assaulted one of my cops!" Sparafucile pointed to Shorty sitting on the grass with a bloody rag on his nose.

"That cop started it," Ryan said, also pointing at Shorty. "He hit my dad with his baton." Ryan glared at Sparafucile, his jaw clenched and face red.

"Shut your mouth, kid," Sparafucile ordered, "or you're next." He waved the Electric Gun at him. Ryan took a step back when the laser dot hit his chest.

"My husband's confused," Melanie said, bracing against Jared. "He's not thinking clearly. You need to take him to the hospital for his seizures. He's a gentle man."

"Gentle, bullshit," Sparafucile hollered. "My guy's got a busted face from your fucking gentle man. I don't give two shits about his seizures. That's his problem, not mine. I'm cuffing him to take him to jail for assaulting a uniformed Hopperville police officer. Now, step aside or I'll take you in too. And don't think I won't fry your little titties with this." He waved the Electric Gun at her.

The cops moved in on Jared, closing the circle around him. Sparafucile watched Jared's pupils dart from one officer to the other and his jaw quiver. Sweat broke out on Jared's forehead. He turned to face the nearest cop and yelled, "Keep away from me!" He pushed Melanie aside and bunched his fists.

She slipped and fell in the wet grass. Sparafucile squeezed the trigger.

The metal probes from the Electric Gun flew at Jared and struck him in the left chest. They pierced his thin shirt and embedded deep in his skin. One hit just beneath his left collarbone, and the other lodged six or eight inches below that, in his lower rib cage. With a tiny spine on the side like a fishhook, the probes dug deep into his skin and stayed securely in place.

Jared stiffened as fifty-five thousand volts of electricity surged over the wires that connected the probes to Sparafucile's gun and tore through his body. The five-second burst left Jared flailing like a caught flounder, mute but standing. He looked around, a bewildered expression on his face. He swatted at the air in front of him, trying to find the source of his pain.

"Stop! Leave me alone!" Jared screamed at Sparafucile. "That hurt. Don't do it again."

Predictable, Sparafucile thought. *One second, a takedown's giving you a nose bleed; the next, he's begging for mercy.*

Ryan, eyes bulging, his face contorted by rage, ran at Sparafucile, shouting, "You son of a bitch, leave my dad alone!"

Diaz sprang to life and tackled Ryan. Bennett helped and jumped on Ryan's back. The two quickly cuffed Ryan's wrists behind his back. They raised the boy, and each held an arm.

"Fisheye, shoot the kid!" Sparafucile yelled.

Fisheye didn't move. Sparafucile shouted again, "Shoot him now, goddammit."

"He's cuffed and under control, Chilli," Fisheye said, shaking his head while one hand gripped the boy's handcuffs, the other his arm. "No need. Jim's got hold of his other arm."

"I don't give a shit," Sparafucile shouted. "I said shoot him. That's an order."

"But he's—"

"Just fucking do it, for Christ's sake! You deaf as well as blind?"

"Yes, sir, Chilli." Fisheye unholstered his Electric Gun, pointed it at Ryan's back, and pulled the trigger.

The probes hit Ryan hard, from less than two feet away. He shrieked, stiffened rigid as a steel pole, and pitched forward into the dirt like a toppled statue.

"Nobody calls me a son of a bitch, kid. Remember that," Sparafucile said.

Jared lunged.

Sparafucile pulled the trigger of his Electric Gun a second time. The current seared across Jared's chest, and he fell onto his knees. This time, Sparafucile overrode the five-second safety stop, and the electricity continued passing through Jared's chest. From the training videos, Sparafucile knew the electric current arced from one barb to the other to complete the electrical circuit, scorching everything in its path.

On his knees, Jared looked up at Sparafucile and twisted his lips to say something. Sparafucile could barely make it out, but it sounded like, "Please stop the hurting."

Jared reached a trembling hand toward Sparafucile, fingers twitching, his face grimaced in pain. Sparafucile kept his finger on the trigger. Jared grabbed at Sparafucile's pants leg, fell forward, and remained on his hands and knees for several seconds. When Sparafucile still buzzed him, Jared collapsed in the mud, hands folded beneath his chest. His legs jerked twice, and he stopped moving.

Sparafucile released the trigger on the Electric Gun. *Not a bad hit,* he thought. *At least thirty seconds.* Later, he'd download the gun's memory chip to see exactly how long he had shocked him.

"Serves you right for striking a cop, you black bastard. Now, put your hands behind your back," Sparafucile ordered, "or you'll get more of the same."

Sparafucile toed him with his foot, but Jared didn't move. "Do it now," he said, "or so help me God, I'll give you another jolt."

Jared still didn't move.

"He's faking it," Fisheye yelled. "Hit him again, Chilli."

"Stop!" Melanie screamed. "You're killing him." She fought the officer holding her arms but couldn't break loose.

Sparafucile squeezed the trigger again. But this time, he showed mercy and delivered only a five-second burst.

Jared didn't budge.

"Cuff him," Sparafucile ordered. "The chickenshit's got no fight left."

Bennett approached Jared, pulled his hands out from under his body, and cuffed his wrists behind his back. He rolled him over and sat him up.

Jared's head hung forward, chin on his chest, pupils turned back in his head, only the whites showing like half-moons in a dark face. When Bennett let him go, Jared collapsed against Bennett's legs behind him. He looked like a puppet with its strings cut.

Jared's breathing came in shuddering, harsh gasps. His legs straightened, and his arms tensed against the cuffs in a repetitive jerking motion.

"See? He's faking it, Chilli," Fisheye said, "trying to break out of the cuffs. I'll show you."

Fisheye disconnected his Electric Gun from the wires still attached to Ryan, bent over Jared, and pressed the tip of his gun against Jared's shoulder. He pulled the trigger, and the five-second electric shock burned a hole in Jared's shirt and skin as the current penetrated his body. The smell of seared flesh rose in a wisp of smoke from the gun's tip.

Jared didn't move.

"Hmm," said Fisheye, "guess he's not faking."

Melanie finally broke free and ran to Jared. She knelt beside him and cradled his head in her arms. "He's not breathing!" she shrieked. "You killed him. You killed my husband."

"Wrong, lady," Sparafucile said. "The Electric Gun can't kill. It shoots electricity, not bullets. Maybe he hit his head when he fell. He'll come to after a while. Your kid didn't die, did he? He got the same electricity."

Still holding Jared, she looked at the boy. "Ryan, are you okay?"

Ryan staggered to his feet, a cop on each arm. Fisheye yanked the probes from his back. "Ow! That hurts!" he yelled.

Melanie turned back to Jared and gently stroked his cheeks.

"Jared, talk to me. Wake up, Jared. Open your eyes. Please talk to me. I love you." Jared didn't respond. When she let go of his head, it fell sideways and then rotated forward, chin on chest, mouth gaping open.

She began to sob, rocking Jared back and forth. "You killed him. He's dead. You killed my husband!"

Ryan, regaining body control, fought Fisheye, but he had a tight grip on his handcuffs, and Ryan couldn't break loose.

"Lemme go, you son of a bitch," he yelled. "You murdered my dad. Lemme go!"

Bennett leaned close and searched Jared's face. "I think he's turning blue, Lieutenant. Maybe he's not breathing."

"You think so?" Sparafucile kneeled and looked at Jared's face. "Doubt it, but uncuff him and lay him down so I can check for a pulse to be sure."

Sparafucile grabbed Jared's right wrist. "He's got a faint pulse," he said. He pressed two fingers against his neck. "Yeah, here also, a faint pulse. And I think I saw his chest move, so he's breathing. But remember the first rule of being a cop, Bennett. ACYA—always cover your ass. They teach you that in the academy? Better call for EMS to be on the safe side."

Three cops carried Jared to his porch, a small wooden deck in front of the house, and laid him on a canvas beach lounge. Fisheye cuffed Ryan to an iron railing at the other end of the porch to keep him out of the way. The kid heaved against the restraint, but the railing held.

They waited for the emergency medical services to arrive. Sparafucile lit a cigarette, one of the four he allowed himself each day, and sat on the porch steps, his feet outstretched. The air had cooled, and it was pleasant after the storm. He loved that musty smell when the rain backed off. It was a perfect late-summer afternoon.

He checked on Shorty. "You okay, buddy? No trouble breathing through your nose? We can have the emergency guys take a look at you when they get here."

"Na, I'll live, Chilli. But thanks for asking."

"Wish I had a beer," Sparafucile said. "A smoke goes best with a cold Bud."

He always felt relaxed after an encounter with bad guys. The adrenalin high of the moment, followed by the calm afterward when the adrenalin tapered, made being a cop the best job in the world.

CHAPTER FOUR

Melanie's frantic moves spoiled Sparafucile's peaceful mood. She raced in and out of the house, tending to the children and trying to revive Jared with a wet cloth to sponge his face. Unnoticed tears ran down her cheeks.

"Call 911," Ryan shouted when she came out.

Melanie glanced at him. "And get more cops here? It's the last thing we need. That's what started this in the first place."

They heard sirens in the distance. Moments later, an ambulance rolled up. Two emergency medical technicians hopped out and ran to the porch. The first EMT carried a small black suitcase, and the other, a defibrillator. Sparafucile briefed them as they performed a quick examination. "A simple takedown," he said, eyebrows raised. "Couple of shots with the Electric Gun. No big deal."

"Nonresponsive, no pulse or respirations, pupils dilated and nonreactive," the first EMT said. "Glasgow Coma Scale 5."

"What's that?" Sparafucile asked.

"Bad," the EMT said, his face grim.

Sparafucile watched them move Jared to the floor. The first EMT dropped to his knees alongside to begin cardiac massage, and the other one ripped open Jared's shirt. He released the top of the defibrillator, tore the paper backing off two circular patches, and stuck them on Jared's chest, one top right and the other lower left.

Melanie hovered over them. "Will he be okay? Can you save him?" she cried.

"I don't know, ma'am. I know you're concerned, but could you please stand out of the way so we can do our job? We need some room here."

Ryan pulled at his handcuffs. "The cops did it. That fucker Sparafucile shot my dad."

The machine analyzed Jared's heart rhythm. "Ventricular fibrillation. Deliver a shock."

The first EMT pushed a red button, and Jared's body lurched as the defibrillator sent a jolt of electricity over the patches.

The machine recycled. "Analyzing rhythm," came the message. "Asystole. Do not shock. Perform chest compressions."

"What's that mean?" Sparafucile asked.

"The shock stopped the ventricular fibrillation," the EMT said as he resumed cardiac massage, "but now there's no heartbeat. Start an

IV," he said to the other EMT, "and give one milligram of epinephrine. Maybe it'll get his heart beating."

"Oh my God," Melanie moaned, collapsing to her knees. "Please save my husband."

The EMT opened the black bag that contained medicines and equipment. He inserted an IV into a vein in Jared's neck and infused the medicine. He recycled the defibrillator to reanalyze the ECG. "Asystole. Do not shock," the computer replied. "Perform chest compressions."

"In three minutes, try another dose of epinephrine." The EMT shook his head. "But I doubt it'll do any good. I think he's been in VF too long."

"Sodium bicarb?" the EMT asked.

"Try it. He's probably acidotic. Can't hurt." The first EMT continued to push on Jared's chest. He looked at the cops standing around watching the resuscitation. "None of you performed CPR, did you?" he asked, more accusatory than questioning.

They all turned to Sparafucile. He took a last drag on his cigarette and flicked the butt into the lawn. It landed with a shower of sparks and extinguished in the wet grass. He shook his head. "No. The guy was unconscious. I felt a pulse, and he was breathing. No need to do CPR."

"When was that?" the EMT asked.

"A while ago. Before you came. That's when I called for you guys, just to be sure."

"Feeling a pulse is often misleading," the first EMT muttered between chest compressions. "You end up sensing your own pulse in the tip of your finger."

"I know I felt a pulse," Sparafucile said, "at his wrist and in his neck. And he was still breathing." He'd be damned if they were going to hang this one on him.

"Maybe," the EMT said, "but I doubt it. More likely agonal gasps as he was dying."

"He fought to get out of his cuffs," Fisheye said, "so he wasn't totally unconscious. Pulled on the cuffs and kicked his feet."

"Hmm," murmured the EMT. "That could've been a seizure from lack of blood to his brain. Didn't you think he might've had cardiac arrest from the Electric Gun when he didn't respond? You carry a defibrillator in your squad car. You could've resuscitated him."

"Yeah, but the Electric Gun is safe," Sparafucile said, with a wave of his hand. "Can't kill. I can show you the manual. The instructor told us it was nonlethal."

"Screw the manual," the EMT said while he pushed down on Jared's chest. "You were taught wrong. Electricity from the gun can enter the heart, trigger ventricular fibrillation, and kill. I bet that's what happened here."

"He most likely hit his head," Sparafucile said. He hated these EMTs. They couldn't resuscitate the guy, so they were dancing to their own ACYA music.

"Doubtful. We'll try to resuscitate him for another five minutes," Aarons grunted as he continued to push. "Give another dose of epinephrine, then load him into the ambulance for University of Indiana Medical Center. But I think he's gone."

"No, no!" Melanie shouted, eyes red and mouth twisted in alarm. She ran at Sparafucile, her fists pummeling his chest. "I called you to help him, not kill him!"

Ryan pulled at his cuffs. "Let me loose, you sons of bitches. Let me loose. You killed my dad!" He broke down, hiding his face with his uncuffed arm. "You killed him … you fucking killed him."

CHAPTER FIVE

Melanie flailed at Sparafucile, her tiny fists pummeling his big chest until she ran out of steam. He just stood there, a bemused expression on his face, letting her hit him. Exhausted after several moments, she fell back into a chair on the porch to catch her breath.

The emergency medical technicians loaded Jared's body into the ambulance. One stayed in the back of the ambulance with Jared, and the other drove. They sped off.

Melanie roused and called a neighbor to watch the children until their mothers came. The cops uncuffed Ryan, and he and Melanie jumped into the family car, a late-model white Honda Civic, and raced after the ambulance.

Melanie could barely keep the car on the road, driving so fast with tears nearly blinding her. All she could think about was that Jared was in that ambulance up ahead, maybe dying or already dead. She was terrified for him … and for herself. What would she do if he died? How could she live without him? What would happen to Ryan? She'd asked the police for help and got hell instead.

She cut across several side streets and caught up with the ambulance as it turned into the hospital emergency entrance.

She parked, and they jumped out of the car. She told Ryan to go to the waiting room, she would join him soon. He protested, but she was in no mood to argue. "I'm going to be with your father. You're going to wait for me. Now do it!"

She pushed into the crowded cubicle in the emergency room and remained in the back, out of the way, hugging the wall. She watched them hook Jared to an ECG machine that recorded his heartbeat, a blood pressure cuff, and an oxygen monitor. They inserted a breathing tube and continued the chest compressions.

She prayed to God and promised she'd go to church every Sunday for the rest of her life if He would let Jared live. She didn't know if God was listening or if there even was a God, but Jared had been without a heartbeat a long time. He needed some sort of miracle.

After ten minutes, she heard the ER doctor in charge say, "Try another bolus of epinephrine. If that doesn't start his heart, we may have to quit. He may be brain dead by now."

"Yes, Dr. Bashir," a nurse said.

She gasped and was about to protest, but Bashir followed it with, "Keep going for now. I've seen some miraculous recoveries—people who seemed brain dead and then fully recovered. We don't want to stop prematurely."

The ER nurse followed Bashir's orders. Moments later, she said, "We have a heartbeat," surprise in her voice. She made the sign of the cross and looked skyward.

Maybe there was a God after all, Melanie thought, and maybe He was listening.

Melanie turned to the ECG screen. Jared's heart had started beating again. Slowly at first, it picked up speed and was soon racing at one hundred beats per minute. "Thank you, dear God," Melanie said under her breath. "Thank you, thank you."

"Blood pressure?" Bashir asked.

"Fifty over twenty," the nurse replied.

"Start a Levophed drip," Bashir said.

"Yes, Doctor," the nurse said, "already preparing it." Several minutes later, she said, "One-ten over seventy and holding."

"Keep the Levophed going for the next hour and then wean it. Too much will damage his heart and kidneys. The big question is whether we've resuscitated a vegetable."

"Yes, Doctor."

"Insert a Foley catheter to follow urinary output. Cool him to thirty-four degrees for the next forty-eight hours to preserve any brain function left."

"Yes, sir."

Melanie slipped out and walked to the waiting room. Ryan was pacing up and down. "He's got a heartbeat," she said, "so there's hope."

Ryan hugged her. "I prayed, Mom. I prayed for Dad. I love him."

"Me too, Ryan. Maybe our prayers did something."

A few minutes later, Bashir entered the lounge with another doctor. "I'm Dr. Mohammad Bashir," he said. "I'm in charge of the emergency room."

He met her gaze with a grim smile.

"I'm so sorry this happened," he said. "I don't want to give you false hope, but we've restored a heartbeat."

She smiled at Ryan and gave him an "I told you so" look. He waved a V of index and middle fingers. But his victory signal didn't reassure her. She was still fearful. Bashir's comment about resuscitating a vegetable frightened her. What would she do if that happened? She'd read about people being comatose for long periods of time. How could she handle it? How could she pay for it?

"This is Dr. Greg Dumont." Bashir indicated the man standing next to him. "He's a heart rhythm expert. I've asked him to take over the care of your husband from here on."

Melanie and Ryan shook hands with Dr. Dumont. He was tall and slim. Streaks of gray laced his blond hair and full beard. Dr. Dumont had kindly blue eyes and a smile to match.

"Any questions for me before I leave?" Bashir asked.

When they didn't respond, he said, "Okay, then, I'll bow out of the picture. I wish you the very best and hope for your husband's recovery." He turned and left.

Dumont chose his words carefully. "Hope for loved ones is critical, but I need to convey optimism mixed with reality."

"What's that mean?" Melanie asked, alarmed. After all, Jared had a heartbeat. Their prayers had been answered. She watched Dumont's eyes. They were the passport to his inner thoughts. Was he telling the truth? Could she trust him? She decided, *Yes, he's an honest man, a straight shooter. He cares.*

Dumont paused. He sat down on the edge of a couch covered in tan leatherette and patted the space beside him. Melanie sat down.

"He has a heartbeat, right?" She fidgeted on the couch and silently thanked God again. "Will he live?" she asked, fixated on Dumont's eyes as he answered.

"Maybe," Dumont said. "I need to be as honest with you as I can. I'd give him a 10 to 20 percent chance—maybe less, not more. After the shooting with the Electric Gun, he developed a lethal heart rhythm called ventricular fibrillation. VF's over four hundred beats per minute, so the heart has no time to pump blood to his body. The brain begins to die after several minutes. That's the major problem."

"The cops did it," Ryan interrupted. He was pacing wildly up and down. A few strides carried him from one end to the other in the small waiting room. He repeatedly drove one fist into the palm of his other hand. The *smack* reverberated in the small room.

"That Sparafucile killed him with the Electric Gun. One of the cops shot me in the back. That was the worst pain I've ever felt. Like holding your finger in an electric socket. How come I didn't die?" His face was suffused with anger, and Melanie could only imagine what he'd like to do to Sparafucile.

"Because you were not shot over your heart like your dad," Dumont said.

Ryan started pacing again.

"According to the report, when the EMTs got there, they found Jared in VF and shocked his heart. They stopped the VF, but then Jared had asystole," Dumont said. "They did cardiac massage until they got to the hospital. We started his heart beating, but the big issue will be how much neurologic recovery he'll have—will his brain get better. It could be he'll remain in a vegetative state, but then again, some people recover after a prolonged cardiac arrest like this. Only time will tell. But the odds are not good."

"What if his heart had been shocked sooner?" Melanie asked.

"The VF would've been stopped without brain damage," Dumont said with a slight smile. "His heart would've started up on its own after the shock. Chances of survival would've been better than 50 percent—even 60 or 70 percent, depending on how quickly they stopped the VF."

"One of the EMTs said the cops had a machine in their car that could've done it," Ryan said. He stopped pacing in front of them. "I heard the cops say so. But they didn't use it."

"Yes, they did have one. In fact, when they first bought it, they asked me to teach them how to use it. It's called an AED, automated external defibrillator. The same thing you see hanging on the wall in many airports and public places."

"Why didn't they use it?" Ryan slammed a fist against the wall.

"Easy, son," Dumont cautioned. "No histrionics here. They didn't use it because they didn't know he was in VF."

"They caused the fibrillation with that damn Electric Gun, and then didn't try to stop it," Ryan said. "They just stood around and let him die." He raised his hand to strike the wall again, but a look from his mother stopped him.

"I can't address that," Dumont said, "because I don't have all the facts. And remember, your dad's not dead yet. I'm sure Sparafucile would've tried the AED if he thought VF was present. He may be a tough cop, but I doubt he's going to let someone die that he could save."

"Maybe," Ryan said, "but you'd never know it. He didn't even try CPR, just loafed around smoking a damn cigarette and wishing he had a beer. My dad deserved better."

"Once we're sure your dad's heart and blood pressure are stable, we'll let you in to see him," Dumont said. "Then we'll move him to the coronary care unit."

Twenty minutes later, a nurse with a pleasant smile led them into the emergency room. The bustle had quieted, and Jared lay still, his face distorted by a breathing tube taped in his nose. The sheet and blanket covering him were a spotless white. A white bandage protected an IV in his neck, into which a pale, yellow liquid dripped. Melanie prayed his brain and heart looked as good inside as he did outside.

"Can he hear me?" she asked the nurse.

The nurse shrugged. "I honestly don't know."

"Can I give him a kiss?" she asked. "Or will I upset some of this medical stuff?" A bank of machines beeping, hissing, and whooshing surrounded Jared.

"Nothing you can do will hurt anything. Go right ahead," the nurse replied, patting her shoulder. "Maybe he'll respond to you."

Melanie leaned over the bed's railing and lightly pecked Jared's cold lips. She prayed he could hear her when she whispered in his ear, "I love you, Jared. I'm so sorry this happened. It was my fault, trying to protect you. I shouldn't have called 911. I was afraid you'd wander onto the highway." She wiped tears trickling down her cheeks as they dripped onto Jared's face.

"Please get better so I can make this up to you. I can't live with this guilt the rest of my life. I need you to forgive me," she cried.

She rose and thought about the last few weeks. It'd been rough since he got fired. They'd argued for several days, and she'd said things she wished she could take back. She'd planned an apology today, but then he'd had his seizures.

BEAR'S PROMISE

She was going to cook a gourmet dinner tonight and afterward send Ryan to a friend's house. She'd put on a lacy pink-and-white, see-through negligée she'd splurged on at Victoria's Secret and planned to just walk into the kitchen wearing that, give him a big kiss, and tell him she understood the pain he was going through and was sorry she'd added to it.

Knowing she might never get the chance to apologize and be forgiven was tearing her apart. She felt a pain in her chest. This was what a broken heart felt like.

Ryan stood behind her and put his hand on her shoulder. "It's okay, Mom," he said. "You didn't know what was going to happen. It's not your fault. It's that damn Sparafucile. He did it. He shot Dad, and he's going to pay for it. I promise you that."

She turned and collapsed into Ryan's arms, sobbing. "I'm so sorry, Ryan … so very sorry."

They stayed in the hospital until visiting hours were over. She had her arm hooked through Ryan's as they walked to the car. The night was cool after the storm earlier in the day. Moonlight reflected off puddles in the parking lot, creating a ghostly shimmering of light. A brisk breeze ruffled the trees, and late-autumn leaves floated to the pavement.

Later that evening, she phoned Bear. Her brother's real name was Jason Judge, but nobody called him that. Bear was the managing partner of Judge, Williams, and Hamden, a large law firm on Sixth Avenue in New York City. She'd once visited and was overwhelmed by its size. They occupied three floors of the fifty-five-story building. Their website boasted they were unafraid to challenge anyone on behalf of "ordinary citizens who have been hurt" by big business or law enforcement agencies.

Helping others was important to her brother. After law school, the FBI had recruited him to be a field agent, but something happened, and he quit after a few years to start his own law firm. He said he could help more people with words than with a badge and never talked about why he quit. She knew that whatever made him leave the FBI had to have been monumental since he loved the agency, but when she tried to get him to open up about it, Bear just clamped down. It was his private pain.

After Jared lost his job, she'd called Bear for a loan. He never asked what for, just how much. But when the $5,000 check arrived, Jared tore it up. "We've always stood on our own two feet," he said, "and we'll continue to do so. I'll find another job."

None of this would have happened had Jared accepted her brother's check. Perhaps being African American made him even more fiercely independent and determined he could and would solve his family's problems without any help from others.

CHAPTER SIX

"Hello." I answered the phone on its first ring, though it was near midnight.

My wife, Kat, and I have a thing about phones. She picks up on the last ring after checking the readout to see who's calling and deciding whether she wants to answer at all. Sometimes she's too late, and the call rolls to voice mail. I always answer—and on the first ring if I'm close enough. I don't want to miss anyone or anything important, and the readout's not always helpful.

"Bear? Hi. It's me, Mellie."

"Mellie! What a surprise. It's not even my birthday or Christmas."

Her tone set off an alarm. Little things upset Mellie, and I often needed to provide Psych 101 support to help her through a mini crisis. A misplaced credit card could trigger an emotional meltdown. But this seemed different.

"I need to talk to you."

"What's going on?" I asked, concerned.

Melanie wept on the phone. "I need help."

This was no misplaced credit card.

"They almost killed him, Bear. They might still."

"Who?"

"The cops. They shot him with the Electric Gun." Melanie explained what'd happened.

"Oh my God. I'm so, so sorry for Jared. And for you and Ryan," I said. "How awful. Is he going to pull through?"

"I don't know," Melanie said, her voice quivering. "His heart's beating, but he may have severe brain damage. The doctors said if he doesn't respond in the next twenty-four hours, they're going to do some sort of a brainwave test. An EEG. And if that doesn't show brain activity, they'll want me to consider stopping his medications and turning off the respirator. If I do that, he'll die, and if I don't do that, maybe he'll live but be a vegetable. Oh, Bear, I don't know what to do. Can you come out? I need you."

"Of course. Hold on just a minute." I opened my computer and checked my schedule. I was between trials. Just meetings and nothing I couldn't reschedule.

"Mellie, I'll check flights and get the first one out. Will you be okay until then?"

I heard a sob. "Yes, but hurry. Text me the flight, and I'll meet you at the airport."

I held the phone, thinking about the agony she had to be going through.

Katherine looked up from her crossword puzzle. "Trouble?" she asked. "Anything I can do?"

Kat and Mellie were fond of each other, but the two were very different, physically and emotionally. Mellie was pleasantly plump—*maternal*, Kat good-naturedly labeled her. Kat was a couple of inches shorter than I, kept her weight at 115 through strict diet control and exercise, had facials and manicures every other week, and had her blonde hair colored monthly.

Kat was strong. She survived alcoholic parents and their rocky marriage that had ended in divorce when she was a teenager. When she lived with her folks, she regularly attended Al-Anon group meetings with them, afraid she'd inherited their genes. Since we'd been married, I'd never seen her drink more than a single glass of red wine at dinner.

She'd been a queen at a Dartmouth College Winter Carnival weekend when I fell in love with her radiant blue eyes. They seemed to take in life's adventures in broad swaths of color and action, and I was mesmerized. It was a thrill to walk into a room as her date and watch all heads swivel toward us. It was an even greater thrill after we were married to know what every man in the room was thinking as they stared at her.

She modeled for a few years after we married. When I needed a paralegal during the firm's early days, Kat gave up her career and pitched in long hours, learning the trade and then working at it for five years until I could afford her replacement. It was a tough decision, but I never heard her complain, not one word of regret or resentment. Now, I gladly paid for her body work and enjoyed the benefits of living with this beautiful lady.

Those early years were the best. Over the last five, our marriage had drifted onto thin ice. We had no children—her choice. We loved each other, but we'd been traveling different paths and had grown apart. I spent too much time working, and Kat spent too much time shopping. We were no longer important to each other or a meaningful part of each other's lives. We didn't talk about it because that would bring it out into the open and require some sort of resolution, but we both recognized it.

She repeated her question about Mellie needing help. I told her what'd happened. "Oh my God. That poor woman," she said, blinking back tears. "What can I do?"

Growing up, Mellie was never strong emotionally. I was three years older and became a parent surrogate. We'd been raised on a farm just south of Bloomington. Nashville, Indiana, was a tiny town that abutted Brown County State Park. Grampa Judge had cleared one hundred fifty acres seventy-five years ago and farmed corn, soybeans, and milk cows. My father ran the farm when both grandparents passed, and Mellie and I grew up there, helping out as soon as we could walk.

I milked cows when I was six, drove a tractor at eight, and hunted squirrels, pheasants, wild turkey, and deer at nine. Mellie wasn't much for the outdoors. She'd do her chores, then hide in her room with her head buried in a book. I often covered for her, milking or mucking out the stalls. Sometimes she'd get angry at me for staying so calm when she'd get upset over every little thing and I'd just shrug it off.

I earned the nickname Bear when I was ten.

One summer, a poacher shot and killed a female black bear, leaving a cub just a month or two old. I'd been in the woods hunting dinner when I heard her crying, wandering about looking for her mother. I picked up the little fur ball and wrapped her in my jacket to take home. As I did, she stopped crying and nuzzled against my neck, and I fell in love with two pounds of black fuzz by the time I got home. I was thrilled that this little wild animal accepted me as her mother.

My dad let me keep her in my room. I named her Snooky and fed her a bottle of milk every four hours throughout the summer. I kept her clean and diapered, and she slept with me, curled up on my pillow. I'd wake with her face pressed on mine, making little purring sounds and dribbling down my neck.

Snooky was not a picky eater. She soon graduated to field grasses, roots, nuts, berries, and red meat. She'd do anything for a lick of honey, and I taught her to flail her paws and snarl real mean. She'd also come running when she heard my voice, expecting a treat. I'd stroke her muzzle and scratch behind her ears, just like she was a dog. She loved it.

When I left for school that fall, she was about six months old and weighed as much as I did, close to one hundred pounds. I'd built a big metal cage, and she'd nap in it until I got home. Then I'd take her for a walk with a collar and chain. Snooky pulled at her chain, and we'd end up wrestling in the field. Or she pulled me to a stream she liked about a mile from the house, where we'd swim together.

As she grew older and tipped the scales at two hundred plus, the wrestling became pretty one-sided. Grandpa and my dad were big guys, well over six feet, and I was slated to be that way as well, but Snooky was overpowering. Sometimes she'd roll on her back with me on top of her, and other times she'd just lie with her head and paw across my chest, pinning me to the ground. She'd make fearsome noises—a cross between a growl and a pulsating moan—open her jaws, and drool on me. It was all great fun.

When she got too rough—tossing me around like a rag doll—I got her to quit most times by holding up my hand like a traffic cop and saying, "Snooky, stop!"

At about two or two and a half, Snooky heeded nature's call and left us for the woods in the park. I worried she might not survive after living with me practically since she was born, but I'd taken her into the woods enough times that she did fine. Instinctively, she knew what to eat and where to go. Periodically, when I'd be hunting near the stream, I'd shout, and she'd track me down. We'd have our play wrestling match. By this time, she weighed over five hundred pounds and was an awesome animal with huge teeth and six-inch, curved claws.

Still, she was gentle with me. She'd barrel out of the woods, stop short, rear up on her hind legs, paw the air, and roar, just like I taught her. Despite knowing she was all show, I had to muster a lot of courage not to run. I'd grab a handful of fur, and we'd tumble in the grass or water. She'd eventually get bored and amble off into the woods. I might not see her again for six months or a year. I'd find her distinctive claw marks—she had one nail on her right paw that deviated at a sharp angle—on the bark of birch trees near the stream, so I knew she remained nearby and probably hibernated in one of the local caves.

The last time I saw her was several years after I finished IU Law School. My dad and I had been duck hunting, and I spotted Snooky in the distance. She had three cubs with her and rose to her hind legs, looking at us from a safe distance, maternal instincts outweighing friendship. I felt emotionally conflicted: sad for me but glad for her. But when I thought about the role I played helping return this magnificent animal to the wild, seeing her become a mother, my sadness lifted, and I felt good inside.

Mellie and I both attended Indiana University in Bloomington, just a few miles away. That's where she'd met Jared. He'd been an outstanding left tackle, but his grades were mediocre. When their relationship turned serious, our parents objected that he wouldn't amount to much. But that wasn't the real reason. He was a good man, loved her to pieces, and would always be there for her. Plus, he was a lot smarter than his grades showed; he was just busy with football.

Our parents' real objection was because he was African American. How could their little white princess marry a black man? Finally—with lots of encouragement from me—she mustered enough courage to stand up to our parents, and they eloped during their senior year at Indiana University. I'd just graduated IU Law School and passed the bar, so I married them myself as an appointed judge pro tem.

My parents were angry at both of us, but they got over it when Ryan was born. Eventually, Mom and Dad retired from farming, though they still lived in the house in which we grew up. They leased the land to neighbors, who did the actual farming, and hired a live-in woman named Hattie to help with household chores.

Kat interrupted my musing. "I can't imagine having to make the decision to turn off a respirator that's keeping alive someone you dearly love, knowing that will kill him. How on earth can you do that?"

"I agree," I said, "but if there's no brain activity, he's basically dead already, and the machines are just keeping a shell alive. What's the point?"

"But do you really know that?" she asked. "Just because he's not responding, does that mean he's not hearing you or feeling your presence or still loving you? What about people who recover from a coma and remember a spouse talking to them when they were comatose?"

"They probably still had brain function during the comatose state," I said. "But if the brain scans show no activity—a flat line— his chances of mental recovery are essentially zero, even if his body survives."

"Hmm. I guess not turning off the machines is almost as bad if he survived as a vegetable." She shuddered. "What an awful position for a wife to be in. Poor Mellie."

I landed at the Indianapolis International Airport at eleven o'clock the next morning. The sky was cloudy and leaden, looking like it was preparing for a downpour or maybe getting ready for winter. The image triggered memories of winter's bleakness in the Midwest, with pewter-gray skies that seemed to last forever.

Melanie was waiting for me at the baggage claim. We hugged, and I held her a long time, not saying anything, just trying to transfer my emotional strength through close physical contact.

We walked toward the Delta baggage section holding hands. The plane had been full, and people jostled to get close to the revolving carousel to grab their bags.

"How's Jared? Any change?" I asked as I hauled mine off the belt. I looked at her with a hopeful expression that faded with her response.

"No," Mellie said, eyes glistening. "They're doing a brain wave test this morning." She checked her watch. "Probably already done. I don't have great hopes for what they'll find." She sniffled. "He didn't move or do anything when I saw him this morning." Her sniffling turned to tears.

"And Ryan?" I hadn't seen him in a while, but he was a really good kid and devoted to his dad. This had to be so hard on him.

"Not well," she said, eyebrows bunched. "We had a big fight this morning just getting him to go to school." Her hand shook as she pushed an errant strand of hair behind her ear. "He keeps saying he's going to make Sparafucile pay. That's the guy who shot Jared. He frightens me."

"Ryan or Sparafucile?" I was trying to make a lighthearted response, but Mellie took it seriously.

"Both, actually."

Melanie settled behind the steering wheel. "Ryan's never been so headstrong. I think he's just as afraid of losing him as I am."

"That's a pretty fatalistic statement. You're sure he's not going to recover?" I asked.

Mellie's sob was an answer. She put her head in her hands.

"Want me to drive?" I asked.

Melanie shook her head, took out a tissue, and wiped her eyes. "I'll be okay. I want to get to the hospital as soon as we can and find out about the EEG."

We rode in silence as she concentrated on the traffic. We took I-465 to the University of Indiana Medical Center, about fifteen miles north of the airport. As she drove, I thought about what had happened and what the future might be like if Jared died. Fortunately, Ryan was a high school senior and would be off to college shortly, hopefully with a full ride on a football scholarship. Mellie would still have her day care center to keep her busy and feeling fulfilled. I had no idea how much money it brought in, but I was prepared to supplement her income with whatever she needed. I'd make sure that money would be the least of her problems.

Melanie drove to the hospital entrance and handed the keys to the valet. One of the hospital perks was free valet parking.

Melanie led us to the Coronary Care Unit. We walked into Jared's room. He was lying on his back, eyelids taped closed, a breathing tube in his nose, an IV in his neck, and another in his arm.

She bent down to kiss him. "Hi, darling," she said. She ran her fingers through his hair. "I guess they already did the EEG," she said, grabbing a washcloth to wipe electrolyte jelly from his scalp. "They weren't too neat."

The room was large, with plenty of space for medical equipment and an extra bed for someone to spend the night. The walls were a cheery robin's-egg blue, with several framed pictures of Indiana pastoral scenes. The hospital seemed pretty new, bright, and airy.

"I'll ask the nurse to find his doctor," she said. "The head of electrophysiology, Dr. Greg Dumont, is taking care of him now."

"Want me to come?" I asked.

"Sure."

We walked to the nurses' station, passing groups of doctors huddled around a computer on a cart. I guessed they were making morning rounds on each patient.

Mellie stopped a nurse walking by.

"Excuse me. I'm Melanie Simpson," she said. "Jared Simpson's my husband in room 538. He was admitted yesterday from the ER. Is Dr. Dumont available?" she asked.

"I'll page him for you."

A vending machine against the wall caught my eye. "How about a coffee?"

"Sounds good," Mellie said.

"Still take cream and one sugar?"

She nodded.

We sipped, and after a few minutes, a tall, middle-aged, bearded man wearing a long white coat strode toward us, a stethoscope dangling from his neck. I glanced twice at his open-toed brown sandals with no socks.

He saw me look down, wiggled his toes, and laughed. "Hippocrates wore sandals," he said. His gaze shifted to Melanie. "Hello, Mrs. Simpson. Nice to see you again."

"Please, I'm Mellie," she answered, turning to me. "This is my brother, Bear."

Dumont took in my six-foot-three frame, shaggy brown hair, beard, and mustache. "Yes, the name fits. I like men with beards." He smiled and stroked his own.

We shook hands, and he tipped his head toward 538. "Let's go to his room where we'll have a little privacy."

Dumont went to the bedside and peered at Jared. He took out his stethoscope and listened to his chest and heart. After several seconds, he straightened and looked at Melanie.

"I'm sorry to have to tell you that the EEG showed no brain activity," Dumont said. His face was sad, filled with concern. "The neurologist examined him this morning and is prepared to declare him brain-dead. I hate to say it, but you need to think seriously about how long you want this to go on."

Mellie gasped. She put both hands to her face and covered her eyes. The creases in her forehead were pronounced, and I didn't remember ever seeing my sister look so old as she did right then. She began to sway as if she were going to faint. I rushed to her side and eased her into a chair, where she sat and wept.

Finally, she took a deep breath and let it out with a long sigh. "What happens next?" she asked Dumont.

"Does he have an end-of-life directive, what his wishes would be in a situation like this?" Dumont asked.

Mellie shook her head. She barely squeezed out, "No."

"We can continue as we are, supporting his breathing and blood pressure with hope he'll recover, that his brain will show activity," Dumont said.

"What's the chance of that happening?" I asked.

"Unlikely," he said. "Very unlikely."

"But a chance?" Mellie asked, looking at him with hope. She mustered a slight smile that ironed out the furrows a bit. "You and Dr. Bashir said you've seen people like this recover."

"I have, but with the flat EEG, I don't think so. His down time without a heartbeat before the EMTs arrived was too long." Dumont tightened his lips, frowning.

"Earlier this morning, we turned off the respirator for almost a minute to see if he would breathe on his own. He didn't. We stopped the IV to see if he could maintain a blood pressure. He couldn't."

He went on to explain that those responses meant Jared's total brain was affected, including the brainstem. His kidney function had worsened, and he'd need hemodialysis soon if they continued to keep him alive. Dumont worried whether he'd be able to tolerate that.

The doctor continued. "Frankly, I think we're reaching a point where his major organs will fail. It may be the kidneys first, but then, like falling dominoes, other functions will shut down—lungs, heart, clotting ability of his blood, and so forth." Dumont's face showed anguish. "I'm sorry to be so blunt, but it's important you have all the facts."

There was silence in the room as we considered what Dumont said. After a bit, Mellie asked, "What would you do if this was your father? Or your brother?"

"I'm asked that question often," Dumont said. "And of course, I can't answer it honestly because he isn't my father or my brother. There's no way I can really experience that emotion, except through you. But that said, if he were, I'd give him a dose of morphine to be sure he felt no pain or anxiety, stop the respirator and medications, and let him experience a gentle, dignified death."

Mellie once again covered her eyes with her hands and began crying. I put an arm around her shoulders and rocked her tenderly.

"I can't," Mellie said. "I can't make that decision now. My son, Ryan, should be here. He'd never forgive me if Jared died before he saw him again. No, not now, Dr. Dumont."

Dumont checked his watch, pulled out his cell phone, and clicked through several screens. "What time does Ryan finish school?" he asked.

"Three fifteen," Melanie said. "I can pick him up at school and be here by three thirty."

"I'll have to be present to write the orders," Dumont said.

"If I agree, how long will it take?" she asked.

"Writing the orders and stopping therapy will take just a few moments."

"That's not what I meant. How long will it take him to ... you know, to die."

"I can't predict that with precision," Dumont said. "But remember, his brain is already dead. We're just talking about when his breathing stops and his heart stops. I doubt that will take much longer than fifteen or twenty minutes—maybe not even."

Dumont started for the door but changed his mind and came back into the center of the room. "One last thing, Mrs. Simpson. It's always a difficult topic to broach at a time like this, but sometimes it helps loved ones come to a decision. Would you want to donate his organs? He could make several people happy by contributing his corneas, liver, and so on. For some families, knowing their loved one can live on in other people eases the burden of death."

"Yes, I think Jared would like that. But I'm not agreeing to stopping, at least not now. Maybe he'll recover. We need to give him every chance to do that."

"Fine. I'll be back at three thirty. You can tell me then what you want to do."

CHAPTER SEVEN

BEAR'S PROMISE

At a quarter after three in the afternoon, Mellie and I picked up Ryan outside Hopperville High School. The overcast sky looked ready to repeat yesterday's storm. There was no wind yet, but I could smell rain in the air.

"Uncle Bear," he said, giving me a hug. "When did you get in?"

"Hi, Ryan. This morning. I'm so sorry about your dad." I held him at a distance and looked him over. "I think you've grown some since I saw you last. You've certainly filled out." I squeezed his biceps.

"Yeah. The football weight room helps a lot. I can do fifteen biceps curls with fifty-pound weights."

"Wow!"

He slipped off his backpack of books and settled in the back seat. "Is Dad any better?" he asked Mellie, leaning forward on the back of the front seat. Through the rearview mirror, I detected a look of pain on his face that brought tears to Mellie's eyes. Good thing I was driving.

She shook her head. "No change. His doctor was not very hopeful. He wants me to stop the respirator."

"What about the brain wave test?"

"No activity," she said, as I put the car in gear and drove off. She blinked back more tears. "But I think we should give him a few more days before we do anything."

"Did the doctor agree?"

"Sort of. I told him I wouldn't do anything until you saw Dad this afternoon. He's going to meet us at the hospital."

Ryan squirmed in his seat, frowned, and smacked the armrest with the flat of his hand. "Why couldn't it be Sparafucile lying there? I'd unplug the respirator in a second." Ryan made a fist with one hand and drove it into the palm of the other.

I flipped the keys to the valet, and we walked straight to the CCU. It was a quarter to four, and Dumont had come and gone. Melanie asked the nurse to page him.

Ryan stood at the bedside, looking at his dad. His eyes watered. He reached down and stroked his dad's face, bent over him and whispered something in his ear, then kissed his cheek. He straightened, came over to Melanie, and put his arms around her. They remained that way, unmoving, a long time. I couldn't remember the last time I saw Ryan so affectionate.

A shrill blast, loud and insistent, erupted from the bedside ECG monitor. Dumont, followed by a nurse, burst into the room.

Oh my God, I thought. *What's happening?*

"He's back in ventricular fibrillation," Dumont shouted. He yanked the blanket off Jared's chest and ripped open the front of his hospital gown. The nurse handed him two paddles with black plastic handles. He placed one near Jared's right shoulder and held the other on his lower left chest. "Hit it," he said to the nurse.

The nurse pressed a button on the bedside defibrillator. Jared's upper body jerked convulsively.

Dumont looked at the monitor. "Still in VF. Increase by fifty joules. Hit it again."

Again, the nurse pressed the button, and again Jared's chest heaved.

"Okay, that got it," Dumont said. Staring at the monitor, he released a loud "Whew."

I think my heart was going as fast as Jared's.

"Give him another hundred milligrams of amiodarone and increase the IV drip to one milligram per minute for the next two hours. He can't afford another VF episode."

"Yes, Doctor," the nurse replied, nodding. For a very rotund lady, she moved pretty fast when she had to.

Dumont turned to Mellie. "That was the heart rhythm that killed him the first time. It almost did again. I'm giving him a medicine to try and prevent another episode, but it may not. So, you see, we're dealing with a brain that doesn't function and a heart that may not as well. You're going to have to decide soon. If you don't"—Dumont tipped his head at Jared—"I'm afraid his heart may decide it for you."

Mellie inhaled sharply and looked at the ECG. "But his heart's still pumping, isn't it, there on the screen?" She pointed.

"Jared's heart has taken a beating, Mellie—first from the Electric Gun, and then the prolonged resuscitation," Dumont said, shaking his head. "And now this. It can't take much more. I can only have an inkling of the pain you must be feeling, but whatever it is, if the next brain test still shows no activity, I don't think you've got a choice. His body will make the decision for you."

Mellie wept quietly against Ryan's chest, their arms encircling each other. She whispered to him, "Ryan, you're my man now, son. You're all I have. Be strong for me."

Ryan peered at his father over her shoulder. I could see his face was angry, a squinty-eyed mask of dark eyebrows and compressed lips. We shared a glance, and Ryan looked away.

We stayed another hour, sitting at the bedside and talking quietly as if we might disturb Jared. We told happy Jared stories, trying to dispel the somber mood, lighten the load, and postpone the time for making a decision. Finally, Ryan said, "I think we should go home. I need to eat something, and I have a lot of homework due tomorrow."

I looked at the young man. His clenched teeth and wrinkled brow seemed to speak of more than hunger and schoolwork.

CHAPTER EIGHT

BEAR'S PROMISE

The kitchen was small but painted in cheery yellows and blues that made it seem larger. A table sat against one wall, and from there I could reach both the sink and refrigerator. We slid carefully past one another as we performed our chores. I made the arrabiata meat sauce, while Melanie boiled the spaghetti for seven minutes, per my instruction. I liked it al dente, and seven minutes was the perfect amount of time to cook spaghetti, keeping it firm and tasty. Mellie tossed a salad and toasted garlic bread. We ate quickly. No one was in the mood to talk.

Ryan finished first and excused himself. "Got homework to do. Thanks for dinner, Mom and Uncle Bear. It was great." He gave her a kiss on the cheek, me a hug, and went upstairs to his room. I always got a kick out of him calling me Uncle Bear. I'd told him often to drop the "Uncle," but he refused.

I watched him leave. I realized how much he'd matured when we picked him up at school, but I saw it even more clearly now. He'd grown into a handsome, strapping young man, popular and doing well in school. If his father's skin was coffee colored, Ryan's had been diluted with milk. Or maybe Jared's was an espresso, and Ryan's a cappuccino. Whatever, he was a good-looking young lad, and I was proud of him. I was confident he'd be a major support for Mellie if his father died. And she'd definitely need it.

I could never replace Jared as his father, and didn't want to, but I'd be there for him in any way he might want. I hoped he'd follow me into law school and then the FBI. He'd be a superb special agent, and I'd help him chart the waters to avoid the mistake I'd made. It was something I lived with and thought about every day. If only I'd given that boy more time to respond ... I'd probably still be a special agent.

Ten minutes later, Melanie left the table and called up to Ryan, "Want some dessert? We've got apple pie with vanilla ice cream, your favorite." There was no answer. She called again. Still no answer. I heard her climb the stairs to Ryan's room.

In a moment, she ran back downstairs into the kitchen. I was pouring the last of the bottle of Amarone. "He's not there," Melanie said, her voice quivering. "He's not in his room."

"Maybe he went to a friend's house to finish his homework?" I said.

Melanie shook her head. "He's never done that without telling me. Besides, his books were in his backpack. Wait a minute," she said, sprinting out of the kitchen. She came back two minutes later, dangling a key in her hand.

Her face was white. "Jared's gun is gone. He kept it locked in a cabinet in the basement."

I jumped up and pulled out my cell phone.

"Who're you calling?" Melanie asked.

"Googling to get Sparafucile's home address." In seconds, I had the results. "It's 2613 Maplewood Lane."

I plugged it into my iPhone GPS. "Three miles west of here. What kind of gun?"

"I don't know," Mellie said. "A rifle, but I don't know what kind. Jared and Ryan used it for target practice in the woods."

"Give me your car keys," I said.

Her eyes flared. "Ryan took them."

"Shit," I said. We needed wheels now. Even the few minutes Uber might take was too long.

"A neighbor? You know the people next door?"

"Yes."

I grabbed her hand. "Let's go."

We ran across the lawn, where Jared had been shot the day before. The air was cold, but the rain had held off. Mellie darted up the path and pounded on her neighbor's front door. I moved some distance away to avoid frightening whoever answered this late at night.

An elderly, gray-haired woman in a blue-and-yellow flowered housedress opened the door. I watched Melanie speak rapidly, point to me and then to the garage. The woman disappeared into the house and returned with a collection of keys. She handed them to Melanie and gave her a brief hug before closing the front door.

We ran to the garage. I raised the garage door to reveal a black vintage Buick Skylark with a rusted fender and cracked windshield. I hoped it would start.

"Mellie," I said, turning to look at her. "I think you should stay here. I don't know what we're going to find when we get to Sparafucile's house. It could be dangerous."

She shook her head. "I'm not staying when Ryan might be in trouble. Let's go." She jumped into the passenger seat.

I took my Glock 43 from my shoulder holster and checked the six-round magazine. I'd gotten into the habit of packing when I was in the FBI and continued after I left. I replaced the agency's 9 mm Glock with my own when I handed in my shield. An inconvenience was flying commercial because I had to check luggage rather than take the gun in a carry-on.

The Buick started with a roar. I backed it out of the garage and into the street. "Make a right at the next intersection," Melanie said, checking the GPS on my phone.

I punched the accelerator to the floor, and, thankfully, the old car responded. "Do you think he'd actually pull the trigger on Sparafucile?"

"I don't know, Bear. He's so angry he just might."

"Frankly, my concern's for Ryan. Sparafucile's an experienced cop. Unless Ryan takes him by surprise, Sparafucile has the upper hand."

"Would he arrest Ryan?" Mellie asked.

"He could." I was thinking of a lot worse.

We reached Sparafucile's house five minutes later. I jammed on the brakes when I saw Ryan pointing his rifle at Sparafucile.

Sparafucile had his hands raised over his head and was standing on his porch, framed in the doorway of his house, backlit by lights in the entrance hallway. I couldn't see clearly because of the dim light and dark night, but there appeared to be a woman standing in the doorway several feet behind him.

We leaped out of the car and ran to Ryan. "Stay away from me," Ryan shouted, "or I'll shoot this son of a bitch." He didn't take his eyes off Sparafucile. We stopped where we were, about twenty feet from Ryan. He stood at the foot of the porch, looking up the three steps at Sparafucile.

"Ryan, please put the gun down," Melanie begged. "This is no way to settle what happened. It was an accident."

"Accident, hell," Ryan shouted, jaw clenched and eyes wide. "This bastard killed my dad, and I'm going to kill him. I just wish I had an Electric Gun to do it, so he could see what it feels like."

"I know what it feels like, you punk," Sparafucile said, flipping the back of his hand at Ryan. "We tested it on each other during training."

"But you didn't die like my dad."

"No, I didn't, and I didn't scream like a candy-assed baby either. I told you, Electric Guns can't kill. Your father died from something else. And besides, I heard he was still alive."

"He's brain-dead," Ryan yelled, "because of you." Ryan's eyes glistened with tears in the reflected light. He was breathing fast.

Sparafucile just shrugged. His face showed no emotion. He did not seem frightened. He slouched against the doorjamb and slowly began to lower his hands.

"Keep your fucking hands up," Ryan yelled. "No tricks, you bastard." Sparafucile complied, still leaning. He glanced over his shoulder as the woman behind him came closer. I could see her more clearly. She was elderly, gray hair in a bun at the back of her head, wearing a pink robe and pink slippers. She appeared to touch Sparafucile's back and then retreated.

Sparafucile tried to hide a smirk.

Ryan was sweating, his forehead beaded with moisture. With his free hand, he swiped at the wetness and ran a fist across his eyes. The rifle shook in his hand. He paced a few feet in one direction, turned and paced back, unwavering vision glued to Sparafucile.

Ryan was no killer. As a kid, he'd bring home strays, homeless dogs wandering the streets, nurse them back to health, and then give them up for adoption. He was acting out his rage against Sparafucile. I needed to talk him down from this crazy ledge he'd blundered onto.

"Ryan," I said, walking cautiously toward him, "put the gun down. Shooting Lieutenant Sparafucile is only going to make the problem worse."

He cocked his head in my direction, listening but still pointing the rifle at Sparafucile. FBI training taught me to watch people's hands at all times. Sparafucile's were at his side, but I could see his fingers twitching, preparing to do something. Ryan didn't even have his finger inside the trigger guard of the rifle. I had to stop this craziness.

"Ryan, your mom needs you more than ever if your dad passes. You're the man of the family now. She needs your strength. Don't do something stupid. You're no good to her in jail, son. Give me the rifle."

His brow furrowed as my words hit home. But he shook his head, dismissing my argument. He looked like he'd made up his mind and was preparing to act. He put his finger through the trigger guard, rested it on the trigger, and leveled the gun at Sparafucile. As he took a step toward the cop, his foot bumped the first porch step, and he stumbled, dipping the muzzle of his rifle.

In a flash, Sparafucile whipped out a handgun tucked in the waistband behind his back and pumped three quick shots into Ryan. The bullets must've been hollow points because Ryan's chest exploded, ripped to shreds. The slugs spun him around, knocking him off the porch and onto the lawn. He was dead before he hit the ground. Though I was not that close, his blood splattered the front of my shirt, and I wiped my face.

"Oh, no!" Mellie shrieked and ran to her son. "No, Ryan, no!" she wailed, kneeling alongside the prostrate, blood-drenched body. "Get an ambulance. Call a doctor. Help!" she cried.

I was already dialing 911, but one look told me it was too late. I went to comfort my sister. She was in a state of shock, hugging Ryan's body close to her, rocking back and forth, oblivious to my presence. She was covered in his blood.

I ran to the porch and up the steps to confront Sparafucile, my hand reaching inside my jacket.

"Hold it right there, fellow," Sparafucile said, pointing his handgun at me. "One step further, and I'll blow you away like I did the kid." He tipped his head toward Ryan's body. "Hands at your sides where I can see them."

I fought to keep calm, though my fingers itched to pull my Glock on this guy. He was a mean cop, the worst kind, but I knew he'd be able to squeeze off several rounds before I could even move.

I dropped my hands to my sides and faced him, standing as close as I dared. The old woman disappeared, fading into the darkness of the house interior. I was breathing fast and could barely contain my anger, but I willed myself to stay cool. He'd use the slightest excuse to shoot me.

"You murdered that kid, Lieutenant," I said, my voice harsh. "You didn't give him a chance. I could have gotten him under control. You didn't have to kill him."

"Who the fuck are you?" Sparafucile demanded, his face contorted into an angry scowl. "What were you going to do? Magically lift the rifle out of his hands? He was going to kill me, buddy. I shot him in self-defense."

"I'm his uncle. You never gave him a chance," I said. "He was just a scared, upset kid. He wasn't going to shoot you. You're a professional. You could've talked him out of it."

"What kind of bullshit is that?" Sparafucile asked, keeping the handgun pointed at me. I saw that it was a Sig Sauer P226, a very powerful gun that shot 9 mm slugs.

"Somebody's got a gun aimed at me, and I give him a chance?" Sparafucile said. "Are you fucking nuts, pal? Leave the police work to professionals. Now get the fuck off my porch so I can call this in." Sparafucile shoved me with his fist hard in my chest. He caught me off balance, and I tripped down the three porch steps. He spun on his heels and withdrew into his house, slamming the front door.

"The kid was right," I said to the closed door. "You are a bastard." I turned and went to Melanie. She was sitting on the grass with Ryan's head in her lap, his face pale as snow. She was moaning, rocking him back and forth.

"My poor baby, my poor baby," she said over and over. She had one hand on his chest, and blood pooled around her fingers. I kneeled alongside, my arm around her shoulders.

Melanie began keening, a high-pitched wail for the dead. Her eyes glazed over, and her rocking increased. I was afraid she was going into shock. I took off my jacket and draped it across her shoulders.

I heard sirens in the distance. An ambulance pulled up, followed by a Crown Vic police car. Two EMTs ran to us and dropped alongside Ryan's body. There was nothing they could do.

A Hopperville police officer came striding up. He stopped and took pictures of Ryan's body with his cell phone.

One EMT returned to the ambulance, removed a stretcher, and pushed it toward Ryan. They loaded his body onto it, wheeled it to the ambulance, and lifted it into the rear.

"Wait," Melanie cried, finally stirring. She stood, her face, hands, and jacket covered in blood. Her movements were slow, catatonic. She wiped her hands on the front of her jacket and then looked at them with a wrinkled brow. I couldn't know what she was thinking, but her vacant look made me wonder if she was questioning how they got so red.

She seemed to shake off the spell a bit, gathered herself together, and said, "I want to go with him." They helped her into the back of the ambulance and sped off.

Sparafucile opened his door and called to the cop. "Hey, Fisheye. That you?"

"It's me, Chilli. Coming right up." Fisheye bypassed me on the lawn and climbed the steps to the porch. "What happened?"

"The kid knocked on my door—"

"This the kid I shot yesterday?" Fisheye interrupted. "Ryan somebody?"

Sparafucile nodded. "When I opened the door, he had his rifle aimed at me, told me to put my hands up and that he was going to shoot me because of his father. I did like he said, but before anything happened"—he pointed to me on the lawn—"his mother and this character showed up. The kid looked away for a second, and I shot him."

"Where's the rifle?"

"On the lawn where he fell," Sparafucile said, indicating the spot with a head nod. "I haven't touched it."

Fisheye walked to where the rifle lay. He took a picture of the gun, pulled on a pair of white plastic gloves, and picked up the rifle. He walked back onto the porch to show it to Sparafucile. I followed at a distance and stood on the path in front of the porch.

I was close enough to overhear him say, "It's a bolt action .22." He read the inscription on the metal plate. "Savage 93 FV-SR."

He pulled back the bolt to eject the bullet loaded in the breech. Nothing popped out. He locked and unlocked the bolt again to be sure. Nothing. Fisheye looked into the breach and shook his head.

The gun wasn't loaded!

I'd never know what Ryan had been thinking. Perhaps he was so rattled and in such a hurry he never checked to see if the rifle was loaded.

"Chilli," Fisheye said in a soft voice, glancing at me. "We may have a problem if the kid was going to shoot you with an unloaded rifle."

"No, we don't," Sparafucile said. "No way I could tell that when he was pointing the rifle at me. Could've been a BB gun, and I'd have done the same thing. Self-defense all the way."

"I agree, but it won't look good in the press," Fisheye said. "They'll have a field day. 'Hopperville cop shoots unarmed kid.'"

"I don't give two shits about the press. Just write your report as I tell you, and we'll be fine."

"Yes, sir," said Fisheye. "I will."

"Wait a minute," Sparafucile said. "ACYA, the first rule of policing."

He disappeared into the house and reappeared several moments later. He dropped his voice so low I couldn't hear what he was saying, but I saw him wipe something small and shiny with a handkerchief and hand it to Fisheye. Fisheye's gloved hand slipped it into the rifle. I suspected the gun was now loaded.

I started to reach for my cell phone to video their exchange but stopped when I realized Sparafucile might think I was going for a gun. He stood on the porch talking with Fisheye, his Sig Sauer prominent in his waistband and one eye on me. Now was not the time to face off with him. I'd lost this battle, but I had a gut feeling I'd have another chance in the future.

CHAPTER NINE

I drove the Buick to the hospital, parked, and went into the emergency room. Melanie was waiting, pale and trembling. Her eyes were bloodshot. Dark mascara smudges snaked down her cheeks.

"He's dead," she said. Her sobs had dried and turned to hiccups. She took deep breaths in between each spasm. "They told me the bullets tore holes in his heart and lungs. I just gave permission for organ transplants, whatever they can salvage."

"Bless you," I said. "Somebody will live better because Ryan died."

"Yes," she cried, "but what will happen to me? I've lost my son. Soon I'll lose my husband. What's next? I can't go on like this, Bear. I just can't. I have no one anymore, no life—"

I put my arms around her and squeezed gently. We stayed that way a moment. Then she drew away, brows knit together in anger. "All because I dialed 911 for help."

"I can't imagine losing a child," I said, my eyes clouding. "No one can know that agony unless they've lived it. But you must go on, Mellie. The kids in your day care center need you, I need you and love you"—I groped for words—"and maybe Jared'll pull through." I didn't really believe that, but I had to say something.

After a bit, Mellie straightened and dried her eyes. She set her mouth in a firm line and gave a little nod, calm as if she'd come to some sort of a resolution, her mind made up about something.

"I want to see him. Now," she said. "I must tell Jared about Ryan."

I checked my watch. "It's late, Mellie, almost eleven. Do you think they'll let us visit?"

"Frankly, I don't care if they will or won't. I want to see my husband now, and I will do that." Melanie squared her shoulders.

I couldn't remember seeing her so determined about anything before. Whatever was in her head didn't need my support. "Okay," I said. "If that's what you want, that's what we'll do. We'll make it happen. Let's go."

We left the ER and took the elevator to the fifth floor. As we entered the CCU, a nurse stopped us. "I'm sorry, but visiting hours were over at nine o'clock."

"I know," Melanie said. "But I want to see my husband."

"Well—" The nurse hesitated.

Melanie brushed past her and walked quickly to Jared's room. She opened the door slowly. A glance in the dimly lit room told us nothing had changed. The whoosh of the respirator, the beep of the monitor, and the click of the timer counting IV drops were the only noises in the room.

Melanie went to the bedside, bent over Jared, and kissed him on the lips. She whispered in his ear a long time. Her tears dripped onto his face and pillow. She finished, wiped his face and hers, straightened and looked at me, a determined expression on her face. She seemed more at peace with herself. "Now we can go."

As we left the room, she said, "Goodbye, my love. I will see you again soon."

We drove by Sparafucile's house to pick up Melanie's car, still parked on the street, and then drove both cars home. I opened the neighbor's garage door as quietly as I could, backed her car into the garage, and left the keys on the front seat. We went into Melanie's house and walked into the kitchen.

"I'd get you a bite, but I'm exhausted, Bear," Mellie said, eyes sad. "There's food in the refrigerator if you're hungry—leftover spaghetti you can reheat. Canned soup and tuna fish in the pantry. Just help yourself to whatever you want." She pointed. "Would you mind terribly if I just went to bed?"

"Of course not, Mellie," I said. "You go on. I'll be fine. I'm too tired to eat anything and still full from dinner. I'm going to open that second bottle of Amarone and then go to bed too."

"Thanks for helping." Mellie turned to embrace me. "You've been my ballast my entire life, holding my hand, giving me courage. Thank you for being you—and for helping me marry Jared, the love of my life. It just didn't last long enough."

Mellie and I wrapped arms around each other and hugged tight. We held each other, no words necessary. Then she pulled away, her face wet. "I love you, Bear, and always will. Good night." She left the kitchen with a tiny wave of her hand and went upstairs.

I found the corkscrew, opened the Amarone, and sat drinking and thinking. It had all started with that 911 call and that goddamn

Electric Gun. The lawyer in me kicked in. The legal possibilities would have to wait until I got home, but they'd be high on my to-do list. First and foremost, however, was decision day tomorrow for my poor sister. That was going to be rough.

I was too tired to call Kat, so I texted her what had happened and fell into bed, blessedly numbed by the Amarone.

I overslept the next morning and grabbed for the clock. "My God, it's past nine," I muttered. I heard no noises in the kitchen. Maybe Mellie had gotten a good night's sleep before decision day.

I dressed and went downstairs, made scrambled eggs for two, coffee, and four slices of rye toast. Finished eating, I put Mellie's share in the oven on a low heat, rinsed the dishes, and had a second cup of coffee.

Fifteen minutes later, Mellie still hadn't appeared. I decided to wake her since it was now past ten. She had to see Dumont and find out about the second EEG. The hospital wanted her decision by noon.

I knocked softly on her bedroom door. No answer. *She must be sound asleep.* I knocked harder. Still no answer. I turned the knob and peeked into the room.

"Good morning, Mellie," I said loudly to give her warning in case she was indisposed. No answer. I opened the door all the way and walked into the bedroom.

Mellie was lying facedown, arms outstretched, her head on the pillow, still sleeping. I went to her and gently touched her shoulder. It felt cold.

"Mellie?" I said. No answer. Louder, I said, "Mellie."

I stripped off the blanket and rolled her onto her back. Her skin was cold and blue. Her pupils were dilated, opaque, vacant. I put my ear to her chest. No heartbeat, no respirations.

An empty pill bottle lay on the bedside table, along with a half-full water glass.

I dialed 911, but the call was out of reflex. There was nothing anyone could do.

My sweet little sister was dead.

BEAR'S PROMISE

I sat down on the bed next to her and stroked her hair. I understood. Her pain had been too great. I bit deep into a knuckle to try to keep my composure.

I noticed a handwritten note propped against the bedside table lamp.

> Dear Bear: I can't go on any longer. The thought of stopping Jared's treatment fills me with dread, and once again I need you to decide for me. Deep down, I know what the decision must be, but I can't face it. I give you total power of attorney to make all decisions for me.
>
> I hope I'm on my way to meet Ryan in heaven and that Jared will join us shortly. If we can't be a family on earth, we'll be one someplace else. It hurts too much to live after someone you love has died.
>
> God bless you. I love you with all my heart. Just promise me you'll go after the people responsible for killing my men and bring them to justice. If I know you'll do that, I'll die and can rest in peace.
>
> All my love, brother dearest,
> Mellie

I sat there holding the note, dazed with grief, tears sliding down my cheeks. The Electric Gun had wiped out my sister and her family. There was an emptiness, a hole in me where they had lived. Nothing could fill it and take their place. I'd miss my sister's bubbly laugh, her mini meltdowns, and her turning to me to bail her out of one crisis or another. I'd miss my nephew's growing up, his future football career, and how he would have lived his life. And I'd miss my brother-in-law, the rock that had anchored the family but had been broadsided by loss of job and an old football injury. Somebody once said that grief sucks. I had to agree. My only solace was to do my sister's bidding.

"I promise you, my lovely, dear sister, I will go after them with everything I have, and I will not stop until they've paid for what they've done. You can rest in peace."

I kissed her cold forehead, held her limp hand, and stroked her eyelids to cover nonseeing pupils. I prayed she'd be reunited with her men in a different place.

CHAPTER TEN

I met with Dr. Dumont later in the morning and told him about Ryan and Mellie. Even though they were not his patients, he became very emotional.

"I have to accept some of the blame," he said with a contrite expression. "Had I been more optimistic about Jared's recovery, perhaps—"

I interrupted him. "No, Greg—may I call you that? I'm Bear," I said, extending my hand and shaking my head.

"You had to be honest with them, and you were. But you were also sympathetic and held out some hope. No, you were the good doctor. The blame lies with the Electric Gun Company and that cop, Sparafucile." I rested a hand on his shoulder.

"Thank you for that," he said with a tiny smile. He went on to tell me that Jared's repeat EEG showed no brain activity. As next of kin and having power of attorney from Melanie's suicide note, I gave him permission to discontinue the respirator and medications. Although the suicide note was most likely not legal since it was not notarized or witnessed, hospital officials didn't quibble over technicalities.

"You're sure about this?" Dumont asked as we stood at the foot of Jared's bed, watching the machines keep alive the shell that was left.

"I am," I said. "I'd want someone to make that decision for me if I were in his place. That's the only yardstick I can use. Do unto others ..."

Dumont wrote the orders. The nurse gave Jared fifteen milligrams of morphine, stopped the IVs, turned off the respirator, and removed the breathing tube.

I watched the ECG on the bedside monitor with a morbid fascination. It's not often you see someone die right before your eyes.

I don't know what I was expecting, but it turned out to be anticlimactic. Jared stopped breathing, and his heartbeat gradually slowed from about seventy to fifty, then thirty, then a beat every ten or fifteen seconds, and finally a flat line after twenty minutes. The shell remaining did not even twitch.

And that was it. He was officially pronounced dead at 2:53 p.m. Hospital personnel swooped in and transported his body to the operating room to salvage his liver, kidneys, corneas, and God knows what else might still be recoverable.

BEAR'S PROMISE

I'd done my grieving earlier this morning, and it was a relief to finish what my sister knew had to be done.

Dumont led me to his office, where he explained that, because of the suspicious or unnatural manner of Jared's death, Indiana law required an autopsy by a certified pathologist. The body would go from the OR to the autopsy room, where the pathologist, acting as a medical examiner, had to determine the cause of death.

"Since Jared was my patient," Dumont said, sitting down at his desk and pointing to a chair for me, "I'll attend the autopsy. You're a lawyer, aren't you, in addition to being next of kin?" he asked.

I nodded.

"This is the third death I've seen after an Electric Gun shooting with the probes in the chest. It can't be coincidental." He went on to explain his idea that electricity from the gun sped the heart rate into ventricular fibrillation and caused cardiac arrest. He rummaged on his desk for a yellow legal pad and, finding it, drew a diagram of what he'd just explained.

"What does the medical examiner think?" I asked, studying his drawing.

"Come with me and find out," he said with a half smile.

"Is that legal? I mean, can a nonphysician observe an autopsy?"

"You'd need permission from the hospital, which I'm here to give. And permission from the family or next of kin. That's it. C'mon," he said and stood. I did also. He put his hand on the back of my shoulder and gave me a gentle push out of his office.

He led the way down the hall, then stopped and turned around. "On second thought—you don't faint when you see blood, do you?"

I shook my head.

"Get sick? Vomit? Queasy stomach?"

"Nope."

"Seen an autopsy before?"

"Once, a long time ago." I pushed the memory away.

"Okay, then you're good to go. Follow me." He resumed walking.

His cell phone beeped, and he stopped again, listened a moment, and said, "Fine. See you in fifteen."

Dumont turned to me. "That was Benjamin Frisson, the pathologist. He's going to be a few minutes late."

We passed a coffee shop. "Want a bit of caffeine to fortify you first?" he asked. Without waiting, he walked inside and ordered a double espresso. "What're you drinking?"

"Same." I was still reeling from the three deaths and found his casualness a little—I don't know—a little disconcerting. But I guess Dumont dealt with death all the time, and life does go on. That started me thinking. Would anyone but Kat and I miss the presence of the Simpson family? Sure, each of them had friends or acquaintances who'd be sad for a short time, but real life would continue as it had before. The Electric Gun Company would sell guns and make a profit, and law enforcement would use them on resisting subjects. And perhaps kill some of them.

Unless I did something about it.

We sat at a table in an alcove sipping our coffees. A sign on the wall over the table said, "Space reserved for medical personnel."

"This has got to be terribly painful for you," Dumont said. "Were you close to your sister and her family?"

"Yes, very. She was my kid sister, and I took care of her lots of times growing up and as adults. And I was very fond of Jared—a real stand-up kind of guy. Ryan was going to be like his dad, and I'd hoped he'd follow me into law school and then the FBI." I looked away as my eyes got moist.

"You were an FBI agent?" Dumont said, brow raised in surprise.

I nodded. "Long story, but yes, before I started my law firm. That's when I saw an autopsy." I wasn't going to explain, and Dumont didn't ask. I think he sensed my discomfort.

We were silent for a moment, drinking our coffees. Dumont continued.

"This autopsy will be tricky for a couple of reasons," he said. The doctors had removed some organs for transplant, but since they could not have played a role in Jared's cardiac arrest, he didn't think that would be a major problem. "The key organs, the brain and the heart, are still in place," he said.

The second issue was that, officially, Jared had died that afternoon at 2:53 p.m., after Dumont had stopped the respirator and meds. But the cause of Jared's brain death—the cardiac arrest—was the major issue. That had happened two days earlier and was what the pathologist had to deal with.

"What do you think he'll conclude?" I asked.

"Dunno. Let's find out," Dumont said. He pushed back from the table and stood. I offered him my Visa card, but he ignored it and tucked a ten-dollar bill under his coffee cup.

The white tile walls and floor of the autopsy room reminded me of a large restaurant kitchen: a walk-in stainless steel refrigerator; bright, fluorescent lights hanging from the ceiling; and five shiny, stainless steel sinks.

Three metal tables, maybe seven feet long and two and a half feet wide, could have been kitchen counters with cutting boards for mountains of veggies or meat. Each had grooves in the sides that funneled debris into a central drain and from there to a collection pail hanging from a chain beneath the table.

Two tables were empty. Jared's body, naked except for a towel covering his groin, lay pale as a ghost on the third table. That, along with the smell of chlorine or some sort of an antiseptic cleaner, shattered my kitchen image. Reminded me of the odor in the dentist's office when I was a kid.

Frisson stood next to the table, already gloved and gowned. He was short and stout, totally bald with a round, almost cherubic face. A bristly brownish-gray mustache drooped over his upper lip, with the ends twisted into half-moons. He didn't fit the mental picture I had of a ghoul who cut up dead bodies for a living.

Dumont introduced me.

"You sure you want to watch?" Frisson asked, creasing his brow. "Most civilians can't handle it."

Interesting that he labeled nonmedical people civilians. When I said yes, he pointed to the closest sink. "If you feel sick, be sure to get to that sink in time. Can't have you puking on the body."

He turned to Jared's body and began dictating into a microphone suspended on a wire from the ceiling over the table. "The body's external appearance is normal except for burn marks on the skin from the Electric Gun probes shot into the deceased's anterior left chest and the gun pressed posteriorly against his right shoulder."

He took pictures and drew blood. "Toxicology screen," he said. He cut into the scalp and peeled it back like an orange rind. He cut through the bone with a circular saw and popped off the skull like the top of a hardboiled egg. He removed the brain and dumped it into a stainless steel pan—the kind used to cook a roast in the oven.

I came close to losing it. This was my brother-in-law he was chopping up. The guy I tossed a football with, drank beers with, ate dinner with. I fought waves of nausea and glanced at the sink. It seemed to beckon me. I held my ground, took deep breaths, and convinced myself it was just a nameless body. The feeling slowly ebbed. I took out a handkerchief and wiped my forehead beaded with sweat. I turned back to the table and—

Almost lost it again—this time for real.

Frisson was cutting a Y incision into Jared's chest, beginning at both shoulders and joining at the midline down his sternum. After peeling the skin back, he chomped through the ribs with a pair of garden shears and lifted the sternum off like a breastplate.

Stale air, trapped in the chest, filled the room with the acrid smell of old blood. Though Frisson had flipped on a fan, which helped a bit, I was hyperventilating so fast I got lightheaded. I had to grab the side of the table to steady myself. The waves of nausea returned, and my stomach heaved and jumped through hoops. I struggled for control and gulped mouthfuls of air.

"Want some Vicks?" he asked. I shook my head. He explained that some attendees applied the vapor rub under their noses to block the smell. "The chickenshit civvies who can't stomach the aroma of death. I ought to write a book about that," he said. "I'd call it *The Aroma of Death*." He laughed at the idea.

We stared at the heart, a fist-sized lump of red meat cradled in a pale-white, glistening membrane. "That's the pericardium," Frisson said, cutting the membrane open.

Frisson dictated, "Heart, like the brain, looks normal on the surface. Under the microscope, both of them will likely show anoxic and ischemic changes." Frisson looked at me. "Changes from lack of oxygen and blood flow," he explained.

"Yeah, but those changes are the result of the cardiac arrest, not its cause," Dumont interrupted. "The microscopics of the brain also might show a scar from Jared's football concussion years before."

Frisson agreed. He gave the abdomen a cursory look and said, "I have enough information. We're done."

Dumont had explained over coffee that Frisson, as the medical examiner, had to fill out three critical lines on the death certificate: *cause* of death, *mechanism* of death, and *manner* of death.

Frisson once again stepped on a floor switch that activated the microphone hanging over the autopsy table and dictated the cause of death: excited delirium; the mechanism of death: cardiac arrest; and the manner of death: natural.

He looked at Dumont and said that Jared's excited, delirious mental state caused the cardiac arrest, which led to the brain death. He made no mention of the role played by the Electric Gun.

"That's absolute bullshit," Dumont said, fuming. His voice rose in volume, and he barely contained himself. He stared at Frisson in disbelief. "I can't believe you said that. Do you even know whether an agitated state can affect the heart? The Electric Gun caused the cardiac arrest, not excited delirium, whatever the hell that is. What's wrong with you? Are you nuts? This was a homicide, not a natural death."

"You can't prove that." Frisson kept his cool. "The heart is grossly normal."

"As I would expect it to be," Dumont said, eyes big and round, lips in a flat line. "The electricity from the gun leaves no trace on the heart. Just the entry burns on the skin. You should know that from autopsies on people struck by lightning. Same damn thing. Lightning enters and exits the body, leaving a skin burn and nothing else. Can still cause cardiac arrest and kill you."

Dumont backed a few feet from the table and took several deep breaths. He ran his fingers through his hair and returned, shaking his head.

"Jared was excited and delirious all morning after the seizures. Why in God's name did he have cardiac arrest at the exact moment he received the jolts of electricity from the gun? Helluva coincidence, don't you think?" Dumont said.

Melanie had witnessed all of it and had been explicit in her description.

"Also, from the police reports," Dumont went on, "you know he was conscious after the first shock, still standing, and was still conscious at the beginning of the second shock while he was upright. After he fell to his knees, he was talking and moving until he pitched forward onto his hands. That's when he lost consciousness."

"So?" Frisson said.

"The heart moves in the chest with different body positions, as I'm sure you're aware," Dumont said, hands wide, palms up.

Judging by Frisson's blank expression, I wasn't sure he was.

"So?" he repeated.

"The heart moves closer to the chest wall when you're leaning forward," Dumont said, demonstrating by leaning on his hands across the autopsy table.

"I took a careful history from Melanie when Jared was admitted to the hospital," Dumont said. "Jared leaned forward when he went from being upright on his knees, down onto his hands and knees. That means the heart was closer to the probes in his chest, making it easier for the electricity to reach and capture his heart. That's when he fibrillated."

"You don't know that," the pathologist said, waving his index finger back and forth.

"Don't know which part?" Dumont asked. His face was getting red, and he was breathing fast.

"The heart being closer to the ribs when he was on his hands and knees," Frisson said.

"I do know that. I can show you cardiac echoes as proof," Dumont said. "Since there was no ECG recording at the time of his death, I can only conjecture when the fibrillation happened. But it's a good bet I'm right, that it started when he fell forward onto his hands. That's when he suddenly lost consciousness, stopped responding, and totally collapsed."

The pathologist glared at him, a doubtful look on his face.

I remembered something else Mellie had told me. I added my two cents. "He'd had this excited, delirious state years ago when the seizures first started. He obviously didn't have cardiac arrest then. So, why now at the precise time of the electric shock?"

"Who the hell asked you?" Frisson snapped. He looked up at the ceiling as if appealing to a higher authority and drew in a deep breath.

"Look, Dr. Dumont," Frisson said in a tired voice, stripping off his rubber gloves. He tossed them into a garbage pail and washed his hands at the sink. I flipped him a towel a little too hard. It bounced off his hands and hit him in the face. He shot me an angry look. I played innocent.

"I respect what you're saying. But let me give you a little history. The last two times I made a diagnosis of cardiac arrest caused by the Electric Gun—situations almost identical to what happened here—the company came after me with a pack of very angry lawyers. They were like attack dogs. They threatened to sue me and the hospital for product denigration unless I changed the diagnosis to excited delirium. They claimed the diagnosis would negatively impact gun sales. They told the hospital administrator it would cost hundreds of thousands of dollars if he went to court to challenge them, and that he'd probably lose in the long run."

"That's bullshit," I said, the lawyer in me kicking in. "There's no legitimate legal basis to sue for product denigration. You have every right to express your opinion about a product. Look at all the negative comments on the internet about all kinds of merchandise, a dining experience, or a hotel. It's called freedom of speech, the First Amendment. Of course, anybody can sue for anything, but you could've told them to go to hell and that you'd countersue for filing a baseless and frivolous claim. Called their bluff."

Drying his hands, the pathologist snorted a short, mirthless laugh.

"Not likely. They had big bucks behind them and very sharp lawyers out for blood. We didn't have either and didn't stand a chance. I checked with several medical examiner colleagues around the country who'd also filled out death certificates blaming deaths on the Electric Gun. Every one of them had the same experience.

"Electric Gun lawyers knocked on their doors and brutalized them into changing their diagnoses. One medical examiner who initially opposed them got his leg broken in what was called a random mugging. The mugger said next time it would be his neck. My hospital administrator folded and made me change the cause to excited delirium."

"You should've fought them," I persisted. "Pushed them to sue."

The corners of his mouth turned down. "You may be a good lawyer, Mr. Judge," the pathologist said, "but you don't know what in holy hell you're talking about."

He turned back to Dumont. "Albert Einstein once said repeating the same thing over and over and expecting a different outcome was the definition of insanity. I'm not insane, Doctor. The diagnosis stays as it is, excited delirium."

"Do you even know what that is?" Dumont asked.

Frisson shrugged. "Go look it up," he said and walked off.

CHAPTER ELEVEN

We were back in the coffee shop, having a second espresso. I needed quiet time to settle my nerves—and my stomach—after the autopsy and Frisson's tirade. It was late in the afternoon. The tiny shop was deserted, long after lunch and too early for dinner.

We sat at a corner table. The waitress brought a plate of crunchy almond biscotti cookies along with the coffee. Aromas from lunch lingered in the air. Fried chicken must've been the day's special. Usually that would rouse my taste buds, but I think they died during the autopsy and were now on life support, recovering slowly. A simple cookie and coffee were about all I could handle.

"What do you know about excited delirium?" I asked Dumont.

"I've spent countless hours researching articles." He stroked his beard, thinking. "I was baiting Frisson to see what he'd say."

"Didn't seem like he knew about it."

"I'm sure he did. Hell, he's a pathologist. He had to know. I think he just was being stubborn."

Dumont explained that the standard definition was a condition of extreme agitation, delirium, and sweating, often mixed with violence and feats of unexpected strength. "A key aspect is a very high body temperature, which Jared did not have."

"The cause?"

"Unknown but may be from drugs like cocaine or amphetamines, or maybe mental illness," Dumont said, taking a sip of coffee.

"How does that cause cardiac arrest?"

"I'm not sure it does, or if it does, how. Many of the individuals dying with this diagnosis were restrained and held lying facedown on the ground, cops on top of them, making it hard to breathe. Lack of oxygen could cause death by asphyxiation."

"But that's dying from the restraint, not excited delirium."

"Exactly," Dumont said. He made circles with his coffee cup on the tabletop, staring at his artwork with half-lidded eyes. He looked up with a slight frown. "Frankly, I think it's a wastebasket diagnosis Electric Gun fabricated to deflect blame from their gun and shield the company. They dug it up from a condition called Bell's mania, described in 1849—death with violent convulsions after a manic attack."

"Nothing like that here."

"True," Dumont said. "Also, Bell's mania was a chronic condition in which people died after weeks or months of extreme agitation."

"What about doctors? Do they think it's legit?" I knew medical societies, like bar associations, often took a stand on new ideas and debunked scams.

"Some do, some don't. The big medical societies like the American Medical Association and the American Psychological Association haven't taken an official position. The fact that shrinks can't agree about a psychological diagnosis makes me doubt it really exists."

"I'm not a physician," I said with a mouth full of biscotti, "but even if excited delirium could cause cardiac arrest, why did the arrest occur precisely when Jared was shot by the Electric Gun? He'd been raving and ranting for some time prior. And he'd had this confused state years before. Why didn't he suffer cardiac arrest then?"

He smiled. "You're preaching to the choir, Bear."

I sipped my coffee, trying to figure out where the discussion should go. Greg could be a valuable colleague when I got ready to sue Electric Gun. I could use him as an expert witness. "Let's say hypothetically"—the lawyer in me was raising its head again—"it was the Electric Gun that killed him. How could it do that?"

"Good question," Dumont said, making eye contact. He explained that electricity delivered to the chest penetrated the skin and could reach the heart to alter the heartbeat.

"We do that routinely in emergencies," he said. "Say someone blacked out from a very slow heartbeat, maybe twenty beats per minute, and needed a pacemaker immediately. We can increase the heart rate from twenty to seventy by delivering electric shocks through patch electrodes on the skin over the heart." He watched my face to be sure I was with him. I nodded.

"That's what the Electric Gun does. The difference is the gun delivers shocks through the probes at much faster rates—over one thousand times a minute. No human heart can go that fast and still beat normally. Ventricular fibrillation results, and with it, cardiac arrest, killing the person unless promptly stopped by a defibrillator."

"So, where do we go from here?" I asked. "What would you do?"

"My advice? Sue the sons of bitches for making an instrument that destroyed an entire family and failing to warn it could kill."

"I plan to sue, but it's more easily said than done," I said, pushing back from the table. "Let's not get ahead of ourselves. I need to be able to prove what you said about the gun causing the cardiac arrest. How do I do that?"

"It's so obvious," Dumont said, exasperated. He walked to the counter, ordered two more coffees, and returned. "Anybody who knows anything about the heart knows that can happen."

"Not good enough, Greg," I said, taking another bite of biscotti. My taste buds were coming off life support and on the way to recovery. "It may be obvious to you, but I need to prove that fact in front of a jury. I can put you on the witness stand to testify the gun caused Jared's cardiac arrest, but Electric Gun will hire their own expert to say you're wrong, that it can't happen. Who will the jury believe? Do you have proof?"

"Animal studies," he said, again playing with his beard, "showing the gun caused ventricular fibrillation in goats and dogs."

I shook my head. "We need proof in humans. How do we get that?"

He shrugged and gave me a sheepish grin. "Going to be tough to ask someone to be shot and killed with the Electric Gun so we can record their heart rhythm when they die. Might be hard to get volunteers to do that."

CHAPTER TWELVE

DOUG ZIPES

I flew back to New York early that evening, sipping a vodka on the rocks. I had a first-class seat—I didn't enjoy chewing on my knees in coach—and was thinking about Mellie and her family.

I'd loved my little sister, loved that she and Jared had had the courage to marry and that Ryan had been growing up as a healthy blend of his African American father and Caucasian mother. He'd have been an outstanding, caring adult. My eyes welled as I remembered when he was born and how Mellie and Jared had doted on the infant. She'd had one miscarriage before Ryan and one after. He'd been the focus of their lives.

I was grieving, but my response was to do something about it, not just mourn. Maybe I was too left-brained. For me, the only way to lighten the load was to fix it—or try to. That was why I'd become an FBI agent, then switched to law. I chased bad guys when I was younger and sought justice for those they'd harmed when I got older.

But if I was honest with myself—really honest—I had to admit I'd grown jaded with the kind of law my colleagues and I practiced. I was making good money, but too often I ended up helping rich people keep wealth they'd gotten by dubious means or suing somebody who'd done nothing more than displease one of the rich guys.

When I was a special agent with the FBI, lines separating right and wrong were pretty clear. Except for that one time, I always felt I wore the white hat. In my law practice, decisions were a lot murkier.

I'd considered returning to law enforcement. Not likely at age fifty, but I needed to do something that made me happy to look in the mirror again.

All that had come to a head in a phone call a month ago from someone in the Kremlin close to Putin, anxious to launder a lot of money. It wasn't clear who the money belonged to, but it was a lot, north of $1 billion. The Moscow man wanted me to fabricate multiple shell companies in countries that didn't ask questions, like Cyprus. My fee would be 5 percent, about $50 million.

Mario Puzo was right on when he said a lawyer with his briefcase can steal more than a hundred men with guns.

I told my partners dishonest clients made dishonest lawyers and I wasn't going there. Moscow wouldn't deal with anyone else at the firm, so when I said no, they went elsewhere.

BEAR'S PROMISE

My partners threw a hissy fit. "You're depriving each of us of an end-of-the-year million-dollar bonus," they said. For them, a summer home in the Hamptons beat wearing a white hat.

Kat was unhappy too. "I like our lifestyle and don't want it to change."

Kat grew up in an affluent household, very different from my own. Though both her parents drank heavily, her father was a successful lawyer, and her mother an interior designer. They lived in a large house in Briarcliff, a wealthy community in Westchester County, just north of New York City, had a live-in maid who also did the cooking, and belonged to Briar Hall Country Club, later bought by Donald Trump and renamed Trump National Golf Club Westchester. Kat graduated from Greer School for Girls in Pennsylvania, where she was a member of the equestrian and fencing teams. Her father was a Dartmouth College grad, and Dartmouth accepted Kat for early admission. We met there in our freshman year.

Kat's mother was not too excited that her daughter was dating a guy on scholarship who grew up on a farm in southern Indiana and was called Bear, but I got along with her dad—we were both hunters—and he overrode his wife's tantrums when Kat and I got engaged. Her parents divorced after eighteen years of marriage and died at early ages from alcoholic complications. Their big house had been double mortgaged, and there was barely enough money left in the estate to pay off debts. Kat easily gravitated to the lifestyle I provided after the law firm took off.

Was I too naïve? I wondered. *Had I made the right decision to turn down all that money? For me? For Kat? For my law partners?* I pulled out a copy of Mellie's suicide note and reread part of it:

I love you with all my heart. Just promise me you will go after the people responsible for killing my men and bring them to justice. If I know that, I'll die in peace.

Maybe that fight would make me feel good about practicing law again.

I had to hit them where they were most vulnerable. For Sparafucile and Fisheye, that'd mean a charge of police brutality or excessive use of force. The Electric Gun, sold with the promise it couldn't kill, fed right into the hands of vindictive police like Sparafucile who used it to punish and terrorize, while hiding behind the company's claims that the gun was a nonlethal weapon.

I wondered how many victims the Electric Gun had murdered, how many families it had destroyed, and how many medical examiners the company had silenced. I'd sue the company for product liability, selling a product that could kill and failing to warn users about it. I knew they were a take-no-prisoner company, but I'd fought bad guys in the FBI, so that didn't scare me.

The management committee of my law firm had final say, and they might not approve taking on this fight for nothing close to the $50 million Moscow offered. At most, we'd get 40 percent of $4 or $5 million if we won. But if we were true to what I put on our website when I founded J. W. & H, it was a battle worth fighting.

The law reached out to me, as pure and meaningful as when I graduated law school. I loved what it represented and what it could do. We were a nation of laws, but laws were empty words on paper unless I applied them to do what was right and honorable, not just expedient and remunerative.

CHAPTER THIRTEEN

DOUG ZIPES

I'd started Judge, Williams, and Hamden, LLP more than twenty years ago, with just three of us. We now had 110 lawyers between our main office on Sixth Avenue in New York City and satellites in Chicago, Houston, San Francisco, and Los Angeles. We specialized in multidistrict litigation cases composed of hundreds of plaintiffs, challenging pharmaceutical giants, car manufacturers, device companies, and whatever needed righting.

I was sitting at a polished teak table—it reminded me of an aircraft carrier when I'd bought it—in our conference room library, surrounded by floor-to-ceiling shelves of burnished leather-bound law books, leather chairs, and rosewood paneling. I loved the smell of musty books and leather.

I'd tried to make the room a quiet chapel dedicated to the law, where we could bring clients and help them deal with their problems. White coasters scattered on the table with the firm's monogrammed initials, J. W. & H, in gold letters, and a sideboard of coffee, soft drinks, cups, and glasses tarnished the subtle magic I'd tried to create.

Across from me sat Mark Hamden, one of my original partners—Bill Williams had died several years ago—who was leading the opposition wanting me out. Though I was the senior partner, Hamden was two years older and wielded his age as if he were the ranking member of our firm.

"I don't much care for your holier-than-thou attitude, Bear," Hamden said, patting down his perfect hair. I'd often wondered if it was a toupee but had never found out. "When did you develop this conscience of yours? It's hurting the firm."

Hamden looked the part of the distinguished litigator: about five feet ten, slim, impeccably dressed in a three-piece, pin-striped, dark blue suit, white shirt—always white—and solid burgundy bow tie—always solid, but colors ranged from burgundy to red to blue. His gray hair was always neatly trimmed. A narrow pencil mustache and matching goatee highlighted a face Modigliani might've painted. I could never look like that, even on a starvation diet.

I'd explained the case over the phone, giving Hamden a summary of what had happened to Melanie and her family. I asked what he thought about taking on the Electric Gun Company and the Hopperville cops. That was a bad beginning since it had given him time to do his homework and the opportunity to lecture me about product liability.

"Manufacturers that make products sold to the public are held responsible for injuries those products cause," Hamden said in a professorial tone. He went on to explain what I already knew: that we'd have to prove injury from shoddy workmanship, design flaws, or misrepresentation of the product by failing to warn of foreseeable risks and potential harm. We had to prove the Electric Gun Company breached an acceptable standard of care and caused that injury. In Jared's case, we'd have to show the Electric Gun directly triggered his cardiac arrest and that the diagnosis of excited delirium was a myth. Since the Electric Gun was not considered a consumer or workplace product, it was not regulated by agencies such as the Consumer Product Safety Commission or the Occupational Safety and Health Administration.

"Mark, I know all that," I said, trying to conceal my annoyance. "The company may be shielded, but they're vulnerable because they failed to warn. And what about the Hopperville police? Killing somebody when they were asked to help is indefensible, even if the guy whacked a cop's face. The guy was out of his head."

Hamden sipped his coffee from a pearl-colored porcelain cup with gold J. W. & H imprinted on the side, more glitz I'd opposed. He leaned back in the leather chair and gazed out the large bay window in the middle of the room that opened onto Sixth Avenue. He was perfectly at ease, as if he were the senior partner, here to lecture me. I suspect that's what he was angling for.

"I think we could sue the Hopperville police force and in particular Sparafucile, under the Fourth Amendment," I said, "prohibiting unreasonable search and seizure. Officers must use reasonable force appropriate for the circumstances and magnitude of the threat."

"Who determines that?" Hamden asked. I guess he hadn't researched that part.

"Each of the eighteen thousand or so police departments in the US has its own protocol outlining use-of-force policies," I said, "or to be more politically correct, 'response to resistance,' as it's now called." I explained that the police department protocol dictated when cops could escalate their behavior from talking to a subject and using mild restraint to using low-level weapons, such as tear gas, pepper spray, or a baton, to electronic control devices like the Electric Gun, and finally to firearms. While protocols for each department differed, deploying the Electric Gun would generally be limited to subjects aggressively resisting in a manner likely to injure the officer, the subject, or others.

"Okay, say you take the case and you win—which I doubt," Hamden said. "The firm will collect a couple of million, maybe more if we're lucky, but have to invest that in time, expert witness costs, court costs, depositions, travel, and so on. You know the drill. The net proceeds to the firm will be piddly. And you're turning down an opportunity worth almost fifty times that and requiring less work and expenses." His eyes narrowed, and he firmed his lips.

"Look, Mark, let me make it perfectly clear I don't appreciate being lectured to by you or anyone else in this law firm," I said, trying to keep my voice even, though I wanted to kick his pompous ass. "When I invited you to join me over twenty years ago, it was with the understanding we helped the little people as well, not just big money."

"Times have changed, Bear," he said, frowning.

"But I haven't." I returned his frown with a smile I didn't feel. My gut told me this was not going to end well.

"Yeah, and that's the problem." He shifted in his chair, took off his glasses, and set them on the table. He took out a handkerchief, buffed the glasses, put them back on, and looked at me. He blinked his eyes repetitively when he was nervous, which is what he was now doing.

"The partners met at an early breakfast this morning. Since you're the founder and senior partner, we voted to give you another chance to reconsider your decision."

"That's big of you," I said in a sarcastic tone.

Hamden shrugged. "You turn down this stupid gun case and accept Moscow, or ..." He left the sentence dangling.

"Or what?" I asked.

"We'll vote you out of the firm. And let me remind you that the compensation package states—"

"I know what it says. I wrote the damn thing." I waved off his response.

"—that you get $2 million severance if you retire," Hamden went on, disregarding my interruption, "but nothing if you join another law firm or start your own. That's a two-year noncompete policy."

He put his glasses down, picked up his coffee cup, and sipped. "We agreed to give you twenty-four hours to rethink your decision."

BEAR'S PROMISE

I stroked my beard, trying to keep my temper in check. I thought back to when I started this firm, built it from scratch to one of the top ten in the city, took on clients rich and poor, and now my partners were going to throw me out. Greed conquers all.

I couldn't do much about it. The firm had grown so large I'd long since relinquished management to a group of senior partners who made the firing and hiring decisions. Still, I was tempted to grab Hamden by his designer bow tie and wring his neck with it.

Instead, I reached across the table and grabbed his coffee cup. He flinched as if I might throw what was left in his face. I ran my finger over the gold initials, J. W. & H, and took out a small gold-plated pocketknife I always carried. It was a gift from my parents on my thirteen birthday.

A look of fear flashed across his face.

I scraped off the J on the cup and tossed it back into his lap. Residual coffee spilled onto his dark blue pants. Nice, right at the crotch.

"You and the partners can shove the two million up your collective asses. I intend to sue those bastards who took out my sister and her family."

I rose, turned my back on him, and stomped out of the room, slamming the door to my quiet chapel.

"How could you quit without talking to me first?" Kat said when I told her what'd happened. "What about us?" She fixed me with an icy stare.

We were sitting at the dining room table, finishing a slightly burned pot roast. Kat cooked dinner one night a week when the housekeeper was off. Even though she'd been the chef tonight, she was wearing a black sequined, off-the-shoulder jersey and matching black palazzo pants, ready to walk down the model's runway in shiny, black, spiky heels. Her nails were bright red, and her blonde hair was in a messy bun with hanging tendrils. She looked lovely, and my heart did a flip-flop, even after a dozen years of marriage.

"What do you mean, what about us?" I asked.

The reality was that an *us*, like when we worked as a team, no longer existed. Those early years, pulling together with an uncertain future, held magic now lost.

"How're we going to live?" Her eyes flashed daggers at me.

"Like we've always lived." I didn't really believe that, and neither did she.

"You can't be serious, Bear. There's no way we can keep up this lifestyle if you're not a top lawyer with J. W. & H."

"Then we'll have to downsize, cut back on a few luxuries. It's not that big a deal." I tried to make light of it, but I knew she wouldn't buy into that idea.

"Maybe not to you, but it is to me. I didn't starve those early years, working my butt off as your paralegal, to have to do it all over again."

"C'mon, Kat. Be reasonable. We're not going to starve."

I gazed out the window of our apartment. We lived in a four-bedroom, forty-five-hundred-square-foot condo on the Upper East Side of New York City, overlooking Central Park. "$10 million is a steal," the real estate agent had said. We were big supporters of the arts and donated to the Metropolitan Opera, Carnegie Hall, and various museums. My monthly expense to garage our two cars was more than 90 percent of what most New Yorkers paid for rent. We had plenty of room to cut back—and she was right, we'd have to.

"What about our trip to the Grand Caymans this winter?" she asked, pouting.

"We may have to cancel." That would hurt. I loved scuba diving, and the Caymans were diving heaven with multicolored corals and exotic fish.

"And what're you going to do? Join another law firm? Start your own? Or do you expect me to go out and find a job?" She dismissed the latter possibility with a downturn of her lips and a head shake.

I went to her and tried to put my arms around her to console her, but she pushed me away. "I'm serious," she said, glaring at me with a clenched jaw. "I do not plan to go back to work again ... ever."

I think the thin ice supporting our marriage was cracking, but my mind was made up. I'd just completed the life-altering decision to leave the law firm I'd started, and now I might have to leave my marriage as well.

"God forbid you'd have to go to work again. To answer your question, I don't know what I'm going to do, but I'm sure of one thing."

"Yeah? And what's that?" Kat asked, a sharp edge to her voice.

"I'm going to honor my sister's last wishes."

"You do that, and I'm also sure of one thing," Kat said, chin thrust forward.

"What's that?"

"You'll be doing it alone." She stalked out of the room.

CHAPTER FOURTEEN

BEAR'S PROMISE

J. W. & H had security escort me out of my office, giving me just enough time to collect a few personal items and say goodbye to one or two colleagues. The firm was afraid if I were left alone, I might download my client list and attempt to take some with me. I had no such intention. I had just one client in mind—my sister's estate—and just one issue, suing the Hopperville cops and Electric Gun.

I moved to Hopperville a month later. Kat and I agreed on a separation that left her the condo, one car, and money in the bank, but no divorce, at least for now. I still loved her and hoped after a while she'd decide I really hadn't betrayed her, and we'd get back together. But for now, she changed the locks and didn't answer her cell phone, so our future was iffy. I half expected divorce papers in the next mail. She'd have to alter her lifestyle, and I had a twinge of guilt about that. But she'd hardly be destitute and certainly would not have to go back to work, either modeling or as a paralegal.

I put Melanie's house up for sale and rented a place on Main Street in the center of Hopperville. The furnished apartment had cream-colored walls, two bedrooms with baths, and a tiny kitchen that opened into a living room, perfect for my needs.

I'd debated moving into Mellie's house, but I couldn't bear to be surrounded by her constant presence reminding me of what had happened.

After living many years in New York City, I'd forgotten how lovely life in a small town could be. I had to adjust to the quiet. The loud silence kept me awake at night. I finally bought a sleep noisemaker and dialed in city sounds. I fell right to sleep.

Shops and restaurants filled every nook along Main Street, always busy with a steady stream of pedestrians. Nothing like the swarms jam-packed along Fifth Avenue in New York but a welcome change to be able to walk and not collide with a wall of people.

The town had commissioned an artist to create life-size statues of people in everyday situations like carrying groceries, sitting on a bench reading a newspaper, and walking a dog. A dozen of these figures peppered the sidewalk along Main Street. They were so lifelike—even to the wrinkles in a man's shirt or the loaf of bread sticking out of a lady's shopping bag—I had to look twice to be sure they weren't real people.

My apartment was a few streets from a municipal building where I rented office space—less ostentatious than J. W. & H but suitable for my purposes. The convenience of free parking and a ten-minute walk to work outweighed any downside.

Indiana offered reciprocity for my New York law license, so I only had to fill out a handful of papers to be admitted to the Indiana Bar Association and obtain an Indiana license to practice law.

The suite had three rooms for offices, a conference room, a tiny kitchen, and a reception area. I shopped at Best Buy for computers, printers, and other office equipment and had everything up and running in two weeks. I placed an ad in the *Hopperville Daily* and on Facebook, Instagram, and LinkedIn for a receptionist, paralegal, and a law partner to join Jason Judge, JD, attorney at law.

My last name had always been the source of comments and amusement. "Suppose you become a judge?" one of my friends teased. "Would you be called Judge Judge?"

The name was not as attention grabbing as someone I'd met while I was still at J. W. & H. I'd interviewed a feisty, recent Georgetown Law School graduate named Gladys Shark. Gladys was a boyish, short, stocky brunette with clipped hair and an attitude to match. During her interview, I asked if she'd ever considered changing her last name, now that she was about to become a practicing lawyer.

"No," she said, "but I've considered changing my first name."

Surprised, I asked, "To what?"

"Great White."

I laughed, hired her on the spot, and always called her GW after that. She developed into a superb trial lawyer, true to her name, and she was one of the few who came by my office to say goodbye.

GW called my cell phone about a month after I'd moved to Hopperville.

"Hi, Bear. How's the new firm going?"

"GW, what a surprise. Looking to move to Indiana? I could use a partner."

"I'm not, but I just spoke with someone who might be. Name's Deroshay Odinga."

"Who?" I was interested. I trusted GW's judgment, and I did need an assistant.

"Deroshay Odinga. He's as unusual as his name," GW said. "Originally from Kenya. Shay's grandfather or great-grandfather was a tribal king or medicine man or somebody important."

She went on to say that Shay had just graduated from Harvard Law second in his class, had been on full scholarship, a member of the law review, the moot court, and was exceptionally bright.

"He passed the New York bar exam with one of the highest scores in the city. I think he's got a photographic memory. But he's a bit of a nonconformist, a little quirky."

"In what way?"

"His appearance, attitude—pretty much everything about him. Maybe because he comes from Kenyan aristocracy. The firm's application committee turned him down because he didn't fit the image of a J. W. & H lawyer. You interested?"

"Intrigued." She'd heard me complain often enough that J. W. & H was getting too staid—that we needed to get with the millennial generation, put away the jackets and ties at work, and end the tuxedo dinners. "Finally creating a new image?"

"Yup. In fact, we recently went to a Greenwich Village jazz cellar instead of the Metropolitan Opera."

"Good start. I'm interested as long as he doesn't use 'like' in every other sentence."

"Shay would be *like* putting your toe in the millennial waters," GW said, laughing.

I debated. I didn't mind the nonconformity as much as I did working with a kid just out of law school as my sole law partner. That was like having a recently minted doctor perform open-heart surgery. I wouldn't want that person holding my heart in his hands. But he'd be young blood to help build the firm. Even from a physical standpoint, he'd be useful, able to work fourteen- and sixteen-hour days when necessary. That was the norm during a court trial that could last several weeks or a month.

GW gave me his contact information, and I arranged for Shay to visit.

Two days later, Deroshay Odinga walked into my office. "Walked" is not quite accurate. He kind of sauntered across the rug to stand in front of my desk.

"Hello, I'm Shay," he said.

Shay was a tall wisp of a guy, ebony black, skinny, wearing jeans, a gray sweatshirt with *Harvard* stitched in bright red letters across the front and a small sparkling diamond in each ear. The jeans were worn but had no holes, and the belt looped around his waist, not his ass.

His most striking feature was his head, covered with curly black hair raked into squares like a checkerboard. A long braid grew from the center of each square, like a rose stem from a square patch of dirt. The braids merged together into a thick single plait that hung down his back in a shoulder-length ponytail. I wondered how many hours his hairdresser took to sculpt that intricate pattern—and what special shampoo was required to clean and nurture this hirsute garden.

I rose and extended my hand. "Hi, Shay. I'm Jason, but my friends call me Bear."

Shay's handshake was firm, almost a knuckle cruncher, but lasted only a second. He pulled out a chair and plunked down, looking at me with brow raised in a questioning expression, silently saying, *Okay, I'm here. What's next?*

CHAPTER FIFTEEN

Shay locked eyes with me, friendly but penetrating, sizing me up. I'd googled him after GW called, and I'm sure he did the same about me. He'd find out that I'd been listed in *The Best Lawyers in America* annually for the past fifteen years and that our law firm had won an impressive number of high-profile judgments. I could teach him a lot of law.

I knew my Google bio didn't say why I switched from the FBI to practicing law, just that I'd been a former special agent in charge. It did include the story about me raising a bear cub as a kid.

I'd found out a lot about Shay, mostly from GW. He'd become friends with her, and she was able to give me insight into his personality from some personal stories he'd related to her.

He was different, she said, a nonconformist—that's why the application committee of the law firm rejected him. They didn't care he was a black guy trying to make it in a white world, trying to live by white men's rules set for black people. He just wasn't J. W. & H material, like it or not.

GW told me that Shay was trying to preserve a sense of self—his own identity—and chose to be different within those constraints, to be true to his Kenyan heritage and to his black brothers and sisters, at least in how he dressed and some of his mannerisms. Most of his external behavior conformed to the white world, but what went on in his head was black.

Black people were held to different standards than whites, he said to her. If they didn't obey white rules, they could get their asses in trouble. He told her the story about driving in New York City when he'd crossed lanes on West Fifty-Seventh Street without signaling. A white cop stopped him, and he was almost cuffed and hauled off to the police station, just for crossing lanes without signaling.

When GW pursued why the cop got so rough, he told her he did give the cop a bit of shit for pulling him over for such a stupid infraction. The cop had no legal right to make him get out of the car, he said, or to do a pat down and search for drugs. Still, Shay knew he should've just shut his mouth, taken whatever abuse the cop was going to dish out, and not dissed him.

But that was not his nature, she told me. You dealt him shit, he dealt it right back.

A short time later, he and his girlfriend stopped at a sidewalk café on Sixth Avenue for a coffee. The girlfriend needed to use the restroom and asked Shay to hold her purse. He said, "No way. Take it with you." He told her a black guy standing on a New York City sidewalk holding a woman's purse was an invitation to disaster. A white guy could do it with impunity.

Shay went on to tell GW a joke about that type of situation.

"What do you call a black kid riding a new ten-speed bike?"

"What?" she asked.

"A thief."

To Shay, that was reality. When he was eight, his family lived in Upstate New York, near Saratoga Springs, in a small house in a mostly white neighborhood. They'd immigrated to the States when his mom was in her ninth month so he could be born on US soil and become a citizen by birth. His folks became citizens through the naturalization process. His dad taught science and math at Saratoga Springs High School.

Shay'd been saving for a new bike by selling lemonade on a street corner in front of their house. He'd already made thirty-three bucks. One day, an African American man stopped his car, came over, and bought a glass of lemonade. He gave Shay five bucks and refused the change. Turned out the man owned a bike shop in town, and he invited Shay to come to his store and pick out any bike he liked. Shay chose a ten-speed Schwinn.

The family moved to New York City a year later when Shay's dad became principal of a high school in Harlem. A white cop stopped him riding in Central Park and grilled him about where he got the bike. His mom had the bike receipt—the shop owner had told her to be sure to keep it handy—and that saved him from being called a thief … just like the joke.

Would the cop have questioned a white kid riding that same bike? he'd asked GW. "No way," he said, answering his own question.

GW had asked him whether he thought it'd be different living in a small Midwestern town like Hopperville. He hoped it would be, he told her, that the racial tensions might be a lot less than in New York City.

"You look like you've pumped some iron," Shay said, staring at me and bringing me back to the present.

"Past tense," I said. "In college and for a few years after that. Too busy now, and just let it go."

I wanted to hear him discuss the Simpson case and gave him all the details. He listened attentively, and when I finished, I asked, "Think we have a chance? How would you approach it?"

"From my vast experience in the courtroom," he said, and we both laughed, "yeah, I do think we have a chance. I'd start out researching excited delirium and learn more about the Electric Gun and its effects on the heart. Maybe find an expert cardiologist to help us. We'd also need to start deposing the players like Sparafucile and Fisheye, get the police and medical reports, talk with the medical examiner, and find any other witnesses."

"Good start. Those are the basics. What else?" I asked.

"I'd file in federal court because we're talking violation of federal civil rights statutes. We need to draft a summons and allegations and then file with the court, serve the complaint on Sparafucile, Fisheye, his police department, and Electric Gun Company, Inc. After that's done, I'd start the discovery process with depositions and fact gathering."

Shay stopped to scratch his neck and adjust the braid. "This damn thing itches where the hair rubs my skin. Cost me two hundred and fifty bucks but worth every penny."

"Why don't you cut the braid off if it's bothering you?"

"I'm tempted, but I have a picture of my grandfather with the same hairstyle at a chief's gathering in Kenya thirty or forty years ago. He was dressed in black, red, and white ceremonial robes and beaded necklaces. The outfit had been part of my family for more than a hundred years. I feel like I owe it to him to carry on the tradition."

"Maybe it's time to give up the past, to go modern? No robes or necklaces but maybe a pair of dress jeans and a nice white shirt?"

He just sat there, not saying anything. I backed off. He could dress any way he liked in the office. In the courtroom, things would be different.

"Okay, back to business. You sound like you know what you're doing," I said, giving an encouraging nod. "But this is the easy part. First-year law school stuff. The tough part will be preparing and proving our case in front of a jury. The cops may settle to avoid notoriety and adverse publicity, but I'm sure Electric Gun won't.

Then again, Sparafucile may not want his police department to settle. They could do it without admitting guilt—settle with an 'admit no wrongdoing' clause—but he may still object."

"How much are we going to sue for?" Shay asked, eyes wide.

I smiled at the *we*. "Sounds like you're on board already."

Shay grinned and nodded.

"Tough call," I said. I explained that there'd really been only one death directly attributable to the Electric Gun. Still, we could argue, but for that death, the other two wouldn't have happened. The loss of earnings from the parents wouldn't amount to much, but the son had a full life ahead with great potential. We'd contend he could've become a football star making millions.

"We'll need a statement from his coach praising his talents, that he was being recruited by three universities, full scholarship, and stuff like that," I said, running my fingers through my beard. "Fifteen million would not be unreasonable. The reality, though, is that one and a half or two million from Hopperville police would probably be their max. If their insurance coverage is more, we'll ask for more."

I said that the Electric Gun Company was a different beast. They had deep pockets, and that's where we'd attack. But they'd be a lot tougher than the cops, not caring about adverse publicity, not scaring easily, and willing to pull out all the stops. Hopefully, we'd get $4 or $5 million from the company. They did have deep pockets but maybe short arms.

I paused, deciding whether to hire him. I liked the young man. I didn't care about him being different as long as he was a good lawyer. "You in?" I asked finally.

"Offering me a job?" he said with a grin.

"Maybe. How about a six-month probation that gets us through this trial? See how well you do, how well *we* do. After all, it's my only case so far. If we win, we'll have others flocking to us."

"Sounds good to me."

"I need to be careful with finances," I said, "since there'll be lots of expenses ahead. I'll start you at thirty-five K for the six months, and we'll see how things work out. Bonus if we win. Deal?"

Shay held out his hand. "You just got yourself a new associate."

"Great. You can move in with me until you rent an apartment. We've got a trial date set, so we start work on this case tomorrow morning at eight."

I stood, stretched, and checked my watch. "Hungry?"

"Yeah," Shay said.

"There's supposed to be a great pizza joint near here. Let's check it out."

CHAPTER SIXTEEN

I'd already finished half a cream-cheesed bagel and a cup of coffee when Shay finally woke and emerged from the spare bedroom. No sauntering this time. More like staggering.

I was taking to the kid already. He was smart, pleasant, and didn't say "like" except when appropriate.

But he couldn't hold his liquor.

"How'd you sleep?" I asked. He was massaging his head and looked pale. We'd been up late last night, debating the merits of the case, washed down with multiple shots of fourteen-year-old Oban scotch. The single malt was my favorite, from one of the smallest distilleries in Scotland, making it sometimes hard to find. One ice cube freed up the smooth West Highland flavor, smoky and sweet.

"Ugh," was his response with a turned-up lip, almost like a snarl. "If this is what it's going to be like working with you, sign me up for a liver transplant."

"Hungry?" I asked, standing to toast the other half of the bagel for him. "Or just coffee?"

"Coffee. My stomach can't handle anything stronger." He waved his hands over my empty bagel plate.

I went to the black wire carousel on the kitchen counter holding pods of Starbucks coffees. "French roast?"

"Okay."

I popped it into the Keurig, brewed a cup, and toasted and cream-cheesed the bagel half in case he changed his mind. I sat with him at the kitchen table. He sipped slowly and ignored the bagel, so I took it.

"Do you remember much of what we discussed last night?" I asked.

"Not a whole lot after the second Oban. Or maybe the third—I forgot which. That scotch has a wicked kick to it." He held his head and closed his eyes.

"Let's review," I said in a cheery voice. I had to dispel the gloomy hangover he was feeling. "Hopperville's defense is going to be that Jared attacked the cop and Sparafucile shot him in self-defense with a nonlethal weapon. The fact that he died was accidental because the gun can't kill. We talked about researching the Electric Gun Company to try and prove wrongdoing, find out maybe if the gun's defective. Remember any of that?" I asked.

"I do, but like I said last night, that logic's not realistic because Shorty provoked Jared with his baton, and so did Sparafucile when he ordered Fisheye to shoot Ryan. The cops incited the whole thing." He held out his hand, finger pointed at me like a gun, and went, "Bang."

Ah, the naivete of a young lawyer. I smiled at him. "Shay, my young friend, you'll soon learn that reason often has very little to do with the law. The United States justice system is not about determining what's reasonable or—too often—who's right and who's wrong. It's only about what you can prove and whether you can convince a jury to believe it. It's all about winning—like that old football quote, 'Winning isn't everything; it's the only thing.'"

That brought him to life. He jumped up, stood straight, and recited as if he were in a classroom. "Vince Lombardi, head coach of the Green Bay Packers, 1959 to 1967. Studied to be a priest. Died of colon cancer in 1970 at age fifty-seven. Nine wins and one loss in postseason play and never had a losing NFL season." He plopped back down, again holding his head.

I looked at him, impressed with his instant recall. Maybe he did have a photographic memory.

"In this case, I think the police and Electric Gun Company could persuade the jury that the use of the Electric Gun was justified in a subject aggressively resisting arrest 'in a manner likely to injure the officer or the subject.' Remember, Jared was a big guy whose appearance alone was threatening. Defense will argue that the provocation was irrelevant and Sparafucile had every right to defend himself against Jared attacking him."

"Maybe Jared wasn't really coming at him?" Shay asked.

"That's not what the police reports state," I said, pointing to my computer.

I'd downloaded accounts by Sparafucile, Diaz—the one they called Fisheye—Bennett, and the fourth cop, a guy named Abernathy, using the Freedom of Information Act that gave me access to public documents. All four reports described the same scene. Jared lunged at Sparafucile after he ordered Fisheye to shoot Ryan. In fact, the wording was so similar in three of them, you'd think one person wrote them. Bennett's was slightly different.

"What about Sparafucile ordering Fisheye to shoot Ryan in the first place?" Shay asked, sipping his coffee. "That wasn't justified since he was already cuffed."

"I agree," I said, taking the last bite of the bagel. I should have made a second one. "That's a weak point for the defense we need to capitalize on, but as I said before, they'll argue that provocation was irrelevant."

"And then Sparafucile killing Ryan?" Shay was showing more animation. I guess his head was clearing. "His gun wasn't loaded, and you could've talked him down."

I shook my head. "Much as I hate to say it, Sparafucile didn't know the gun wasn't loaded, and once again, he had every right to defend himself."

"What about product liability and a failure to warn of potential harm?" Shay asked, brow raised.

"Good question." GW had been right about Shay. The kid was a quick study. It was going to be fun working with him. "Electric Gun will claim excited delirium killed Jared, not the gun. They've successfully used that defense many times. It'll be difficult to prove that the gun did it."

Shay gazed out the window, sort of trancelike. His face showed a look of concentration, forehead wrinkled, eyes focused, and lips pursed so tightly they blanched. My eyes followed his, but all I saw was an early-morning blue sky with white, fluffy clouds wandering among the buildings.

"What?" I asked. "Where's your head?"

"Where's my head? Actually, it's in Kenya with my grandfather, Nyundo Odinga. Nyundo means hammer in Swahili, and that's what he was, a hammer. Anything got in his way, he hammered and shaped it into what he wanted."

Shay formed a fist and mimed hammering on the table.

"You didn't mess with the chief and live to talk about it. But when I was in my teens, he told me the days of the hammer were ending, which was why my parents moved to the US. Right now, I wish I could use a hammer."

"Hammer out justice?"

"Yeah, something like that," he said, grinning.

We showered, dressed, and walked to work. On the way, we passed a JoS. A. Bank men's store.

"I'll stake you to a new pair of pants and shirt, sort of a signing bonus," I said.

He smiled. "Haircut to follow?"

I ignored the sarcastic tone. "Your call. But maybe a blue suit, white shirt, and red tie before we go to court. I think they're on sale this week."

Once we hit the office, I sent Shay to find an apartment.

I dialed up Google and from there went to the Electric Gun Company's website. Very impressive. Headquartered in Framingham, Massachusetts, about twenty-five miles outside Boston, the company had a workforce of a thousand, including executives, engineers and factory workers, trainers and sales force. Net sales for 2017 were more than half a billion dollars, selling to thirty thousand police departments around the world. That was a lot of Electric Guns. The company prided itself on supplying law enforcement with a reliable weapon safe for users as well as for the suspects it was used against. Their major competitor was the other electric gun manufacturer TASER, International. The Electric Gun Company, Inc. did everything they could to distinguish themselves from TASER.

Use warnings said nothing about the Electric Gun provoking cardiac arrest. Because it produced neuromuscular incapacitation, the company did warn against shooting someone who could fall onto a sharp object, from a great height, or into water, and not to aim at the face. But instructions were to target the "largest part of the body accessible," which, naturally, included the chest if the subject was facing the shooter.

I wondered why they had no oversight organization, like the Drug Enforcement Agency or the Bureau of Alcohol, Tobacco, Firearms, and Explosives. It seemed the Electric Gun Company did whatever it wanted. Why didn't the ATFE oversee the Electric Gun as it did other firearms?

I had many questions that needed answers before we went any further. I couldn't imagine the CEO, a guy named Slaughter, would talk to me if he knew I was planning to sue his company. But I needed to get a feel for him, see what kind of leadership he provided and why he didn't warn the gun could kill. I'd have to set the lawsuit in motion so I could question him at deposition.

Shay, returning successfully from apartment hunting, thought otherwise.

"We need to talk to this guy in a friendly manner," he said, brow creased in a knowing look. "Disarm him without his lawyer present. That way, we'll really find out what the company's like."

"And how do you propose we do that?" I asked.

Shay pursed his lips again. I was to learn that when he made that face, he was deep in thought.

"How about we pose as reporters? Tell him we're considering a front-page story for some law enforcement magazine." He checked Google on his iPhone. "*Police* magazine looks like a good one. You be the reporter, and I'll be the photographer."

"Nice thought and technically not illegal but definitely unethical. No, we can't do that. Maybe it's best if we don't say anything, just tell him we're interested in hearing his story behind starting the company. Play to his ego. He might go for that."

CHAPTER SEVENTEEN

DOUG ZIPES

Ego trumped better judgment, and Beverly Slaughter, CEO of Electric Gun Company, Inc., agreed to an interview.

From his picture on the internet, I knew Beverly was a man, despite his name. I couldn't help imagining what it must've been like growing up with that moniker. How many fights had he gotten into? Did his friends call him Beverly? Bev? Lee? Maybe a lot of worse names than those.

We flew to Boston, rented a car, and drove to the company's headquarters in Framingham, Massachusetts. The twenty-five-mile drive from the airport took an hour and a half because of traffic. Tunnels built beneath the city failed to alleviate the congestion of cars on the streets. The day was gloomy with clouds and a light rain that worsened traffic delays and chilled our bones. March in Boston was definitely not spring.

Beverly Slaughter sat behind a mahogany desk and didn't bother getting up as his secretary led us into his office. His clingy green T-shirt—at least one size too small—outlined a thick neck, reasonable biceps, and flabby pecs. Since his internet picture had been posted, he'd shaved his head. His scalp shimmered a bright pink in the overhead fluorescent light. It reminded me of a polished bowling ball: his dark eye sockets would be the two finger slots, and I'd put my thumb in his mouth.

"You got ten minutes, maybe fifteen tops," Slaughter said by way of greeting, glancing at his watch. "I got a busy morning and can't waste any more of it. I don't usually grant interviews like this. Don't make me regret it." He motioned to two chairs in front of his desk, and we sat down.

"Thanks for agreeing to meet with us, Mr. Slaughter," I said. "I'm Jason Judge, and this is my partner, Deroshay Odinga. I'll get right to the point. Can the Electric Gun cause cardiac arrest?"

His raised eyebrows and open mouth conveyed his surprise.

"You two cops?"

I shook my head.

"Lawyers?"

"Yes."

He scowled at me through beady eyes. "I need my lawyer present? I don't know if I should talk to you alone."

"Up to you, but we just want to chat informally, find out about your incredible invention and the very successful company you founded," I said, looking around his office. "You've redefined the use of restraint in the field of law enforcement."

He barely suppressed a smile. I repeated my question. "Can your gun cause cardiac arrest?"

"That's bullshit," he said, running a hand over his bald pate. The fingers stopped halfway across to pick at something, maybe a razor nick, and moved on to scratch an earlobe. "Who's feeding you crap like that?"

"We've been reading police reports." I told him about Jared but not that he was my brother-in-law.

"Sounds like a classic case of excited delirium," he said, pushing back from his desk and standing. He was medium height, five nine or ten, with a huge gut that flopped over his belt. I could see why he'd want to remain sitting, shielding that belly behind a desk.

Slaughter pulled over a metal stand that held a flipchart. "Look here," he said, indicating the chart. "We figure the Electric Gun's been deployed at least five million times around the world." He pointed to a rising curve. "I'm pretty proud of those numbers."

I suspected he'd had that chart prepared for a presentation about the Electric Gun to some group, perhaps as a sales pitch to sell guns to a police department.

"There've been less than fifty reported deaths, and all were due to injuries after the combatant was immobilized and fell, or was inadvertently shot in the eye or throat, or a fire triggered from the spark of the Electric Gun. None"—he slammed a flat hand on the desktop—"were due to cardiac arrest caused by the Electric Gun. Whenever anyone died suddenly from cardiac arrest, it was always triggered by excited delirium, not the gun. And they had it coming. Like your guy, Jared, for slugging a cop. You can't hit a cop and not expect them to hit back." He shrugged and held his hands out as if to say, "What the hell would you expect?"

"Of the five million deployments, how many probes were shot into the chest?" I asked.

"How the hell do I know?" Slaughter said, sitting down with an angry look.

"Wouldn't that affect the safety numbers?" Someone shot in the buttocks, legs, or back wouldn't have electricity going near their heart and wouldn't be at risk for cardiac arrest. Those deployments would artificially jack up the safety factor.

Slaughter shook his head. "We don't have records of chest shots."

"When the cardiac arrests occurred," Shay said, "how do you know they were all due to excited delirium? Who made the diagnoses?"

Slaughter looked at Shay and paused. It seemed to me he was deciding whether to answer this young kid who'd just butted in. Finally, he did. "The local medical examiner, of course, but our in-house expert, Dr. Jeremiah Verity, reviewed each case and concurred."

"Is Dr. Verity employed by you?" Shay asked.

I watched Shay's face and then Slaughter's. Shay seemed excited, eyes wide, mouth open, on to something. Slaughter seemed to withdraw, eyes narrowed, mouth shut, and lips in a tight line. Finally, he answered.

"Not directly. He's an adjunct professor at the University of Biomedical and Scientific Chemistry in Boston and chairs our scientific board of advisers."

Shay scratched his head. "What's an adjunct professor?" I couldn't tell if he really didn't know or whether he was jerking Slaughter around. The CEO gave him a straight answer.

"It's some sort of an unfunded teaching position—like a student adviser—at the university, not part of the actual faculty," Slaughter said.

"So, not a real university association with salary?" Shay asked, eyebrows raised.

"It's exactly as I said," Slaughter responded, looking annoyed.

"Did Electric Gun donate to the university to get him that position?" Shay asked.

"Absolutely not," Slaughter answered too quickly.

I needed to shift Slaughter's attention. He seemed to be getting too riled at Shay. But I thought Shay uncovered a chink in the company's armor with this guy Verity.

"Your company pay Dr. Verity to head your scientific board?" I asked.

"Yeah, you expect him to work for free? So what?" Slaughter said.

I didn't bother pointing out the obvious conflict of interest. "Has he been given stock options in your company?"

"I suppose so," Slaughter answered, appearing unhappy with my question.

"I assume he's a physician, an electrophysiologist expert in heart rhythm disorders?" Shay asked, jumping back into the fray.

"Not exactly," Slaughter said, fidgeting in his chair. He checked his watch.

"What do you mean, not exactly? What kind of doctor is he?" Both Shay and I inched toward the edge of our seats.

Slaughter didn't answer but stared at me and played with an earlobe. He took out a handkerchief and blew his nose. Finally, he said, "I think I should have my lawyer present. I don't like the way these questions are going."

"Don't answer if you don't want to," I said, sitting back to defuse any suspicion. I crossed my legs and tried to look bored. "I'm just curious is all. Your invention's revolutionized police work, made it much safer for the cops and the takedowns, and we want to find out as much about it as we can."

Slaughter perked up. "Verity's mainly a chemist and does some research on dogs."

I could hardly believe what I was hearing. Slaughter was using a non-MD—paid by the company and given company stock—as a scientific expert to judge probable cause of death after an Electric Gun shooting. I was amazed any jury would buy what a chemist had to say, but they obviously had.

Slaughter explained why.

"Verity's an expert witness who's got a PhD in chemistry," Slaughter said with a dismissive wave of his hand. "He's called doctor; that's all I care about. I don't give a damn whether it's an MD or a PhD. He could be a PhD in garbage collecting, for all I care, but still a doctor. He writes detailed reports supporting the diagnosis of excited delirium that he signs with his name, *Doctor* Jeremiah Verity, and he testifies for us at depositions and in court as *Doctor* Verity. The jury hears *Doctor* Verity, and that's all they need to know. If they think he's a medical doctor, that's their problem."

Slaughter just blurted this out. I'm sure had his lawyer been present, the lawyer would have shut him up pretty fast. This was a deceptive tactic and incredibly unethical, even if it wasn't illegal. I looked forward to ripping Verity and his credentials to shreds on the witness stand. He was responsible for Frisson and his medical examiner buddies getting cold feet, making them diagnose excited delirium as the cause of death instead of the Electric Gun.

"Do you pay him extra for writing those reports?"

"Yeah."

"How much?" I asked. I didn't really expect him to tell me, but I wanted to give Slaughter an opportunity to say no to me and distract him from what he'd just revealed.

"None of your goddamn business," Slaughter said.

I was sure I could find the answer in their end-of-the-year financial statement they had to post as a publicly traded company.

Shay pursed his lips. I liked this kid even more. His questions were right on the mark. "Earlier, when you used that chart, you said, 'reported deaths,'" Shay pointed to the chart. "Could there be unreported deaths? Is reporting mandatory?"

"I suppose there could be but not likely," Slaughter said with a head shake. "No, there's no mandatory reporting, except, I think, in Connecticut."

"Should there be?" Shay persisted.

"No need. The gun is safe," Slaughter replied. "We sell it as a nonlethal weapon. I said it doesn't kill. Period. End of discussion." He slammed his hand down again.

Slaughter's actions didn't appear to intimidate Shay, and he continued his questioning without showing any emotion. "Wouldn't you like to know where the probes ended up after each encounter and the outcome of each deployment?" he asked.

"I really don't give a damn," Slaughter said. "Sales are climbing through the roof, like I showed you." He pointed to the chart. "That's all I care about. What the cops do with the guns is their business. Once the shipment leaves my factory, it's someone else's worry, not mine."

"You don't care that people are killed by a product you make that you tout as safe?" I bit my tongue after I said that, but I couldn't stand his superior attitude any longer, his lack of remorse and refusal to take any responsibility. He remained aloof, untouched by the mayhem he founded, a smirk on his face. My response didn't faze him a bit.

"I suppose I'd care if it were true. But it's not. They die of excited delirium."

"All the time?" Shay asked.

"All the time, every time. Absolutely. There's never been one report—not one—showing that the gun produced cardiac arrest. Until that happens, the diagnosis stays excited delirium."

"Suppose you get sued?" I asked. I knew he had, plenty of times. But their defense record was envious. They'd rarely lost a court battle.

"It happens. I got a team of very smart and very tough lawyers. They cost me a mint, but they're worth every penny. I figure it's just the price of doing business. Because of them, we rarely lose a case. And when we do, we appeal and always get the court to reduce the award to a fraction of what the jury awarded, an amount my insurance easily covers."

"Do you settle claims or go to court with all of them?" I asked.

"That's confidential," he said with a smug look. "I will tell you this, though. We've got a litigious reputation that scares off most challengers who don't have lots of bucks to cover the legal fees. They know not to mess with us. We mean business, and we go to the mat every time. They can't afford to take us to court, and they back off."

I wanted to change the subject. "You don't list any warnings about the gun triggering cardiac arrest in the brochure posted on your website," I said.

"Something wrong with your hearing, pal? What did I tell your friend?" He tipped his head at Shay. "That doesn't happen. The gun is safe. Nonlethal. If people die, it's always excited delirium triggering cardiac arrest, not the gun. Always, like I said before."

He sat back in his chair and put his feet on his desk. "What did that first Bush guy say about taxes when he was president? 'Read my lips.' So, read them. The gun's never been shown to affect the human heart. Never." He slammed his fist on the desk again. "Ask Verity or our lawyers."

"Human hearts," Shay said. "What about animals? Any animal studies showing cardiac arrest?" Shay had done his homework.

"Some, but a cat or a dog isn't a man, so I don't really give a damn what they showed. The jury doesn't either." Slaughter's face was getting red, and he was frowning. I figured we were reaching his limit.

"Is there any governmental oversight?" Shay asked. This was an important question. We knew the answer was no but didn't know why.

"No."

"Why not?" Shay asked. "These are guns. Why doesn't ATFE exert oversight control, like with other guns?"

"Because these are not guns," Slaughter said with a wave of his hand. "We call them guns because we've designed them to feel, look, and handle like a gun. That's what cops want. That's what they know how to use. It's really an electronic control device, an ECD."

"That's semantic bull," I said.

"No, it's not," Slaughter said.

"Doesn't the Electric Gun use gun powder to propel the probes?" I asked.

"No," Slaughter said, smiling for the second time. He took his feet off the desk and sat upright. "That's where we're one step ahead of everybody—smarter than all of you. The Electric Gun uses compressed nitrogen to drive the probes forward. No explosives, so we avoid tangling with the ATFE, and users don't need a gun permit."

"Clever," I said. So that's how they'd been able to bypass one of the most important regulatory agencies, the ATFE.

The CEO puffed out his chest. He looked at his watch, looked at me, and then back at his watch. He didn't say anything but didn't need to.

I felt we'd done okay for starters, just to get a feel. We were a good team. I'd debated a good-guy / bad-guy routine but had thought the bad-guy questions might turn him off. Softball queries to gather information were best now. I'd leave the hardball stuff for deposition or in court.

But the guy was so arrogant I couldn't deny myself one bad-guy question. "One last question, Mr. Slaughter," I said.

"Yeah?" he said, ignoring us and starting to read a file on his desk.

"How do you handle the name Beverly? Was it tough growing up?"

Slaughter's face turned dark, his eyebrows crunched together, and his eyes became narrow slits barely visible.

"Get the hell out of my office while you can still walk, or I'll throw you out on your ass." He rose and started to march around the corner of his desk toward us.

Shay jumped out of his chair.

I got up slowly. "It's okay, Bev," I said, my hand extended, palm up like a traffic cop. "We'll see you in court, and maybe you'll answer that question from the witness stand."

"I can't believe you asked him that." Shay laughed and shook his head in disbelief as we walked to our rental car.

"It'd been buzzing around in my brain ever since I read his name. I had to let it out. He's got the conscience—or lack of one—of a psychopath, and I bet the name has something to do with it. I wonder what his parents were like, to saddle a boy with Beverly."

"Probably weird," Shay said.

"Crazy how things turn out," I said, stopping to look at Shay. "Name a kid Beverly, and he ends up running a company making legal weapons that kill without oversight, and the guy could give two shits about it."

CHAPTER EIGHTEEN

BEAR'S PROMISE

Shay and I were a couple of months into preparing our case against the cops and Electric Gun, working fourteen-hour days. I needed a paralegal to help with grunt work like searching for publications about the Electric Gun, finding previous lawsuits, setting up appointments for depositions, and so on. We needed help searching for and collecting medical records of other Electric Gun victims, drafting some simple motions, and making appointments to interview witnesses.

And somebody to answer the office phone. I'd amended my answering policy and let the damn thing ring and ring until finally Shay picked it up. But it always interrupted my train of thought and cost valuable time.

It was past midnight when my cell phone rang. I was in the kitchen reading the cops' reports for the zillionth time and eating a home-delivered, soggy pizza that tasted like the cardboard box it came in. I checked the caller ID.

Kat.

I hadn't spoken to her since I left the city more than two months ago. Why would she be calling so late? "Hello, Kat."

I heard only weeping. Finally, "Bear?"

"It's me. What's wrong? How are you?"

"Drunk. I miss you." I could hear the alcohol in her slurred response.

"I miss you too," I said. I really did. It was lonely without her, even though I was working so hard.

She'd obviously fallen off the wagon, big-time.

The weeping intensified. "Oh, Bear. I'm so sorry. So, so sorry."

"For what?" I asked. "What did you do?"

Silence.

"Kat. Are you okay?"

The line went dead.

Shit. Not now. I didn't need emotional stuff in my life, now of all times.

I called her back but got no answer. I waited five minutes and tried again. And again. No answer. I called Shay. From the sound of his voice, he'd been asleep.

"Hey, chum, sorry to wake you, but something's come up. I've got to go to New York for a couple of days. I'll leave first thing in the morning. Hold the fort. Hope to be back by the weekend."

I arrived at LaGuardia Airport late the next morning. Early April showers were bringing May flowers, and the plane ride was bumpy. My stomach was queasy by the time we landed.

I grabbed a cab to our apartment. I didn't expect my key to work, and it didn't. I rang the bell. The security peephole flashed, and Kat opened the door.

She looked like hell. She was wearing an old Chinese kimono with red dragons on a white-and-black background. I'd bought it in Chinatown when we were first married. She'd thrown it over a pink silk nightgown that had a round, wet stain down the front. I couldn't help noticing how the wet silk clung and outlined her breasts, still full and firm. I'd had no sex since I left and felt a stirring. But she smelled of stale booze. Her eyes were puffy and red, ringed by dark mascara that reminded me of a raccoon. Her blonde hair was pancaked in the back from sleep. Bed hair, she called it.

I bent to kiss her cheek, but she pulled away.

"Wanna drink?" she asked.

"No," I said, "and I don't think you do either."

"Yeah, I do." She walked barefoot and unsteady to the small bar in the living room. Two dirty glasses, one lipstick rimmed, sat on the polished brass surface. Kat grabbed a half-empty bottle of Oban and poured two fingers into the lipstick tumbler.

"I can't talk to you if I can't drink," she said, taking a long swallow and plopping down on one end of the love seat.

I sat down on the sofa across from her and scanned the room. Her clothes were scattered about. A blue dress draped over the back of a chair, black high heels on the floor, and a white bra crumpled on the coffee table. Her pink lace panties were half shoved under the sofa cushion. I pulled them out and held them up.

"Who was he?" I asked, looking around.

"Well, aren't you the smartassed detective," she sneered. "FBI training coming to the fore? If you're so clever, you tell me."

BEAR'S PROMISE

"My guess would be Mark Hamden."

"And you'd be right," she said.

Her facial expression said, "Who gives a shit. What are you going to do about it," but then the mask crumbled, and she dissolved, crying into her hands.

I remained seated, unmoving and unmoved, unsure what to do. She was obviously distraught, but I was pissed. We were still married. And Hamden of all people. I hated the sonofabitch even more. Yet Kat and I were separated. I wondered whether I would have slept with a woman in Hopperville had the opportunity presented.

I finally went to her and put a hand on her back.

"Oh, Bear," she sobbed. "I'm so sorry. I feel terrible." She got up, unsteady, and wrapped her arms around me, burying her face in my chest. "I'm so bad. I fought the booze for so long. I love you, only you."

I took out a handkerchief and wiped her eyes. She took it, blew her nose, and we both sat down.

"So, how did it happen?" I asked, not sure I really wanted to know.

"He came over last night to help me with divorce papers."

I stiffened. She looked away, first staring at the ceiling and then at the rug.

Her vision returned to me, tearful. "I changed my mind and couldn't go through with it. I still love you. He got angry, and to appease him, I offered him a drink and had one too. One thing led to another, and ..." She swept her hand around the room.

She leaned across the space between us, snatched her panties from the sofa, and held them in her lap, twisting them into a tight braid with her fingers. Then she stood, turned her back to me, hiked up her kimono and nightgown, and bent over to slip on her panties. Her movements were slow, theatrical, probably a combination of alcohol and showtime for me. It had her desired effect, but I fought it off.

"In our bed?" I asked, trying to force from my mind the image of her with Hamden, slipping off her panties as she'd just slipped them on, lying nude next to him.

She turned around and nodded, dabbing my handkerchief at her drippy eyes and nose.

"And after he left, you called me, guilty and upset."

Another nod.

I studied her face, cheeks swollen and whites of her eyes bloodshot. Gone was the beauty I'd married. I suspected she'd been hitting the sauce more than just last night and this morning—perhaps since I left. It occurred that maybe this wasn't the first time with Hamden. Or maybe someone else. I didn't want to know. I still loved her, and I thought she'd beaten the bottle.

"What do you expect me to do?" I asked. "Kick his puny ass?"

"What do you want to do?"

"I don't know, Kat. You're the one who decided to end our relationship, to become separated."

"I want you back. You're the only man I want to be with, to love." She stood and slipped out of the kimono. Her fingers played with her nipples until they got hard and pressed against the silk. She slid one nightgown strap off her shoulder.

I was tempted, but I couldn't shake the Hamden scene from my mind. I got off the couch and stepped back.

"No, Kat. Don't demean yourself"—I looked around—"any more than you already have."

Her face hardened, and the tears stopped. She grabbed the empty tumbler from the table and threw it at me. I ducked. The heavy glass flew past my head, careened off a lamp, and shattered against the wall.

"Get the hell out of here," she yelled. "Go back to your rinky-dink town and your stupid case. Hamden will send you the divorce papers next week."

CHAPTER NINETEEN

I caught an afternoon flight back to Indy and got to the office around five.

"Back so soon?" Shay greeted me when I entered the room. "Didn't trust me alone?"

"Nope. Anything happen while I was gone?"

"That heart rhythm doctor called, the one who took care of Jared. Greg Dumont. He had some new ideas about the gun and asked if we could meet in his office at UIMC tomorrow morning at six, before he starts seeing patients."

"Six's pretty early."

"That's what I told him, but six was the only open time he had. I don't think the guy sleeps. He wanted to meet at five thirty, but I got him to delay it until six."

I met Shay in front of the UIMC coffee shop about ten to six the next morning. My double espresso failed to suppress my yawns.

"Glad I became a lawyer," Shay said. "Doctors' hours suck."

"I agree," I said, draining my cup. "Let's go see what the good doctor has for us."

The door to room 316 was wide open. Greg Dumont sat behind a large desk cluttered with empty Starbucks cups, papers piled high and scattered over the surface, and two large textbooks opened to passages highlighted with a yellow marker.

"Good morning, gentlemen," Dumont said, rising to shake hands. "Sorry for the mess." He swept a hand around the office. "Let me clear off a couple of chairs." He removed more of the clutter from two bamboo slatted chairs and stacked the papers and books on the floor. We sat down.

"Nice to see you again," I said.

"You too," Dumont said, smiling.

"You met Shay"—I pointed at him—"over the phone yesterday. He's my new law associate. He said you might have some interesting information for us."

"I might. I've been doing a lot of thinking about the Electric Gun and the fact that there's never been a human electrocardiogram recording of it causing ventricular fibrillation."

I leaned forward, attentive. He told us the animal studies he'd researched confirmed that the electricity from the gun fired into the chest can speed up the heartbeat to cause VF. Frisson knew that, but the company's lawyers scared him into submission. If we could show the gun caused VF in a patient, we might be able to change everybody's thinking. Get people to testify against Electric Gun and stop some of the abuses.

Shay and I exchanged enthusiastic glances. "We're with you, Greg," I said, "100 percent. How're you going to do it?"

Greg rose and went to a small blackboard hanging on one wall of his office. He picked up a piece of yellow chalk and drew the stick figure of a man. He drew a circle where the chest might be and labeled it ICD. He told us that when he implanted a cardioverter defibrillator in a patient—the ICD was an advanced type of pacemaker that detected ventricular fibrillation and terminated it with an electric shock—he had to start VF in the patient to test that the ICD functioned properly. He did this by pacing the patient's heart at rates similar to the Electric Gun. If he could get a patient to volunteer, he could use the Electric Gun to start the VF. The ICD would terminate it.

"That wouldn't prove that's what happened to Jared," Shay said, standing next to Dumont and pointing at the blackboard.

"True, but it would prove the gun can trigger VF in a human," Dumont said, "not just an experimental animal."

"How would you do this?" I asked.

"I'd anesthetize the patient, stick the probes through the skin over the heart—the same spots Jared's probes hit—and pull the trigger. The patient would be asleep and wouldn't feel anything." Dumont added Xs to the diagram where the probes would hit.

"Why not tape the probes to the skin?" Shay asked with a shrug. "Spare the patient puncture wounds."

Dumont shook his head as he reached for one of the coffee cups collected on his desk. He sipped and grimaced. "Cold. Must be yesterday's."

He held the cup out to me, but I declined with a grin.

"The skin provides high resistance," Dumont said. "Probes penetrating the skin bypass that resistance, so the electricity gets to the heart. That may be why the human tests turned out negative."

"Who'd volunteer for this?" I asked. I stood beside Shay, took a piece of chalk, and added a big question mark over the figure's head.

"Good question. I don't know. My patients have heart problems, or they wouldn't be getting the ICD. I guess it just depends on who'd offer to help. I'll send out a flyer to my referring doctors and hospitals to let them know I'm looking for volunteers and ask them to refer the patients to me."

CHAPTER TWENTY

I'm scared, Dr. Dumont, really scared, but I want to help. I *have* to help. Will it hurt much?"

It was Dumont's day to see patients in his hospital office, a cubicle barely large enough to hold an examining table, sink, two chairs, and a tiny desk. He'd asked me to sit in with this particular patient to provide legal advice if needed. He told me his patients were usually booked at fifteen-minute intervals, but he'd carved out an hour for this man.

His new patient, Gerald Carpenter, had been referred by an internist in town. Carpenter was a fifty-nine-year-old accountant, short and stocky with a kindly face and deep-set, soft brown eyes. He'd suffered two heart attacks and a recent episode of ventricular fibrillation that caused cardiac arrest. According to Dumont, Carpenter couldn't have picked a better time or place for the VF: a slow Friday afternoon at a gambling casino not far from Indianapolis.

When I asked why, Dumont told me that ceiling cameras focused on gamers 24-7, so when Carpenter lost consciousness and crumpled to the floor, he figured casino spotters saw it immediately. They would've notified the medical office adjacent to the casino. The resuscitation team would've been at Carpenter's side in less than two minutes. A single shock from the defibrillator would've stopped the VF. In fact, Carpenter told Dumont that he regained consciousness so quickly he wanted to continue playing the slots. After all, he said, he was down forty-five bucks and wanted a chance to win it back. The Super Grand Jackpot slot machine was his favorite, and he was certain it was about to pay off.

The EMTs overruled and whisked him to a local hospital for monitoring. He stabilized, and two days later, they referred him to Dumont, who saw him as an outpatient.

"Mr. Carpenter"—Dumont insisted everyone in his group address patients with dignity and respect; no first names unless the patient was a friend or asked for that—"this is Mr. Jason Judge, the lawyer I told you about. He's here to answer any legal questions you might have about what we're planning to do."

I shook hands with the patient. "Good morning, Mr. Carpenter. It's nice to meet you. I'll just hang in the background and let you and Dr. Dumont carry on." I smiled at Carpenter, stepped to the back of the small room, out of the way, and let Dumont do his thing.

"Thanks, Bear," Dumont said. He turned to the patient. "Mr. Carpenter, you need a defibrillator implanted because there's no way to predict if or when you might have another VF episode. The ICD will monitor your heartbeat and stop the VF in seconds should it recur."

"Yes, that's what my internist told me at the other hospital. Where do you insert it?"

Dumont explained that it went under the left collarbone and connected to the heart with a long wire called a lead that was threaded into a blood vessel. The entire assembly sat under the skin and was like having your own emergency room in your chest.

Carpenter laughed at that last phrase. He asked, "I'm asleep through the implant?"

"Yes, we'll give you a medicine called propofol that puts you to sleep. By the time you wake up, it'll all be over." Dumont explained how the ICD worked, Carpenter's chances of getting shocked in the future, and potential complications. He drew a diagram of the assembly on a pad on his desk.

"Thanks. The picture makes it clearer than what they told me in the other hospital," Carpenter said.

"Did they tell you I have to start up your VF after the ICD is implanted to make sure the ICD works in your heart?"

Carpenter grimaced. "Yes. That's really why I wanted to be referred to you, Dr. Dumont. They told me you were looking for volunteers for your study of the Electric Gun. I want to volunteer."

"Why?"

Dumont's why was a simple query, but it struck me as really profound. Why would anyone volunteer to be killed? I watched Carpenter try to answer.

First, he went silent. Then tears flooded his eyes, and his face crumpled into a sad expression, aging him. He ran a hand through thinning gray hair, took out a handkerchief, wiped his eyes, and blew his nose. He struggled finding an answer.

"May I tell you a story, Dr. Dumont and Mr. Judge"—he checked his watch and looked at Dumont and me questioningly—"if you both have the time?"

"We do," Dumont said, pulling up a chair, motioning for me to do the same. "This is too important to rush. We'll take as much time as you want."

He nodded a thank-you. "I'm almost sixty. Betty and I have been married thirty-three years, and we have four children. I make eighty-five thousand a year, which was enough to live on until a year ago."

Dumont smiled, encouraging him to continue.

"Our oldest, Tom, was kind of a wild kid. Smart but a real wiseass. He's a skinny kid, but that didn't stop him from flaunting authority—mine, his teachers, anybody's. A year ago, just after he graduated from Purdue with a major in government, he had a few late-night beers with his buddies in a downtown Hopperville bar. Apparently, the kids got a bit rowdy talking politics. I guess they offended a few Trump supporters sitting at the bar—Indiana's a solid red state—and the owner asked them to leave.

"Tom had been repainting his room in our home and had a leftover can of red spray paint in the trunk of his car. After the kids left the bar, he got the can and spray-painted the front window of the bar—it's the building on the corner of Main and Rangeline—with the statement, 'Trump is a racist pig. Impeach the bastard.'"

Greg and I laughed. "Some would agree, but not many in Indiana," Dumont said.

Carpenter brushed aside his comment. "I suppose, but that's not the point," he said. "The bar's security camera nailed Tom plain as day, and two Hopperville cops—one named Sparafucile and the other Diaz—pounded on our door at five o'clock the next morning. They were there to arrest Tom on misdemeanor charges filed by the bar's owner."

Carpenter paused to catch his breath.

"And that's why I'm here."

He went on to tell us that he and his wife and Tom were standing in the doorway of their home, responding to the banging. The other kids were still asleep in their rooms at the back of the house. He and Betty had thrown on robes, but Tom was just wearing pajama bottoms. The two cops pushed their way in, and Sparafucile told Tom he was under arrest. He unclipped a pair of handcuffs from his belt and ordered Tom to turn around and put his hands behind his back.

Tom told Sparafucile to fuck off. The cop pulled out his Electric Gun and shot Tom in the bare chest with no warning at all. Just unholstered his weapon, pulled the trigger at close range, and said, "Nobody tells me to fuck off."

Carpenter's eyes filled with tears. He bobbed his head to clear his vision and paused again to regain control.

"The probes hit Tom's bare chest, right over his heart. He fell immediately and didn't move." The other cop handcuffed Tom, and still he didn't move. Carpenter and his wife tried to get Tom to stand, but his legs were like rubber, and he collapsed to the ground. They didn't know what had happened to him or what to do. Betty called 911. When the EMTs finally arrived, they found Tom's heart in ventricular fibrillation.

"Had it happened at the casino, like mine did—" He broke down, shrugged helplessly, and left the sentence unfinished. "They were able to resuscitate my son, but he suffered irreversible brain damage."

Carpenter began sobbing and couldn't continue. Dumont passed him a box of tissues. After a while, he regained control and resumed.

"Tom was in VF too long. We didn't know he was, and no one tried to do CPR. The EMTs stopped the VF—it took four shocks from the defibrillator and some IV medicines—and Tom remained comatose five days. They cooled his body during that time. He woke with severe brain damage. Now, he's like a two-year-old," Carpenter said, his head in his hands.

"Diapers, spoon-feeding, full-time care, and temper tantrums. Try to bathe him, shave him, or give him a haircut, and he fights like a madman. Needs constant tranquilizers, or he goes bonkers. And his erections. Poor guy. His hormones are probably raging, and what can we do about it? Imagine for a moment how difficult it would be to care for a twenty-three-year-old man who has the mentality of a two-year-old."

As I tried to visualize that scene, Carpenter said, "Tom needs full-time care. The city supports part of it, but the expenses are bankrupting me."

"Did you sue the Hopperville police or the Electric Gun Company?" I asked.

Carpenter made a wry face and nodded. "Both. The police settled for seven hundred and fifty thousand to hush it up as quickly as possible. That money sits in a special bank account and spins off 3 percent interest. Helps pay some of Tom's bills. We got nothing from Electric Gun. At trial, their lawyer—a guy named Papageorgio—claimed excited delirium caused Tom's cardiac arrest."

Dumont shook his head in wonder. "Excited delirium? He'd just woken up. How the hell could he have had excited delirium?"

"They had some doctor named Verity swear that's what happened."

"Amazing," Dumont said, standing with his hands on his hips. "That's absolute bull crap."

Carpenter shrugged. "Papageorgio convinced the jury the gun couldn't have caused the cardiac arrest because there's never been a documented instance of the Electric Gun ever initiating VF in humans. That's why I'm here."

He gripped each side of the front of his shirt and ripped it open. Buttons flew like tiny missiles as he exposed his chest.

"Put the ICD in while I'm asleep, Dr. Dumont, but I want you to shoot me with the Electric Gun while I'm conscious, fully awake, standing like any guy resisting arrest—like Tom did and countless others. I want to feel the pain my Tom felt. I'm an ex-Marine, Doctor. I can take that pain and more. I want to experience the loss of consciousness Tom had—and then, please God, the ICD will kick in and stop the VF."

He stood and paced the small room, breathing fast and trying to keep his anger in check.

"We need to put an end to this police insanity and show the world that the Electric Gun can cause VF. We need to prove it could've triggered cardiac arrest in my son and turned him from an honors Purdue graduate into a two-year-old. I want to be the one—I *need* to be the one—the guinea pig you use to prove it."

Dumont sat back down at his desk and checked his operating schedule. "I've got an opening in ten days. Does that work for you?"

"You bet, Doctor. Schedule me."

CHAPTER TWENTY-ONE

Ten days after Greg Dumont examined Gerald Carpenter, we were in the electrophysiology operating room for the defibrillator implant. Knowing I was ex-FBI, Greg had invited me to observe the implant and do the shooting. He'd never even held a gun before, electric or otherwise.

The operating room was a large rectangle, almost seven hundred square feet, with green tile walls and a rubber tiled floor. Three surgical lights, looking like big TV dishes, hung from the ceiling, making the room bright as midday.

All OR personnel wore blue operating room T-shirts and pants, specially cleaned to reduce infections. Paper booties covered street shoes. Personnel directly involved with the implant donned hats and masks.

Carpenter was resting on the OR bed. Dumont had given him a mild sedative to take the edge off his anxiety, so he was relaxed, watching as they got ready.

"You sure this won't affect what I'll feel?" he'd asked about the sedative. Dumont promised it wouldn't.

Dumont had tried talking him out of being awake during the shooting, but Carpenter had been adamant. "Not going to happen, Dr. Dumont. We do this my way or not at all."

Dumont told me he'd had to get special approval from the medical center's Institutional Review Board to do it Carpenter's way. He assured the IRB members that the implanted ICD would resuscitate Carpenter promptly. If it didn't, Dumont had two backup defibrillators sitting on tables in the room, charged and ready to shock. There was no way Carpenter was going to die during this test. His heart would be in VF less than fifteen seconds if the first shock from the ICD was successful, and up to thirty seconds if he needed a second shock. That was short enough to ensure no brain damage.

The chair of the IRB had asked about the pain Carpenter would feel. Dumont had told her honestly the five-second shock would be excruciating, like holding a finger in a live electric socket for five seconds.

The IRB had deliberated an entire afternoon about whether to approve this unusual and potentially dangerous study. They had Dumont bring Carpenter to the meeting, and the IRB chair questioned him to be sure he understood the risks. The final vote was close, nine approvals to seven disapprovals. Dumont told me he left the meeting feeling elated but nervous that something might go wrong, despite his assurances to the IRB. Carpenter ended up reassuring Dumont that he understood the risks and still felt compelled to go ahead.

Dumont's guess was that Carpenter needed to do this to help him live with the pain of what happened to his son Tom, like a survivor's guilt. When Dumont tried to help him work through his reasons, Carpenter shut him down, saying he had his own motives and they were personal.

"Where'd you get the Electric Gun?" I asked, opening the package in the OR and turning the gun over in my hands.

"Bought it online from the company's website," Dumont said. "No questions asked, no forms to fill out, just had to pony up eight hundred fifty bucks on my Visa card. Holster was thirty bucks extra, but shipping was free. The gun came in four colors: black, red, yellow, and blue. Blue's my favorite color. The Electric Gun Company shipped it in two days."

"That was it?" I asked. "Hard to believe it was that easy."

Dumont nodded. "Anybody can buy one. Easier than a firearm. Legal in practically all states without any permit. No warnings. Just get it, aim it, and shoot it. You can carry the gun concealed or open. Smaller sizes and pastel colors for women. Blue or pink velvet holster fits in a purse. Check out their website."

I held up the gun for the OR crew to see. A small group crowded around, fascinated by what we were about to do. Legally shooting someone in the UIMC hospital OR was unheard of. We were making history.

"Can I see it?" Carpenter asked, sitting up in his bed.

I walked over to him. "You're going to be the shooter?" he asked. "I thought you were a lawyer."

I smiled and nodded. "I'm ex-FBI, Mr. Carpenter. You okay with that?"

"I am," Carpenter said, looking at the gun. "Where will you aim?"

"At your chest. I'll be standing several feet in front of you, so the probes will hit you about six inches apart, one above and the other below your heart on the left side of your chest."

"Like they did to my boy Tom," Carpenter said, eyes welling up.

"Yes, just like that," Dumont responded, putting his arm across Carpenter's shoulders. "That has the best chance of capturing your heart and inducing fibrillation."

"Exactly how the Electric Gun Company should be instructing cops *not* to shoot," I added. Carpenter's eyebrows bunched together, and his breathing quickened. I think the sedative was wearing off. Poor guy. I'd be scared to death. He had guts.

"How does the gun work?" Carpenter asked. "Where are the probes?"

Amazing, I thought, that he wanted to know about the gun. I would have just closed my eyes and said, "Shoot." Actually, I wouldn't have agreed to being shot in the first place.

"This is a replaceable cartridge," I said, pointed to the front of the gun. "It contains compressed nitrogen. When I pull the trigger, the cartridge doors blast off, and two metal probes shoot out to penetrate clothing and skin. Thin wires connect the probes to the gun."

I went on to explain that electricity from two lithium batteries stored in the gun passed between the probes in the skin and made the person's muscles contract very rapidly.

"That's called tetany," Dumont said. "Locks up the muscles, freezes them like someone having a seizure. Police then can handcuff the immobilized person."

"If I touch that person on the arm, will I get shocked?" a nurse asked. "I'm one of two people who'll be standing next to Mr. Carpenter, holding him up to be shot."

"No, not unless you touch the wires or probes," I said.

She shuddered. "Not a chance. You can be sure of that." She hid her hands behind her back.

"Will the shock damage my ICD?" Carpenter asked.

"Great question," I said and turned to Dumont for an answer.

Dumont looked around the OR and motioned to a young man with sandy hair holding a leather tool bag. "Andy, you want to answer that question, or should I?" He explained that Andy was his chief electrical technician and responsible for setting up the OR equipment.

"Very unlikely," Andy said, walking over. "The ICD's well insulated from outside electrical interference. Thirty or forty years ago, microwave ovens and stuff like that were problems. Not today. ICDs and pacemakers have been safe a long time."

"What about hackers?" Carpenter asked. "I read some place they could reprogram the ICD and kill somebody."

Dumont laughed. "So far, just the stuff of spy novels. Manufacturers have upgraded the software with safeguards to prevent unauthorized access."

"How do you aim the gun?" a technician asked. The tech reached out to take the gun, but I pulled it away.

I saw Dumont look closely at the guy. He seemed not to recognize him. An OR mask and hat covered the guy's face and head. Average build, dark eyes, large steel-rimmed glasses with thick lenses. Must be new to the team, I concluded.

"The gun has sights on top," I said, pointing, "and also a laser beam to guide you." I described how the probes left the gun at a seven-degree angle to each other, so they spread apart with distance. The farther away the target, the wider the area captured between the probes when they hit.

"That's a good thing," I said, "because the more muscle mass included in the electric arc between the probes, the greater the paralyzing effect."

"Can I touch it?" the tech asked, again reaching for the gun. I glanced at Dumont.

Dumont hesitated and looked at me. I shook my head. If he said yes, others might want to also. That could delay the procedure, and perhaps someone might accidently pull the trigger or even drop the gun.

"No, I think it's best if Bear's the only one to handle the gun. Maybe when we're finished, you can hold it." The tech turned away.

"Ready, Mr. Carpenter?" Dumont asked. "We've used up enough time with all the explanations."

Carpenter nodded.

A nurse shaved Carpenter's chest hairs and swabbed his left shoulder and chest with betadine antiseptic. It looked like someone had spilled Worcestershire sauce on his skin.

Carpenter looked around the room at the ten to fifteen people busy with individual tasks. "So many folks," he said, "for one minor operation."

"It's not so minor," Dumont said. "The only minor operation is one that happens to the other guy."

Carpenter laughed.

"And, obviously, we've made this one even more complicated than usual."

"Then let's get on with it. You ready, Doctor?" he asked.

"I am. You?"

Carpenter lay back down on the OR table and closed his eyes. He began an off-tune whistle and said, "Do your business, Dr. Dumont. Do your business, and don't fuck it up!"

CHAPTER TWENTY-TWO

The anesthesiologist infused propofol. Dumont had told me it was nicknamed milk of amnesia because of its milky consistency and white color. Carpenter fell asleep in five or six seconds. As soon as the drug hit the brain, it was lights out.

I waited at the side of the room and watched Dumont implant the ICD. His rubber-gloved hands traveled with sure, quick moves, perfectly coordinated with the nurse standing alongside, handing him instruments.

He made a small incision beneath Carpenter's left collarbone, found a vein, threaded a long, insulated lead into it, and snaked the lead into Carpenter's heart while watching the image on fluoroscopy. Dumont connected the end of the lead to the ICD, a roundish metal disc. It looked like a stack of three or four silver dollars. He made a small depression in the chest muscle beneath the skin incision and placed the ICD there. Then he brought the skin edges together to cover the lead and ICD and sewed the incision closed.

Carpenter had a slight bulge in his skin beneath his left collarbone where the ICD assembly was placed, monitoring every heartbeat and ready to intervene if the heartbeat got too fast or too slow. The whole procedure took less than forty-five minutes.

After some programming adjustments, Dumont turned to the anesthesiologist and said, "Let him wake up." Dumont removed his gloves and handed them to a nurse, who tossed them into a receptacle. The anesthesiologist stopped the propofol, and Carpenter gradually stirred. We waited until he was conscious.

"How was your nap?" Dumont asked.

Carpenter mumbled an incoherent response.

"Wait another five minutes," Dumont said. "I want him totally coherent before he's shot so he can still change his mind."

After five minutes, Dumont said, "Ready to be shot, Mr. Carpenter? You can still stop this, and we can put you back to sleep."

Carpenter struggled to sit up. "Not a chance," he said, his words now clear. "Help me stand."

Two nurses walked over, a male and female, and each took hold of one of Carpenter's upper arms. They tugged him upright. He was a bit wobbly but able to stand with his back braced against the OR bed for support. Except for a metal shield and sterile dressing covering the site of the ICD implantation, Carpenter's chest was bare.

"A little nervous, but my mind's crystal clear, and I want to do this. I *must* do this," Carpenter said, pulling his shoulders back and expanding his chest like a soldier at attention. "Fire when ready."

He stared at the gun in my hand, eyes wide open, brow taut, and lips compacted in a tight, determined straight line. His hands trembled, and he clenched them into fists, his knuckles white.

I stood a few feet in front of Carpenter and pointed the Electric Gun at his chest. It was a weird feeling, aiming a gun at someone eager to be shot. I'd never experienced that before. My only concern was to avoid hitting his ICD even though a metal shield protected it.

I looked at Dumont to see if he was ready. He was standing beside an ECG monitor on a metal stand—like a big TV screen—and watched Carpenter's heartbeat flit across the screen. He held a cell phone in his hand. Dumont glanced at the two defibrillators, making sure they were charged and ready. He scanned the OR to be certain the entire team was on alert and got an okay signal from the anesthesiologist and Andy.

Finally, he gave me the go-ahead.

OR personnel stood still as statues, shifting their gaze from me to Carpenter and back. The ping of Carpenter's ECG monitor was the only noise.

I pointed the laser dot at Carpenter's left chest beneath his nipple, took a breath, and pulled the trigger.

The front of the gun exploded with a loud bang as the cartridge doors shot off. The prongs were a blur, flying too fast to be seen clearly, but we heard Carpenter grunt—"Ugh!"—when they hit his chest.

A loud clicking sound filled the OR as electricity flowed over the wires and burned through the prongs into Carpenter's chest. Electrical signals registering each pulse of electricity from the Electric Gun flooded the screen Dumont was studying, totally obscuring the ECG.

"Aaaaiiieeee!" Carpenter screamed, clutching his chest. "Stop! I can't take—" His body stiffened in midsentence, and he toppled forward, taut as a tree trunk. He would have fallen but for the two nurses holding his arms.

At the end of the five-second shock, Carpenter collapsed, unconscious, rigid muscles turned to jelly. A third person ran over, grabbed his feet, and the three hoisted Carpenter back onto the OR bed.

"He's in VF, cardiac arrest!" Dumont yelled when the screen cleared to show Carpenter's ECG again. Dumont hit the stopwatch on the cell phone in his hand.

"Three seconds for the ICD to detect VF ... Done! Eight seconds to charge the capacitors ... Done! Shock should occur ... now!" Dumont signaled with his hand like a conductor leading an orchestra.

Carpenter's body lurched as the ICD discharged 750 volts. The surge of electricity momentarily blanked out the ECG screen, but then the rhythm reappeared.

"Still in VF," Dumont shouted. I heard a note of panic in his voice, and my heart jumped. "Be ready with the external defibrillators," Dumont said, eying the two nurses standing next to each defibrillator, paddles in their hands. "We'll give the ICD another chance."

I watched OR personnel look at one another, unease in their faces.

"The ICD's recycling now," Dumont said. "Recharging the capacitors ... Here comes the shock ..."

Carpenter's body jerked.

A moment later, Dumont's voice rang out, "Normal sinus rhythm!" He let out a long breath. "Okay. Everyone, relax. He's back among the living—thank God."

CHAPTER TWENTY-THREE

I watched Carpenter struggle on the OR bed as consciousness returned. His eyes wandered around the room, unfocused while his brain recovered from the impact of the VF. The process reminded me of rebooting my computer. His brain was rebooting. He finally focused on one of the nurses who had helped keep him upright.

"Don't shoot," Carpenter garbled in a hoarse whisper, barely recognizable. "I changed my mind. Hurts too much … no more."

The OR exploded into applause and high fives. Dumont went to Carpenter, leaned over him, and gripped his shoulders, his happy face inches from Carpenter's.

"You're done, Mr. Carpenter. It's over," Dumont said, his voice bubbling. "The Electric Gun triggered VF, and your ICD stopped it. We've got all the proof we need. Your son's tragedy is vindicated. No crazy diagnosis of excited delirium causing VF this time. The Electric Gun did it. We've got those guys—finally."

Carpenter closed his eyes and slowly turned his head from side to side, as if he couldn't believe what he was hearing. He blinked back tears and attempted to sit up. "Show me," he whispered.

Dumont pushed him back down on the bed. "I will in a minute. You're still connected to the gun. Let me get these probes out of your skin. They're embedded pretty deep, so I'll have to inject a local anesthetic. Otherwise, it'll hurt like hell when I pull them out."

"Do it now," Carpenter said. "Just yank the bastards out. I want what the cops did to Tom."

"You're sure?" Dumont asked.

"I'm sure. Just do it." His face showed that same determined look he had just before he was shot, with taut brow, eyes wide, and lips compacted.

"Okay," Dumont said. He held up his cell phone. "First I need to document the position of the probes."

Dumont snapped several pictures from different angles and then handed his cell phone to me to hold. He donned a fresh pair of rubber gloves and lifted a hemostat from the OR tray. "Grit your teeth. This is going to hurt."

Dumont clamped the hemostat—like a miniature pair of pliers—onto the end of one probe and twisted. The move reminded me of a fisherman using pliers to yank a fishhook from the jaw of a trout he'd just caught.

"Oh shit!" Carpenter yelled as the probe popped loose. His face blanched, showing the agony he had to be feeling.

"One out, one to go. You okay?" Dumont asked.

"No, but don't stop," came the answer through tight lips. The pain had to have been more tolerable than the electric shock, but Carpenter's eyes watered. Whatever was driving this man wasn't letting up. He seemed determined to relive all his son's agony.

Dumont clamped the hemostat onto the second probe and tugged. This time Carpenter just clenched his teeth, and only a *grrr* emerged.

"Done," Dumont said. He straightened and held the probe up for Carpenter to see.

"I want to take those little fuckers home with me," Carpenter said, relaxing his mouth and extending his hand for the probes. "I'm going to mount them in a picture frame as reminders of how much agony—not just the pain from the shock—but how much total agony these fishhooks have caused my family."

"And other families as well," I added.

A nurse swabbed each puncture site with fresh betadine solution and then applied burn cream. She covered them with small sterile dressings. She removed the metal plate covering the ICD.

Dumont turned to the nurse. "Is his hospital room ready? I want him admitted and his ECG monitored overnight after all he's been through."

"Yes, sir, as soon as you give the word that he's ready to go."

"Not before I look at the electrocardiogram," Carpenter said. "I want to see the heart rhythm that almost killed me twice and my son once. Show me how the gun started ventricular fibrillation and explain what I'm seeing."

Dumont returned to the ECG screen he'd been monitoring and hit "replay."

Nothing happened.

He pushed the replay button again. The screen remained blank. He struck the top of the screen with the heel of his hand and hit the replay button a third time.

Still nothing.

He called over his head technician. "Andy, what in hell's going on here?"

Andy walked to the screen and pushed "replay."

Nothing.

He removed a Phillips screwdriver from the black tool bag he was holding, went to the back of the ECG console, and unscrewed the rear panel.

"Holy shit," Andy said. "We've got a problem."

"What?" Dumont asked, dread in his voice.

Andy beckoned Dumont over. "Look here," he said, pointing. "The wire to the recording function of the monitor came loose. The screen showed the live ECG okay—the display function worked—but it didn't record."

"How could that be?" Dumont asked, a stunned look on his face.

"Damned if I know," Andy said. "I checked everything in my electronics shop before we moved the screen down here. It was all working fine. Maybe the screen got jarred en route and the wire came loose. All I know is we've got no recording of anything in the OR."

The OR became graveyard silent. All eyes focused on Dumont.

Finally, Carpenter shattered the spell.

"No!" he cried, shaking his head. "No, no, no!"

He staggered off the OR bed but tumbled to the floor on rickety legs before he could reach Dumont. Two nurses lifted him to his feet and held him upright.

"No!" he shrieked again, breaking down in tears. "I can't go through it a second time. The pain was excruciating. I told you not to fuck it up, Doctor!"

He slowly sank to the floor and buried his head in his hands. "My poor Tom. My poor boy. I told you not to fuck ..." The words faded to silence.

CHAPTER TWENTY-FOUR

It was five in the morning—an ungodly hour except for crazy lawyers and hardworking doctors. I stood in front of a full-length mirror in my room at the Holiday Inn in Framingham, Massachusetts, with Shay alongside me, practicing questions that Shay would be asking Slaughter in a few hours. We'd filed the complaint for damages and all the necessary paperwork to initiate the lawsuit. Slaughter was the first to be deposed. I wanted Shay to handle as much of the deposition as possible. I'd be there to help if needed.

After rehearsing for an hour and then refining questions we had prepared, we broke for breakfast. Shay returned to his room, and we both showered and dressed. Shay had talked about cutting his braid but decided the Hammer wouldn't like it. His grandfather wore the braid, and so would Shay—at least for now.

Shay did sacrifice his jeans and sweatshirt for a charcoal-gray suit I bought at JoS. A. Bank. He wore a white shirt and a striped blue and yellow tie. He'd taken out his earrings and tucked his braid inside his jacket collar. He told me at breakfast that the tie knot took him forever to get straight. Finally, he googled instructions on how to tie it. It was still skewed, so I retied it for him over coffee.

"I miss my jeans," he said with a tiny smile, pulling on the seat of his pants to get some freedom as we sat down to breakfast. "They were easy on the crotch. These pants ride too high."

The deposition was to be held in the law offices of Casey and Harold, a small firm of six lawyers in Framingham, about three miles from the Electric Gun headquarters. They'd offered us use of a spare office. Law firms did this for one another. If Casey and Harold had a deposition in Indy, they could call me to lend them one of our offices.

The room was small, just large enough for a conference table, six chairs, a window, and a side table. Two prints of downtown Framingham hung on beige walls. The side table held ice cubes, soft drinks, and coffee.

We arrived before Slaughter and his lawyer to make certain all was in order. I positioned the video technician at one end of the conference table. Slaughter would sit at the opposite end, so taping would be head-on. The court stenographer would sit to Slaughter's left but back from the table so his lawyer could sit next to him. Shay would be on Slaughter's right, and I would sit next to Shay.

I'd heard from Slaughter's lawyer, Achilles Papageorgio, that Slaughter was upset because we'd baited him into giving an interview without the lawyer present. Slaughter fumed at my last question about his name. I anticipated him to be an uncooperative witness.

Slaughter and Papageorgio arrived a half hour late—close to ten thirty. Not a good start. They made a point of not saying hello or acknowledging our presence—not even eye contact—and just took their places around the table. Their disagreeable attitude charged the room with an air of hostility before the first words were spoken.

Papageorgio was a short, stout, dark-featured man of Greek descent, reputed to have a hair-trigger temper and equally quick intellect. He headed Electric Gun's legal team of five lawyers and three paralegals.

He wore jeans with a blue, plaid cotton shirt opened at the neck and what must've been a two-day beard. Papageorgio wouldn't be in the video, so how he dressed didn't matter. We wouldn't be in the video either, but we still wore suits.

Slaughter wore brown slacks and a khaki-colored golf shirt. That surprised me since he'd be the star of the video. I wondered if he wanted to convey an air of casualness, that the whole deposition wasn't very important and certainly not worth getting dressed up for.

No one said a word as Slaughter and Papageorgio clipped tiny microphones onto their shirt collars, arranged some papers in front of them, and whispered to each other. They looked at the stenographer, ready to begin. I nodded at Shay to start.

Shay turned to the video tech. "Please begin taping."

The tech clicked on the video recorder, went through preambles, and asked the stenographer to swear in the witness.

After she did, Shay began.

"Good morning, Mr. Slaughter. My name is Deroshay Odinga. As you know from our previous meeting, I am with the law firm of Jason Judge and Associates. I am here with Mr. Judge. We represent the estate of Jared and Melanie Simpson, and their son, Ryan, on behalf of Melanie Simpson's nearest surviving relative, her brother, Jason Judge."

Slaughter remained mute. Papageorgio had tutored him well. A cardinal rule in testifying was not to say anything if you didn't have to. When you did respond, you kept your answers as brief as possible to give the other side as little information as necessary. Lawyers try to cherry-pick statements made at deposition so they can turn whatever you said against you in court.

"Impeach the witness" was a fundamental courtroom concept: get the witness to make statements in court that contradicted statements made at deposition. Shay knew his job was to prod Slaughter to open up.

"In the Notice of Deposition and subpoena we sent to your lawyer, which I'm sure he shared with you," Shay said, "we listed several documents you were to produce for today's deposition. Did you bring them?"

"No."

"Why not?" Shay asked. His lips curled down, annoyed.

"Couldn't find the copies," Slaughter said, showing no emotion.

"You don't have the records of the early safety tests performed on the Electric Gun?"

"That's right."

"How can you not have kept these important records?"

Slaughter shrugged. "That's just the way it is."

"Did you have a fire, and they were burned? A robbery, and they were stolen? A move, and they were lost? What happened to them?" Shay asked.

"Objection," Papageorgio said, his hand raised like a traffic cop. "Asked and answered. He's already told you he doesn't have them. Stop badgering the witness."

"I'm hardly badgering—oh, let it go."

I'd bet the farm Slaughter destroyed them. Or maybe he still had them and was lying.

"When was Electric Gun incorporated?" Shay asked.

"December 1995," Slaughter said.

"How did that come about?"

"Objection," Papageorgio interrupted, hand raised again. "Question's overly broad and vague. Focus your question, Counselor," he said. "Didn't they teach you that in law school?"

I was about to object, but Shay handled it well.

"I don't need your instructions, Mr. Papageorgio," Shay said, brow arched and face red. "The question may be broad, but if he can't answer it, I'm sure Mr. Slaughter will let me know, and I can rephrase. Or are you instructing the witness not to answer?"

"Not at all, Counselor. I'm just trying to help an inexperienced fledging do his job better," Papageorgio said with a wave of his hand.

"And I'll remind you that you're not entitled to speaking objections, Mr. Papageorgio," Shay said. "You want to object, fine. Do so, state your reason, and then be quiet. If you have a problem with that, we can call the judge for clarification."

Wow. Good show, my young friend, I said to myself. Lawyers are not supposed to give more information than needed by the judge to sustain or overrule the objection since it might influence the jury. Shay caught him on that, and Papageorgio flinched at that rebuff. Fledgling or not, Shay wasn't going to be bullied.

Shay turned to Slaughter. "If you can answer the question, Mr. Slaughter, please do so."

"I bought the patent from the electrical engineer who invented it."

"Was the gun ready to use?"

"No. I improved it."

"How?"

"The gun's output was too weak, didn't lock up muscles," Slaughter answered, still showing no emotion. "We changed its shape, made it more powerful."

"How did you do that?"

"Increased its electrical output with lithium batteries in the handle of the gun."

"What is the electrical output of the gun?"

"Less than the output of a cattle prod."

"That's not what I asked," Shay said, shaking his head. "The output of a cattle prod is irrelevant. We're talking about humans. Please listen carefully to my question. What is the Electric Gun's output that shocks people?"

Slaughter looked at Papageorgio, who mouthed, "Answer him."

"Each pulse delivers an electrical charge of one hundred thirty microcoulombs. The pulses are twelve hundred a minute."

I'd coached Shay to think of a deposition as taking place in front of a jury. All questions and answers were for the jury's enlightenment.

"Please explain for the jury what a coulomb is," Shay said.

"It's a quantity of electricity."

"Like a package of electricity, a packet of electrons?"

"Yeah, like that."

"One hundred thirty microcoulombs is enough to paralyze muscles, make a resisting subject compliant, correct?"

Slaughter nodded.

"Please answer out loud," Shay said. He pointed at the stenographer. "She can't write down your head nod."

"Yes. They collapse. Cops can then handcuff them."

"Any other major changes?"

"We switched from using explosive gun powder to compressed nitrogen to propel the probes," Slaughter said.

"And that eliminated the Bureau of Alcohol, Tobacco, Firearms, and Explosives from requiring oversight and approval, correct?"

"Yes."

"How did you test the safety of the gun?"

"We tested the Electric Gun on two goats and three dogs," Slaughter said after a moment, "and some human volunteers."

"That's all?" Shay shook his head in amazement.

"It was enough. We shot each animal twenty or thirty times, and they had no ill effects," Slaughter said.

"Were the animals anesthetized?"

"Of course. The shock's quite painful. What do you think I am, cruel? Besides, I didn't want any animal rights group coming after us." This was as animated as Slaughter had been until now. He looked Shay in the eye, took a deep breath, and huffed out the air.

"Did you record blood pressure, an electrocardiogram, and check blood for oxygen content?"

"No. We just watched the animals, saw their muscles lock up, that they continued breathing and woke up from anesthesia without problems. That was enough animal testing for me. It proved the gun was safe and there was no reason to warn anybody about anything."

"What kind of human testing did you do?"

"We taped electrodes on the backs or thighs of ten police volunteers and shocked them. The shock immediately immobilized them without harmful effects."

"Were these normal-size police officers?"

"Yes." Slaughter thought a minute. "Well, one was a weight lifter, a big, huge guy, a self-defense expert. He bragged he could fight through the effects of the Electric Gun. I bet him a case of beer he couldn't."

"Who won?"

Slaughter smiled for the first time. "I did. Shut him down just like it did the other cops."

Amazing, I thought, how little premarket testing they did. That's what comes from having no oversight. They didn't need anyone's approval before going commercial. The Food and Drug Administration would never allow a new drug or medical device sold to the public with such woefully inadequate testing. Nor would the Consumer Product Safety Commission, without extensive testing and warnings. While no animal or human died during the testing, they couldn't know what the shocks did to the heart without recording a blood pressure and ECG.

"Would you agree that, if the risk of death from an Electric Gun shock was, say, one in a thousand—or even one in ten thousand—the few animals and humans tested were clearly insufficient?" Shay asked.

"There's no risk of death," Slaughter said.

"Just accept the question as a hypothetical. Suppose there was a risk, wouldn't it have been much more scientifically valid to shock twenty animals one time than one animal twenty times?"

"How the hell do I know?"

"Well, you're the CEO and responsible for the safety of the gun."

"The gun's safe. How many times do I have to say that?"

We'd debated whether to ask this next question or save it to broadside Slaughter at trial. I wanted to wait. Shay didn't.

"Do you know the TENS device?" he asked Slaughter.

"Yeah," Slaughter said. "It's used to treat people with back pain."

Shay agreed. The Transcutaneous Electrical Nerve Stimulator, known as TENS, was FDA-approved to treat severe muscle pain. Skin electrodes connected to a battery gently stimulated superficial nerves in the skin over areas of painful tissue, suppressing pain signals to the brain.

"Do you know the amount of electrical charge TENS uses?" he asked.

"Nope," Slaughter said, dismissing the question with a hand wave. "Less than ten microcoulombs."

Slaughter shrugged. "So?"

"The TENS company published a warning in 1994—a year before you started your company. It says that a charge of seventy-five microcoulombs would be hazardous if delivered through the chest because it only took one hundred microcoulombs to capture the heart from the skin. Do you know what I mean by the word *capture*?"

"Yeah. The electrical stimulus could take over the heartbeat, make the heart race, go faster."

"Correct." Shay handed him a piece of paper. "I represent to you that this is the warning section recommended by the United States Food and Drug Administration for the TENS device. It says in part that if a device is capable of delivering a charge of twenty-five microcoulombs or greater per pulse, that may be sufficient to cause electrocution and cause a cardiac arrhythmia. What is a cardiac arrhythmia?"

"An irregular heartbeat."

"Please remind the court how much charge your Electric Gun delivers."

Slaughter mumbled a response, his hand covering his mouth.

"Would you repeat that please? I don't think the jury could understand what you said."

"One hundred and thirty microcoulombs, damn it all," he thundered. Shay didn't need a video for the jury to note this response.

"So, the Electric Gun delivers more than five times the upper safety limits of electricity set by the FDA for TENS and 30 percent over the amount of charge needed to capture the heart," Shay said.

"Objection," said Papageorgio. "That's not a question."

Shay ignored him. "Would you repeat for us the rate at which the Electric Gun delivers these one-hundred-thirty-microcoulomb pulses, please."

"Twelve hundred a minute," Slaughter said.

"What's a normal heart rate?"

"I don't know."

"Take a stab at it."

"Maybe seventy or eighty," Slaughter said.

"What would that do to the heart," Shay asked, "being stimulated twelve hundred times a minute by one-hundred-thirty-microcoulomb charges?"

"How the hell do I know? I'm no doctor."

"Do you agree with me that stimulating the heart that fast could start the lethal arrhythmia, ventricular fibrillation?"

"I already told you I'm not a doctor. How the f—" Slaughter caught himself in time. "How the hell would I know?"

"Based on the TENS document, don't you think you had a duty to warn Electric Gun users about the potential harm of electrocution?"

"Objection," Papageorgio said. "Calls for a legal conclusion. The witness is not qualified to answer."

Shay turned to Slaughter. "If you didn't feel there was legal reason to warn, did you at least feel a moral or ethical obligation to warn?"

"Hell, no. The goats, dogs, and cops all survived and did fine. No reason to think a suspect zapped in the field wouldn't also. Don't you listen to me? Have I been unclear? There was nothing to warn about." Slaughter, half standing, shouted the last sentence.

"Why didn't you test the Electric Gun with the patches—or better still, the probes sticking though the skin—on the chest, over the heart?"

Slaughter was now boiling mad. His face was red, he was breathing fast, and his eyes were shooting daggers. He made a fist, leaned across the table, and shook it in Shay's face.

"Why should I?" he yelled.

"Wouldn't that have been more appropriate to test for safety and maybe simulate field conditions more accurately?"

"No, it wouldn't, you b—" Slaughter again caught himself in time.

The f earlier was certainly for fuck, but the b here could have been lots of things—most likely a racial epithet, I thought.

"I did what was necessary," Slaughter concluded, sitting back down, scowling at Shay, still red-faced.

Shay and I held a brief conference. I felt he'd pushed Slaughter to the limit and gotten what we needed. I decided we should quit while ahead. "I have no more questions at the present time," Shay said.

"I have several," Papageorgio said, "but I'd like to take a fifteen-minute break first." Slaughter needed time to cool off.

Shay said to the video tech, "Off the record." He switched off the recording.

Papageorgio and Slaughter stormed out of the conference room. Papageorgio returned without Slaughter about ten minutes later, picked up the microphone, and said, "Back on the record."

The video tech started recording.

"I have no further questions for Mr. Slaughter. This deposition is over." He marched out of the room.

We stood and glanced out the window of the conference room. Slaughter was standing by the building entrance, smoking a cigarette. He looked up and flipped us the finger, then tossed his cigarette butt into the street and walked away.

CHAPTER TWENTY-FIVE

DOUG ZIPES

It took us fifteen minutes to gather our papers and pack them into our briefcases. We left the deposition elated, eager to get on with the lawsuit. Electric Gun didn't seem so tough after all.

A four-door black Mercedes sedan was parked in the slot next to our Hertz rental. It overflowed its space and was inches from our Nissan. Heat radiated from its hood, so it had just been parked.

Shay shimmied between the cars and tried to open the Nissan's door.

His hip bumped the big car's door handle, and he triggered its theft alarm system. A shrill wail erupted, and he jumped away.

Pedestrians on the sidewalk parallel to the parking lot paused and stared at us.

"Oh, shit, this is not good, Bear. A black man standing next to a Mercedes with its alarm blasting—not a healthy scene." He grabbed his briefcase and moved away from the car. His eyes darted from the Mercedes, to me, to the sidewalk.

I took hold of his arm. "Nothing's going to happen. You're not alone. I'm here with you."

"Won't matter," he said, shaking loose.

Three white guys in matching red, sleeveless gym shirts that showcased bulging steroid muscles came to an abrupt halt on the sidewalk, exchanged words, pointed, and started toward us. I felt a rush of adrenalin and clenched my fists. Maybe Shay was right.

"Trying to steal the car, guys?" the first man shouted as he neared. One man slid behind Shay's back, in between him and his car, and the other stood behind me.

"Like that Mercedes, do you? Want to take it home?" the first guy asked.

"No, we just came here to get my rental," I said. "Back off before I call the cops."

The first guy was in Shay's face, his alcohol-laced breath enveloping Shay like a cloud that I could smell standing a few feet away. "Bullshit," Alcohol Breath said. "Then why'd the alarm go off if you wasn't trying to steal it? Show me your car keys to prove this rental is yours."

Before Shay could answer, one guy grabbed me in a bear hug from behind. He pinned my arms to my sides and lifted me off the pavement. I struggled but couldn't break free. The other guy grabbed Shay the same way.

Alcohol Breath smiled, flexed his biceps, and raised his fist in front of Shay ... when the alarm suddenly stopped.

Alcohol Breath lowered his hand and glanced over Shay's shoulder. Both guys released us.

Slaughter and Papageorgio emerged from behind a car parked several feet away. Slaughter was flipping a Mercedes key up and down in his hand.

"Trouble, Counselors?" Papageorgio asked. "Or maybe you don't want to hear my speaking objections?"

We stood there, Shay trembling and me seething, as Slaughter walked over to the three guys, shook hands with Alcohol Breath, and whispered something in his ear. A flash of green changed hands, and Slaughter smiled. The three men strolled back toward the sidewalk laughing, without a backward glance.

"You're in way over your heads, gentlemen," Slaughter said, coming back to stand in front of us. He was a little shorter than Shay, but his shoulders seemed twice as wide, and his protruding gut made him look like a sumo wrestler.

"You better back off. Those guys"—he pointed as the three merged with other pedestrians on the sidewalk—"would've hurt you pretty bad if we hadn't just happened to come along. They were doing their civic duty, trying to prevent you from stealing my car. You would've resisted, and they would've resorted to physical violence to restrain you until the cops came."

Slaughter ran his hand over his shaved head and pulled at an earlobe. "I hate to think what you would've looked like when they finished, your faces all busted up, probable concussion, bleeding. Very nasty. No way to continue lawyering." He shuddered. "I could even call the police on you now for trying to steal my Mercedes. How'd you like that? Couple of Framingham cops arrive with Electric Guns drawn that I sold to them?"

I could hear Shay's teeth chattering.

"You can go fuck yourselves," I said, breathing fast. I felt hot, and my heart was pounding. "You try any shit like this again, and I'll have your lawyer disbarred and you both arrested and thrown in jail. We don't scare." I pushed Slaughter hard in the chest, and he stumbled backward, almost falling.

"Really? On what charge?" Papageorgio asked, stepping forward. "Trying to prevent somebody from stealing our car? Consider this a wake-up call, Counselor. Make no more mistakes. You might not be so lucky next time."

Slaughter recovered his footing and turned to Papageorgio. "Let's go, Papa. I think they got the message. And if they didn't, they sure as hell will next time." They piled into the front seat of the Mercedes and drove off.

"I don't feel good, Bear," Shay said, swaying on his feet. He fell back against the side of the car. I caught him before he hit the ground. I opened the car door for him, and he tumbled in. I got in and locked the doors. Shay remained motionless, his head resting against the back of the seat, eyes closed, his breathing in fast, little breaths.

"Shay, that was just intimidation. You don't really think they would've given us a beating, just because we were next to the car?"

"A black guy standing alongside a Mercedes with a beeping car alarm?" he answered without moving or opening his eyes. "Hell, yes. A perfect trap, even with you there. Slaughter paid them off. I'm just glad it wasn't a cop. He might've shot me."

"I think you're a little paranoid."

He sat up and opened his eyes. "Am I? Wear my skin, Bear. You have no idea how your whole world changes. That was only one example. There're lots."

"Like what?"

"Wander through Nordstrom searching for the perfect gift for your girlfriend, and the store detective will trail you. Discreetly, of course, but close enough to be sure you don't pocket anything.

"Or leave your table in a fancy restaurant to go to the men's room before you've paid, and suddenly the manager needs to take a leak at the urinal next to yours. Or be a black guy fumbling with his house key late at night and get arrested as a burglar."

He shook his head, his eyes downcast, dejected. "And good luck flagging a taxi after dark, even wearing a jacket and tie. The examples are endless, and sadly, many end violently. Look at all the shootings of young black men."

BEAR'S PROMISE

"Win this case and your color won't matter," I said. "You'll be a hero."

"Yeah, right. You still don't get it, do you?" Shay said. "I'll always be black, Bear, and you'll always be white. I have to work twice as hard as you to get half as far. And no success, no matter how great, will change that. Obama will always be a black president, not an American president who happened to be black."

"You want to quit?" I asked.

"I'm thinking about it, but the Hammer would never back down and would never forgive me if I did. No, I'm still on board."

"I guess we'll have to be more careful, especially as the case heats up. Electric Gun's a lot rougher than I thought," I said.

CHAPTER TWENTY-SIX

BEAR'S PROMISE

For months, I'd tried scheduling depositions with the cops and Verity, but they gave excuses about how busy they were, or were on vacation, or that their defense team had conflicts with the suggested dates. Finally, the court got fed up with the delays and issued orders for the trial to move ahead with the original date.

Shay and I were at lunch at Mulligans, a café on Main Street in downtown Hopperville, where I'd become a regular. The food was great, service prompt, and not too pricy. Wine and oysters were half-price on Sundays. The café even reserved an outdoor table in my name since I ate lunch there so often during the week. It was just a couple of blocks from my office.

Spring had arrived, and a warm May sun was ironing out winter's last wrinkles. Hopperville closed Main Street to auto traffic from June 1 to September 1 so pedestrians could enjoy the carless atmosphere. It also made eating at outdoor tables next to the road much more enjoyable. We had to contend with car exhaust for just a few more weeks until road closure took effect.

"The court issued its pretrial order this morning," I said to Shay as we sat down at my regular table. "The judge hasn't changed the trial date he gave us. We begin in four weeks."

"Not much time left." He let out a "Whew."

"Papageorgio called me after he got the order, bitching and making like it was my fault, that I'd delayed scheduling depositions on purpose. He appealed to the court for a continuance but got stonewalled. 'The trial will commence when I said so,' the judge responded." I grinned, anxious that the trial date was so close but happy the judge had stiffed Papageorgio.

"Tough judge?" Shay asked. I nodded.

A small diesel-powered truck drove by, spewing black exhaust into the air. I tried holding my breath but started coughing as soon as I exhaled and sucked in the fumes.

"That smell's awful," I managed to gasp. "The exhaust will kill you." I took out a handkerchief and blew my nose. I breathed through the handkerchief until the air cleared.

The waiter came running over with a glass of water. "I can move you to the other side of the café, away from the road," he said, pointing to a distant table shaded by the adjoining building. "You'll lose this nice sun," he said, "but no car exhaust."

I looked at Shay.

"I'm okay here," he said. "I don't mind the cars."

"I do," I said, standing. "Let's switch tables."

We gathered our water glasses and napkins and moved several tables away, back from the road.

After we settled in, I said, "We're not going to have time to depose anyone else before the trial date. It'll be trial by ambush." I smoothed my napkin and placed it on my lap.

"What's that?" Shay asked, doing the same.

"Neither side has time for discovery, and we'll have to get all the information in court."

"Weird," Shay muttered.

"Some states still do that," I said. I remembered an article in the *American Lawyer* several years ago featuring trials by ambush in Oregon. No depositions and no interrogatories, so information about the opposition's case remained hidden right up to the day of the trial. That made for less prep time but increased anxiety because lawyers couldn't plan for what the other side was going to throw at them.

"Isn't that good for us?" Shay asked, elbows leaning on the table. "From their reports, we know what the cops'll say. And you know Verity's going to lie and take a bullet protecting Slaughter. He'll testify it was excited delirium no matter what. They don't know about Dumont."

"Yeah, but I wanted to question that cop, Bennett."

"You got a thing about him," Shay said.

"I do." I thought Bennett was different from the others, more honest. He might be the chink in their armor. I wanted to question him before trial, but I'd have to wait until he was on the witness stand.

Shay looked up from the table at a woman approaching in the distance.

"Looks like we got a beauty queen joining us," he said, tipping his head at her.

She was walking toward the table we'd just vacated. I put down the menu and rose, waving.

"Kat, over here."

She saw me and quickened her pace.

BEAR'S PROMISE

Approaching, she gave me a hug, Shay a smile, and sat down. "Not your usual table," she said, scanning the restaurant and seeing the waiter lead another couple to my regular spot.

She looked radiant in a skintight black miniskirt, off-the-shoulder sheer blouse, and black leather boots. For the life of me, I couldn't understand why women wore boots in the summer. Feet sweat, legs sweat, and boots are clunky, but I guess making a fashion statement outweighed comfort. I often teased Kat about wearing boots when there was no snow.

Kat had become quite ill after our encounter six weeks earlier. She'd ended up depressed, drank heavily, and landed in Columbia Presbyterian Hospital with jaundice from painful hepatitis. The doctors told her that her inflamed liver was failing from the booze and her future guarded if she continued drinking. Her liver was scarred—cirrhotic—and could not withstand much more abuse.

She'd cold-turkeyed on the spot, spent a week in the hospital and two weeks at an Al-Anon spa to dry out. She emerged as an older but more brittle version of the beauty I'd married. More importantly, the scare made her rethink her life and where it was going. She called me when she left the spa, crying on the phone. "I want to be back in your life, Bear. I want it to be like the old days, when we were a team, important to each other."

I invited her to join me in Hopperville. I now had my paralegal as well as my lovely wife back.

She'd changed her lifestyle and cut her personal expenses. Gone were the hair salons, manicures, and facials. Her blonde hair had become streaked with gray, nails a bit frayed, and clothes, except for one last splurge that she was wearing today, came off the rack at Nordstrom. She said Saks, Bergdorf, and Tiffany would likely remain solvent without her.

She worked eight to five alongside me, like when we were first married. As we neared the trial date, those hours ballooned to seven to six, and then seven to seven, or even longer. But she seemed to love every minute, sharing our lives and doing something meaningful, fighting injustice together. We were back on the same page, loving the law and each other. She attended Al-Anon meetings twice weekly.

She told me Mark Hamden texted and called, but she didn't answer. She wished she could hit the delete button for that chapter in her life. We talked about it just once. I wanted to move on, to chalk it up as part of her alcoholic past.

The waiter took our order, and we chatted until our food arrived. The café was crowded, but we were in no particular hurry. The day was bright and lovely, and the upcoming trial consumed most of the conversation. Our food arrived in about fifteen minutes.

My back was to the street, so I didn't know anything was wrong until I'd taken a bite of my blackened grouper sandwich and heard Kat scream.

I turned and saw a large van hurtling down Main Street, scattering folks in its path. It gained speed until it was about even with Mulligans, when it swerved from the road and careened into my usual table. People, food, and furniture exploded. The van braked and, with a squeal of tires, roared back onto the road. It disappeared around the next corner. We were only two tables away and sat stunned as the carnage splattered us with blood.

The couple sitting at my regular table had been hurled into the air like bowling pins, their table and chairs flattened.

"Call 911," I shouted at Shay and ran to try to help them.

An elderly, gray-haired man and a young woman—perhaps his daughter—were in death throes. His leg was twisted at an impossible angle, and the side of his head bashed in. She'd been thrown onto the adjacent table, and as I approached, she rolled off and onto the ground, unmoving and glassy-eyed, her arm dangling by a piece of skin.

The guy sitting at that table just gaped at her in shock, his mouth slack and eyes wide, his face and shirt dripping red.

In minutes, the shrill blast of sirens erupted, and police cars and an ambulance descended on the restaurant. Chaos replaced the quiet spring day in sleepy Hopperville.

EMTs barreled out of the ambulance and ran to the man and woman. They administered first aid, halted bleeding, and inserted IVs but quit after a half hour. The people were dead at the scene. The EMTs loaded the man and woman onto stretchers, and the ambulance carried them away. The police cordoned off the café and questioned all of the diners. We weren't much help, and I suspect the others weren't either. The slaughter was over so quickly we couldn't even remember the color of the van, how many were in it, or whether a man or woman drove. We didn't get the license plate number.

We huddled in a corner of the café, trying to calm down, settle our jittery nerves. After the police and EMTs drove off, we rose and left as the café personnel began to clean up. We walked back to my office deep in thought but keeping an eye out for speeding cars. An event like that makes you realize life can change on a dime. You become hyper acute about ordinary happenings like hearing a loud noise or seeing a car drive too close to the sidewalk. I knew it'd impact where I chose to sit at my next outdoor café.

"But for that diesel exhaust, we'd have been sitting at that table," Shay said, pointing. "Two near misses. I'm not looking for a third."

"Did you believe the police?" Kat asked, her face still ashen despite her makeup. "A random act of terror?"

"No," I said, taking her hand and nudging her to walk away from the road, in between Shay and me. "I bet the cops will find the van several miles away, abandoned, and wiped clean. No link to Slaughter, but my guess is he's responsible."

"That's a long reach from Framingham," Shay said.

"Not really. A phone call to the right local person is all it takes," I said.

"Why didn't you tell that to the police?" Kat asked.

"To the Hopperville police? You got to be kidding, Kat. From what I've learned, they'd be the first to protect their own. Probably arrest Shay or me instead," I said.

The incident made front-page news in the *Hopperville Daily* the next day. The article noted that the cops found the van but had no further leads. "We'll continue to investigate and search for the perpetrator or perpetrators of this horrific act," they said.

An investigative reporter for the paper wrote a compelling piece after interviewing our waiter and finding out we'd switched tables moments before the hit-and-run. The reporter called my office for a statement, but I told him, "No comment." I didn't want to say anything that might get printed and jeopardize our case. That only made him more curious.

He'd dug deep—found out I'd grown up in Brown County, near Bloomington, recently moved to Hopperville after losing my sister and her family, and was preparing for an upcoming trial. He researched the court docket and came up with *Simpson v. Hopperville Police and Electric Gun Company*. His piece got more provocative as he speculated whether it wasn't a random terror act but meant for me, and it questioned whether the Hopperville police knew more than what they were saying publicly.

When I read that last statement, I googled the reporter, a guy named Bradford Hillsdale. Turned out his house burned down five years ago after he wrote an article about how tough the Hopper*vile* police were. He put two l's in this article, however.

CHAPTER TWENTY-SEVEN

DOUG ZIPES

Two days after the *Hopperville Daily* ran the hit-and-run story, Kat answered a phone call from a woman asking to speak with me.

"Hello, I'm Attorney Jason Judge. May I help you?"

"My name's Cynthia Griffin. I'd like to speak with you about a personal matter."

I explained we were busy preparing for trial, but the woman said what she wanted to discuss might help. She insisted I had to meet with her.

Kat answered the knock on the office door and ushered in our guest. Cynthia Griffin arrived in dark blue shorts, a striped white-and-blue tank top, and sandals. She looked to be in her early thirties. I'd bet she was once a knockout. She had a cute turned-up nose, blue eyes, and blonde hair but had let her beauty go to pot. Her face was pudgy, her full chest sagging, and what might have once been a narrow waist, thickened.

"Please sit down," Kat said, guiding her into the conference room. "Can we offer you anything? Coffee? Water? Juice?"

Cynthia shook her head. Her downturned expression showed the emotional strain she must've been feeling. She took a handful of Kleenex from her pocket, blew her nose, pulled her legs beneath her on the chair, and rested her arms on the conference table.

I sat across from her, Kat next to me. "How can I help?" I asked.

"The reverse," Cynthia said with a slight smile. "I think I can help you."

I leaned forward, interested. "Okay, let's hear it."

"I read the story about you almost getting killed the other day." She stopped and dabbed at her eyes. "The reporter didn't come right out and say it, but it seemed like he wondered if the cops had anything to do with it, or at least knew more than they were telling."

I gave her an encouraging look.

"Did they catch the guy yet?"

"They found the van but not the driver."

"I doubt the Hopperville cops are very good detectives. I don't know about all of them, but I know this one cop who's a bad apple."

My ears perked up.

She stopped again, mouth open, but no words emerged. She rearranged her feet beneath her, flicked a piece of imaginary lint from her shorts, and pressed her lips together. Her eyes grew moist.

She seemed to need a moment alone to gather her thoughts.

"Let me bring you some water," Kat said, rising. "I'll be right back." Kat went into the kitchen and returned several moments later with a plastic water bottle. She unscrewed the top and handed it to Cynthia. "Glass?"

"No thanks," Cynthia said, and took a sip, setting the bottle down on a coaster. After a deep breath and a long sigh, she began again.

"It happened about fifteen years ago. I'd snuck out my father's car on a Sunday morning while he was playing golf." She paused and sucked in her belly. "I used to have a pretty figure back then, before the kids came."

I returned her smile.

"A Hopperville cop named Sparafucile stopped me for speeding on Route 31 ..."

Cynthia went on for about twenty minutes. "Since then, I've heard rumors he still does it, lies in wait on Route 31. It's usually Friday afternoons but sometimes Mondays."

"Why're you telling me this? If you wanted to sue him, the time has long since expired," I said.

"This isn't about me anymore. Well, it is, but it isn't. Women are coming forward finally to accuse men who've molested them. It's time I did this too. It's festered in me so long it feels like I have a disease, an infection or something, deep inside. Every time my husband and I"—she stopped, searching for words—"well, you know, when we do it, I think of that cop touching me. I don't know how many other girls he's molested, but it has to stop. Reading the newspaper story the other day started me thinking, gave me enough courage to come here."

"Have you told anyone else about this?"

She shook her head. "Too embarrassing."

"What do you want me to do?" I asked.

"Make him stop."

━■━

After Cynthia left, Kat and I talked about what we should do. The statute of limitations had long since expired to bring sexual harassment charges against Sparafucile. Even if we found someone who'd been molested more recently and was willing to testify, it would still be her word against his. He'd bring a gang of his buddies to swear on his behalf, and it'd be a he-said-she-said slugfest.

I always thought those trials were the riskiest since a jury could be swayed either way. Plus, it would subject the woman to the harsh glare of public exposure and likely a withering cross-examination by a good defense lawyer like Papageorgio. Defense strategy was always to go after the woman, find anything to make her look like a slut. That or make it seem consensual. Either way, it took a strong and courageous woman to testify.

Kat brewed us both a cup of coffee and came back into the conference room. "What about if I got him to arrest me for speeding," she said, sitting down next to me, "and was able to get him to talk about the Electric Gun and shooting Jared? Maybe he'd reveal something you could use at trial—or he might let something slip about Cynthia or one of the others." Her eyes glistened. "I want to help you win this trial, Bear. I need to do something to become an equal partner again, to make up for ... well, you know."

She reached out and squeezed my hand. I squeezed back. We used to play a silly game when we were first married. Four hand squeezes were, "Do you love me?" Three in response meant, "Yes, I do." Then, two squeezes, "How much?" One long squeeze, "Lots!"

We did that now.

I stared into her lovely eyes, those beautiful blues that'd transfixed me years ago at Dartmouth. "You are my partner, Kat, my life's partner. You've been doing more than your share since you moved back. You don't need to—"

She shook her head, tears dripping. "Not enough, Bear, not enough. I need to do more ..." She looked at the clock. "It's 11:00 a.m. Friday. He could be waiting."

"No, Kat, absolutely not. It's too dangerous. I will not let you do this—whatever wild notions you have."

CHAPTER TWENTY-EIGHT

DOUG ZIPES

Sparafucile sat at the side of the road in an unmarked police car on the northern outskirts of Hopperville. Route 31 ran through Indiana from Kentucky to Michigan, bisecting the center of Indianapolis on its way north to Hopperville. Shortly after it left town, Route 31 became a four-lane, three-mile stretch of black macadam, straight as an arrow, with an on-off ramp to Interstate 65. Drivers hurrying north to Chicago or south to Louisville liked to press pedal to metal, exceeding the forty-five-miles-per-hour speed limit. Sparafucile led the squad in speeding ticket income from those three miles alone.

But that's not why he was a traffic cop a half day a week. And it wasn't to show the guys he was one of them either.

The first time it had happened was about fifteen years ago. He'd moved to Indiana three or four years before and joined the Hopperville police force. Cynthia somebody—he'd forgotten her last name—had just gotten her driver's license. She was a pretty little sixteen-year-old blonde with blue eyes, a tiny nose, pixie ears, and a full figure, surprising for one so young. She'd snuck her father's blue Chevy convertible out for a spin on a Sunday morning while he was playing golf, and her mother was at a church meeting. Sparafucile clocked her doing sixty. When he pulled her over, she became hysterical—totally lost it because she knew how her father would react.

"I'll be grounded for life," she wailed. Her hand trembled as she passed him her driver's license and registration.

Sparafucile went back to his patrol car, stayed in the front seat, and pretended to enter her information into the computer. This was just for show. He kept her waiting ten minutes to build anxiety. He could see her pounding the steering wheel as she waited.

He returned to her car and leaned close to her face through the driver-side window.

"I just checked," he said. "This'll cost you $150 and three points on your license. The judge might even suspend your license a year to teach you a lesson."

The fine really was only seventy-five, and no judge was going to revoke her license for driving fifteen miles over the speed limit. But what the hell. Gotta nip speeders in the bud.

She gasped, and her pretty blue eyes filled with tears. She looked desperate.

"What would you do if I didn't write it?" he asked.

"Anything," she said, almost before he'd finished the question.

"You mean that?" he asked. "Anything?"

She nodded. He took off his sunglasses and stared into those blues to make sure she wasn't bullshitting. She didn't blink and, in fact, had a slight smile on her face. Or maybe it was a scared look? He couldn't tell. Whatever, he figured Cynthia was no Virgin Mary. She had to know what she was doing.

"Okay," he said. "Follow me."

She stayed fifty yards behind his car all the way. He drove to a Super 8 motel two miles away, managed by a guy who owed him lots of favors. Sparafucile let Mousey use his hotel basement as a drug parlor where locals could shoot up. As long as they were quiet and didn't bother anybody, Sparafucile didn't bother them. If they got too stoned to drive home, Mousey rented them a room to sleep it off. He called Sparafucile if they got unruly, and he bounced a few heads. It was a good deal for everybody.

"The Iceman cometh," Mousey said, smiling, as they walked in. Mousey was thin, short, and mostly bald but had a wiry mustache resembling a mouse's whiskers. "How you doing, Chilli?"

"Great, Mousey. You?"

Mousey gave Cynthia a good look-see. "I guess you want a room. Overnight or just a couple of hours?" he asked.

Cynthia's eyes flared. "My father—" she started to say.

"An hour should be enough," Sparafucile said.

Mousey pulled a key off a hook on the wall behind his desk. "Room 110. Booked for a late check-in, but you'll be done by then?"

Sparafucile nodded.

"First floor. Queen-size bed with a soft mattress." Mousey looked at Cynthia and then back at Sparafucile. "No need to register. Just don't break anything or steal the towels," he said with a laugh.

"Thanks, Mousey," Sparafucile said, taking the key from his outstretched hand. "Owe you one."

"Na," Mousey said, with a head shake. "Anytime."

Cynthia and Sparafucile walked side by side down the hall to room 110. He felt a little awkward with jailbait but what the fuck. She'd asked for it. He draped his arm across her shoulders. She stiffened at first but then relaxed and tentatively put her arm around his waist. He pulled her close, and they bumped hips.

"Why'd he call you Iceman?" she asked.

"Long story. Maybe later."

When they got to 110, he put the key in the lock with his free hand, opened the door, and led her in. He closed the door, made sure it was locked, and set the chain in place. He didn't expect to be interrupted, but no sense taking chances.

The room was small, with the queen-size bed taking up most of the space. A bathroom was off to the right, and a metal coat rack leaned against the wall with a cluster of empty black wire hangers. A dresser with a mirror on top was against the wall opposite the foot of the bed.

They stood face-to-face, looking at each other. Cynthia dropped her gaze to check her watch. "I don't have too much time before my father gets home."

"Okay, let's turn it on." Sparafucile reached for her.

He got a flared look, and she backed away, shaking her head.

"I changed my mind. I need to go home. I can't do this." Her voice cracked and ended on a high pitch, almost a scream. She looked toward the door.

"You want the ticket and lose your license?"

"No." Her eyes teared as she shook her head.

"That's what'll happen. And remember what your father'll do to you."

A moan escaped her lips. He reached for her again, but she pulled loose. "You're not a virgin, are you?"

She shook her head.

"Then what the fuck's your problem?"

"It was different then—with my boyfriend. We were in his car, and it was dark."

"I'll turn out all the lights, and you pretend I'm your boyfriend."

"Yeah, right," she said with a short laugh. "Not hardly. You're almost old enough to be my father."

Sparafucile was getting pissed. He was hard as a rock, and no way he was going back to work like that. "Cynthia, enough of this bullshit. You should've said no back on 31. It's too late to chicken out now."

He didn't want to use force, but she was pushing his limits. He grabbed her and tugged her to him. She was wearing a pale blue silk blouse and a dark blue linen skirt. He took the top button of her blouse in his fingers—it was pearl shaped—and slowly pushed it through the buttonhole.

There were six. She closed her eyes and chewed her lower lip as he worked them and then slid the blouse off her shoulders. He let it fall to the floor. With the tips of his fingers, he traced the top of her bra where her breasts fought loose from the lacy pink constraint. Her skin was snowy white, soft, yielding.

Her skirt had a zipper in the back. He reached behind her, pulled it down, and made her step out of it. Standing there in her bra and panties, her eyes were still closed, and her wrinkled brow was a look of fright.

"It's okay," he said, whispering in her ear. "I promise I won't hurt you if you do what I tell you."

She was breathing fast and close to panicking. Sparafucile didn't want her to start screaming. As much as he liked to beat up bad guys, he didn't enjoy violence during sex. He liked harmony, not brutality; the softness and yield of a woman's flesh, not taut muscles resisting his advances.

But he'd use force if he had to. No way in hell was she going to walk away from this.

"Your turn," he said.

She didn't move, eyes still scrunched tight. He took her hand and placed it on his tie. "Undo it," he said.

She opened her eyes, and her trembling fingers fumbled with the knot. Tie undone, she pulled it from his collar and let it fall to the floor on top of her clothes.

"Now the shirt," he said, guiding her hands to the first button.

She unbuttoned each one and slid his shirt off like he had done hers. She ran her fingers over the tattoos on his biceps. "Iceman? Ice cubes?"

He ignored her. "The belt next."

She unbuckled his belt, unbuttoned the top of his pants without being told, and pulled down his zipper. The pants fell with a thud, dragged down by the weight of the law enforcement duty belt with its assorted attachments, his Electric Gun, and the .38. She jumped at the noise.

He put a hand on each shoulder and drew her close. He didn't try to kiss her but took her hand and ran her fingers over the prominent bulge in his boxer shorts.

An hour later, Cynthia left without a speeding ticket.

Since then, there'd been lots of Cynthias, most of them older. Sparafucile didn't mind those who refused. They just got ticketed.

When he stopped a guy, he asked the same question but expected a different payoff. Minimum two hundred bucks, depending on how fast he was going. Most paid up without a squawk. It was not much more than the price of the ticket these days, and they avoided points on their license.

Sometimes he caught a speeder with drugs on board. That's when it really got interesting. They often had lots of cash and were only too willing to part with half or more, or samples of their product, to avoid arrest.

So, all in all, his half day as a traffic cop spun off lots of interesting experiences, most of them rewarding—at least for him. But he figured it was a win for the speeder as well.

He'd always remember Cynthia as the first. When they finished, lying next to him in bed, she asked again why he was called Iceman.

"I love encounters that call for brute force," Sparafucile said. "I work out a lot. My chest's almost as big as yours."

"Yeah, right." Cynthia laughed and pulled the sheet to her chin.

"My biceps are eighteen inches. Cassius Clay's biceps—I hate the name Muhammad Ali—his were only seventeen inches."

He flexed, making the tattoos dance, the pair of ice cubes on the right and picture of the Iceman on the left. She traced the images with the tip of her finger.

"Enough stalling. Tell me the story," she said.

BEAR'S PROMISE

He sat up straight in bed, leaned back against the headboard, and arched his knees. He looked at the mirror on the dresser on the opposite wall. His eyes stared at his own reflection as he remembered.

"Several years ago, we busted a drug gang called the Assassins on Hopperville's lower east side—the wrong side of town unless you were Hispanic or black. We had them outnumbered and outgunned, but it was still headed to a bloody firefight. They were well protected, holed up in a vacant tenement building, and I didn't relish having to fight them room to room. The stairwells were the most dangerous, especially if they held the higher floors. I could lose guys that way.

"The leader of the Assassins was a real tough black named Razor— his favorite weapon. Razor was a born-again Bible dude. An ornate gold cross dangled from a braided leather necklace around his neck. I found out later he read Bible stories to his gang every night and led them in prayer. Razor especially loved the story of David and Goliath.

"He knew he might lose men in a gun battle, so he threw out a challenge.

"'I'll fight any one of you, one on one, no weapons. I lose, you take us in without a gun fight. I win, we walk.'

"Man, to me that was a made-for-TV script. In fact, channel 8 was there covering the drug bust for the Ten O'clock Evening News. That made it even more fun. I'd be the TV hero like all the video games I watched growing up. I spent hours mesmerized by the big guy beating up the little guys. Loved every minute of it."

He glanced away from the mirror and looked down at her, making sure she was paying attention. Her head rested on her pillow, but her face showed excitement with big, round eyes and a slightly open mouth. "Keep going. Don't stop now," she said, a little breathless. The top of the sheet had drifted down, exposing her breasts, but she didn't seem to notice or care. He bent down and kissed each nipple. Then he stared back at the mirror and continued.

"I took off my jacket, unstrapped the belt, and stepped forward. Razor had his back to me and real casual-like, slipped off the leather necklace, kissed the cross, and handed it to one of his gang.

"Then, in an instant, he spun and came charging, fists flailing like a young Mike Tyson. Big, looping rights and lefts whistled through the air. He was tough, but he didn't know how to fight my way.

"I dodged his fists, whirled, and hit him with a spinning judo kick to the side of his face. The heel of my boot caught him totally by surprise, and I heard the crunch as his jaw shattered."

She gasped and sat up. "Holy shit."

"That part was over in less than ten seconds.

"Then, when he was down, I picked up his right arm and snapped it in two. I just cracked it at the elbow over my knee like a piece of kindling. That took another ten seconds.

"Finally, a toe kick to his left gut sent him to emergency surgery for a ruptured spleen. Maybe five seconds for that. So, less than half a minute, and the fight was over, probably faster than David beaned Goliath with his slingshot."

"You're a brute," Cynthia said, awe in her tone. She propped herself on an elbow, pulled up the sheet, and studied him. "Then what?"

"The good thing is that all this happened in front of his own guys. The gang laid down their guns, meek as lambs, and we cuffed them without a fight. I got a letter of commendation from the chief. But more important, I got status from my squad. You can't buy that kind of prestige or order it. You got to earn respect in battle like any warrior.

"My guys had always stumbled over my last name, not pronouncing the "c" at the end as "ch." I don't know where in Sicily Sparafucile originated. My mom didn't either. I once looked it up on Google, but all I got was some Italian opera about a hunchback and a hired killer named Sparafucile. After I chilled Razor and the Assassins, that's what my guys started calling me: Chilli or Iceman."

"I was right. You are a brute," she repeated, smiling.

He reached for her.

CHAPTER TWENTY-NINE

DOUG ZIPES

The day was overcast as cottony clouds flirted with the sun, creating impressionistic images on the countryside like Seurat paintings.

Sparafucile watched as the woman drove by in a late-model silver BMW, headed north at five miles over the speed limit. Nothing unusual about that. His gaze shifted to the cars coming after her. When she passed the sign, *Goodbye, come back soon to Hopperville,* and made a U-turn to drive south on 31, that drew his attention. She blew past the entrance to Interstate 65, where he sat in the police cruiser, concealed between a large clump of bushes and a low-slung billboard advertising a Super 8 motel. He clocked her doing almost seventy, and he swung into action with flashing lights and a blasting siren.

He pulled her over and parked close behind. He waited a full five minutes, then got out of his car, put on his hat, adjusted his utility belt, and walked deliberately to the driver's side of her car. He saw she was an attractive blonde, and his interest heightened. He stood tall, rapped on her window, and motioned for her to roll it down.

"I clocked you doing sixty-seven in a forty-five-mile-per-hour zone, lady. That's more than twenty miles over the legal speed limit. Put down your cell phone and hand me your license, registration, and proof of insurance, please," Sparafucile said, holding out his hand.

She put her cell phone at the top of her purse and rummaged around to find her papers. She handed them to him. He noted her trembling hand. After reading the documents, he said, "Please remain in your car."

He walked back to his vehicle, entered the driver's side, and sat down. He glanced at her car and saw she was watching him in her rearview mirror. He entered her name, license, and registration into his dashboard computer. The response surprised him, and he began to make plans.

After ten minutes, he walked back to her car and said, "Please step out of your car and keep your hands where I can see them."

"What did I do that I have to—"

"Just get out of the car as I asked," he said, his tone now harsher.

"You don't have the right to order me to do that."

"Lady, get out of your car." His tone was severe, and his face a dark mask. "Hands where I can see them," he repeated, an even sharper edge in his voice.

"You are Mrs. Katherine Judge," he said, returning her license and registration.

"Yes."

"You're the wife of the man suing me and my friends for police brutality. Is that correct?"

Her face turned ashen, and she sucked in a mouthful of air. He figured she hadn't thought he'd make the connection. But how dumb can you be? Drive north scouting the landscape, turn around and race, expecting to be stopped. Stupid lady! He was bound to check and recognize the last name. But what did she want from him?

"Yes, I am." Her voice was a quivering whisper.

"Turn around and put your hands behind your back. I'm arresting you—"

"For speeding? You can't do that. I want to call my husband."

"Lady, I'm telling you once more to put your hands behind your back. If you don't, I will also cite you for resisting arrest. You want to escalate this further?"

"You can't—"

He grabbed her shoulder and spun her around. He seized one hand, twisted it forcibly behind her back, and then the other hand, in a practiced, fluid motion. He clicked the cold metal handcuffs against her wrists. She shuddered and winced at the pain.

He whirled her around to face him. "Mrs. Judge, you are under arrest for reckless driving at speeds exceeding twenty miles an hour over the official speed limit, as well as for resisting arrest."

He pushed her back against the car and figured, especially with a lawyer husband, he'd better read her her rights. He pulled a plastic card from his pocket and read the Miranda text. "Do you understand what I've just read to you?"

She was speechless. He hoped she was good and scared. An *excellent beginning*, he thought.

"Mrs. Judge, do you understand your rights?" he asked in an irritated tone. His facial expression, dark deep-set eyes, forehead contorted into a scowl, and mean, thin-lipped mouth made her shiver.

She still couldn't speak. He turned her around, and with one hand on her bound wrists, he pushed her toward his police car. He opened the back door, put his hand on top of her head, pushed it under the door frame, and forced her into the back seat. He slammed the door shut, walked to her car, and came back with her handbag.

He opened the opposite back door, placed her handbag on the floor, sat down, and closed the door.

He slid next to her. She pulled away with a look of panic. She groped for the door handle, but it was locked. "Get away from me," she yelled.

"Sorry, but I've got to pat you down," he said, unsmiling. "You might be carrying concealed weapons. I checked your handbag and found none. But you may have concealed one or more on your person."

"No. You can't do this," she screamed, her cries muffled in a car with the doors and windows shut.

He wedged her into a corner of the seat and looped a seat belt around so tight she could barely move. When she opened her mouth to scream again, he stuffed in a piece of cloth.

"No more noise," he said, unbuttoning her blouse. With gentle, lingering moves, he ran his hand inside her bra, under and around her breasts. "No guns or knives there," he said, now smiling. He reached beneath her skirt and slid his hand up her thighs and over her buttocks. "None there either. I guess you're clean."

He stopped and pulled back. "Sad to quit now," he said a bit breathless, his hand pulling on the bulge in his crotch, "but I think we'd better go to the police station and book you for reckless driving and resisting arrest, and maybe we'll find more infractions."

As soon as he removed her gag, she yelled, "Help! Somebody, help me!"

He leaned over her, his face inches from hers, as he rebuttoned her blouse with careful fingers. "So far, I've been very gentle with you, Mrs. Judge. I don't like to beat up women. Yell like that again, and things will change very quickly. Do I make myself clear?"

She could only nod.

"I want you to be quiet and cooperative from now on. Do you agree, or don't you understand?" The tone in his voice was sinister.

She managed to stammer, "I agree. What about my car? I want to call my husband. You can't do this," she said. She bit down on her tongue, and he figured she was fighting the urge to scream again. Her teeth chattered, and her body shook.

"One question at a time, Mrs. Judge," he said in a calm voice. "I will send a tow truck for your car, you can call your husband after we book you, and I very well can do this, all quite within the law. You brought it on yourself."

He drove to the Hopperville police station. It occupied the ground floor in the same municipal building where the Judge law office was located.

A young cop named Bennett was at the front desk and took mug shots and fingerprints and booked her on charges of reckless driving and resisting arrest.

"Anything else, Chilli?" Bennett asked Sparafucile.

"I haven't searched her purse yet, Jim. Let's take a look."

Sparafucile upended Kat's purse and dumped the contents on the sergeant's desk. Lipstick, compact, Kleenex tissues, keys, and her cell phone spilled out.

"What's this?" Sparafucile asked, removing two cellophane envelopes from a zippered partition in her purse. Each held a tiny amount of white powder.

Sparafucile opened one envelope, sniffed, put a finger into the white powder and tasted the residue. "I'd say she's got two bags of cocaine in her purse, maybe half an ounce in one and an ounce in the other. Agree, Jim?"

"That's what you pulled out, Chilli," Bennett said.

"Those aren't mine," she yelled. "I've never seen them before. Somebody put them in my purse."

Sparafucile opened a zippered bag lying on the desk. He took a glass slide from the bag and shook a sample of powder from one packet onto it. Then he squeezed a drop of liquid from a dark bottle onto the powder.

"If this powder turns blue, Mrs. Judge, it's a positive identification for cocaine. We'll need to add another charge of illegal possession of a controlled substance, with intent to use or sell."

In moments, the white powder turned blue.

"What do you think, Jim?"

"Definitely blue."

"Wait! They're not mine. You planted them," Kat shouted.

"Sure, Mrs. Judge, sure I did. Just like you weren't speeding, right?"

"No, I was speeding, but those are not mine. I swear it."

"You know, Jim, she may have more hidden on her person. I think a strip search is in order, don't you?"

"Oh my God, no. Please, no. They're not mine. I don't have any on me. Please, no. Let me call my husband. He's a lawyer. He'll know what to do."

"We'll definitely let you call your husband, Mrs. Judge. You're entitled to call your lawyer, just as soon as we finish our investigation. And that includes a body search. Now, you can come along nicely and cooperate, or you can scream and fight, and I'll have to subdue you," Sparafucile put his hand on the butt of his Electric Gun. "You don't want me to do that, now do you?"

"I'm begging you, Officer Sparafucile. Please stop this insanity. Those bags are not mine. I don't know how they got into my purse. I have none in my possession. Dear God, please don't do this to me. I can't—"

"I don't believe much in God, Mrs. Judge, and I suspect the feeling's mutual, so don't count on Him for help."

Kat collapsed to her knees, weeping uncontrollably.

Sparafucile watched her, unmoved. She seemed spaced out. He had to speak to her twice before she responded.

"What would you do if I didn't do a strip search?"

"Anything. What do you want?" she moaned.

"I want the lawsuit against me and my buddies to go away."

"I can't control that. My husband's the lawyer."

"I know. But a good wife has a lot of influence on her husband."

She shook her head. "He won't stop. His sister and her family—"

Sparafucile grabbed her by one arm, and Bennett by the other, and they hauled her to her feet. As they began to drag her away, she shouted, "Where are you taking me?"

"To a nice, quiet back room where we'll have a nice, quiet body search. Just you and me," Sparafucile said. "Officer Bennett will go back to his desk to take care of the front office."

"Chilli, maybe we shouldn't—"

"Shut up, Bennett. I'm running this."

"Stop! Stop!" Her knees gave way, and she collapsed to the floor again. "I'll do whatever you want. Just stop."

"I told you what I want. Make your husband end the lawsuit. Will you promise to do that?"

"Yes. Yes. I promise. I promise."

They lifted her to her feet. Sparafucile unlocked the cuffs. He stood in front of her, a rocky monolith, and took hold of her arms with big, beefy hands, his thick fingers encircling her biceps. He glared at her.

"Mrs. Judge, you're free to leave. However, please believe me when I say that if you do not live up to your side of our bargain, I will come after you. I promise you that—and the strip search will be the least of your worries. I will see to it that you're convicted for drug trafficking and sent to prison on a narcotics charge of selling cocaine. I promise that your sentence will be a minimum of ten years in the worst prisons in the US, places like Attica or Leavenworth or Sing Sing. Do you understand me? In places like that, you'll have a strip search and more daily."

Kat nodded.

"Do not tell your husband what happened today. Just convince him to drop the suit. Understand?"

She nodded again. Words didn't come.

"If I end up in court, you end up in jail. Hear me?"

She blinked a response.

"The jury's going to believe two police officers who removed cocaine packets from your purse rather than an alcoholic with a drunk and disorderly conviction and two DUIs on her past record."

She gasped.

"Yes, I know about your boozy past. Your D and D and DUIs are part of your police rap sheet. Now, get out of my sight. If you ever see me again, prepare for the worst."

Chapter Thirty

BEAR'S PROMISE

Shay and I returned to the office after a meeting with the judge and lead defense counsel, Achilles Papageorgio, to work through several pretrial motions. Papageorgio was defending Electric Gun as well as the Hopperville police.

I expected to find Kat at the office typing briefs I'd left her but instead found a message on my computer saying she expected to be away most of the afternoon and would meet me at home for dinner around six. "I hope to have a wonderful surprise for you," the message ended.

Shay and I spent the afternoon discussing jury selection. The court had summoned thirty people to fill six jury slots and an alternate. Voir dire, jury vetting, would begin Monday and was expected to finish by noon or early afternoon. Each side had three unconditional peremptory strikes we could use to remove a juror without cause. We could also challenge an unlimited number to remove for cause.

Jury selection was critical. Any edge to legally turn them in our favor, to get them to sympathize with the Simpson family, was crucial at any cost. To do that, we needed to know as much about each juror as possible.

I'd hired a professional company, JurySelect, to do the legwork. They'd investigate the entire jury pool—at a thousand bucks a head—as soon as the prospective jurors filled out a basic questionnaire and registered with the court. JurySelect guaranteed we'd know within an hour where each one lived, how they voted, their occupation, debts and liens, health, income, and religion. We'd learn what they wrote on Facebook, or any webpage, what and where they ate, where they shopped, important relatives, legal encounters, and practically everything else about each one, except maybe what they dreamed last night. We'd have all that information downloaded to our computer or phone. In one hour! Amazing.

Shay would keep track of the records as I interviewed each juror to get to know each one personally, and for them to know me. Establishing a trusting bond was critical.

Papageorgio and his team would be doing the same thing. We could save a lot of money if we shared the data, but that wasn't going to happen.

I returned home around seven.

"Kat, you here?" I called out as I entered the kitchen.

No response.

I walked into the bedroom and called again. "Kat, are you—"

Kat was sprawled half in and out of a chair, shoulders on the seat of a recliner and her butt on the floor. She clutched an empty bottle of Macallan scotch in one outstretched hand and an empty glass in the other. She had on the same dress she'd worn to work this morning. It was stained with vomit in her lap that had spilled onto the rug. She had a shoe on one foot but none on the other. Her lipstick was smeared, eyes closed with mascara smudges, and she was snoring in loud, fitful bursts, sounding like gasps for breath. The room reeked of vomit and booze and some other strange odor I couldn't identify.

I took the bottle and glass from her hands and set them on the table. "Kat, are you okay? What happened?"

She mumbled something incoherent.

"Kat, talk to me."

She bolted upright and retched. Not much was left in her stomach, and only a little spittle came out. She fell back onto the recliner.

Calling 911 was my first thought, but I couldn't tell if she was sick or just drunk.

I lifted her from the floor and laid her on the bed. I sat down beside her.

"Kat, Kat. Say something. How much did you drink?"

She no longer responded to her name. I pried open her eyelids and saw the whites had a yellow tint, her breathing shallow. I felt her pulse. It was fast, like 130. Her breath smelled like—that was the weird odor. It smelled like ammonia.

This was more than an alcoholic stupor. I remembered the warning from the Columbia doctors and dialed 911.

"Your wife has alcoholic hepatoencephalopathy," Dr. Alex Abraham said, after examining Kat in the emergency room of University of Indiana Medical Center and checking the results of her blood tests. Abraham was the liver specialist on call.

"What's that?" I asked.

"She's developed fulminant liver failure from excessive alcohol. Her liver can no longer remove toxins from her blood. That's why her eyes have turned yellow—jaundice. It's also why you smelled ammonia on her breath and why she's comatose. The toxins have altered her brain function, put her into a coma. Her pancreas is also affected, so she has trouble secreting insulin and regulating her blood sugar."

"How could that be? She didn't drink that much. Only a couple of binges since we've been married."

Abraham's face showed compassion. "That you know of. She could've been drinking during the day while you were at work and hiding it by the time you got home. Or maybe she was a big drinker before you even met. Drinking as a teen is particularly dangerous. The toxic effect of alcohol at that age is ten times as bad as in an adult."

I started to protest, but Abraham waved me off.

"Mr. Judge, you don't need to defend her. It is what it is. Perhaps she did drink as little as you say and was just more vulnerable to the toxic effects of alcohol."

"What's the ammonia smell? She couldn't be drinking ammonia, could she? Maybe that caused the liver failure, not the alcohol."

"No. During digestion, bacteria help break down proteins in the intestine and produce ammonia that's degraded by the liver. Obviously, her liver can't handle that, so the ammonia builds up and can affect the brain and other organs. That's what you smelled on her breath."

"What happens now?" I asked.

"I'll admit her to the hospital, of course, and we'll detoxify her over several days. Abrupt cessation of alcohol could bring on DTs. We'll sedate her if that happens, support her nutrition, regulate her insulin, and hope for the best."

"Predictions?"

He spread his hands, palms up, and shrugged. "None. The liver has an amazing capacity to regenerate, the pancreas less so, and the adult brain virtually none. Brain damage could be permanent. We'll just have to wait and see how much function she recovers."

"How soon will you know?" I asked.

"Again, hard to predict. As short as several days to a week, or maybe as long as a month or two. One day at a time, Mr. Judge. One day at a time."

I remained by Kat's bed, watching the instruments that had kept Jared alive try to save her. As I listened to the same beeping, hissing, and whooshing, I felt unreal, transported into some sort of dream world—nightmare—reliving those days after Jared's cardiac arrest. I prayed for a different outcome. Kat and I had just reconnected and now were being driven apart.

The looming trial date magnified everything. How the hell could I function in a courtroom knowing my wife was fighting for her life in a hospital a mile away? I'd ask the judge for a delay, but I wasn't optimistic.

The court responded as I'd predicted.

"No, you may not have a continuance. This trial will proceed according to the dates I laid down originally. Jury selection begins Monday at 9:00 a.m. sharp. Make sure you're ready."

CHAPTER THIRTY-ONE

"**A**ll rise for the Honorable Felix J. Maplethorpe III," the bailiff intoned in a loud voice.

We stood as Judge Maplethorpe, black robe fluttering, strode into the courtroom through a rear door. He was an impressive-looking man, tall with broad shoulders and a dark, bristly mustache that contrasted with a full head of silvery-white hair. Shaggy salt-and-pepper eyebrows—more pepper than salt—hooded intense, deep-set hazel eyes that portrayed an intelligent, no-nonsense demeanor.

The Silver Fox ran a skintight courtroom.

Lawyers knew that when his eyebrows arched—they looked like two black crows flapping wings and ready to fly away—in response to "Objection, Your Honor," they'd just blundered into quicksand. He used those eyebrow crows as weapons of management. Rescue would come only after a lecture on why the objection was so stupid. The Fox wanted everyone to know he was the smartest person in that courtroom. Most of the time, he was.

He sat down in a high-backed, black leather chair behind an impressive oak desk, improbably called the bench. The tallest structure in the courtroom, the bench and leather chair kept Maplethorpe's head higher than all others. Old Glory to one side, the state flag of Indiana on the other, and the state's seal in between created a picture postcard of Indiana justice in action.

Shay and I sat at one of two identical long, dark wooden tables that divided us from Papageorgio with his associate lawyer, Harold Bosworth. Had Melanie been alive, she'd be sitting with us, while Slaughter, representing Electric Gun, sat with Papageorgio. The Hopperville police chief chose to be less noticeable and sat in the back of the courtroom.

A collection of large cardboard boxes holding critical files and papers we'd need during the trial were stacked beneath the table. We'd spent long hours indexing every item in each box, so we could pull them out at a moment's notice to support a statement.

I eyed the witness stand near the judge's desk where I'd be questioning Slaughter, Verity, and the cops. The name, a holdover from when witnesses stood to testify, was an enclosed wooden booth with a straight-backed wooden chair in the center, hardly an impressive site to host the bloody clashes I envisioned over the next few days.

BEAR'S PROMISE

My batteries were charged, weapons loaded, and I couldn't wait to do battle with Slaughter, Verity, and friends.

"All rise," the bailiff called out. We all stood, including the judge, as twenty-nine of the thirty people summoned for jury duty entered the jury box—not really a box but three rows of dark, polished wooden benches reminiscent of church pews, opposite the witness stand.

"Good morning to the best potential jurors in the state of Indiana and maybe all of the US," Maplethorpe said, smiling with enthusiasm. "Thank you for fulfilling one of the most fundamental duties as citizens of our great country. Jury duty and voting make us a democracy even though Mark Twain once said, 'If voting really made a difference, the government wouldn't let us do it!'"

Maplethorpe guffawed at his own joke and continued, "I hope your weekend was as grand as mine. We had a wonderful outdoor barbecue for our neighbors and friends."

The potential jurors murmured, and some smiled back at the judge, returning his good-morning greeting. His "I'm no different than you" approach was calculated to put them at ease.

He smiled again, finger-combed his hair, took a sip from a coffee mug on his desk—my heart did a little flip when I saw it was a Dartmouth mug—and his demeanor shifted, became serious, an abrupt transformation from an affable friend to a strict parent.

"This court has earned the nickname 'rocket docket' because it will not tolerate unnecessary delays. And most delays requested by counsel are unnecessary motions for this or that, or the lawyers stray from the facts and confuse you with irrelevant details. I will try not to let any of that happen in my courtroom."

Maplethorpe turned from the jurors to face us.

"Counselors, we will proceed in an expeditious manner, selecting jurors this morning and hearing opening statements this afternoon. I caution both plaintiff and defense counsels to be brief in questioning prospective jurors and refrain from making bold assertions in your opening statements. Rather, keep your story simple and stick to the facts. Save your big guns for examining the witnesses."

He turned back to the jurors.

"This trial has two parts. The first is whether a weapon labeled safe, nonlethal if used as directed, can kill a person and if that's possible, whether the police deployed the weapon in a judicious and appropriate manner. The second part is whether the company making the weapon behaved in a careless or negligent manner, making them responsible for the outcome. You will render a verdict in favor of plaintiff or defense, based on a preponderance of the evidence. From what I've told you, is there a reason any of you feel you cannot serve as a juror in this matter?"

Three hands shot up.

"Juror number twelve." He was a middle-aged man with dark, wavy hair, clean shaven, wearing a sports jacket over a white shirt without a tie.

"I cannot take time away from work, Your Honor."

"What is it you do?"

"I'm a cardiac surgeon at the university medical center, and I have a dozen patients scheduled for heart valve replacements over the next two weeks. Some may not survive if I have to delay their surgery."

"No one else can operate?"

"Not as well as I can, sir. People may die if—"

Maplethorpe laughed and held up his hand. "Enough. That seems like a pretty valid reason to me. Counselors, any objections to excusing the doctor?"

Shay hit the JurySelect tab on his computer, and his screen lit up. "Checks out," he whispered. "Jonathan Schroeder. Chief of cardiovascular surgery at UIMC."

"Too bad," I said, my hand covering my mouth. "Would've been nice to have had a juror who understood the heart rhythm problem."

"Not all's lost," Shay said. "Two nurses are still potentials."

"Excuse me, counselors," Maplethorpe interrupted. "Have we lost your attention or are you going to invite us to join your little soiree?"

"Sorry, Your Honor," I said. "No objection to dismissing this juror."

Papageorgio agreed.

"You are excused, Doctor. Thank you for coming. Bailiff, escort the doctor from the courtroom." The bailiff, an elderly, gray-haired man with a limp, motioned for the doctor to follow him out of the courtroom.

Another hand went up.

"Hello, juror number eight." Maplethorpe glanced at a paper in front of him. "And welcome to the court. Why can't you participate?"

I read the computer screen. Jordan Smith, divorced, McDonald's manager.

"I'm a single parent, Your Honor. I can't be away from home." Smith was short, with a potbelly, wearing jeans and a yellow golf shirt.

"Do you work outside the home?"

"Yes, sir. I manage a restaurant in downtown Hopperville."

"Who takes care of your children while you're at work?"

"I pay a sitter."

"This is no different than going to work. You can pay the same sitter while you're here. You're not excused. Anybody else unable to participate?"

I felt neutral about Smith. He'd probably be an okay juror.

The third hand did not reemerge.

The bailiff came back into to the courtroom and caught the judge's attention.

"Excuse me a moment," Maplethorpe said to the jury. The bailiff whispered to him, and he said, "Bring him in."

The bailiff returned with a young man in his twenties wearing jeans torn at the knees and a white T-shirt that said in bold red letters, *I'd like to challenge you to a contest of wits, but I can see you're hopelessly unarmed.*

The bailiff placed him in front of the judge.

The judge scanned the T-shirt, and his brow rose, but he said nothing. He read a sheet of paper the bailiff handed him.

"Juror number thirty, you're late for jury selection. Reason?"

"Overslept. I forgot to set my alarm clock." His tone, confrontational rather than apologetic, was not lost on the judge, whose brow arched a second time. The crows were beginning to twitch.

"This court does not tolerate tardiness, juror thirty, especially with such a lame excuse. You could have been more creative and at least said your dog ate the alarm clock." He waited for laughter from the jurors.

"You have two choices. You can spend the duration of this trial in jail with a contempt of court citation, or attend the entire trial as a spectator, arriving on time and spending the day sitting quietly in the back of the courtroom. If you're late again, you'll be sent to jail for the remainder of the trial. Which will it be?"

Thirty stood there, a shocked look on his face, mouth agape and about to protest. He turned his head slowly from side to side, bewildered, as if trying to clear it from Maplethorpe's pronouncement.

Before he could say anything, Maplethorpe held up his hand. "Arguing will add two days to your sentence. I'd advise you to keep your mouth shut, accept one of the options I offered, and show up on time. But, again, that's your choice."

Thirty was speechless. He turned as if to leave the courtroom, but the bailiff stood in his way. He turned back to the judge, red-faced and mouth drawn into a tight grimace. He clenched and unclenched his fists. Finally, he snapped, "I'll sit in the back."

"Wise decision, Thirty. Life's all about making choices and living with the consequences. You've made yours. Now live with it." Maplethorpe paused and added, almost as an afterthought, "Oh, and one more thing. Don't come back wearing that ridiculous T-shirt. In my courtroom, you're hopelessly outgunned."

Shay and I exchanged amazed looks. In my experience, late jurors were just seated at the end of the line. Maplethorpe was a no-nonsense judge, maybe a bit heavy-handed.

The bailiff escorted Thirty to the back of the courtroom, passing through a gate in a hip-high slatted wooden fence—the bar—that served as a barrier separating the front of the courtroom from spectators in the back. Only lawyers or participants in the trial could pass the bar to enter the front of the courtroom. The term "passing the bar" was applied to newly accredited lawyers after successfully taking a state examination that licensed them to practice law.

Maplethorpe cleared his throat, sipped from the mug, and addressed the potential jurors.

"Participating as a juror is both a blessing and a curse. The blessing is that you help decide right from wrong, help condemn or exonerate, and participate in the tradition of laws that underlie our democracy. You get to be a part of justice being done and contribute to our democracy. That's a big responsibility.

"The curse is that this takes you from your work and your family to discuss someone else's problems, with little reward except personal satisfaction. That's our system, and we have to live with it. Winston Churchill once said, 'Democracy is the worst form of government except for all others.' The same can be said about our legal system. It has its flaws, but it's the best in the world.

"The lawyers will have questions for some of you as they select whom they want on the jury. If they do not want one of you, do not take it personally. They may feel you'd be better as a juror in a different case."

He turned to me. "Now, let's get on with it. Counselor, you may begin questioning the jurors."

CHAPTER THIRTY-TWO

BEAR'S PROMISE

Shay and I had discussed the characteristics we wanted in a juror: a woman, black, older, a mother, and ideally someone with a medical or science background. The reality would likely be a compromise, with those qualities scattered among several jurors.

I started my interviews at the top of the list with juror number one, James Cooper. Maplethorpe, except for his barbecue story, had been impersonal. I needed to change that. Shay pulled up Cooper's stats from JurySelect. He was white, forty-three, a firefighter, father of two, and had voted for Trump. He had a $50,000 mortgage, owned a 2016 Chevy Malibu, and had no police record.

I walked to the podium placed at the end of our two long tables. Papageorgio and I would take turns asking questions from here. I adjusted the microphone, tapped it to be sure it was working, and greeted the first juror.

"Good morning, Mr. Cooper. My name is Jason Judge. Thank you for coming today. I represent the family of Jared Simpson. I'd like to ask you a few questions."

Cooper moved to the edge of his seat as I said this, elbows perched on his knees, staring at me with a frown. Dressed in blue slacks and an open white shirt, he was muscular and bald and had an oval face flanked by prominent ears.

"Okay. Go ahead."

"How long have you been a firefighter?"

"Five years."

"Before that, what did you do?"

"I was an EMT."

"Do you have any experience with the Electric Gun?" I asked.

"What do you mean, experience? I never used one."

"As an EMT or firefighter, were you ever called to treat someone shot with the Electric Gun?"

He sat up straight. "Yes, once."

"What happened?" This could be important. I left the podium and walked to the jury box to observe his facial expressions up close.

"A young kid snatched a purse. Ran from the cops. They cornered him, shot him in the chest, and he had cardiac arrest. We were called, tried to resuscitate him, but couldn't." His eyes showed no emotion as he said this, and no body language suggested remorse.

"Was the boy white or of color?"

"White."

"What do you think caused the cardiac arrest?"

"Most likely excited delirium," Cooper said, nodding with conviction in his tone.

"Not the Electric Gun?"

He shook his head. "No, it can't do that. It's not lethal like a real gun."

"How do you know?" I asked.

"Cops told me and showed me the manual."

"So, if I understand what you're saying, even if the evidence shows the Electric Gun can produce cardiac arrest, you are not going to accept that. Correct?" I kept my facial expression neutral, but I was already deciding I didn't want this juror.

"I'd say you probably were wrong." His lips were firm.

"Will you be able to listen to the evidence and the judge's instructions to follow the law and render an impartial judgment?"

"Sure," he said, smiling, "as long as you don't blame the death on a gun that can't kill."

"Thank you, Mr. Cooper. I have no more questions." I sat down.

Papageorgio introduced himself to Cooper, asked no questions, and just made nice chatter. Cooper was perfect for their case, and he wasn't going to ask anything that might cause his dismissal.

When Papageorgio finished and sat down, I rose and said, "Your Honor, this juror has already made his mind up. I move to strike for cause."

"I expected you would," Maplethorpe said. "Mr. Papageorgio?"

"Objection, Your Honor. The juror left doubt in his answer, saying 'most likely excited delirium' and that Mr. Judge was 'probably wrong.' That leaves open the possibility of a skilled litigator such as my honorable colleague"—his voice dripped with sarcasm as he tipped his head toward me—"convincing him otherwise."

"Objection sustained."

"Your Honor," I said, "the juror clearly stated he wouldn't be able to follow the law and find the Electric Gun as a cause of death if the evidence so warrants. I'll use my first peremptory strike to dismiss." I wasn't about to take a chance with this juror.

"Accepted. Bailiff, escort juror one from the courtroom."

BEAR'S PROMISE

Juror two, Janet Hastings, was Caucasian, a retired pharmacist who spent most of her time caring for her grandkids. For some reason, her personality reminded me of a beige living room wall: bland, the color could go with anything in the room. She was a blank slate on which Papageorgio and I would compete to write the final decision. We both accepted her.

The same went for juror three. Henry Sanders was a golf professional at the Indianapolis Country Club, thirty-eight, with a benign background posing no problem for Papageorgio or me.

Juror four was a different story and rated a ten in my scorebook.

"Hi, Mrs. Donahue," I said, making eye contact and smiling at the stout black woman, forty-eight and mother of three. "My name is Jason Judge, but people call me Bear." I stroked my beard, smiling. "Maybe because of this."

That drew a short chuckle.

"You're a nurse at the medical center, correct?"

"Yes," she said. Her voice quivered, and her eyes darted about the room.

"What kind of nursing do you do?"

"I'm an LPN, a licensed practical nurse."

"Thank you. Have you ever been a juror before?"

"No, and I'm a little nervous about doing it." She cracked a tiny smile.

"Trust me—you're not alone. I'm sure the other jurors are nervous too." I walked to the jury box and rested my hands on the railing to be close to her and offer some reassurance. "I'm always nervous at the beginning of trials, even though I've done many. It's like stage fright, and once you start talking, the nervousness will disappear." I smiled. "Let me ask you about your role as a nurse. Have you dealt with lethal heart rhythms like ventricular tachycardia and ventricular fibrillation?"

"Yes, when I worked in the cardiac care unit about five years ago."

"Any nursing experience with the Electric Gun?"

She shuddered. "No." She tried to hide the response by shifting in her seat and crossing one leg over the other, but I caught the movement.

I debated following up but decided to let it go. I figured Papageorgio would zone in on that. And if he didn't see it, tough.

"Did you know Jared Simpson when he was hospitalized?" This was critical. If she had, it could be a conflict of interest, and Papageorgio would move to strike her.

"No."

"Any problem finding someone responsible for not doing the right thing?"

She squirmed a bit, lips downturned. "I don't like to pass judgment on others. That's a job for the Lord. But in this situation, I expect I could do it."

"Do you have any relationship to any of the parties to this lawsuit, the Electric Gun Company or the Hopperville police?"

"No."

"Thank you, Mrs. Donahue. I have no further questions. I think you'd make an excellent juror." I sat down.

"Objection, Your Honor," Papageorgio said.

"Sustained. Counselor, in the future, refrain from such extraneous comments."

He was right. Stupid mistake. I bit my tongue. "Sorry, Your Honor. It won't happen again."

Papageorgio rose and addressed her. "Mrs. Donahue, why did you shudder when Mr. Judge asked you about the Electric Gun? Have you had a personal experience with it?"

"No, nothing personal," she said, shifting her gaze from Papageorgio to me.

"Uh-oh," Shay whispered. "Evasive. We're about to lose juror four."

"Anyone you know been shot with it?" Papageorgio asked.

She paused, a frightened look on her face. Her color drained, as if she'd been caught stealing.

Finally, "My sister's son."

"What happened?"

"He was robbing a house. Somebody called the cops, and they shot him."

"Did he have cardiac arrest?"

"No. He collapsed. They handcuffed him and took him to jail."

"Do you have a problem with the police using the Electric Gun because of your nephew being shot with it?"

She paused, a second too long.

"No," she said slowly, her hand to her mouth. "My nephew said it was the worst pain he'd ever felt. Excruciating." She took out a handkerchief and dabbed at the corner of her eyes.

Before she could answer further, Papageorgio asked, "Do you think the police were wrong using the Electric Gun on your nephew?"

"I don't know the answer to that," she said, crossing her legs and folding her arms across her chest. "But I think it's better than a real gun. He'd probably be dead if they shot him with that."

"Thank you, Mrs. Donahue. No more questions."

Papageorgio turned to the judge. "Your Honor, I move to strike this juror for cause."

Maplethorpe turned to me, a questioning look on his face. "Mr. Judge?"

"Objection, Your Honor. May we approach for a sidebar?"

"Yes."

Papageorgio and his cocounsel, Bosworth, Shay, and I walked to the side of the judge's desk. He flipped on a white noise machine that broadcast a steady hum to drown out our conversation to all but the five of us with heads huddled together and the court stenographer.

"Mr. Papageorgio, you moved to strike for cause. Reason?"

He creased his brow and shook his head. "She's prejudiced against the police and Electric Gun, Your Honor, because of what happened to her nephew. She'll not be an unbiased juror."

"Mr. Judge?"

"Bias will not be an issue, Your Honor." I looked at Maplethorpe. "If she follows your instructions and follows the law, she will overcome her bias, if any exists—which I doubt. I think she shuddered being reminded of the excruciating—her word, excruciating—pain it caused her nephew. She said very clearly the Electric Gun"—I read from Shay's notes—"'was better than a real gun. He'd be dead if they shot him with that.' That's hardly prejudicial."

"Objection sustained."

"If I cannot dismiss on cause, then I'll use my first peremptory strike to dismiss," Papageorgio said, mirroring my response to the first juror.

"I object to that also," I said. "Counsel is obviously dismissing her because she's African American and no other reason. Dismissing her would violate *Batson*, Your Honor. In *Batson*—"

"I know the holding in *Batson*, Counselor," Maplethorpe snapped. "Be quiet."

Shay and I had done our homework and were prepared for this challenge. We'd reviewed the landmark 1986 trial *Batson v. Kentucky*, in which a black man named James Kirkland Batson was convicted of burglary and receipt of stolen goods by an all-white jury. Prosecutors had used four peremptory strikes to eliminate any black jurors. Subsequently, the US Supreme Court found it unconstitutional to remove a potential juror based on ethnicity, race, or sex. The ruling was initially applied to criminal cases but broadened to private litigants in a civil case.

I watched Maplethorpe's face and tried to read his mind. I intended to fight for this juror. She had all the qualities we wanted. If Maplethorpe agreed with Papageorgio and dismissed her and we subsequently lost the case, I'd use that decision as grounds for appeal, that the case was not decided by a jury of peers, as guaranteed by the Sixth Amendment, and denied us equal protection under the law in the Fourteenth.

Maplethorpe had to know my thinking. No judge wanted an appeals court to overturn a verdict. Maplethorpe had one of the best records of not being reversed. His outspoken comments often led losing lawyers to appeal, claiming he'd influenced the jury's decision, but in the end, the appeals court almost always sided with him, citing reasons such as he was just clearing up ambiguity in the service of clarity or that a tart remark or two was needed to keep a lengthy trial on track. I'm sure he wanted to maintain his excellent record.

"You may return to your seats," Maplethorpe said to us. He sat back, stroked his mustache, took a sip from the coffee cup, and fiddled with the computer on his desk. I could almost see and hear the cogwheels spinning in his head.

Finally, he said, "Objection sustained. She may serve as a juror."

"Thank you, Your Honor," we both replied in even tones.

Papageorgio's face did not change, nor did mine, though inwardly he had to be madder than hell—raging, in fact—while I was jumping for joy.

But we both knew the cardinal rule of the lawyer's ten commandments: thou shalt never display emotion in court; neither anger, joy, nor disappointment shall ever cross a lawyer's face.

Shay was grinning from ear to ear. I guess they hadn't taught that commandment at Harvard Law.

I struck jurors five and six, five because her husband was a cop and six because a second cousin worked for Electric Gun. Papageorgio objected, but the judge overruled. Papageorgio struck juror seven peremptorily and never gave a reason. I think he just didn't like the guy.

After we'd selected juror eight, an African American male CPA, and nine, a white male barber, without objections, I asked Shay if he wanted to select the last juror and alternate. It'd be good practice for him, and I'd be there to help if needed.

CHAPTER THIRTY-THREE

Maplethorpe called a fifteen-minute break, which gave Shay a little time to steady his nerves. I knew he'd practiced jury selection in law school, but this was the real thing.

We downloaded information about juror ten from JurySelect.

Aristide Demetrios was fifty-six years old, born on the island of Rhodes. He owned a large restaurant in Indianapolis, another one in Bloomington, and a third in Fort Wayne, each specializing in homemade Greek cuisine. He was a bachelor, didn't vote in the last presidential election, had no debts, owned a house in Indianapolis and another in Bonita Springs, Florida, and drove a 2018 BMW.

I gave Shay a nod and mouthed, "Good luck." He rose to question Aristide Demetrios.

Demetrios had a swarthy complexion and a small port wine birthmark on his right cheek. He was the only juror dressed in a dark suit, white shirt, and tie. I noted a gold Rolex on his left wrist and a thick gold chain bracelet on his right.

"Mr. Demetrios, good morning. Thank you for coming. My name is Deroshay Odinga. I'm cocounsel with Mr. Judge. I'd like to ask you a few questions. You were born in Greece, correct?"

"Yes. I came to the US when I was five, so"—he quickly calculated—"fifty-one years ago."

I handed Shay the JurySelect printout. "And you became a naturalized citizen when you were ten, correct?"

"Yes."

"You've been a successful restauranteur."

Demetrios showed a smile with lots of teeth and nodded. "My restaurants prepare fresh foods using recipes that have been in my family for several generations. My mother—she's almost eighty—cooks in the kitchen of the Indianapolis restaurant and taught all the chefs how to cook Greek food. People like our food. You should come for dinner some night. We make a superb spanakopita."

"Mr. Judge and I will do that after the trial, Mr. Demetrios, I promise."

Shay checked the printout and continued.

"Mr. Demetrios, I think you know most people have certain biases, but in court we have to put those aside and be totally fair. Is there any reason you cannot be completely objective in this litigation?"

Demetrios shook his head. "None."

"Have you ever had any contact with the Hopperville police or people from Electric Gun?"

He paused, scratched an earlobe. "Not that I remember. Some may have eaten in one of my restaurants. But other than that, nothing."

"What about opposing counsel, Mr. Papageorgio. Do you know him?"

"No. Perhaps he's eaten in my restaurant. I don't know."

"Do you know anything about the Electric Gun?"

He scratched his ear again. "Only that it beats being shot with a real gun, like the lady said earlier."

"You're on the board of the United National Council of Greek Descendants and a major benefactor. Is that right?"

"Yes."

Shay read from the printout. "In fact, you just finished your term as president, correct?"

"True."

"And this organization has chapters throughout the United States, true?" He waved the printout in the air.

"Yes."

"If I'm not mistaken, Mr. Papageorgio is a member of the Indianapolis chapter." Shay turned and pointed at Papageorgio.

"I don't know. We have over twenty-five thousand members."

"Assume for the moment that he is. Do you know him personally?"

"No."

"Will the fact that you're both members influence your decision in this case?"

"It shouldn't."

I didn't like that answer, but Shay let it go. "Thank you. No further questions." He sat down as Papageorgio went to the podium.

"Kaliméra sas, Mr. Demetrios." Good morning. "Pos iste?" Papageorgio said. How are you?

"Kaliméra sas," Demetrios replied. "Náste kalá!" May you be well.

"Hold it, both of you," Maplethorpe interrupted. "You must speak English. The court stenographer cannot record other languages, and the court needs to understand every word you're saying."

"Sorry, Your Honor," Papageorgio said. "We were just greeting each other. Nothing important."

"I don't care what you were doing, and I'll decide what's important. Use English from now on. Understood?"

"Yes, Your Honor." Papageorgio turned to Demetrios.

"My colleague"—Papageorgio tipped his head in my direction—"intimated that, since we're both Greek and belong to the same Greek organization, you might have a problem being totally objective in this trial. I want to clear up any confusion in that regard, especially with your answer 'it shouldn't.' Will the fact that we're both Greek at all influence your decision in this trial?"

He shook his head again, more forcefully. "Not in the slightest."

"You are sure?"

"Quite sure."

"No further questions. Thank you." He sat down.

"Your Honor," I said, standing, "may I have five minutes to confer with Mr. Odinga?"

"Granted, but keep it brief."

I whispered to Shay, "What do you think?"

"I think we should move to strike for prejudice. There's no way this witness can be impartial."

"Because he and counsel are both Greek?"

"Yes, that and the warm relationship they seem to have."

"Because they both spoke Greek? Papageorgio will object, and Maplethorpe will sustain his objection."

"Then I'd use our peremptory strike. We can't let them pack the jury with ringers."

"He's not a ringer. He clarified his 'it shouldn't' response. You can't strike because he and counsel are both Greek. We just cited *Batson* against striking for ethnicity and race. We can't have it both ways. No, just accept him."

"Bear, I'm not going to let them push us around."

"They're not pushing us around. What's gotten into you?"

"I'm just remembering that scene in front of Slaughter's Mercedes. Slaughter and Papageorgio made me cave then, scared the shit out of me, and I'm not going to let it happen again. We can't let them intimidate us."

"It's okay; they're not. Calm down. I hear you, but I think Demetrios will be fine."

DOUG ZIPES

I accepted Demetrios, agreed on juror eleven as the alternate, and completed the voir dire. The remaining people were excused.

"Ladies and gentlemen of the jury, you have all been sworn in and know your responsibilities," Maplethorpe said. "You are not to discuss the case with each other or anyone else. You are not to read or listen to any news reports about the trial. Any and all questions must be directed to me alone. Understood?"

Head nods and murmurs of assent rose from the jurors.

"We shall break for lunch and then begin with brief opening statements from the lawyers. I will give you an hour to devour the sumptuous meal provided by the court."

Maplethorpe motioned to the bailiff. "All rise," he said as the jury filtered out of the courtroom, followed by the judge via the back door to his chambers.

As we gathered up a few papers, I mused about the selection process. Overall, I thought it went well. Shay and I had disagreed on Demetrios, but I didn't think he'd be a problem. I was surprised Shay felt so strongly. He wasn't happy. We ended up with two black and four white jurors. Two of them were women. I wish we'd gotten to call up the second nurse. Two nurses on the jury would've been awesome. I was glad we had *Batson* ready. I thought Mrs. Donahue would be the best juror.

CHAPTER THIRTY-FOUR

Judge Maplethorpe said, "Whenever you're ready, Counselor, you may begin your opening statement."

"Thank you, Your Honor." I gathered my notes, rose, and went to the podium. I was a bit nervous, just as I had told the juror, and made a conscious effort to control my breathing and appear relaxed.

"Ladies and gentlemen of the jury, I want you to forget everything you may have seen on TV or read in the newspapers about the use of electronic control weapons. I want you to keep an open mind about what you will hear in this courtroom." I looked from face to face as I talked, trying to make personal contact with each juror, to make them become an extension of the Simpson family so they could feel their pain.

"Mr. Papageorgio and I will tell you entirely different stories. It will be up to you to sift through what you hear and determine whether this weapon"—I held up the Electric Gun for them to see—"was capable of wiping out an entire family: a father who suffered from mental illness and had a cardiac arrest after being shot with the Electric Gun, a son seeking retribution and killed by the very same police officer who shot his father, and a mother so grief-stricken at the loss of her husband and son that she took her own life."

I left the podium and walked in front of the jurors, my hands in my pockets, casual-like. I wanted them to think this was an intimate chat among friends, not a lecture by a lawyer.

"It's our position none of this would have happened had this weapon, the Electric Gun"—I held it up again—"not been sold with the false assurance of being nonlethal, had users been instructed that it was capable of killing if the probes embedded in the chest over the heart. We will prove to you that the Hopperville police used excessive force, way beyond what was called for, when they shot Jared with the Electric Gun. The Electric Gun did not just inflict excruciating pain and immobilization, but—"

"Objection, Your Honor. There's no need for inflammatory rhetoric," Papageorgio interrupted.

"Sustained. Counselor, stick to the facts without embellishments."

Shay jumped up. "Those *are* the facts, Your Honor," he said. "The Electric Gun *does* inflict excruciating pain and—"

I couldn't believe what'd just happened, what Shay'd just done! I turned and looked at him in amazement, my mouth open. What had gotten into him? The Mercedes thing? I think what he did just hit him because his face turned red, and he buried it in his hands.

"Counselors, approach the bench—now," Maplethorpe ordered, his voice stern. His eyebrows looked like the two black crows were ready to pounce. We slowly walked to the bench, trailed by Papageorgio.

Maplethorpe turned on white noise. "Mr. O *din* ga. Have I got that right?" he asked. "With emphasis on din?"

"Yes, sir. That's fine," Shay managed to say. My heart was pounding, and I suspect his was also. The outburst was inexcusable, and we were now going to catch hell from the court.

"What's not fine, Mr. O din ga, is your eruption." He stared at Shay and repeated the word. "Eruption, that's what it was. You don't ever do that in my courtroom. And you don't ever argue with me about my decision to sustain or overrule a motion. When I hand down a decision, the issue is finished. Done. Do you understand?"

"Yes, Your Honor, but—"

"Damn it, Counselor, there is no 'but' in my courtroom. My ruling is final. I'll cut you slack this one time, seeing you're in your first case. But you've used up your only 'get out of jail free' card. Make no more mistakes. Next time I will reprimand you in front of the jury, not in our cozy little conference at the side of my desk. After that, it will be a contempt citation. Is that clear?"

"Yes, sir." Shay's head hung on his chest, his eyes on the floor.

"Now, let your colleague finish his opening statement without interruption and don't argue with me again." Maplethorpe turned to me. "You're ultimately responsible for his behavior, Mr. Judge. I'll give you five more minutes, and then your opening is closed."

"Yes, sir." As we returned to our table, I caught a barely perceptible smirk on Papageorgio's face.

I walked to the lectern and took a deep breath. I picked up the gun again and held it in front of the jurors.

"This gun shoots two metal probes that embed in the clothes or skin of its target. Batteries in the gun then transmit electricity over wires that connect the gun to the probes. The electric current shot into the chest reaches the heart and speeds its rate so high, cardiac arrest and death result. That's what happened to Jared Simpson. The death of his son, Ryan, and his mother, Melanie, occurred as a result of Jared's death.

"What I want you to remember is this: but for Jared being shot with this weapon, all three Simpsons would be alive today. The take-home messages are, one, this gun can kill." I held up one finger. "Two, police used it inappropriately." Two fingers. "Three, the company had a duty to warn." Three fingers. "And, four, the company breached its duty to warn." Four fingers. I collapsed my fingers into a fist and shook it in Slaughter's direction. "Thank you for your attention."

I sat down, and Papageorgio stalked the lectern and stood, feet wide apart, large hands gripping each side of the stand, not to still any nerves but to claim ownership, the image of the confident lawyer.

"Mr. Papageorgio, proceed."

"Thank you, Your Honor. Ladies and gentlemen, my name is Achilles Papageorgio. People call me Papa. Despite claims from this young lawyer—"

"Objection, Your Honor," I said. "There's no need—"

"I agree. Sustained. Counselor, stay with the facts of the case. Only the facts."

"Yes, Your Honor," Papageorgio said in a contrite voice.

He turned back to the jury. "I will show you clear proof that never—not once, not ever—has this law enforcement instrument"—he reached over to his table and held up his Electric Gun—"ever been shown to cause cardiac arrest in a human. Without that proof, plaintiff's arguments are nothing more than a smoke screen that facts will blow away.

"We will provide ample evidence that the unfortunate death of Jared Simpson was due to excited delirium. No one can deny that he was excited and also delirious. In fact, Jared's brother-in-law, who just happens to be lead counsel with Mr. Odinga here—"

"Objection, Your Honor," I said. "My relationship to Jared Simpson has nothing to do with these proceedings."

"I disagree. Overruled. Continue, Mr. Papageorgio."

"Mr. Judge was the brother of Melanie Simpson, brother-in-law to Jared Simpson, and uncle to Ryan Simpson. Mr. Judge chose to pursue this lawsuit not because it was justified but because it was a promise to his sister, to satisfy her dying wish."

"Objection, Your Honor. That's pure speculation," I said.

"I agree. Sustained. The facts, Counselor. My last warning," Maplethorpe admonished.

"Yes, sir," Papageorgio said, barely slowing down. "I will show you incontrovertible evidence that Lieutenant Vincenzo Sparafucile, one of the most decorated officers on the Hopperville police force, was defending himself when he shot Jared Simpson with the Electric Gun—he could have used his firearm but chose a nonlethal instrument instead; that he was again defending himself when Ryan Simpson, Jared's son, came to his home to kill him with a rifle; and that he played no role in Melanie Simpson's suicide."

Papageorgio left the lectern and now stood in front of the jury. This was a good move, to get up close to them, make eyeball contact as I had done.

"I'll conclude this opening statement by giving you three facts you can write down and take to the bank. Number one." He held up one finger. *Damn*, I thought, *he's copying what I did*. But Papageorgio did it parading from one end of the jury box to the other. "The Electric Gun is safe. Number two"—two fingers in the air, walking—"the Electric Gun has saved countless lives by providing law enforcement with an instrument that detains and immobilizes to facilitate capture without killing." Three fingers up, still walking, "And number three, the Electric Gun played no role in the unfortunate series of events leading to the deaths of these three people. I will prove each of these points to you during the trial. Thank you for your attention."

I watched the jury's response. Papageorgio was good. He had a commanding stage presence that came from years of courtroom experience. Several jurors, including the nurse, were taking notes. Two had locked vision with him and were nodding, and even the golf pro was paying attention.

Between this judge and that lawyer, I feared this was going to be an uphill battle.

CHAPTER THIRTY-FIVE

BEAR'S PROMISE

Shay and I walked back to our office. He apologized for his outburst. "I just lost it, Bear. I'm sorry. Papageorgio's objection to 'excruciating' triggered a momentary meltdown."

"I understand. You've got to remember a good lawyer shows no emotion. It pisses off the judge, screws up your reasoning, and God knows what impact it has on a jury."

"It won't happen again. I promise."

As soon as I sat at my desk, my cell phone buzzed. It was a message from Kat's doctor, Alex Abraham. "Come to the hospital immediately." Kat had taken a turn for the worse.

I raced to the hospital, heart tripping. The thought of Kat dying made me realize how much I loved her. It was like a room seeming darker after losing the light than had the light never shown.

Dr. Abraham was waiting for me as I walked into the intensive care unit and led me to a visitor's lounge off the main floor. He went straight to the coffee machine. "Want some? Makes talking easier."

I suspected he needed the coffee diversion to tell me some bad news. He brewed two Keurig cups, and we sat on a Naugahyde couch facing each other. The brown vinyl seat displayed spiderwebs of cracks and creases. I fidgeted until he started talking.

"She's comatose and having grand mal seizures," he finally said, sipping. "I've given antiseizure medications, but the convulsions keep breaking through. We've put her in soft restraints and inserted a mouth guard, so she doesn't hurt herself."

"All from the liver failure?" I could feel the color drain from my face and a cold sweat begin. She was really sick.

"Yes," he said, shifting on the couch. "Her liver's continuing to deteriorate, despite nutrition, vitamin supplements, and medications. Her pancreas has stabilized, and we've stopped the insulin, so at least that's not a problem anymore. But the toxins keep building up in her blood and are poisoning her brain and kidneys." His face wore a worried look.

"How can you get rid of them?" I was ready to pull out all the stops for her.

"That's what I wanted to discuss with you. We need to use a special dialysis machine to cleanse her blood of toxins. But that has risks."

"Patients with kidney failure are dialyzed all the time. What's the difference?"

"Big difference," he said. He explained that toxins from kidney failure dissolved in the blood and were easily removed. Liver toxins became bound to blood proteins, which made them much harder to get out. They had to infuse another protein called albumin and use it to attach to the bad stuff. "I need your permission to do this," he concluded.

"How risky is it?"

His hand absentmindedly ran over the vinyl cracks, pressing and smoothing the bumps. He reeled off a list. "Low blood pressure and shock, worsening liver failure, bleeding, even cardiac arrest and death—none likely, but you need to know they are possible."

I finger-combed my hair, thinking. "What choice does she have?"

"None, really. Her liver must've have been limping along for many years before this. You didn't know?"

"I had no idea." She'd told me her folks had been alcoholics, but that's all I knew. She'd never mentioned drinking before we were married.

"Her recent bouts with the bottle pushed her over the edge. I hope the dialysis stabilizes her long enough for her liver to regenerate—or if it doesn't, at least prevent further deterioration and buy us time to find a donor for a liver transplant."

A chill ran through me. "It's that bad?"

"It is. She's near death unless we reverse the downward spiral."

I felt drained as reality hit me. She'd never let on how precarious her life had been. Initially, I was angry that she'd started drinking again, but that changed to guilt. I thought I was the cause of her recent binges, that I was the one who almost killed her. But maybe she'd been an alcoholic years before.

"How quickly will the albumin work?" I asked, fighting back tears.

"Pretty fast." He flashed a grim smile. "We should know within a couple of hours if it's helping."

I checked my watch. Fortunately, Maplethorpe had called an early recess, and court was over for the day. Regardless, my place was with Kat even though there was nothing I could do. Hopefully, I could be back in court by morning. If not, Shay would have to start without me.

"When would you begin?"

"As soon as you say so."

"Do it now. Can I see her?"

"Of course."

Abraham gave an order to a nurse for the dialysis equipment and led me to her room on the ICU ward.

I gasped when I saw her. Soft white cotton straps bound her wrists and ankles to the bed rails. A red, rubber mouth guard was set between her teeth, while an IV infused fluid into a vein in her arm. Her face was gaunt, her eyes glowed yellow like a cat at night, and her hair was stringy with sweat. The skin on her arms was tinted a gray yellow, like an old piece of dried-out parchment exposed to the sun. It was hard to imagine the beauty I'd married.

I went to the bedside and gently kissed her lips. "I love you, Kat. Don't leave me." I choked up and could barely speak. "I promise I won't ever leave you. Please get better." I pulled up a chair and collapsed into it.

A nurse wheeled in a large machine containing two flat, circular pumps and a cluster of tubes. Abraham was right behind her.

He explained the procedure, how they'd connect her to the dialysis machine, infuse the albumin, and suck it back with the toxins bound to it. Sounded simple, but I knew it wasn't.

He flipped a switch, the pumps whirred, and the dialysis began.

I prayed.

CHAPTER THIRTY-SIX

BEAR'S PROMISE

I stayed at Kat's bedside, mesmerized by the noise and motion of the dialysis machine. My gaze flicked from the albumin infusion trickling drop by drop into the vein in her arm, to the blood being withdrawn via the needle in her groin. I followed the whirring of the pumps round and round as they pushed the blood through the dialysis machine, where it was detoxified, and then pumped it back into her. I imagined the albumin leaching off the ammonia and other poisons, making her blood clean again and sparkling, like a dirty car emerging spotless from the automatic car wash.

"Get off me!" she screeched, jarring me from my trance.

I flew from my chair to her bedside. "Kat, what's the matter?"

"They're all over me," she yelled, struggling. "The bugs and cockroaches, crawling all over me! Get them off! For the love of Christ, get them off me!"

She tried to brush off whatever was on her, but her hands were bound to the bed's side rails. She tugged at the ties and thrashed her feet, trying to break loose.

"What is it, Kat? There's nothing on you. You're okay. Calm down."

"Calm down? Are you crazy? They're eating me alive! Get them off … get them off, for God's sake! I can't stand them!"

I pushed the emergency buzzer for the nurse. She came running, and I explained what was happening.

She smiled!

"How can you smile at a time like this? My wife's out of her head."

"Precisely," the nurse said, checking to make sure the restraints were intact. "That means she's no longer comatose because the dialysis is working. These are withdrawal hallucinations, which means her brain is functioning again, though abnormally." The nurse gave her a sedative to calm her down and told me to be thankful she'd responded to the dialysis.

I watched Kat gradually stop trying to brush off fantasy creatures as she drifted to sleep. Her breathing slowed and regularized. I kept an eye on the monitor to be sure her blood pressure and heart rate stayed normal. If Kat continued to improve, as the nurse suggested, I hoped to be back in the courtroom tomorrow morning.

There was a brief knock on the door. Dr. Abraham came in.

"The nurse just paged me." He went to the bedside and listened with his stethoscope to Kat's lungs and heart. "She's much improved,

Mr. Judge. The albumin dialysis was the right decision, and, thankfully, she's tolerated it without any complications. I think we can stop it in a few more hours."

"Thank God. What happens then?"

"She'll be out of the woods but will require several months of recovery. She'll be weak, need lots of careful nutrition, and we'll see if her liver has the ability to regenerate or whether we should put her on the transplant list. We might want to do that anyway, just to secure a place in the transplant queue. We can always cancel if it turns out she doesn't need it."

I told him I had just the place. My folks owned a farm in southern Indiana that had been passed on to me and my sister. I leased the land for farming, but the house stayed empty except for a housekeeper. Once the trial was over, it'd be perfect for her to recuperate.

"Excellent," Abraham said. "Bloomington Hospital should be pretty close if you need it, and I'm sure you could get visiting nurse support there. Good idea."

I stood and extended my hand to the doctor. "Many thanks for your help. You saved her life."

Abraham smiled. "All in a day's work, Mr. Judge. It's what I do. I'm just glad it all turned out so well. This could've gone sour."

"But it didn't, thanks to you."

"I'll be popping in each day while she's here to check on her progress, but I think she'll do fine—as long as she doesn't hit the sauce again. One more binge, and it could be her last."

Abraham left, and I returned to my vigil. I thought about his parting comment. I'd do everything I could to stop "one more binge," but I couldn't be with her 24-7. Maybe I'd need to hire someone to be there when I wasn't.

The monotonous sounds in the room, along with Kat's steady breathing, made me drift off.

I woke to the nurse jostling my arm, pointing. There in the bed was my wife, smiling, her hair washed and shining to match her pretty face. The whites of her eyes were still yellow, but less so, and now created an exotic look, straight out of *Kismet* but fragile, like an eggshell that might crack.

"You've been asleep forever," she said, her voice weak. "I woke an hour ago, and the nurses have been helping me get cleaned up.

I've missed you." She held her arms out to me, fingers beckoning. I went to her and kissed her tenderly.

"I won't break," she said with a laugh as she pressed our bodies together. Then, more seriously, "We need to talk about canceling the trial."

"What did you say?" I backed out of her arms, astonished at what I'd heard.

"We need to talk about dismissing the case," she repeated, a worried look on her face.

I adjusted her pillows. She leaned back and closed her eyes. A long sigh escaped her lips. She was obviously exhausted but seemed distressed as well.

"What?" I said, sitting down on the side of her bed. "We've got a jury sworn, and opening statements were today. I plan to call our first witness tomorrow."

"Oh, no," she gasped, mouth open and eyes wide.

"Kat, what's wrong?" I couldn't believe what I was hearing. She'd been working as hard as I to prepare for this.

"Who," she asked in a whisper so soft it was like a breeze, "are you calling?"

"Jeremiah Verity's first up. He heads Electric Gun's scientific board of advisers and has been their star defense witness."

She sat up straight in bed and leaned into me for support. I held her in my arms. "What about Sparafucile? Are you going to question him?"

"Of course. He's the damn shooter. What in God's name is bugging you?"

"Don't," she said, tearing up. "Please don't."

"Kat, what are you talking about?"

She shook her head side to side and fell back against her pillow. "Just trust me. Don't put him on the stand."

"We've got no case without him."

"Then lose the damn case." She slapped a weak hand against the sheet.

"Kat, what's gotten into you?" I got up and checked her monitors to be sure her heartbeat and blood pressure were okay.

"I need a drink," she said. "I've got to get out of here." Before I could stop her, she slid her legs off the side of the bed and tried to stand. She was too weak, and her knees buckled. I lifted her back onto the bed.

"Kat, you can't have another drink of alcohol, ever. Not if you want to live. Dr. Abraham said your liver won't tolerate another binge. He's not even sure it'll recover from the last one, and you might need a liver transplant. You've got to give the booze up forever."

She sat there, head in her hands. "You're killing me," she said, looking up. "Do you know that? You're killing me."

"I'm sorry. I didn't mean to." I reached for her, but she pulled away. "I'll do whatever I can to help you beat this. I love you."

"It's not the alcohol that'll kill me. If you love me, don't put Sparafucile on the witness stand."

"Then I might as well not have the trial. Without him, we can't win."

"Then lose the damn thing."

"Kat, what's gotten into you? You were my staunchest ally when you came back into my life—our lives. What's happened? What's changed?"

She gasped, almost a shriek. "Lose the trial or lose me. Your choice."

I spent the next hour trying to persuade her to tell me what was wrong, but she wouldn't say anything except I could not call Sparafucile to the witness stand. No reason, just that I had to trust her.

I stayed with her through her dinner. She nibbled a bit but finally, with a sigh, pushed her dinner tray away, lay back in bed, and closed her eyes. I tried again to get her talking, but she lay silent, moving her head back and forth. Finally, she fell asleep.

I slipped out of the room and went to my office.

Shay was hard at work, preparing for the next day in court. We talked about what had happened.

"Maplethorpe's something else," I said. "You can argue with some judges and not others. He's the last word in that courtroom, and whether you agree with him or not, you just shut your mouth, bite the bullet, and move on. That's another one of the lawyer's ten commandments. Thou shalt not argue with a know-it-all judge."

CHAPTER THIRTY-SEVEN

Shay and I finished about one in the morning. I got up at five to review my notes and visit Kat before trial. She looked better, with some color in her cheeks and the yellow in her eyes all but gone. Her skin was still dry but had lost the gray. She still seemed weak, breakable.

She nibbled on some toast and sipped coffee as she again implored me not to call Sparafucile as a witness. She still wouldn't give me a reason.

Court started right on time.

"Is plaintiff ready?" Judge Maplethorpe asked.

"We are, Your Honor," I replied.

"Call your first witness."

"Thank you, Your Honor. Plaintiff calls Jeremiah Verity to the witness stand."

Verity rose from a spectator bench in the back of the courtroom. He walked through the wooden gate of the bar, made his way to the witness stand, and sat down.

He was medium height, with dark eyes and hair, and wore a blue blazer, white shirt without a tie, and khaki pants. His round, pixie-like face reminded me of one of Disney's characters in *Snow White and the Seven Dwarfs*, or one of the little people in Tolkien's *The Hobbit*. No, more likely Doc in the *Seven Dwarfs* because of the large steel-rimmed glasses and thick lenses that made his eyes bulge like saucers.

Despite his appearance, I knew he'd be a formidable witness. I'd read reports he'd written for past cases. He was dangerous because he peppered his statements with half-truths that seemed real but were actually lies. He was expert at composing compound sentences, using the first half as factual foundation for the second that was a total lie. He'd say something like "The Electric Gun uses special probes"—true—"that cannot cause cardiac arrest"—false.

I'd try to phrase as many of my questions as possible to be answered "yes" or "no" and not give him the opportunity to mix facts with fantasy.

He was also good at schmoozing and could ooze charm, which made him even more convincing. A very slippery guy, smart and oily, one of the worst combinations for a lawyer to deal with when trying to get at the truth. I had to strip away his façade and lay bare the rot underneath for to the jury to see, and not give him a chance to lie and deny.

Maplethorpe said, "Dr. Verity, please stand, face me, and hold up your right hand." Verity did as requested.

"Dr. Verity, do you solemnly swear to tell the truth, the whole truth, and nothing but the truth so help you God?" Maplethorpe asked.

"Yes, sir, I do, Your Honor," Verity answered, smiling at the judge.

"Please be seated. Counselor, you may begin."

"Thank you, Your Honor." I turned from the judge and faced the witness. "Mr. Verity," I began and paused, waiting for the objection I knew would follow.

"Objection," Papageorgio rang out, standing so abruptly he tipped over his chair. Unfazed, he continued, "The witness is a doctor and should be addressed accordingly."

Before Maplethorpe could sustain Papageorgio's objection, I said, "Withdrawn," and started again.

"Dr. Verity, please state your name, address, and occupation."

He gave his name and said, "I'm an adjunct professor at the University of Biomedical and Scientific Chemistry in Boston and chair the Electric Gun Company's scientific board of advisers. My home is in Framingham, Massachusetts."

"You're a chemist, not a doctor, correct?"

"Objection, Your Honor," Papageorgio said. "He's—"

"Sustained, Counselor," Maplethorpe said, "but the witness is capable of correcting Mr. judge's question. You don't need to keep interrupting with objections."

"Yes, Your Honor," Papageorgio said, "thank you."

"So, you're a PhD, not a real doctor, correct?" I looked at Papageorgio, but he heeded the court's warning.

"No, I'm a real doctor," Verity amended, not showing the slightest annoyance I'd hoped to generate.

"But a PhD, not a medical doctor, true?"

"Yes, that is correct, sir. You see—" His glasses slid to the end of his nose, and he pushed them back.

I held up my hand. "Thank you. You've answered my question."

I glanced at the jury to make sure my message was clear.

"Dr. Verity, an adjunct professor is not a teaching position, correct?"

"I serve as an adviser to the many bright students at the university."

I held up my hand again, stopping him. "Please answer the question yes or no. Do you teach any classes?"

"No."

"Do you perform any medical work?"

"No."

"Any chemistry?"

"No."

"Are you employed by the university, paid a salary?"

"No."

I smiled at him, more of a sneer. "So, you're a volunteer with a title?"

"Objection, Your Honor," Papageorgio said.

Maplethorpe's eyebrows rose. "Counselors, sidebar."

The four of us walked to the side of the judge's desk. He turned on the white noise machine.

"Mr. Judge, how much longer do you anticipate for this line of questions?" The black crows over his eyes were bunched together like folded wings ready to take off.

"Several more minutes, Your Honor, until I establish for the jury the witness's credentials, or lack thereof."

"Haven't you done that already?" Maplethorpe asked, wings unfolding, relaxed.

"Almost, sir. Just a couple of more questions."

"Well, finish up soon." He turned to Papageorgio. "Mr. Papageorgio, I suggest you stop objecting. You can raise any issues you want on cross-examination. We need to move this trial along at a faster pace. Understood?"

"Yes, Your Honor," Papageorgio said, glancing at me.

We returned to our places, and I resumed. "Mr.—I'm sorry. Dr. Verity, if the university does not pay you a stipend, how do you support yourself and your family?"

"I consult for Electric Gun."

"How much did you earn consulting last year?"

"I don't remember." He slouched back in the witness chair, arms crossed, confident in his answer.

"Your Honor, permission to approach the witness."

"Permission granted."

I left the lectern, picked up a booklet from Shay, and walked toward the witness stand, holding it in the air. "If I told you, according to this end-of-the-year public filing by the Electric Gun Company, they paid you $450,000 in salary, plus stock options worth more than $3 million, would you have reason to disagree?"

Verity squirmed in his chair and looked at the ceiling, as if calculating. "No, I think that might be accurate."

"Do you own stock in Electric Gun?"

"Absolutely not," he said with conviction and a self-assured smile. I was prepared for that answer.

"If I told the jury that you sold all your Electric Gun stock for $5 million last year when the stock price peaked, would I be wrong?"

When he hesitated, I waved the booklet in front of him for the jury to see. "No, that's right."

"And if I said the Electric Gun Company donated $500,000 to a general research fund at the University of Biomedical and Scientific Chemistry in Boston just prior to your appointment as an adjunct professor, would you have any reason to disagree?"

"No," he said, frowning.

I handed the booklet back to Shay, walked in front of the jury, and made eye contact with as many as I could. "I know you chair the scientific advisory board, Dr. Verity. What else do you do for them?"

"I evaluate the cause of death associated with the use of the Electric Gun, write reports, and testify in trial. Given my experience, education, and background—"

"Thank you, Dr. Verity," I interrupted. "Evaluating the cause of death is part of the salary they pay you. Yes or no?"

"Yes."

I shook my head with a frown. "Isn't that a conflict of interest, to take money from the Electric Gun Company and then adjudicate causes of death in lawsuits against them? Wouldn't you agree that's not being impartial?"

"It's not a conflict of interest because I am impartial," he said, tipping his chair back on two legs. "People who sue us, like you,

Mr. Judge, hire their own experts to claim the Electric Gun caused somebody's death. You pay your experts. Electric Gun pays me."

"Not so," I said, walking back to the lectern. "The experts I retain are paid for their time to give me an unbiased, impartial expert review. How can you be unbiased, receiving so much money and chairing their scientific advisory board?"

"I'm as unbiased as your own experts, sir. I have no problem being objective because the Electric Gun can't cause cardiac arrest."

I read my notes. "Have you ever been to medical school? Taken any medical classes? Gotten a medical degree of any kind? Yes or no?"

"Objection, Your Honor. Compound question," Papageorgio said.

"Overruled. Answer it if you can, Dr. Verity."

His chair flipped forward on all four legs, landing with a bang. "No, I've not been to medical school or taken medical classes."

"So, you have had no medical training to evaluate the cause of death associated with use of the Electric Gun. Correct?"

He spread his hands in front of him, palms up. "I've read medical books and medical journals and written many articles. With my chemistry background, I'm able to put two and two together, Counselor, and arrive at an accurate conclusion."

"Have you published your findings or opinions in scientific medical journals?"

"No."

"How many deaths have you evaluated?"

"Hundreds." His hands came together, fingers interlocked, and rested on his chest.

"And of those hundreds, how many did you conclude were caused by the Electric Gun?"

He formed a zero with his thumb and index finger. "None. They all died from excited delirium or an accident from the shooting, like a fall."

"Don't you find that a bit unusual?"

"No," he said with emphasis, looking at the jury. "The Electric Gun was created to be a nonlethal instrument. It cannot kill. So, something else must've caused the deaths, and excited delirium is most likely."

"And that's how you've testified in depositions and in court?"

His head bobbed. "That's correct, sir."

"And you've disagreed with the diagnosis of many medical examiners who have blamed the deaths on the Electric Gun, correct?"

"Yes," he said, failing to conceal a smile, "but they changed their conclusions after we talked with them and educated them as to the cause of death."

"Talked with them or threatened them?"

Before Papageorgio could object, I said, "Question withdrawn. Have you reviewed the information relating to the death of Jared Simpson after he was shot multiple times with the Electric Gun?"

He nodded.

"The jury needs a verbal answer," I said.

"I have, sir."

"And what is your conclusion regarding the role played by the Electric Gun in his death?"

He set such a firm line with his lips that they disappeared, becoming just a crease in his face. "I'm quite confident the Electric Gun had nothing to do with his death. He died from excited delirium."

"On what do you base that conclusion?"

"I already told you. The Electric Gun cannot kill. Therefore, it must've been something else."

"Did you review the autopsy findings?"

"No."

"Review the medical reports?"

"No."

"Review the police reports?"

"Yes, I did review those."

I suddenly remembered where I'd seen the steel-rimmed glasses. "May I have a moment with my cocounsel, Your Honor?"

"Very brief," Maplethorpe said.

I conferred with Shay.

"One last question, Doctor," I said, giving Shay a head nod.

Shay put up a picture of the electrophysiologist, Dr. Greg Dumont, on the TV screen. "Have you ever seen this individual before? Ever met him or helped him during an electrophysiologic study in an operating room?"

Verity's eyes flashed wide, then clouded over as he studied the picture. His face drained of color, and he glared at me, then looked at Slaughter. I thought I saw Slaughter give a tiny head shake, but I couldn't be sure. After several moments, he said, "No, never."

"I remind you, Dr. Verity, that you are under oath. Perjury, which is lying about facts material to a case, is a felony that carries a prison sentence of up to five years. Do you wish to change your answer?"

Verity's face blanched white as snow, his mouth open and eyes wide. Again he looked at Slaughter. This time I was sure Slaughter shook his head.

"No," he said in a shaky voice.

"Or this person?" Shay flipped up a picture of Gerald Carpenter, the patient shot with the Electric Gun.

"No," he said more confidently, color now returning to his cheeks.

"You're absolutely sure?" I asked.

"Yes." He had to be lying, but I suppose there could've been another person in the operating room wearing similar steel-rimmed glasses. Yet, Verity's presence in the OR when the ECG machine failed to record could not have been a coincidence. Somehow he'd been able to disconnect the recording cable.

"I haven't checked the employment records of UIMC, but if I did, would I find your name listed, perhaps helping out the electrophysiology group during a defibrillator implant? They keep pictures of all employees." I didn't know if the picture bit was true, but it was likely because most wore an identifying badge with their picture on it. I paused to search the jury, study their faces. "Again, I remind you of the penalties for perjury."

He hesitated a long moment, looked at Slaughter, and said, "Not to the best of my recollection."

"To the best of your recollection," I echoed, surprise in my voice. "Surely you'd remember if you were ever employed by UIMC, wouldn't you?"

"Then the answer is no."

"Thank you, Dr. Verity. I have no more questions at this time."

Shay slipped me a note as I sat down. "A pack of lies! Good job. He's toast." I could only hope so. I'd recall him if I had to.

Papageorgio went to the lectern.

"Dr. Verity, have you personally done research on the Electric Gun?"

"Yes," he said, sitting forward, elbows on the wooden railing surrounding the witness stand, much more relaxed. I could almost picture the two of them over a beer talking about a round of golf at their favorite country club.

"What did you do?"

"I performed experiments on goats and dogs to test whether the Electric Gun could cause cardiac arrest."

"And did it?"

"Never," he said, index finger waggling back and forth. "Not once."

"Do these animal hearts and human hearts function in essentially the same or similar ways?"

"Yes."

"And cardiologists often perform studies on animal hearts to help them learn about the human heart, do they not?"

"Yes."

He left the lectern, as I had, and walked in front of the jury, searching faces. "The fact that your studies on animal hearts did not produce cardiac arrest would be proof the Electric Gun cannot cause cardiac arrest, correct?"

"Yes."

"Did you publish your results?"

"Not yet, but I plan to."

"No more questions, Your Honor."

"Smart," I said in a note to Shay.

He sent it back: "Why?"

I wrote, "No sense asking further questions of a witness on your side that may cause him to stumble and give plaintiff any help. Quit while you're ahead."

Maplethorpe turned to the jury. "Do any of the jurors have questions? Write them down, and the bailiff will collect them."

This was unusual in my experience. Maplethorpe was one of the few judges I knew who permitted jurors to submit questions.

Two jurors handed questions to the bailiff, who passed them to Maplethorpe.

"Here's the first question, Dr. Verity. 'Please define excited delirium and explain how it causes cardiac arrest.'"

He turned to face the jurors. Using a professorial tone, he said, "It's a state of extreme agitation, delirium, and superhuman strength.

No one knows exactly how it causes cardiac arrest, but it does, without any doubt."

"And the second question," Maplethorpe said. "You said you're 'able to put two and two together' to make a diagnosis, yet doctors go four years to medical school and require additional training after that to gain diagnostic skills. What makes you qualified to determine the cause of death without any medical training?"

He smiled confidently at the jurors and sat up straight, hands on knees. "As a chemist, I've studied the heart's chemical makeup and have become an expert in that area. The Electric Gun does not alter the chemistry of the heart. I also know a great deal about how electricity affects the heart—more than most physicians—and have determined the Electric Gun cannot affect the human heart electrically. It can't cause cardiac arrest."

"Any further questions, Counselors? Yes, Mr. Judge."

I stood and went to the lectern. "Thank you, Your Honor. I have one question. Dr. Verity, you said that you, and I quote, 'know a great deal about how electricity affects the heart—more than most physicians,' unquote. Since you're an expert on electricity, would you explain Ohm's law for the jury?"

"Who?" Verity asked, eyes big and jaw hanging.

"Ohm's law, named after the German scientist, George Ohm, who studied many properties of electricity over two hundred years ago."

"It's … it's, uh … it defines how fast electrons travel in a substance when it's in a solid state versus a liquid state. You know, like ice and water."

"No, Mr. Verity. It's the formula used by electricians to calculate the relationship between voltage, current, and resistance in an electrical circuit. Ohm's law states that voltage equals current times resistance, or V equals C times R."

"Yeah, you're right, that's what it is. I just forgot for a moment."

I stared at Verity and just shook my head. "No more questions, Your Honor," I said.

"Thank you, Dr. Verity. You may step down," Maplethorpe said. "This would be a fine time for a fifteen-minute break." He checked the wall clock. "We'll resume at ten thirty."

Shay and I retreated to the tiny conference room we'd been given by the court. Defense had an identical room opposite ours.

"What do you think?" I asked Shay.

"Going great. How did you know Ohm's law?" he asked, smiling.

"First-year physics at Dartmouth. About the only thing I remember from that class. Hated every minute and was bad at it." We both laughed.

"I've been watching the jury," Shay said. "The nurse is paying very close attention, jotting things into a notebook. So is the Greek, Demetrios. They may be the deciding influences for the rest of the jurors. I guess you were right about him."

CHAPTER THIRTY-EIGHT

"You may call your next witness, Counselor," Maplethorpe said.

"Thank you, Your Honor. Plaintiff calls Beverly Slaughter to the stand."

Slaughter looked dapper for his court appearance. He wore a chocolate-brown herringbone suit, white shirt, and vanilla-and-rust paisley tie. The suit jacket was well tailored, and when buttoned, as he did walking to the witness stand, it reduced his gut overhang to a slight midriff bulge.

After he took the stand, was sworn, and went through preliminaries, I asked, "At your deposition, I asked you about the early safety tests performed on the Electric Gun. Do you remember that?"

"Yes."

"What tests or experiments did your company perform?"

"Like I told you at my deposition, Counselor, we tested the Electric Gun on animals—similar to what Dr. Verity reported—and humans." His face wore a smug expression that said, "We've been here before; I beat you once, and I'm going to do it again."

"What were the results?"

He looked at the jury for emphasis. "No episodes of cardiac arrest occurred. None at all in the animals or humans."

"Did you feel these findings supported your conclusion that the Electric Gun was safe?"

His head nod was vigorous. "Yes, most definitely."

"And you recorded those findings, correct?"

"Yes."

"And I'm sure you brought the documents to court so we can all see the results, correct?"

"No." He shook his head. His confidence seemed to evaporate, and his eyes shot daggers at me.

"Oh, you didn't bring them? Something happened to these critically important records?"

"We lost them," he mumbled.

"What do you mean you lost them?"

"I couldn't find them." His tone was now exasperated, his voice loud. I'd bet he really wanted to say, "I couldn't find them, you son of a bitch."

"So, you want this jury to believe that a sophisticated company like Electric Gun simply lost critical records proving the safety of your product?"

He shrugged like he couldn't care less what the jury believed.

"We need a verbal answer, Mr. Slaughter," Maplethorpe said.

"The records were lost. Can't you get that through your head?" he shouted at me.

I watched Papageorgio. He was mouthing "no" to Slaughter. He spread his hands out, palms down, and motioned up and down, trying to lower the volume and level of hostility. I paused to let that scene play out in front of the jury. I debated whether to ask the court to designate Slaughter a hostile witness. If Maplethorpe did, that would allow me to ask leading questions to which Papageorgio could not object. I decided to wait and see how the next series of questions played out.

After several moments, I said, "Let's turn to what tests you performed. From the deposition, you said the entire safety testing of the Electric Gun prior to commercial sales amounted to testing the gun on two goats and three dogs, correct?"

"And some human volunteers," he said, voice calmer. "Don't forget that part."

"Thank you for reminding me. How did you test the gun on humans?" That's the advantage of pretrial depositions. I knew what his answer was going to be, and I had a line of questions ready to follow. Trial by ambush eliminated that ability to prepare.

"We taped electrodes on the backs or thighs of ten police volunteers and shocked them."

"Interesting, Mr. Slaughter. Electrodes taped to the back or thighs. In the field, how is the Electric Gun used by law enforcement against a resisting subject?"

"What do you mean, how?"

"When a subject is shot with the Electric Gun, what happens to the probes?" I held up my thumb and index finger in the form of a gun and waved it at the jury.

"They penetrate the clothes and skin."

"Right, they penetrate the skin. And in testing the safety of the Electric Gun, did you penetrate the subject's skin with the probes to replicate the field situation?"

"No."

"In the field, what part of the body gets hit with the probes?"

"Any part. Depends on what the subject is doing—running away or attacking—and where the officer aims."

I left the podium, walked in front of the jury, and stroked my beard as if I was considering a new question. I turned and faced Slaughter. "Let's consider the subject who is attacking a police officer. What part of the body would the probes most likely hit?"

"The chest."

Shay handed me a copy of the Electric Gun manual, which I held up for the jury to see. "And, in fact, your manual instructs users to shoot for the largest body mass, correct?"

"Yes."

I turned to a page earmarked with a Post-it. "And that would be the chest, as in this picture of someone attacking a police officer, correct?"

"Yes."

"Where is the heart located?"

"In the chest."

"More on the right side or the left side?"

I got that exasperated look again. "How would I know? I'm no doctor."

"If I represented to you that the heart tends to be more on the left side than the right, would you have any reason to disagree with me?" I pointed at the picture.

"I guess not."

"If the Electric Gun were to affect the heart, would it more likely do so with the probes on the right or left side of the chest?"

"From what you said, I guess on the left."

"Did you test the safety of the Electric Gun with probes shot on the left side of the chest, penetrating the skin?"

"No."

All this foundation led to a critical question: "Would you agree that the testing you did does not replicate what happens in the field when law enforcement deploys the Electric Gun against a resisting subject?"

He shook his head, sending his jowls quivering. "No, I wouldn't agree. The discharge from the Electric Gun is the same, whether in the lab or in the field."

I held out my hands, palms up, and raised my eyebrows in a questioning look. "How can you compare the effect of electrodes taped to the skin on the back or thighs versus probes that penetrate the skin on the left side of the chest?" I asked.

He shrugged.

"Please answer the question," the judge said.

"They're pretty much the same thing," Slaughter responded.

"Doesn't the skin have high electrical resistance the probes would bypass?" Maplethorpe asked. I was to learn later he'd been a physics major in college. He had a reputation for asking witnesses questions.

"I guess," Slaughter said.

"A decrease in resistance would increase the current in a circuit, would it not?" Maplethorpe asked. "Ohm's law?"

Slaughter pivoted in his chair to look up at the judge, unable to hide his annoyance. "Maybe."

"Mr. Slaughter, does this weapon have any governmental oversight, like for firearms?" I asked. Once again, I was prepared for his answer.

"None, since the gun uses compressed nitrogen, not gunpowder. I am the oversight committee."

Maplethorpe's brow rose at the arrogant tone. I hoped he'd comment on Slaughter's answer, but he remained silent.

I questioned Slaughter about the Transcutaneous Electrical Nerve Stimulator to educate the jury what it was.

"What is a coulomb?" I asked.

"An amount of electricity, like a bundle of it."

"The TENS package insert warns that an amount of electricity of seventy-five microcoulombs would be hazardous if delivered through the chest, correct?" I said.

Slaughter rested his right index finger across his lips, as if he was thinking, then said, "I don't remember."

"And the FDA warned that any device capable of delivering an electrical charge of twenty-five microcoulombs or greater may be sufficient to cause electrocution, correct?"

The finger remained, garbling his answer. "I don't remember."

"Would you remind the jury of the output from the Electric Gun, please?"

His hand fell into his lap. "One hundred thirty microcoulombs."

"Five times the safety limits recommended by the FDA, correct?"

His face darkened. "I didn't do the math."

"And its firing rate?"

"Twelve hundred a minute."

I stood facing the jury, my hands on my hips and feet planted to emphasize my words.

"So there's enough electricity coming out of the Electric Gun to take over the normal heartbeat and rev its rate high enough to produce cardiac arrest. Yet the Electric Gun literature has no warnings about cardiac capture or cardiac arrest, correct?"

"You don't listen, Counselor. I said it's never been shown to cause capture or cardiac arrest in a human, so my company had no duty to issue any warnings." His voice volume rose again.

"Let me repeat my question, Mr. Slaughter. Does the Electric Gun literature include any warnings about cardiac capture or cardiac arrest?"

"No."

I turned back to Slaughter and shook my head in disbelief. "Do you recognize the name Gwendolyn Zabriskie?"

"Yes."

"Will you tell the jury who she is, please?"

He inhaled sharply, brow drawn together in a worried look. "She was my first secretary when I started the company and for the next three years when she retired."

"What would you say if she had records of some early tests that showed the Electric Gun caused cardiac arrest in humans?"

Slaughter's face blanched. He went silent, gulped, then held his breath. This was a hunch Shay had raised when we'd come across her name in the few documents Slaughter did produce. However, we'd not been able to locate Zabriskie or any records she might have hidden. Tracking her down was to have been Kat's job until she got sick.

"Mr. Slaughter, do you want me to repeat the question?"

"No, I heard it." He shot Papageorgio a pleading look.

"Objection, Your Honor," Papageorgio said. "This line of questioning is not relevant unless plaintiff plans to produce Ms.

Zabriskie as a witness or show the court the records to which he is referring."

Maplethorpe considered the objection for several moments and checked something on his computer screen. When I made no response, he said, "Sustained."

I'd planted a seed in the jury's mind but couldn't go any further without the witness or her records. This was a dangerous tactic. If the jury felt I was bluffing, they could become angry. I could only hope they saw Slaughter's response and figured there was something he might be concealing. I switched topics.

"Did you review the information surrounding the death of Jared Simpson?"

I heard Slaughter's sigh of relief as my line of questioning changed gears. "Yeah."

"I take it you don't think the Electric Gun played a contributing role in his cardiac arrest?"

He turned his gaze to the jury. Papageorgio had taught him well. Slaughter had to convince the jury—not me—and therefore they were the ones he should be engaging. "You heard the testimony of Doctor Verity. I agree with him. Excited delirium. That's also what the medical examiner wrote."

"Suppose I showed you evidence of the Electric Gun producing cardiac arrest in a human. What would you say to that?" I asked.

"Objection, Your Honor. You already ruled on the supposed Zabriskie records," Papageorgio said.

"This has nothing to do with that line of questioning, Your Honor," I said, looking at the bench.

"Overruled, but be sure it is different," Maplethorpe said. "The witness may answer."

"I'd say it was fake news," Slaughter said, laughing and smiling at the jury. "Just like the supposed records of my secretary that you can't find."

I watched the jury. Demetrios and the golf pro were smiling. Mrs. Donahue was writing in her notebook. The other three showed no emotion.

"Mr. Slaughter, following your deposition, my cocounsel"—I pointed at Shay—"and I had a harrowing experience in the parking lot. Three young men accosted us and threatened bodily harm after your car alarm activated. Do you remember that incident?"

Mrs. Donahue gasped and covered her mouth with her hand. She stared hard at Slaughter.

Slaughter smiled. "Yeah, I do. I saved your butts from a beating."

"Did you arrange that interaction and pay those men for what they did?"

"Absolutely not." The head shake was rapid.

"So, if I question the men in court, they will say you did not pay them, correct?"

Slaughter shifted in the chair, crossed and uncrossed his legs. He looked at Papageorgio.

"Your Honor, those men are not named on the witness list," Papageorgio said. "If plaintiff does not plan to question them in court, I object to this line of inquiry."

"Do you plan on questioning them, Mr. Judge?" Maplethorpe asked.

"No, Your Honor." We'd tried to find them and failed.

"Objection sustained."

"Thank you, Your Honor," Papageorgio said.

"Mr. Slaughter, did you warn Mr. Odinga and me that we should back off from this litigation?"

"No. More fake news," he said, again smiling at the jury.

"Thank you, Beverly Slaughter. No more questions."

Papageorgio replaced me at the lectern.

"Mr. Slaughter, since you began Electric Gun in 1995, how many deployments of the gun have there been?" He held up the same chart Slaughter had showed us in his office.

"Over five million."

"And how many reported deaths from the gun?"

"Fifty-three but none related to cardiac arrest." Slaughter smiled for the first time.

"How many lives do you estimate the Electric Gun has saved by giving law enforcement a nonlethal weapon to replace a handgun?"

He looked at the jury and spread his arms wide. "Ten percent of the five million, so easily five hundred thousand. All saved by my gun."

"Thank you. No further questions." He walked back to his table.

I rose from my seat. "May I ask a redirect question, Your Honor?"

"Go ahead, Mr. Judge."

"Mr. Slaughter, where do those numbers you cited come from since there is no required national or international reporting of Electric Gun use?"

"They are estimates."

"Guesses, in other words, to support your position."

"Objection, Your Honor," Papageorgio said.

"Sustained." Maplethorpe took a sip of water. "Questions from the jury?" he asked.

The bailiff collected one piece of paper and handed it to Maplethorpe. "This juror asks, 'Because of the issues raised here and I guess in other trials, would you now conduct human tests with impaled probes over the heart to see if the Electric Gun could cause cardiac arrest?'"

"No. That would be unethical," Slaughter responded.

I jumped up. "Your Honor, may I ask a follow-up question?" I asked.

"Yes, Mr. Judge."

I walked slowly in front of the jury, letting his "unethical" response sink in. I thought I now had the son of a bitch by the balls. "Mr. Slaughter, why do you think it would be unethical to conduct human tests with impaled probes over the heart?"

"Well, because it ... it would hurt a lot, and since we know the Electric Gun cannot cause cardiac arrest, it would be unnecessary." He ran his tongue over his lips and looked a little pale.

"Do you think such testing would be unethical because you think the Electric Gun might cause cardiac arrest when used in a situation that replicates field use?"

Slaughter went silent and started at me with an angry look—eyes tiny slits, brow drawn—until Maplethorpe prompted him to respond. He struggled with his answer and looked at Papageorgio, who remained mute. He gripped the sides of his chair so hard his fingers turned white.

"No, it just—" He paused and looked bewildered. "It just means I don't think it's ethical to shoot probes into volunteers."

"How else can you test the gun's safety?" I asked.

"You heard me say it, and you heard Dr. Verity say it." Slaughter's conviction seemed to have returned. "The Electric Gun has never been shown to affect the human heart; therefore, it cannot cause cardiac arrest. And if it cannot do that, shooting people over the heart is a waste of time and money."

I searched jurors' faces to see if that response hit home. Several cocked their heads and wrinkled their brows, but I couldn't tell believers from nonbelievers. I had to drive the point home.

"Isn't that circular logic, Mr. Slaughter? Not testing in a situation that might provoke cardiac arrest because you have decided beforehand that it cannot cause cardiac arrest? Isn't that what testing should prove or disprove?"

"No. The gun is nonlethal. How many times do I need to say that? Further testing is unnecessary."

"We'll let the jury decide that one. No more questions, Your Honor," I said.

"The witness may step down," Maplethorpe said. "Mr. Judge, do you have another witness, or would this be a good time for lunch?"

"We plan to call Lieutenant Vincenzo Sparafucile to testify next, Your Honor," I said. "We can do that after lunch. Thank you."

"That'll be fine. I have some business to attend to for another case that will require about an hour, so we'll take a two-hour lunch break and reconvene at two o'clock," Maplethorpe said.

We stood for the jury and judge to exit. As we walked out of the courtroom, I said to Shay, "I'm going to the hospital to see Kat. Back in a couple of hours."

CHAPTER THIRTY-NINE

BEAR'S PROMISE

I walked down the stairs from the courthouse to the street. I'd had trouble finding a parking space before court and had to park several blocks away. It was a toss-up whether to walk to my car or walk to the hospital about a mile away. With a two-hour lunch break and a pretty fall day, I decided to stretch my legs and walk to the hospital to see Kat. I could catch an Uber ride to get back if I was running late.

The sun shone bright in a cloudless sky, warming the noon air as I set off, thinking about Kat and her issue with Sparafucile. I had to get her to tell me what was going on.

Hanging baskets of red and white chrysanthemums, alternating with baskets of purple lavender, dangled from streetlamps along the sidewalk, their perfumes brightening my spirits.

I'd walked about half a mile and was entering the park near the hospital when I heard footsteps gaining on the sidewalk behind me. I looked over my shoulder and saw a broad-shouldered man approaching. He wore large sunglasses and a black hoodie that hid most of his face. I was alone on the street and fingered my cell phone, ready to call 911.

He quickened his steps and edged alongside me. "Don't put Sparafucile on the witness stand this afternoon," he said. "Sue Electric Gun but leave the Hopperville cops alone."

I came to an abrupt stop and tried to see his face. He was about my height with a muscular build that filled out his black sweatshirt. Only the lower half of his face was visible. His nose had a bump on the bridge below his glasses and bent to the right, probably from a previous break. Thick lips barely moved as he talked.

"Who are you?" I asked.

"That doesn't matter. Just drop the lawsuit against the Hopperville police."

"And if I don't?"

"I'm giving you a chance to do this in a friendly manner," he said, pushing a finger into my chest. "I can get very unfriendly if I have to." He opened and closed a fist with his other hand.

I shoved his hand away and reached for my cell phone. "Back off, or I'm calling 911. The trial goes on as scheduled. Sparafucile is the next witness."

Before I could react, he grabbed my phone, crashed it onto the sidewalk and ground it to pieces with the heel of his shoe.

"Bad decision, Counselor. You're overruled." He laughed, turned, and walked quickly away.

I stood shocked, mouth open. I was now in the park, closer to the hospital than to any store where I could borrow a phone. My best option was to get to the hospital as quickly as I could. I broke into a jog.

A couple of minutes later, I heard a buzzing motor. It sounded like a lawn mower, but no one was mowing the grass. As the sound intensified, I realized it came from overhead. In the distance, I spotted an object flying through the air above the treetops. It was too small to be a helicopter and too noisy to be a bird. I moved off the path, and the thing changed trajectory, veering with me and diving closer to the ground. I moved back on the path, and it changed direction again.

My hard jog turned into a sprint, but the thing was flying too fast for me to outrun. The object was now close enough to identify as a large drone a hundred feet away and plunging right at me.

I looked around for shelter. Ahead to the side of the path was a dense thicket of pine trees with heavy, outsized branches spreading like fingers from the trunks. I raced toward them.

The drone followed until it was directly overhead, hovering like a hummingbird above a flower. Then it dove at me.

I plunged under the lowest pine branches, barely two feet off the ground, and frog-crawled to the trunk.

The last thing I remember was the sharp, fresh smell of pine needles and sticky pine resin on my hands, followed by a loud explosion and then ... nothing.

I woke four hours later in a hospital bed, an IV in the crook of my arm, a bandage around my head, and a pounding headache. The room was deathly quiet. A doctor and nurse at the foot of my bed were talking to me or to each other. I couldn't tell. Their lips moved, but I couldn't hear what they were saying. It was as if someone had turned my audio to mute.

"I'm deaf," I shouted, motioning them to come closer. "I can't hear a word you're saying." My deep breath and shout triggered sharp pain in both sides of my chest.

The doctor walked to my bedside and bent close to my face. He spoke loudly and slowly so I could read his lips. "The explosion knocked you unconscious and traumatized your eardrums. They didn't rupture, so you'll likely regain hearing in few hours as the swelling dissipates. We've started prednisone for that."

"What the hell happened?"

"An explosion in the park. We don't know how or why but—"

"It was a drone," I said, "carrying a bomb meant for me." I realized I was shouting.

"How do you know?" he asked, a finger to his lips and patting the air to reduce my vocal volume.

I spoke softer and told him what had happened.

"That explains why you were beneath the tree—or what was left of it." He explained the Hopperville cops had been the first responders—found me sprawled on the ground and brought me there. I had a scalp laceration where a tree branch must've bounced off my head and superficial burns on my arms. And two cracked ribs on each side of my chest.

"Took four cops to lift a huge tree limb sitting on top of you."

I gingerly touched my head where it hurt. My fingers came away bloody.

"Fifteen stitches. You must've been underneath the bottom tree branches when the bomb exploded. The drone propellers probably got tangled higher up, so the tree took the brunt of the hit," he said.

I shuddered, thinking about the café scene and now this. These guys played for keeps.

"You need to let the court know what happened and that I'm here," I said.

"I did when I found the business card in your wallet. The judge put the trial on hold until you return."

"Did you tell my wife? She's a patient here." Kat had to be worried, expecting me to visit hours ago.

"I didn't know that." He said something to the nurse. "We'll tell her."

There was a knock on the door. I couldn't hear it, but I saw the doctor and nurse turn, and she pulled open the door. A Hopperville cop came in. He stopped to talk with them and then came to my bedside.

He leaned close. "I'm Jim Bennett," he said. "What happened?" He pulled up a chair alongside the bed and sat down.

I went through the story again.

"Was he wearing a police uniform?"

"No, he's not that stupid."

"But you think he's one of us?" His face showed compassion but also worry, with his eyes hooded.

"What else if he's trying to protect Sparafucile? If he's not a cop, someone on your force hired him."

"Could you ID the guy in a police lineup?" he asked.

"Maybe. His nose was pretty distinctive."

Bennett rubbed his own nose. "I'm one of the three cops you're suing."

"I know. I need to get your version of what happened, but it's Sparafucile and Fisheye I'm really after."

Bennett spoke briefly to the doctor and nurse and pointed to the door. They left the room, and he came back to my bedside.

"Maybe we should talk," he said, moving to the edge of his chair.

CHAPTER FORTY

The hospital released me after my hearing returned later that afternoon. Except for the scalp cut, cracked ribs, and minor burns, the rest of me seemed in one piece. The nurse taped my chest and said the ribs would heal on their own. No lifting anything heavier than ten pounds and no deep breaths or coughing. I figured a sneeze would about kill me.

I took the elevator to the ICU floor. I panicked when I saw Kat wasn't there and grabbed the arm of a passing nurse who'd taken care of her. "Where's my wife, Kat?" I asked, dread in my voice.

"Easy, cowboy," she said, pulling free. "She's fine. We moved her to a stepdown unit when the dialysis finished. She'll stay there until we regulate her diet, make sure the DTs don't recur and she regains some strength."

"Where is it?"

"Just down that hall," she said, pointing. "She's a lucky lady—or you're a lucky man."

"Both," I said, fingering my bandage.

Kat collapsed into my arms. "Oh, Bear … Bear, are you okay? I was so worried when you didn't show up. Then they told me."

I winced when she wrapped her arms around me and squeezed.

"No Bear hug, darling," I said with a slight laugh. "Couple of cracked ribs."

She saw the head bandage. "And this?" She pointed.

"Bump on the noggin from a tree branch. A few stitches. Not a big deal." I sat on the side of her bed and held her hand as I told her what happened.

"And you're still going to question Sparafucile?"

"Absolutely. I won't let him intimidate me or the law."

"What about me?" She sucked in a deep breath. "Can he intimidate me?"

"What're you talking about?" I asked.

"He's going to send me to prison," she said, a hand over her mouth to muffle a cry.

"What're you saying?"

BEAR'S PROMISE

Over the next twenty minutes, Kat related her speeding encounter with Sparafucile, ending with her alcoholic binge and hospitalization. She started shivering as she said, "I was going to call you on my cell phone, but then he was knocking at my window …

"His hands, Bear, his hands—they were all over me. Inside my bra, up my legs. And then the threat of the strip search. And you weren't there to help me. I wanted to die." Remembering, she started to lose control, and the tears flowed.

"That sonofabitch!" I jumped up and paced the room. I struck out at an imaginary face and triggered needle-sharp pains in my chest.

"He did this!" I said, pointing to the monitors and IV still dripping in antiseizure medicine. "He's responsible for you almost dying."

Kat fell back in bed, crying softly into a pillow. "I tried to help you," she said, "maybe get some inside information about the police department. I love you and wanted to make up for … Hamden. Instead, I'll go to jail."

"That's not going to happen, Kat. The packets were planted."

"How're you going to prove that? It's his word and that of the other cop against mine."

"The other cop at the desk—was it Jim Bennett?"

"Yes. How did you know?" I told her I had just talked with him.

"You've no history of drug use, so—"

Her brow wrinkled, and tears welled up again. "Bear, I've not been honest with you," she said. She smoothed the sheet covering her and fiddled with the IV in her arm, trying to find words.

My heart skipped a beat. "What?"

"It's hard for me to—"

"What?" I repeated, a bit harsh, thinking of the last time she confessed, that she'd slept with Hamden. What was coming now? Sparafucile?

"I was a drunk before we met. I started before Dartmouth and have two DUIs and a drunk and disorderly arrest. Sparafucile dug them out when he stopped me for speeding."

I breathed a sigh of relief, then thought, *That could complicate a defense.*

"But no drug history?"

She shook her head, jarring loose tears that slid down her cheeks. "None. I never did drugs, not even marijuana."

249

"Kat, you're not going to jail on a trumped-up drug charge. I promise you that. I won't let it happen."

She reached for my hand and brought it to her lips. I sat back down on the edge of the bed and leaned over to kiss her. I tried to suppress the shooting pain, but she saw it in my face and met me halfway.

"Hurts a lot?"

I straightened and smiled through the pain. "Going to be like this for four to six weeks they told me. Can't lift, can't bend, can't do this, can't do that. A big pain in the ass."

"Pain in the ribs," she said, smiling through her tears.

"That too," I said, laughing—and then grunting with the pain.

"No treatment?"

"Pain meds, but I can't take them while working the trial. Screws up my thinking. I've got to remember not to bend over in court."

"Maybe a corset to help keep the ribs from moving?"

"Thank you, Dr. Judge. That's actually a good idea. I'll stop at CVS to get something."

CHAPTER FORTY-ONE

O n doctor's orders, I rested two days at home before resuming the trial. It gave me a chance to regroup with Shay, and we plotted a strategy for Sparafucile's testimony.

Lieutenant Vincenzo Sparafucile looked impressive as he walked to the witness stand in full police regalia. Handcuffs, a holstered 9 mm Glock, nightstick, flashlight, pepper spray, and, of course, the Electric Gun all dangled from the wide, leather law enforcement duty belt. The assembly knocked against the arms of the narrow, wooden chair when he sat down, and he had to swivel around to make room.

I was amazed court officials let him in with those weapons. The security people told me later they had challenged him during screening at the courthouse entrance and initially barred him from entering with the weapons. He told them he was always on duty, even in court, and he might need a weapon to subdue an assailant; you never could tell where or when that might happen, and he wasn't about to go anywhere unarmed. Didn't they agree, or didn't they understand? They agreed.

His cool confidence, puffed-out chest, and smug look infuriated me. He was as relaxed on the witness stand, as if he owned it, legs splayed, looking around the courtroom, smiling at the spectators, the jurors, the judge. *This is my domain*, his body language said. *Try to do something about it.* I intended to do that.

I seethed thinking about what he did to Jared and Ryan and to my poor wife. And how many others? I didn't believe in the devil or hell, but if he or it did exist, I was staring it in the face. This was why I became a lawyer. I was going to use everything I knew to get this evil cop, no matter what it took. One of us was going down, and it wasn't going to be me.

After he was sworn in, I went straight for his jugular. "Lieutenant, have you ever been convicted of a crime?"

"No, never." He smiled at the jury. It was a fake smile, like saying "cheese" when you have your picture taken. Only his mouth moved, with no crinkling around the eyes as in a true smile.

"Interesting," I said. He was lying. "Where did you work prior to joining the Hopperville police force?"

"Pleasantville police."

"Where is Pleasantville?"

"A town about forty miles north of New York City, in Westchester County."

I held out my hand to Shay as he riffled through one of the boxes beneath our table. He pulled out a folder and handed me four copies of its contents—one each for the judge, Papageorgio, Sparafucile, and me.

"Your Honor, may I introduce into evidence this court document from when Lieutenant Sparafucile was Patrolman Sparafucile with the Pleasantville Police Department?"

"This should have been disclosed pretrial, Counselor," Maplethorpe said.

"I realize that, sir, but as you know, defense provided no time for depositions or disclosing information."

"Any objection, Mr. Papageorgio?" the judge asked, shifting his gaze to Papageorgio.

"May I read it first?" Papageorgio asked, taking the document from me.

"Of course," I said.

As he read, his eyebrows drew together. "May we have a sidebar discussion, Your Honor?" he asked.

"If it's to discuss this document," Maplethorpe said, finishing his reading, "no. The document may be introduced."

"Yes, Your Honor, thank you," Papageorgio said. He had no choice but to agree with the court.

"Do you recognize this document, Lieutenant Sparafucile?" I asked.

He skimmed it. "Yeah," he said.

I'd caught him in an outright lie. "You testified a moment ago and told the jury under oath—with a penalty of perjury for lying—that you'd never been convicted of a crime. Was that answer true?"

"I guess I forgot about this."

"You forgot. Remarkable," I said sarcastically. "So, is your answer that your prior testimony was not true?"

"Objection, Your Honor. Counsel is badgering the witness," Papageorgio said, a worried look on his face.

"Overruled. The witness may answer."

"Yeah, I was convicted of a crime," Sparafucile said with a backhanded wave. "No big deal."

"So, a jury of six good people like those sitting here heard your side of the story and convicted you anyway? Do I have that right?" I asked, leaving the podium to walk in front of the jury, trying to get a feel for what they were thinking.

"Yeah, so what?" He flipped the jury a "who cares" look and leaned forward, his elbows resting on the wooden railing of the witness stand and his chin in his hands.

"And what crime was that?"

He drew his feet in and sat up straight. "Excessive use of force."

There were murmurs from the jury that a look from Maplethorpe silenced.

"And was your conviction so insignificant that you just happened to forget about it?" I asked, palms up, questioning.

"It was all a bunch of bullsh—none of it was true." Sparafucile shifted in his seat.

"What is your understanding of excessive use of force?"

"Like using pepper spray or a baton when you shouldn't."

"Do you know how your own department defines excessive use of force?"

He was silent.

"Let me read it to you," I said, opening up a Hopperville Police Department pamphlet. "'The excessive use force can be either physical, verbal, and/or psychological that is inappropriate and excessive for the situation.' Do you take issue with that definition?"

"I already told you what it is."

"So, from your previous answer, I take it that the crime you 'forgot' to tell the jury was inappropriate use of pepper spray?" Though I'd not been able to depose Sparafucile pretrial, the document gave me all I needed, and I intended to drag it out of him, bit by bit.

"No."

"So, what was it?" I asked, acting surprised. "Maybe using a baton?" I walked back to the podium.

He scowled with a face filled with hate. He had to know where I was going. He shifted again and slid his wide belt around, moving the Electric Gun holster from sitting on his hip to his lap.

I waited. "Please tell the jury of what excessive use of force you were convicted," I said, waving the paper in the air.

He paused, looked at Papageorgio, and ran his fingers through his hair. "Excessive use of the Electric Gun."

"The Electric Gun. Interesting. How many times? Once?" I held up one finger.

"Four."

"Four times?" I feigned surprise, held up four fingers, and turned to the jury. "So, you shot one individual four times inappropriately?"

"No, four individuals."

"Ah, at last it becomes clear." I'd told Shay that trial lawyers had to be good actors. I knew the jurors were listening, but they were also watching. It was important my body language conveyed confidence. I placed my hands on my hips as I asked the next question.

"Four separate convictions for excessive use of the Electric Gun on four occasions on four different people. And what race were these four individuals? White, I presume?"

"No."

"So, all four Electric Gun convictions were for shooting African Americans? Really?" I ended the "ly" on an ascending note of surprise.

"Yeah, so what? They commit most of the crimes."

"Like in this case?" Before Papageorgio could object, I said, "Withdrawn."

I observed the jury's reaction to his statement. Both black jurors physically recoiled, and the nurse, Mrs. Donahue, put her hand to her mouth. Three jurors remained impassive, and the Greek, Mr. Demetrios, scribbled in a notebook.

"Why did you leave the Pleasantville Police Department, Lieutenant?"

He didn't answer.

"Did you want to retire and move to beautiful Hopperville to live out your days?" I asked, faking a smile.

He still didn't answer.

"Or maybe because you were fired for this?" I said in a stern voice. I waved the paper at him.

He nodded and shot daggers through wide-open eyes.

"The jury needs a verbal response, Lieutenant."

"Yeah." The answer came out more as a feral snarl than an answer. That was fine with me. I wanted the jury to experience the real Sparafucile.

I returned the document and pamphlet to Shay and changed topics.

"Lieutenant, I'd like to discuss the incident that took place on the morning of September 15 when you were called to aid a fellow officer in distress, Chester Devine, nicknamed Shorty. Do you remember that incident?"

"Yeah." Another snarl.

Rather than stand at the podium, I paced in front of the jury and tried to be as animated as I could. Recounting history could be boring, and I needed them to pay close attention to what I was saying. I knew I was taking some liberties with the court, but I hoped Maplethorpe would be flexible.

"Apparently, Melanie Simpson called 911 seeking help for her husband, Jared, who'd become psychotic after a series of seizures, and she feared for his life. Shorty responded, and in the course of their interaction, Shorty struck Jared Simpson on the shoulder with his baton. Jared grabbed the baton and hit Shorty across the face with it. Have I related that correctly to the jury?"

"Objection, Your Honor. Assumes facts not in evidence," Papageorgio said.

I was afraid he'd object. I hadn't established foundation for all of the facts.

"Overruled. The witness may answer." That was a gift. I think the story sparked Maplethorpe's interest.

"Yeah, you told it okay," Sparafucile said.

I continued with the narrative, still pacing and trying to make eye contact with each juror, especially Mrs. Donahue. Her eyes seemed glued to mine, her expression sympathetic.

"Shorty called for help, and you and three other officers showed up. Jared resisted when you attempted to arrest him for assaulting Shorty, and you shot him in the chest with a five-second burst from the Electric Gun. True?"

"Yeah, so far." He again shifted in his seat.

"Then you ordered Jose Diaz, also known as Fisheye, to shoot Ryan Simpson in the back with the Electric Gun after he attempted to come to the aid of his dad. Even though Ryan was already handcuffed and restrained by an officer holding each arm, you ordered Fisheye to shoot him. Do I have that right?"

Sparafucile folded his arms across his chest, went silent, and glared with curled lips.

"Answer the question," Maplethorpe said.

Sparafucile remained silent.

"Answer the question or you'll be held in contempt of court," the judge said, his black crows ready to pounce.

"Yeah," Sparafucile said under his breath, scowling.

"Louder," Maplethorpe said.

"Yeah, dammit." Sparafucile bit down on his lower lip, but it was too late.

Maplethorpe's eyes flared, and his eyebrows flew up, crows taking off. "The witness will refrain from using profanity in my courtroom. Do you understand, Lieutenant?" Maplethorpe's voice was harsh, no-nonsense.

"Yeah," he said, scowling again.

"Would you consider that an act of police brutality?" I asked. "Shooting a handcuffed and restrained young boy in the back with the Electric Gun—a youngster who posed no threat to you or your officers?"

"He had it coming," Sparafucile said, waving his hand dismissively in another I-couldn't-care-less response.

"That wasn't my question. Answer my question, please."

He stared at me for a moment before he shook his head and said, "No, it was appropriate for the situation."

"Well, we'll let the jury decide that." I stopped pacing, looked at them, and gave a brief nod and smile. I returned to the podium.

"You shot Jared continuously for thirty-seven seconds. He lost consciousness, was no longer responsive, and you shot him again with the Electric Gun for another five seconds. Then Fisheye added five more seconds with a shot to Jared's shoulder. Was that not excessive use of force?"

I heard a gasp from the jury bench and looked at them. I think it came from Mrs. Donahue, but I couldn't be sure.

"He lunged at me, attacked me, and I was just defending myself. I was fighting for my life." Sparafucile gestured, using his arms and fists as if he was fighting off an attack. I didn't think his pantomime was very convincing. "He was a big guy. Might've had a weapon and could've killed me. Clear case of self-defense," he said, looking at the jury.

I made a theatrical show of studying Sparafucile's muscular build. I flexed my biceps, looked at mine and then at his. I assessed him up and down and then gave a short, derisive laugh.

"You say Jared attacked you. He had to have been wobbly from your first Electric Gun shot, and still you feared for your life. Do I have that right?" I imitated a wobbly walk in front of the jury and mock-grabbed at the railing for support. Several jurors smiled, and Demetrios laughed out loud.

"Yeah," he said, the corners of his mouth downturned.

"I read that in your and Fisheye's report. However, the report by Jim Bennett was not so certain about the attack. Who's Jim Bennett?"

"A new guy on the force."

"Was he at the scene with you, Officer Diaz, and Jared Simpson?"

"Yeah."

"He completed a report summarizing the events, just like you did, correct?"

Sparafucile nodded.

"You have to—"

"Yeah," he said in a loud voice, cutting me off. He knew he had to answer verbally. I think he was just trying to bug me. I had to keep my cool.

"Do you agree it differs from the report you and Officer Diaz wrote?"

"Yeah, but he was new, and you can't believe what an inexperienced officer says he saw." He gave the jury another plastic smile. Sparafucile was trying to throw Bennett under the bus.

"You do have the video of the encounter," I said, nodding, "so the jury can judge for themselves which report to believe, correct?"

"No." He smiled again, a confident look on his face.

"No? I'm surprised." I rolled my eyes in mock astonishment. "What happened to it? Doesn't shooting the Electric Gun automatically trigger your body camera to record?"

"Yeah, but mine malfunctioned." He shrugged and gave a not-my-fault look.

"I see," I said, drawing out the "see." "Your camera malfunctioned but not your gun. How about Fisheye's camera? Did he record the encounter?"

"His broke too." Another confident smile.

I met that with my fake eye roll. "Isn't that interesting that both your and Fisheye's body cameras malfunctioned at the same time. How convenient."

Papageorgio stood. "Objection, Your Honor. No need for sarcasm."

"Sustained. Continue."

"But you know whose body camera was working?" I said, my tone bright, happy, a real smile on my face.

Sparafucile stiffened, the creases in his forehead deepening, and looked from me to Papageorgio.

"Jim Bennett's," I said.

The silence broke with murmurs among the spectators.

Slaughter's whisper to Papageorgio was louder than the rest. "Object, Papa. Don't let him show it," he said, a frantic look on his face.

Before Papageorgio could object, I turned to the judge. "Your Honor, if it pleases the court, I have just obtained the video filmed by Officer James Bennett." I held up the video. "Bennett will be questioned later in these proceedings and will state under oath that he videoed the entire interaction by manually triggering his body camera. In the meantime, I have here his sworn affidavit, appropriately witnessed, that this is the video he filmed. With the court's permission, I'd like to offer this into evidence and play the video for the jury."

"Mr. Papageorgio?" Maplethorpe asked.

I felt sorry for Achilles. He sure as hell didn't want to see that video, but if he objected, Maplethorpe would simply overrule, and that wouldn't play well for the jury.

"No objection, Your Honor," Papageorgio said. Smart lawyer. Just suck it up when you have no other choice. Looks better that way in front of the jury.

I handed the video to Shay.

"Lieutenant, we'll play Bennett's video in short segments and ask for your comments after each segment. Here's the first." Shay ran the video. It was displayed on a TV screen in front of the judge, two screens for the jurors, and one each in front of the defense and plaintiff tables. Spectators had to move around to find a screen they could see from the back of the room.

"Lieutenant, would you agree this segment shows you shooting Jared Simpson in the chest with a five-second shock from the Electric Gun after you ordered him to get down on his knees and put his hands behind his head?"

"Yeah. He resisted arrest." His face showed no emotion, eyes heavy lidded, seemingly disinterested.

"Thank you, Lieutenant. Shay, the next segment."

After it ran, I asked, "Would you agree this next segment shows you ordering Fisheye to shoot Ryan in the back?"

"Yeah." Again, no facial emotion, but he shifted in his chair and opened his eyes.

"Why would you do this?"

"Because I thought he was going to attack me after I shot his dad." He ran the back of his hand across his mouth.

"With his hands handcuffed behind his back and one cop on each arm restraining him?"

"He could've broken loose."

"You didn't have him shot because he called you a son of a bitch?"

"No." The no came out low pitched and didn't sound convincing, but that would be up to the jury to decide. He licked his lips and looked at Papageorgio.

"Then why on the video did you say, 'Nobody calls me a son of a bitch, kid. Remember that'?"

Sparafucile was silent. Finally, "I don't like anybody calling me names, but it had nothing to do with me ordering Fisheye to shoot him."

"I see. Another question we'll let the jury answer." I asked Shay to play the next segment. What followed drew a collective gasp.

"Lieutenant, would you agree this segment shows Jared lunging— *but not at you? He lunged at his son*—to try to hold him up after Fisheye shot him."

"No, he's coming for me." Sparafucile's eyes were wide open now, flicking from me to the jury to Papageorgio and back to me. One hand rested on the handle of his Electric Gun, and the other on his thigh, middle finger protruding at me.

"Did Jared make any threatening gestures toward you or just extend his arms to his son?"

"He was coming after me. You can see that in the video."

"Shay, please replay that segment in slow motion."

The segment ran.

Sparafucile was silent.

"Would you point out for the jury at what point Jared was attacking you, please?"

Sparafucile remained mute. He was breathing fast, and his forehead was moist. I turned to the judge for help to get an answer.

"The witness will answer the question," Maplethorpe said.

"It's easy for you smart-assed lawyers to second-guess me. You stand here safe and sound in the courtroom, expecting us cops to do the dirty work. I thought he was attacking me, so I shot him. It was self-defense."

Maplethorpe's gavel rang out to silence gasps and mumbling in the courtroom. "Order, order. I warned you once, Lieutenant Sparafucile, about using profanity in my courtroom. I'll not warn you again. The next time, you'll be hauled off to jail with a contempt of court citation. Is that clear?" The crows were flying.

"Yeah." He sank down in his seat and turned his shoulder away from Maplethorpe.

"Be sure it is." The crows came back to roost.

The next segment showed Sparafucile depress and hold down the Electric Gun trigger, Jared fall to his knees, reach out to Sparafucile and plead to stop the hurting, then fall facedown in the mud and stop moving.

"Was it necessary to deliver a shock lasting thirty-seven seconds, Lieutenant, until Jared was no longer responsive?"

"Yeah. Self-defense, like I said." He seemed to be regaining some composure—or was putting on a good act hiding his emotions.

"For thirty-seven seconds, even after he fell to his knees?"

Sparafucile shrugged. "That's just the way it was. I thought he was trying to kill me."

I looked at the jurors. Half of them were shaking their heads.

The next segment played, and the court heard Sparafucile say, "Serves you right for striking a cop, you black bastard. Now, put your hands behind your back, or you'll get more of the same."

"Would you explain that comment to the jury, Lieutenant?"

"I just lost my temper." His feet splayed out, and he slouched in his chair.

"You just lost your temper. Would you agree that does not justify using the racial epithet?"

"The racial what?"

"The racial slur."

He gave a hand-wave dismissal. "Just cop talk."

"And that justifies it?"

"You wouldn't understand if you've never been a cop. Like locker room talk."

In the next segment, the jury heard Fisheye say, "He's faking it. Hit him again, Chilli." The video showed Sparafucile deliver a five-second shock to Jared's inert body and Fisheye press the electrodes of his gun directly against Jared's right shoulder and pull the trigger, with no response.

"Would you agree with me, Lieutenant, that the subsequent two shocks, one by you and one by Officer Diaz to an unresponsive subject, constitute excessive use of force?"

"No." He shook his head. "I don't agree. We had to be sure he wasn't faking."

"Wasn't faking?" I said, surprise in my voice. "The video shows the man was unconscious, Lieutenant. How could he be faking?"

"You never can be too sure."

I watched the jurors. The two women dabbed at their eyes, and Demetrios looked astonished. His jaw hung as if he couldn't believe what he was seeing. The golf pro wrote something on a piece of paper, and the last two jurors stared at Sparafucile in apparent disbelief.

Sparafucile was stone-faced in front of the jury. Not a flicker of emotion showed, as if he'd read the first rule of the lawyer's ten commandments. He gazed straight ahead, eyes vacant. But gone was the arrogant, confident, smug demeanor. He'd taken some big hits, and more were coming.

"Counselor," Maplethorpe said. He looked at the wall clock and then at me. "I think we might all use a leg stretch."

"With your permission, Your Honor, might I finish with just a few more questions? That will end this line of inquiry."

Maplethorpe again looked at the clock. "Proceed, but finish in the next ten minutes."

"I will, Your Honor. Thank you." I figured Maplethorpe's bladder was talking to him.

"Lieutenant, you shot and killed Ryan Simpson, Jared's son, correct?"

He sat up straight, and I saw his jaw muscles tighten. "He was pointing a rifle at me, intending to kill me."

"Was the gun loaded?"

Sparafucile ran his tongue over his lips as he'd done earlier and paused before answering. "There was no way for me to know whether the gun was loaded or not. It could've been a toy rifle or a BB gun, and I would've still been within my rights to protect myself."

"Do you know if the gun was loaded or not, after you shot and killed Ryan?"

"I'm not sure," he said.

"Let me remind you I was there and saw your fellow officer, Fisheye, retrieve the rifle and find the breech empty." It was obvious he was lying, but I had no proof. I wish I'd videoed the interaction, but that might've gotten me shot. And he was right. This was self-defense, but I pushed it anyway.

"I don't give a sh—I don't care that you were there. When the gun was inspected later, there was a bullet in the breech," Sparafucile said.

"True, but that bullet had no fingerprints on it. How might that have happened if Ryan had loaded the gun before coming to your house?" I asked.

His eyes flared. He was getting angry. Good.

"I don't know. Maybe he wiped the bullet before he inserted it into the rifle, or maybe he wore gloves. How the hell can I be in the head of a teenager?"

"Or maybe you wiped the bullet before you or Fisheye—Officer Diaz—inserted it on your porch?"

"Are you accusing—" He shot me that venomous look again.

I saw the fingers of his hand twitch on the handle of his electric gun. *No*, I said to myself, *he wouldn't dare*. Or would he?

"I'll have Officer Diaz on the stand next, and we'll see what he has to say." I checked my notes. "One last thing, Lieutenant. Did you know that Ryan had an unopened box of Colt .22 longs at home?"

"How could I know that?" He shrugged.

"I'll represent to you that he did. What type of bullet was found in the breech?"

"I don't remember."

"I'll refresh your memory. It was a Winchester .22 short-caliber bullet. Wouldn't it be unlikely for someone trying to kill you to leave all his bullets at home in an unopened box and load his gun with one bullet—a different type and brand—that didn't even have his fingerprints on it?"

"The kid was crazy. How the hell do I know what he was thinking? All I know is that he came to my house to kill me, and I shot him in self-defense."

"Thank you, Lieutenant." I turned to the bench. "If it pleases the court, Your Honor, I'm finished with this line of questioning. We can break whenever Your Honor wishes."

"Fifteen minutes, everyone. All back at ten thirty," the judge said.

"Your Honor, a personal matter has come up. Might I ask for an hour recess instead of fifteen minutes?" I asked. "I'll make up for it by cutting out some questions, so we'll still end at the regular time."

Maplethorpe looked at the clock on the wall and then at his watch. "Granted. One hour, sharp. Everybody back by one thirty."

Shay and I did a quick review of Sparafucile's testimony, but I didn't have much time to talk. I needed to get to my apartment quickly.

"Got enough to request a directed verdict?" Shay asked.

"Not yet, but that's where I'm headed," I said.

I drove home, changed clothes, called Kat, and told her what happened.

"Did you bring up my speeding?"

"Not yet. Coming up next." I heard a sharp intake of air.

"Bear, Sparafucile said if he went to court, I'd go to jail." I heard her sob. "He's going to make sure I end up in prison ten years for selling drugs. You've got to save me, Bear, please." She began to cry. "I don't want to go to jail. I'll die in jail."

"You won't go to jail, darling. I promise. No way that's going to happen. Calm down and try to get some rest. I'll see you later tonight. Trust me. You will *not* go to jail."

"I remind you that you're still under oath, Lieutenant Sparafucile," Maplethorpe said as court resumed. "You may proceed, Counselor."

"Thank you, Your Honor." I shifted my gaze from Maplethorpe and zeroed in on Sparafucile. He was relaxed, like at the beginning of his testimony, slouching in his chair, feet splayed out. I suspect he'd talked with Papageorgio, and that'd calmed him down. I intended to disrupt that demeanor.

I stood in front of the podium. "Lieutenant, I understand you take traffic duty half a day a week, correct?"

"Yeah."

"Why do you do that?"

"Why not?"

"I would've thought your rank and position in the squad got you out of details like that, no?"

"It could, but I choose to do what my men do."

"Is that the only reason?" I locked eyes with him.

"What're you driving at?" he asked, his eyes squinty and forehead creased.

"Do you know a woman named Cynthia Griffin?"

"Should I?"

I shook my head. "I get to ask the questions, Lieutenant, and you get to answer them. That's how our system works." I repeated, "Do you know a woman named Cynthia Griffin? A simple question. Yes or no?"

"Objection, Your Honor," Papageorgio said. "There's no need for counsel to lecture the witness."

"Counselors, sidebar."

I knew what the reprimand would be, and I guess I shouldn't have been so snippy.

"Gentlemen, I'll not let this become a circus. We're here to get facts and resolution." He looked at me. "Do not provoke the witness with irrelevant commentary." Then he looked at Papageorgio. "Do not be so quick to take offense and object. If you both follow those simple rules, we'll get to the end of this trial a lot quicker. Am I clear?"

"Yes, Your Honor," we both said and returned to our seats.

I resumed. "So, do you know Cynthia Griffin?" Sparafucile sat back, squared his shoulders, stared at me, and put his hand on the handle of his Electric Gun. From where he was sitting, I was the only one who could see the hand motion. He was sending me a clear danger signal: don't go where you're going.

"No, I don't know her."

"She'll be testifying in the next day or two."

"So?"

He was so calm I felt the first twinge of doubt whether he really did lay traps for speeders.

"Cynthia Griffin will testify you traded sex to forgive a speeding ticket and that you've continued that practice over the last fifteen years or so." That drew gasps from the two women jurors.

Sparafucile didn't respond, but his face grew dark. His bunched eyebrows created deep forehead grooves, and his compressed lips were a slit in his face. His eyes were menacing. Finally, he said, "Is that a question or a statement?"

"A question. Is that what you do? Trade sex for speeding tickets?"

He thrust out his lower jaw, like a boxer challenging his opponent. "Counselor, if you're making accusations, back them up. No, that's not what I do. I take traffic duty rotations like my men to keep me close to them and involved in their lives and what they do."

"We'll find out. Once Cynthia Griffin's testimony becomes public, I expect there'll be a host of women coming forward. And maybe a few men."

"Objection, Your Honor," Papageorgio said. "Counsel is making allegations without foundation, without witnesses, and with no regard for my client's past history of being an exemplary traffic officer."

"Sustained. The jury is instructed to disregard Mr. Judge's last comment."

"Thank you, Your Honor," Papageorgio said.

Sparafucile remained motionless, his face now blank, inscrutable.

I debated how to launch the next series of questions. I had to protect Kat, but I had to get this bastard to admit what he was doing.

"You stopped my wife for speeding recently on Route 31, correct?"

He nodded. "She was doing sixty-seven in a forty-five-mile-per-hour zone."

"And you arrested her for that?"

Sparafucile addressed the jury. "Speeders traveling more than twenty miles an hour over the speed limit are subject to arrest."

"In handcuffs?" I asked.

He shrugged, a what-was-I-supposed-to-do look on his face. "She resisted arrest and required handcuffs."

"Interesting. A hundred-and-fifteen-pound woman resisted you. What do you weigh? Twice that?"

He remained silent. The eyes of every juror were focused on him.

"Did you record the arrest with your body or car camera?" I asked.

He shook his head. "No."

"Why not? Another camera malfunction?"

"I didn't think it was necessary."

"She'll testify you handcuffed her and then wedged her into the back seat of your police car where you molested her, running your hands over her breasts and up her legs. Is that true?" I was boiling inside, but I had to control my emotions. The jury—and the court—needed to see me as an objective lawyer trying to get at the truth, rather than an angry husband bent on revenge. Papageorgio might object that I was not impartial. I didn't know how Maplethorpe would rule.

Sparafucile withdrew the Electric Gun from the holster on his belt and laid it in his lap, a move concealed by the wooden slats of the witness stand from all but the judge and me. I glanced at Maplethorpe, but he was busy with his computer. I debated whether to notify him to call the bailiff but decided not to.

"No, that's a lie," he said, fingering the gun.

"Then, after you took her to the police station, you threatened her with a strip search if she didn't get me to drop the charges against you. True?"

"That's a lie also." He gripped the handle of his gun.

"I'm sure Officer Jim Bennett will support her claims and will testify you threatened her, exactly as I've said."

"Jim won't do that. He won't testify against me. Not one of my cops," Sparafucile said with confidence. He lifted the gun slightly and looked at me.

"How can you be so sure he won't testify?"

"We protect each other."

"I see. That's interesting. You need him to protect you?"

"That's not what I meant."

"Whether he does or doesn't, my wife's cell phone recorded every word of your interaction. She was going to call me when you pulled her over, but you ordered her to put her phone away and give you her license and registration." I spoke slowly, emphasizing every word. "She did as you requested—after she hit the record button." I took the phone from my pocket and held it up for the jury to see. "I intend to play that in court for the jury to hear what actually took place."

Sparafucile's body language now betrayed him. His face turned scarlet, brows drawn and eyes intense, staring at me with dilated pupils. His lips were drawn into a bared-toothed grimace, and he was breathing fast. The devil incarnate had caught fire, his rage almost palpable. I'd lit his fuse, and he was ready to explode.

I deliberately turned my back and faced the jury to ask my next question. I braced myself against the wooden handrail of the jury box.

A moment later, a loud bang exploded in the quiet courtroom, and I felt a thud against my back, followed by a series of clicking sounds for five seconds. The force of the probes drove me toward the jury box, and I teetered over the railing. Demetrios jumped up in time and pushed against my chest, bracing me before I fell. My cracked ribs sang out as I regained my balance, and I chewed my bottom lip to keep silent.

I turned in time to see Sparafucile pointing the Electric Gun at me. He dropped it and vaulted out of the witness stand. In three giant strides, he reached the bar, leaped over it, and tore from the courtroom before anyone could react. The old bailiff limped after him, but Sparafucile was already gone.

Every eye in the courtroom now focused on me. Papageorgio and Slaughter stood and stared. So did Shay. I hadn't told him beforehand what I'd planned to do.

"Mr. Judge, are you all right?" Maplethorpe asked, rising from his chair and peering over his desk, concern coloring his voice. He pounded his gavel to silence the screams and the "Oh my God!" and "Christ, did you see that!" exclamations from the jurors and spectators in the courtroom. "Bailiff," he shouted over the noise, "call 911 for the police and medical help. Immediately!"

I turned to the judge, tried to smile and reassure him. "I'm fine, Your Honor," I said, slipping off my jacket and tie and unbuttoning my dress shirt. "If it pleases the court, may I take a break and ask my cocounsel to help me out of my Kevlar vest? The probes are embedded in it."

"Certainly, take all the time you need," Maplethorpe said, sitting back down, relief in his voice. He returned my smile and nodded, realizing what I'd done. "I guess we won't need a doctor." He pounded his gavel again to silence the courtroom still buzzing, but this time half-heartedly.

Shay unzipped the front of the bulletproof shield, and I shrugged out of the heavy protection. As I did, the Electric Gun probes fell to the floor.

"Your Honor, I'm also wearing a thin rubber wet suit that I use when I scuba dive. If Your Honor wishes to continue the trial, I'll have to go to the men's room to take it off and redress. It's very warm."

"No, I think we've all seen and heard enough for today. I expect the police to have Lieutenant Sparafucile in custody by nightfall. We'll resume tomorrow if you feel up to it. Bailiff, excuse the jury. Court will resume tomorrow morning at nine."

Maplethorpe stood, looked down at me, smiled again, shaking his head, and left.

Hopperville police, aided by Indianapolis police, cordoned off the courthouse and surrounding neighborhood as they searched for Sparafucile. Coming up empty, they monitored the airport, set up roadblocks, and enlisted help from police forces as far east as Cincinnati and west to St. Louis, south to Louisville and north to Chicago, also without success. Chilli had pulled a Houdini and disappeared.

My guess was he couldn't vanish like that without the help of his buddies. But no one was talking. For all I knew, he could be living in one of their homes in Hopperville right under our noses. Fisheye would be my first bet, but I had no proof, certainly not enough for a search warrant.

The police also made little headway investigating the drone strike. They determined the drone had carried a one-inch wrought steel pipe bomb filled with gunpowder that had been ignited by an electric fuse. They said the materials were available in any hardware store or over the internet, and that was as far as they got.

"I can't believe you let him shoot you!" Kat said when I told her what happened. "That's the craziest thing you've ever done."

"Maybe, but it worked."

I'd broken him. I'd broken the devil himself.

CHAPTER
FORTY-TWO

We were seated in the judge's chambers at nine o'clock the next morning. The room was large and square, with floor-to-ceiling shelves of leather-bound law books, dark wood paneling, and a thick maroon rug. A mahogany desk sat against one wall. A high-backed black leather chair similar to the one in the courtroom was placed behind the desk, with three wooden chairs in front. Heavy maroon drapes partially covered one window.

I'd spent a sleepless night—initially up late with Shay, drafting a motion for a directed verdict, and then twisting and turning with aching ribs that Tylenol barely touched. I wasn't going to use anything stronger, so I just toughed it out—along with a glass or two of Oban.

Maplethorpe entered from a door in the back. Papageorgio—he was alone—Shay, and I stood. We greeted the judge and sat down.

"Your Honor," I said, "to expedite this trial, consistent with your view of a rocket docket, this morning we submitted a motion asking the court for a directed verdict of police brutality against Lieutenant Vincenzo Sparafucile and the Hopperville Police Department. In view of the testimony the court has heard, the obvious implications of the Bennett video, and the defendant's horrific action against me, we hope the court will recognize these realities and agree that, in sum, they constitute a body of evidence proving police brutality and inappropriate use of force."

The crows were positioned at liftoff, but Maplethorpe remained silent.

I continued, "It's our opinion that defense has no alternative but to agree with these incontrovertible facts. A directed verdict would speed the trial by eliminating our need to question on the witness stand Jose Diaz a.k.a. Fisheye, James Bennett, Cynthia Griffin, and my wife, Katherine Judge. She's been ill, Your Honor, and I'd like to spare her the stress of having to testify."

"Mr. Papageorgio, what says defense?"

True to the lawyer's covenant, Papageorgio showed no surprise. "I need to talk with my client, Your Honor, to see if he agrees."

"Is the police commissioner available?"

"Yes, sir."

"Bring him in."

Papageorgio returned several minutes later with Hopperville Police Commissioner Richard Dawson, a burly, middle-aged man with a bulbous nose. The commissioner wore a blue police uniform sporting a gold epaulet on each shoulder and a gold brimmed hat he carried under one arm. Papageorgio pulled up another chair, and Dawson sat down.

Judge Maplethorpe explained the legal issues to him. "For a directed verdict to be executed by the court, the plaintiff—Mr. Judge—needs to present facts proving that the defense—Hopperville police and Lieutenant Vincenzo Sparafucile—have broken the law and that the defense has no reasonable alternative explanation. The court is inclined to agree with plaintiff's position.

"You've been sitting in the back of the courtroom during the trial, Commissioner Dawson, so I know you've heard and seen the evidence on the use of force. This has nothing to do with the lawsuit against the Electric Gun Company. That will resume once we've settled the present matter. My question to you, as the representative for the Hopperville Police Department, is whether you'd be willing to accept a directed verdict of police brutality?"

Dawson was quiet, one finger alongside his nose, apparently weighing what he'd just heard. "May I have a moment to speak with Mr. Papageorgio, Your Honor?"

"Of course. Use the small conference room next door." Maplethorpe pointed to a door in the wall opposite his desk.

Once they'd left, Maplethorpe asked me, a questioning look on his face, "I'm curious, Mr. Judge. How was it you came into my courtroom suited up, so to speak?"

"Just before the midmorning break, Your Honor, I knew Sparafucile was itching to attack me. I figured if I could bait him enough to blow his cool, he'd go for the Electric Gun.

"After the court was kind enough to grant an hour for the break, I returned to my apartment to put on the Kevlar vest I'd kept from my FBI days. I figured if it could stop a bullet, it could stop the probes. But I was concerned it might not block the electricity, so I wore my rubber scuba wet suit under it for insulation."

"Pretty gutsy move," Maplethorpe said. "He could've shot you in the legs."

I shrugged. "I guess, but I bet he'd go for the largest body mass, as he'd been taught. It worked."

"Yes, I'd say it did," the judge said, crows half rising. "But you took a calculated risk. He might have hit someone in the jury had the probes missed you."

I hadn't even considered that possibility. "I apologize, Your Honor. I didn't think of that. You're quite right."

The judge gave me a I-know-I'm-right nod, and the crows relaxed.

Dawson and Papageorgio returned and sat back down.

"What have you decided?" Maplethorpe asked.

"If you rule in favor of plaintiff's motion, defense will not object, and my client will accept the judgment, Your Honor," Papageorgio said.

The judge smiled. "Then we have a decision. Let's go back to the courtroom and bring in the jury."

"Wait a moment," Shay said. "What about killing Ryan? Is that part of this judgment?"

We all turned to Maplethorpe. "Good question. It can be, if you wish. In my view, Sparafucile was justified in defending himself. He had no way of knowing whether or not the rifle was loaded. Questions about loading the gun with a single bullet after the fact are really irrelevant. I believe they probably did plant the bullet, but it doesn't matter. However, if you don't wish to accept my decision and want to put it to the jury to decide, I'll go along with that."

"Shay, you brought it up. What do you want to do?" I asked.

"I agree with the court. Let it go."

"Ladies and gentlemen of the jury, may I have your attention," Maplethorpe said as the jurors took their seats. They filed in according to a strict order so that they kept the same seat each time.

"Plaintiff has filed a motion for a directed verdict," Maplethorpe continued. "That means plaintiff has concluded they have a preponderance of evidence to find a verdict in their favor that the Hopperville police, namely Lieutenant Vincenzo Sparafucile, has committed an act of police brutality by means of inappropriate use of force, and defense has no recourse but to concur. When the parties agree that there are no important facts in dispute, the court can decide to accept with the plaintiff's motion and avoid prolonging that aspect of the trial. The parties have agreed, and the court has ruled in favor of the motion. You will have an opportunity to determine the damages later. We will now proceed with the issue of product liability. Please call your next witness, Counselor."

CHAPTER FORTY-THREE

BEAR'S PROMISE

"Thank you, Your Honor. Plaintiff calls Dr. Greg Dumont to the witness stand."

Greg was wearing black loafers. I hadn't relished explaining his open-toed sandals to the jury. He wore a white turtleneck shirt under a blue blazer with gray slacks.

After swearing him in and establishing his credentials, I asked, "Dr. Dumont, do you have an opinion whether the Electric Gun, under appropriate circumstances, can trigger cardiac arrest in a human?"

"I do," he said, looking directly at the jury as I had instructed.

"What is that opinion?"

"That it can do so." Mrs. Donahue nodded, and Mr. Demetrios half smiled.

I walked in front of the jury. "Defense has claimed that is impossible. Both the CEO, Beverly Slaughter, and the head of their scientific board of advisers, Jeremiah Verity, have testified under oath in this courtroom that there has never been a recorded episode of the Electric Gun causing cardiac arrest." I turned to Dumont. "Apparently, you disagree with them."

He nodded. "I do."

"On what do you base that opinion?"

"Personal observation."

"Please explain that to the jury."

Dumont kept his gaze fixed on the jurors and related how the Electric Gun delivered sufficient electrical charge through the skin to capture the heart and increase its rate to unsustainable levels that triggered ventricular fibrillation, which led to cardiac arrest. He talked with animated gestures, enthusiastic, his hands moving in all directions. He personified the professor he was and radiated an image of trust that said, "If I tell you something, you can believe it."

Donahue and Demetrios seemed to buy what he was saying. I couldn't tell about the others.

"That's an interesting theory, Doctor. What's the proof?" I asked.

At this point, Dumont smiled at the jury, exactly as we'd rehearsed, and talked to them as a doctor would address a patient, slowly and thoroughly. He explained in great detail what happened in the EP operating room to his patient Gerald Carpenter after being shot by the Electric Gun.

"And, of course, you recorded that singular event with an ECG machine, correct?" I said.

"I tried to."

"You tried to?" I feigned surprise. "Please explain that to the jury."

He looked from me to the jury. "My recording equipment failed. The recording cable became disconnected from the ECG machine for some unknown reason. We saw the VF develop but didn't record it."

"If you didn't record it, then you're asking the jury to take your word for it, correct?" I said. That drew nods from the golf pro and McDonald's manager.

"No, I'm not. The implantable cardioverter defibrillator, or ICD as we call it, has a built-in ECG recorder similar to a regular ECG machine. The ICD can record and store in its memory any abnormal heart rhythms it detects."

"So, assuming the ICD was functioning properly—" I turned to look at Slaughter. He was mouthing the word "no" and trying to hide a smile. "It would have recorded the Electric Gun triggering ventricular fibrillation in Mr. Carpenter. Correct?"

"Yes."

"And did it do so?" I asked.

"Yes."

"No!" Slaughter burst out. His hand shot up to cover his mouth, and he dropped his head, embarrassed. His bald pate took on a reddish hue. I never knew an embarrassed blush could spread to the scalp. Papageorgio viewed Slaughter with a stunned look.

Before Maplethorpe could admonish Slaughter, Papageorgio stood and said, "Please excuse my client's eruption, Your Honor. I apologize to the court. He was caught up in the moment. It won't happen again." He sat down.

"It'd better not, or he'll be removed from the courtroom and cited for contempt," Maplethorpe said, crows at full height.

"Yes, Your Honor," Papageorgio said. He turned and whispered to Slaughter, shaking his head no.

"Dr. Dumont"—I pointed at Slaughter—"Mr. Slaughter seems to disagree about what function Carpenter's ICD performed. Would you explain what actually happened?" I asked.

Dumont took the jury through Carpenter's back story of his son being shot by Sparafucile, Carpenter volunteering to be shot, and the results. He told the jury I'd been present during the entire procedure and that I'd done the shooting.

"So, after you implanted the ICD, you reprogrammed all its features before Mr. Carpenter was shot?" I asked.

"Yes. I do that routinely after implant, prior to inducing VF in a patient, to be sure the ICD is functioning properly," Dumont said, waving a hand for emphasis. "I never trust what's been programmed by the device company during manufacturing when the ICD arrives from the factory."

"Was there anything unusual about the ICD before you did that?" I asked, looking at him.

"Yes." He nodded. "It's a good thing I checked because the ECG recording function had been programmed off. Usually when the ICD comes from the manufacturer, that feature is programmed on for safety reasons. Someone had turned it off."

"Reason?" I asked.

He looked at the jury as he answered. "I tracked down the Cardiostim salesman who delivered the ICD to the hospital that morning. The salesman told me he'd been requested by one of our OR personnel to turn off the recording feature."

"Did the salesman say who it was?"

Dumont pursed his lips and shook his head. "He couldn't remember his name."

"How about what he looked like?" I asked.

"Nothing ..." Dumont paused and massaged the bridge of his nose, thinking. "Oh, wait a minute." He held up his index finger. "He said the guy wore steel-rimmed glasses with thick lenses. The guy told the sales rep that I had made that request."

"Had you?"

Dumont shook his head. "Of course not."

Naturally, that was Verity, but I had no proof. Even if I did, there was nothing illegal about reprogramming the ICD. But it all fit. Somehow Slaughter had found out what we were planning—perhaps via the sale of an Electric Gun to Dumont—and had Verity try to sabotage us.

"What happened next?" I asked. Dumont started answering while looking at me. It was hard not to, since I was the one asking the questions. But I nodded toward the jury, and he turned to talk to them.

"I asked you to shoot Mr. Carpenter, and you shot him in the left side of his chest. He developed ventricular fibrillation leading to cardiac arrest. The ICD detected the VF and terminated it with the second shock. Mr. Carpenter recovered without any complications."

I turned to Maplethorpe. "Your Honor, if it pleases the court, I'd like to offer into evidence Mr. Carpenter's ICD and ask Dr. Dumont to print out the ECG recording and explain what happened when Mr. Carpenter was shot by the Electric Gun."

"The court will agree to that. Mr. Papageorgio, any objections?"

Papageorgio was again caught in a bind. He had to agree. "No objection."

I continued, addressing the jury as well. "The problem, Your Honor, is that the ICD remains implanted in Mr. Carpenter's chest, and the only way to interrogate the ICD and retrieve the recorded ECG information for the jury is to bring Mr. Carpenter into the courtroom and do it here."

"This is a bit unusual, but I see no reason not to do it." He looked at Papageorgio. "Mr. Papageorgio, any objections?"

"None, Your Honor."

"With your permission, Your Honor, may Dr. Dumont bring Mr. Carpenter into the courtroom and proceed with the ICD interrogation?"

"Permission granted."

CHAPTER FORTY-FOUR

Dumont left the witness box, walked out of the courtroom, and soon returned, wheeling in a large machine with an array of buttons and wires. He placed it in front of the jury.

"This machine is called a programmer," Dumont said. "I'll connect it to Mr. Carpenter and his ICD and then print out the ECG."

Dumont left again and returned, pushing a stretcher and leading Gerald Carpenter with a hand on his shoulder. Carpenter was nervous, with perspiration dotting his forehead and a worried look on his face. Dumont wheeled the stretcher in front of the jury alongside the programmer.

"Your Honor, for the record, this is Mr. Gerald Carpenter," I said. Carpenter gave a small wave.

"With the court's permission," I said, "I'd like to now turn this over to Dr. Dumont to take us through the recording."

"Permission granted."

"I'm going to ask Mr. Carpenter to lie down on the stretcher and open his shirt," Dumont said. "I'll connect him to this machine and print out the recording."

Dumont helped Carpenter climb onto the stretcher. He lay down on his back and unbuttoned his shirt. Dumont placed a metal electrode on each arm and leg and connected the wires to a cable that he plugged into the programmer. He set a metal disk about the size of a thick drink coaster on Carpenter's chest over the bulge where the ICD was implanted. A second cable connected the disk to another slot in the programmer.

"We're ready, Your Honor," I said. "We'll televise the recording, so you'll see it displayed on the TV monitors. Dr. Dumont will walk us through what we're seeing."

Dumont hit the record button, and the only noise in the large courtroom was the whirring of the programmer printing out the ECG. All eyes were glued to the TV screens around the courtroom as Dumont described the ECG.

"This is Mr. Carpenter's normal heart rhythm prior to the Electric Gun shot," Dumont said, his voice calm, soft. "Regular heart rhythm at around seventy-five beats per minute."

He stopped the recorder. "Now, watch what happens when he gets shot," he said, restarting the recorder.

The ECG changed. Dense, dark vertical lines bunched close together obscured the screen, replacing the regular rhythm.

"The action begins," Dumont said, excited, rubbing his hands together. "These heavy lines"—he pointed to the ECG—"represent the five-second burst from the Electric Gun at over one thousand times per minute when Mr. Judge shot Mr. Carpenter," he said.

The vertical lines suddenly stopped, revealing a horizontal line that rapidly dipped and climbed in a sawtooth fashion, like the jagged outlines of mountains and valleys.

"This is the ECG picture of death, ladies and gentlemen," Dumont said dramatically, his breathing fast and voice high-pitched. He halted the recording again. "We call it ventricular fibrillation. Mr. Carpenter has lost consciousness and will die unless the VF is stopped by a large electric shock."

I watched Carpenter as he closed his eyes and rolled his head from side to side, maybe reliving that moment.

Dumont restarted the recording. A thick vertical line appeared eleven seconds later, followed by the same squiggly sawtooth line.

"The first shock from the ICD failed, and the VF continued, as you can see," Dumont said, voice swelling almost to a shout. "Mr. Carpenter is still unconscious and could die if his ICD fails again. We won't let that happen, of course, because we're ready to shock his heart with an external backup defibrillator."

A second vertical line appeared, this time followed by a normal heart rhythm.

"Whew!" Dumont let out a dramatic sigh and wiped his forehead with the back of his hand. "As you can see, the second shock from the ICD terminated the VF, restoring Mr. Carpenter's regular heart rhythm and saving his life."

Dumont's voice went soft again. "His heart rhythm is now back to the nice, regular beat he had before he was shot. Consciousness has returned, and he sat up in his bed in the OR."

Carpenter mimicked the description and sat up on the stretcher. His smile lit up the courtroom, and he gave a little wave. Several of the visitors clapped.

Maplethorpe rapped his gavel. "Silence in the courtroom. Mr. Judge, are you done with the demonstration?"

"Yes, Your Honor. The bailiff can help Dr. Dumont wheel the stretcher and programmer out of the courtroom. Mr. Carpenter may wish to sit in the back as a spectator, with your permission."

"Fine. Let's get on with it. Are you finished with your witness?"

"Just a few more questions for Dr. Dumont, Your Honor."

Dumont returned to the witness stand holding the ECG printout in his hand.

I took it from him. "Is this the first ECG ever, showing that the Electric Gun can capture the heartbeat of a human and cause ventricular fibrillation and cardiac arrest?"

"To the best of my knowledge, it is," Dumont said with a smile.

"With the court's permission, I'd like to offer this ECG into evidence."

"Any objection, Mr. Papageorgio?"

"None, Your Honor."

"Dr. Dumont, is it your medical opinion that excited delirium is a real psychological entity?" I asked.

His face grew dark and serious. "No, I think it's a diagnosis contrived by the Electric Gun Company to explain away deaths after an Electric Gun shooting."

"What then is the cause of death in subjects who die in cardiac arrest after being shot with the Electric Gun?"

His eyes got big, and he smiled. "We've now shown in that ECG you're holding"—he pointed to it—"that it's the electricity delivered by the Electric Gun."

"Did the warnings contained in the Electric Gun literature adequately explain this risk?" Shay handed me the Electric Gun brochure, and I waved it for the jury to see.

He shook his head. "No. They never mentioned that possibility."

"What warnings would you suggest they write?" I asked.

Papageorgio jumped up. "Objection, Your Honor. Dr. Dumont is not an expert in writing warnings."

The crows never budged. "I'll allow it. Overruled. I want to hear his answer. Go ahead, Dr. Dumont."

Dumont became the professor in front of a classroom again. "I would advise three things. First, avoid chest shots if at all possible. Second, don't shoot longer than five seconds. And third, if the victim becomes unresponsive, think of cardiac arrest and begin resuscitation."

"Thank you, Dr. Dumont," I said.

I paused to let that sink in. "You took care of Jared Simpson after he was resuscitated, correct?" I said.

"Yes."

"And you reviewed the events surrounding his Electric Gun shooting, including the autopsy, correct?"

"Yes."

"What is your opinion about whether the Electric Gun was responsible for his cardiac arrest and subsequent death?"

He firmed his lips and nodded. "It's my opinion the Electric Gun was responsible for causing ventricular fibrillation that produced his cardiac arrest and subsequent death." Watching his face, I felt the sincerity of his response. I hoped the jury did also.

"And is it further your opinion that Lieutenant Vincenzo Sparafucile killed Jared Simpson with the Electric Gun?"

"Yes, it is."

"Thank you, Dr. Dumont." I turned to the judge. "I have no further questions, Your Honor," I said and sat down.

"Mr. Papageorgio, cross-examination?"

Papageorgio rose and replaced me at the lectern.

"That was very dramatic, Dr. Dumont." He left the lectern, clasped his hands behind his back, and paced in front of Dumont. He reminded me of a stalking tiger. "Did Mr. Carpenter have any heart problems that might have made him especially susceptible to the effects of the Electric Gun?"

I watched Dumont. His eyes followed Papageorgio. I hoped Papageorgio's behavior wouldn't distract him. Dumont had been testifying for almost two hours, and I was sure he was tired. The emotional toll of being on the witness stand took a lot out of a person.

"Yes, he'd had two previous heart attacks," Dumont said.

"Did he ever have cardiac arrest unrelated to the Electric Gun?"

Dumont nodded. "Yes, from the second heart attack."

"So you agree the Electric Gun was not necessarily responsible for this cardiac arrest and it could've been another heart attack, correct?"

This was a trap, and I was about to object when Dumont answered.

"I do not agree. The timing of the ventricular fibrillation by the ECG makes it clear it was initiated during the shooting."

Papageorgio stopped pacing and stood directly in front of Dumont, staring intently at him. I had to give Papageorgio credit. He was intimidating. "*During* the shooting but not necessarily *by* the shooting. Couldn't the pain caused by the Electric Gun have triggered another heart attack, and it was the heart attack that caused the ventricular fibrillation and cardiac arrest, unrelated to any electricity affecting his heart?"

Dumont brushed the statement aside with a head shake. "In my opinion, it would be extremely unlikely—less than a 5 percent chance—for such a coincidence to occur. A heart attack would take some time before it triggered ventricular fibrillation. In addition, there was no evidence he had a heart attack after he was shot, only the ventricular fibrillation and cardiac arrest. That makes it even less likely," Dumont answered.

"As you said in the beginning of your lengthy reply, Doctor, that is your opinion, not fact, correct?"

Dumont was silent, considering his answer. Papageorgio was good, drilling down at the core of the problem. Did the timing of the shock immediately preceding the VF and cardiac arrest prove that the shock caused the VF and cardiac arrest, or could it have been a coincidence? Did temporality establish causality?

"I cannot say 100 percent, but to a reasonable degree of medical certainty, I think it probably did."

I breathed a sigh of relief. Dumont answered with the magical words, *to a reasonable degree of medical certainty.* That was what the court was looking for. No one can be 100 percent certain since anything could be possible, but to assign blame, one had to be reasonably certain. And he used the word "probably," meaning a 51 percent or greater chance that it did, rather than "possibly," meaning 50 percent or less. That's what the law called for.

"If you cannot say with 100 percent certainty that the Electric Gun caused the cardiac arrest in Mr. Carpenter when you had an actual ECG recording of the event, how sure can you be in Jared Simpson's case, when you had no ECG recording?"

Dumont smiled his you-can-believe-me smile. "My answer is basically the same. To a reasonable degree of medical certainty, it is my opinion that the Electric Gun most likely caused the cardiac arrest in Jared Simpson, which subsequently led to his death."

"Again, your opinion." Before I could object that he was badgering the witness, Papageorgio concluded, "Thank you, Doctor. No more questions."

Maplethorpe looked at the jury. "Any questions for this witness?"

The bailiff picked up several sheets of paper and handed them to the judge. He read from the first one: "Was Mr. Carpenter excited or delirious when he was shot? Could excited delirium have played a role?"

Dumont answered, "No, absolutely not. He was nervous about the pain involved but calm and resolved otherwise. In fact, I had given him a medication to take the edge off any anxiety. His heart rate, as you saw from the ECG, was only seventy-five or so, hardly the heart rate of someone excited or delirious."

Maplethorpe read from the second paper: "Has Mr. Carpenter had any other episodes of fibrillation since the shooting?"

"None."

The judge looked at the jury for any other questions, but they were silent.

"Thank you, Dr. Dumont," Maplethorpe said. "You are excused."

Maplethorpe turned to me. "Any other witnesses, Mr. Judge?"

"No, Your Honor. Plaintiff rests."

"Fine. The court will take a thirty-minute break and resume again at eleven."

Shay and I walked to our small conference room, a tiny, windowless rectangle just outside the courtroom where we had privacy and could unwind a little. We invited Dumont and Carpenter to join us. Wooden chairs lined one wall, with a small table pressed against the opposite side, holding drinks and snacks.

"Anybody want something to drink?" I asked as we took chairs. "I have water or Coke. And some chips."

There were no takers. The excitement of the past couple of hours had supplanted feelings of hunger or thirst.

"Good job, both of you," I said to Dumont and Carpenter. "Your testimony was riveting and is certain to win the day for us."

"I sure hope so," Dumont said. "That was exhausting, but it did seem to go well. Our preparation helped immensely. Papageorgio's good, though. He got to the heart of the issue."

"He did," Carpenter said. "But it's time to stop this lunacy. I want my boy Tom vindicated."

"He will be, Mr. Carpenter," I said. "He will be."

CHAPTER FORTY-FIVE

"**I**s defense ready to start?" Maplethorpe asked Papageorgio.

"We are, Your Honor," Papageorgio said. "Defense calls its only witness, Mr. Mark Hamden, to the stand."

This was an absolute blindside, classic for trial by ambush. I couldn't imagine what Papageorgio wanted with my former law partner.

After swearing in, Papageorgio asked, "How long have you known Jason Judge?"

Hamden stared at me. I couldn't read his expression, but it didn't seem friendly. No sign of recognition. Maybe he was just nervous. "About twenty-five years."

"In what capacity?"

His gaze shifted back to Papageorgio. "After he left the FBI over twenty years ago, Mr. Judge approached me about starting a law firm."

Papageorgio left the podium and walked to the front of the jury. "And did you do that?"

"Yes, we founded Judge, Williams, and Hamden."

"Is the firm still in existence?"

"It is, but without Mr. Judge," Hamden said with a fake smile. "He left to start his own firm here in Hopperville."

"Why did he leave?" Papageorgio asked, looking at me with interest.

"The managing partners had a difference of opinion with Mr. Judge, and we asked him to leave."

"'Asked him to leave'? Is that a euphemism for saying you fired him?"

"Yes, in a manner of speaking," Hamden said.

"Reason?"

"We no longer agreed on how we wanted to practice law," Hamden said, "and the direction of the law firm."

"You mentioned Mr. Judge left the FBI to start the law firm. Why did he leave the FBI?"

Now I understood where this was going. I needed to object because my background had nothing to do with the case. But I was speechless, despite knowing what was coming.

Shay looked at me, silently asking why I wasn't objecting. But I couldn't move. He stood. "If it pleases the court, Your Honor, defense objects to this line of questioning. Events that happened more than twenty years ago have no direct bearing on the facts of the present case."

"Mr. Papageorgio?" Maplethorpe asked, crows ready to fly.

"If the court grants me a little latitude, I will show Your Honor and the jury that these past events directly impact the present proceedings."

"Very little latitude, Mr. Papageorgio. Objection overruled." The crows rested for the moment.

"Thank you, Your Honor. Mr. Hamden, my question to you was why Mr. Judge left the FBI."

"He told me the FBI asked him to turn in his badge," Hamden said, staring at me.

"So, another firing, this time by the FBI?" Papageorgio said. He said this looking directly from me to the jurors.

"You could say that," Hamden replied with a slight nod.

"What happened?"

"Mr. Judge told me it was because of a swatting prank."

"Please explain to the jury what that is."

Hamden faced the jury as he explained.

"A group of kids at a home party got into a fight over a video game and ganged up on one of the guys for cheating. They beat him up pretty good and threw him out the door of the house. For revenge, the kid called the cops and said he and his family had been kidnapped and were being held at gunpoint for ransom. He gave the cops the names of his former friends and the address where the party was being held. The SWAT team called the FBI to join in the rescue because of the kidnapping claim, and they raced to the house."

Hamden sipped from the water glass the bailiff had placed in front of him. He ran his tongue over his lips and seemed embarrassed.

"Mr. Judge was the first one through the door of the house. When one of the kids reached into his pocket for something—turned out later he was reaching for his wallet to show identification—Mr. Judge shot and killed him. The FBI held an inquiry and decided Mr. Judge's action was an excessive use of force, that he should've given the kid a chance to explain what he was doing. Mr. Judge was tried for manslaughter—a 'reckless disregard for life' was the charge—but it ended as a hung jury. In return for not pressing for a new trial, the FBI asked for his badge."

"One last question, Mr. Hamden." Papageorgio paused and let the question hang dramatically for a moment, his eyes scanning the jury. "Was the boy Mr. Judge shot black or white?"

"Black."

I studied the faces of the jurors, especially Demetrios and Donahue. I was counting on the two of them, but they sat grim-faced, Demetrios shaking his head and Donahue holding a tissue to her eyes.

"Thank you. No further questions," Papageorgio said. "Your witness, Counselor." He sat down, a self-righteous look on his face.

I still couldn't move. I'd told Hamden that story in strict confidence, when we were still close friends. We'd met in law school; he was in his third year, and I was just starting. He acted as a big brother, helping me adjust to school, learn the ropes. Later, when I had the FBI trouble and he was a junior partner in another law firm, I asked him for advice about what to do prior to my manslaughter trial. After the trial, when I gave up my FBI shield, I invited him to join me in starting a new law firm.

I just stared at him, not so much angry as numb. I didn't know what to do or to say.

"Counselor, cross-examination?"

My brain wouldn't engage, couldn't form a coherent thought. I began to tremble and hid my hands beneath the table, pressing them between my knees. It took every ounce of control to remain sitting at the table. I felt gutted, naked. Papageorgio had found the one horrific event that had shaped the rest of my life, made me who I was, and exposed it to the world. Kat had hidden her alcoholism before we got married, but I'd hidden a homicide. Accidental to be sure, but I'd killed an innocent young man and would be forever scarred by it.

CHAPTER FORTY-SIX

I watched Shay purse his lips. He looked at me as though he knew what he had to do. He adjusted his tie, rose, and went to the lectern. "If it pleases the court, due to an obvious conflict of interest of my partner, I will conduct the cross-examination."

"Fine, Mr. Odinga. Proceed."

From the look on his face, Shay seemed furious at Hamden for stooping to this level, and maybe disappointed in me for not telling him about this ugly part of my life. But I couldn't talk about it, not even with Kat. I'd buried it in a dark recess of my brain, closed the door and locked it, and tried never to go there. I couldn't even come to my own defense. I hoped Shay knew he had to conceal his emotions and try to repair the damage by finding a way to discredit Hamden's statements.

"Mr. Hamden, when did Mr. Judge tell you what happened at the FBI?"

Hamden squinted and put a finger on his chin, as if trying to remember for the first time. I suspected this was playacting for the jury. Surely he'd thought about this before today. "Just before his manslaughter trial. As I remember, we were at a bar, drinking."

"He did not try to hide his past, correct?"

"Correct."

"He told you that story in confidence, true?" Good for Shay. He sensed Hamden's weak spot and was going for it.

Hamden shifted in the witness stand, glanced at Papageorgio, and took a sip of water. "Maybe."

Shay left the podium and walked in front of the jury for the next questions. He was a quick learner. "Did he ask for your advice at any time about what to do?"

"Yes."

"And did you give it?"

"Yes."

Shay nodded as if he expected this answer. "Were you a practicing lawyer at the time?"

"Yes."

"Did you bill him for the advice?"

"No. We grant each other professional courtesy."

"So, in addition to a friendship, you established an attorney-client relationship with Mr. Judge at that time, correct?" He'd set Hamden up perfectly and had driven in the final nail to seal the deal.

"Objection, Your Honor," Papageorgio said. "This was an informal chat over a few beers."

"Not so, Your Honor," Shay responded. "They may have been drinking beer, but Mr. Hamden just testified he was a practicing lawyer at the time and granted his friend professional courtesy instead of a bill. That would signify an attorney-client relationship and with it, attorney-client confidentiality."

"Overruled. Continue, Mr. Odinga."

"That relationship, Mr. Hamden, as you know, is privileged and prevents you from divulging any confidences, correct?"

Hamden toyed with the glass of water and blinked his eyes repetitively. "Yes."

"So, you breached the legal code in volunteering this information to the court and could be sanctioned by the New York State Bar Association, even disbarred, correct?"

"Objection, Your—"

"I'll withdraw that comment, Your Honor," Shay said before the judge could respond to Papageorgio's objection. But the jury heard it, and the Maplethorpe didn't strike it. Hamden's eyes darted around the courtroom, flickered a second or two at Papageorgio, the jurors, Shay, and then landed on me. I wondered what he was thinking. I'd bet it was revenge for Kat calling off their affair. I stared back at him until he blinked and looked away.

"You related to the jury in great detail the circumstances surrounding why Mr. Judge left the FBI. Let's talk about why he left Judge, Williams, and Hamden." I'd told Shay all about this Russian episode.

"Isn't it true that a potential client close to President Putin in Moscow wanted Mr. Judge to fabricate multiple shell companies to launder over $1 billion in countries that didn't ask questions?"

Shay walked back to the podium, perhaps to be closer to Hamden in the witness stand. He was doing a great job.

"I don't remember the exact details," Hamden hedged, squirming in his seat.

"Isn't it also true that the firm's fee would have been 5 percent, about fifty million, and that you and the other directors were upset when Mr. Judge turned down this request because of its illegality?

In fact, didn't Mr. Judge say that 'dishonest clients made dishonest lawyers' and he wasn't going to participate?"

"Objection, Your Honor. Compound question."

The crows didn't budge. "Overruled. The witness may answer."

"There was more to it than that," Hamden said, his voice growing weaker, eyelids fluttering.

Shay barely gave him time to answer one question before launching the next. I saw a great future ahead of him as a trial lawyer. "Didn't you and the other partners complain that Mr. Judge was depriving each of you of an end-of-the-year million-dollar bonus?"

"I don't remember."

"Isn't that the real reason he was fired?"

"I don't remember."

"And when he started his own law firm, you prevented him from receiving any severance payment, correct?"

"That's what the noncompete clause in his contract stipulated."

Shay walked to the jurors, leaned back against the jury box, elbows on the railing, and faced Hamden. "One last question. How did Mr. Papageorgio discover why Mr. Judge left the FBI? Did Mr. Papageorgio contact you, or did you contact him to tell the story?"

"I contacted him."

"Why would you do that?" Shay asked, looking at Hamden quizzically.

"In the spirit of transparency, openness." He tried to smile. "The jury should be aware of all the issues surrounding Mr. Judge."

"And maybe to extract a little revenge?" Shay said in a harsh tone.

"Objection, Your Honor," Papageorgio said.

"Sustained."

"No further questions, Your Honor," Shay said, sitting down.

"Any questions from the jury?"

The bailiff picked up a single sheet and handed it to Maplethorpe. He read it several times before asking the question.

"I'm not certain about this question," Maplethorpe said, looking first at the jury and then at Papageorgio and me. "But I think it provides background as to motive, so I'll allow it. Mr. Hamden, one juror wants to know whether you dislike Mr. Judge—and if so, why."

"Yes, I … no, I … I don't know." He crossed and uncrossed his legs. "I can't answer that question." Then he put a hand over his eyes.

BEAR'S PROMISE

Maplethorpe gazed at Hamden with raised brow—the crows flying—and a disgusted look on his face. "Thank you, Mr. Hamden. You may step down," the judge said.

I placed my hand on Shay's shoulder and managed a weak smile that said thank you.

Maplethorpe addressed the court. "We'll break an hour and a half for lunch and resume at two o'clock for closing statements."

CHAPTER FORTY-SEVEN

BEAR'S PROMISE

Shay and I sat in our tiny conference room. He gobbled down a pepperoni pizza delivered by Puccini's Pizza, and I just drank coffee. I was still upset by Hamden's testimony and had no appetite.

"You should've told me about the FBI shooting, Bear," he said with a mouth full of pizza. "I could've been more prepared as I was with the Russian thing."

"You're right, but you did darn good without preparation. It's not something I talk about, not even to myself. I can't stand to go there. I killed an innocent kid, Shay. You cannot know what that feels like."

"No, but—"

"It's a weight around my neck I carry every day, and nothing I do can change it." I sipped my coffee. "I've apologized to his family several times, and they've been gracious about it. I set up college scholarships for their other two kids, and I check on the family every several months to be sure they're doing okay. The father's got steady factory work, and the mother is an elementary school teacher. Not much more I can do. But they know I'm there for them if they need me."

"Would it help if—after the trial—you introduce me to them? Maybe a sympathetic black face would help, especially if they know you're my friend." He finished the last bite of pizza.

I nodded. "Thanks. Good idea. Let's plan on that."

The bailiff's knock on the door told us the judge was ready to start.

"Mr. Judge, you may begin your closing argument."

"Thank you, Your Honor. Ladies and gentlemen of the jury," I said, leaving the lectern and walking in front of the jury box, "we've laid out our case before you. Half has been decided already, as you know. Police brutality, especially that committed by Lieutenant Sparafucile, is now an established verdict of this court, with a monetary judgment to be decided by you and paid by the Hopperville Police Department. We hope the court's decision and the compensatory damages will instigate law enforcement reforms at Hopperville Police Department to eliminate the inappropriate use of force directed primarily but not exclusively toward people of color. Perhaps law enforcement agencies around the US will emulate that example. I hope so."

I paused, placed my hands on the wooden railing in front of the jurors, and leaned toward them. I smiled, and Mrs. Donahue and the golf pro smiled back. Demetrios sat quietly, a pensive look on his face.

"The issue now before you is to decide whether the Electric Gun Company"—I pointed at Slaughter, sitting next to Papageorgio—"is responsible for a share of the blame by selling a product that can kill without warning users of that risk. We're now talking about product liability and whether their behavior was careless, negligent, and unreasonable."

I went back to the lectern to check the outline Shay and I had prepared, then returned to my walking vigil in front of them. Questioning a witness from behind the podium was fine, but now I had to make contact with six people deciding the outcome of the trial.

"We've shown by a preponderance of the evidence that the Electric Gun can provoke the life-threatening heart rhythm called ventricular fibrillation that leads to cardiac arrest and death unless promptly terminated.

"We're indebted to Mr. Gerald Carpenter, seated in the back of this courtroom, who was so overcome by what happened to his son Tom—another police brutality episode perpetrated by Vincenzo Sparafucile—that he volunteered to be the first person ever to have ECG documentation of these events."

I stopped, turned, and looked at Carpenter. I pointed my finger at him and gave a thumbs-up. Once again, a smattering of applause rippled across the spectators that Maplethorpe's gavel quickly extinguished. I turned back to the jury, walked with deliberate steps in front of them, and, as before, tried to make eye contact with as many as possible, lingering my gaze on Demetrios and Donahue. Their faces now seemed impassive, though I thought Mrs. Donahue showed a flicker of compassion.

"We've also revealed that the Electric Gun Company misrepresented their product by failing to warn of this foreseeable risk and potential harm, thus breaching an acceptable standard of care. They trained police, via instructional booklets, slides, lectures, and promotional material, to believe that the Electric Gun was a nonlethal weapon and could be used with impunity. They failed to instruct users to avoid chest shots, avoid long trigger pulls, and to begin resuscitative procedures for any victim unresponsive following an Electric Gun shooting.

"How and why did they conclude their gun was safe? Because they failed to test it adequately prior to launching on an unsuspecting public." I lightly pounded the jury box railing with my fist. "They could have replicated what Mr. Carpenter bravely endured had they wanted to rigorously prove the gun's safety. But they failed to do so and based their conclusions on a few paltry and inadequate animal and human studies. They used phony experts to support phony claims. Who would employ a chemist to decide medical matters?"

I searched their faces. "Would any of you seek medical help from a chemist if you suffered chest pains or palpitations or had a blackout spell? I think not." Mrs. Donahue, Mr. Demetrios, and the golf pro shook their heads in agreement. Maybe I was getting through.

I resumed pacing. "You'd go to a medical expert, like Dr. Greg Dumont. His testimony leaves no doubt that, to a reasonable degree of medical certainty, the Electric Gun was responsible for the death of Jared Simpson. The diagnosis of excited delirium is a myth concocted by defense experts, like that chemist, *Mr.* Verity"—I looked at Papageorgio to see if he'd object, but he remained silent—"to shield the Electric Gun Company from liability. Their lawyers led by Mr. Papageorgio"—I pointed at him—"even sued medical examiners to change the cause of death from the Electric Gun to excited delirium." I shook my head in disbelief.

"It's also our claim that Jared's death by electrocution with the Electric Gun set into motion, like tumbling dominos, the deaths of his wife, Melanie, and his son, Ryan. But for the death of their husband and father, they would still be alive, a caring mother and a future football star being recruited by three world-class universities. The Electric Gun wiped out an entire family. We ask for compensatory damages for all three lives lost because of the Electric Gun Company's failure to warn."

I resumed pacing. "We've learned the Electric Gun Company plays hardball. Mr. Odinga and I were threatened by three thugs while we stood next to Mr. Slaughter's Mercedes when the theft alarm went off. He, my wife, Kat, and I were almost killed sitting at a sidewalk café here in Hopperville by a hit-and-run driver. And a bomb-carrying drone almost killed me just a few days ago."

"Finally, it's hard to talk about my FBI tragedy, but I must. We all make mistakes, and I've dedicated my life to helping the family of the boy I shot, and others, as pay back for my heartbreaking misjudgment. I try to be a good and decent person in every way I can, but I'm an imperfect human being." I shrugged and blinked back tears.

"Thank you for your attention. Please do your duty, apply your common sense, weigh the facts, and return with a verdict in favor of the plaintiff." I sat down, relieved it was all over. I'd dreaded the last statements, but the jury needed to hear them.

Shay whispered, "Well done. Just the right tone." I smiled a thank-you and looked at the judge. He was staring at me but said nothing. The crows were still.

"Mr. Papageorgio, you may proceed."

"Thank you, Your Honor." Papageorgio rose and walked straight to the front of the jury box. He placed both hands on the railing and looked at each juror, taking his time, I'm sure trying to connect as I had.

"Ladies and gentlemen, you've heard plaintiff's argument. Despite his assertion to the contrary, the Electric Gun Company provided many warnings. They included warnings about not shooting pregnant women, the elderly or infirm, and those mentally challenged; to avoid shooting at the head and groin; and to avoid shooting someone who could fall onto a sharp object or from a great height. They trained police properly on all these issues. What more could you ask for?"

He began pacing in front of them. "What you didn't hear my colleague say is that, prior to the theatrics that defense has staged in this courtroom, the Electric Gun Company had no information upon which to base a warning. They rigorously tested the Electric Gun in goats and dogs and human volunteers, and not once—I repeat, not once—did they show any cardiac effects in humans. How could they warn about the risks of an event that hadn't taken place?" He shrugged and elevated his brow in an incredulous look.

"And even today—the point I raised with Dr. Dumont—one cannot exclude a coincidence that the pain of the Electric Gun triggered a heart attack that then caused the ventricular fibrillation in Mr.

Carpenter. Remember, it was Dr. Dumont's *opinion*"—Papageorgio searched the faces of the jurors—"that the Electric Gun caused the ventricular fibrillation. It was not fact. Temporality does not prove causality." He struck the railing with the palm of his hand to emphasize his statement.

Mrs. Donahue creased her forehead and shook her head almost imperceptibly, perhaps disagreeing with Papageorgio's last assertion.

"And with Jared Simpson, the association is even less certain because there was no ECG recording. Jared Simpson was excited, he was delirious and, despite counselor's disparaging remarks,"—he pointed at me—"excited delirium was the most likely cause of death. Another expert—ridiculed by Mr. Judge but in reality a doctor of chemistry with expertise in electrical matters of the heart—concluded that excited delirium was the cause of death." He emphasized that point with a raised index finger.

"Further, I remind you that the unfortunate death of Jared Simpson occurred *prior* to the courtroom drama enacted for you earlier today. So, even if the Electric Gun can cause ventricular fibrillation—and I do not accept that as fact—that knowledge was unavailable at the time Jared Simpson was shot. Therefore, no warnings could have been issued that might have prevented his death."

He stopped, planted both feet firmly in front of the jurors, hands on the railing, and addressed each one. "Finally, to conclude that the deaths of Jared's wife, Melanie, and his son, Ryan, were due to the Electric Gun is preposterous and challenges the imagination. This is a claim without substance to justify an increase in the compensatory award plaintiff has requested.

"I say to you what defense has said. Do your duty but remember, based on the preponderance of the evidence presented, the Electric Gun Company could have had no reasonable expectation that a shooting from its gun would prove fatal. There has been no evidence the Electric Gun was unreasonably dangerous, and the company did not breach its duty by failing to warn. It cannot be held responsible for deaths that coincidentally occurred when someone was shot with the Electric Gun. How can you believe a lawyer suing for excessive use of force when he himself has been accused of that crime?" He stopped and stared dramatically at me. "That's like believing a convicted sex offender suing another person for sexual assault. You must find in favor of the defense. I ask you to do so. Thank you." He sat down, his face reddened and forehead wet. He shook out a handkerchief and wiped his head and neck.

"Thank you both," Maplethorpe said. "This trial is concluded, save for the jury's deliberation and verdict."

He turned to the jury. "You must now select one of your members as the presiding juror to manage your deliberations. As I have instructed you, the liability issues with regard to the claims against the Hopperville Police Department have been resolved, and your deliberations in that regard should only concern damages. You are to reach a verdict regarding the liability of the Electric Gun Company and for the total compensatory damages to be awarded. That amount should be divided between the defendants, depending upon each defendant's percentage of fault—that is, how much each contributed to cause the plaintiff's damages. Punitive damages are designed to punish and deter future similar conduct, and those would be separate and entered against each defendant individually, dependent upon how egregious the defendant's conduct was and also taking into account the amount that would sufficiently punish.

"Once you reach a verdict by unanimous agreement, hand it to the bailiff, and I will read it in open court. You are to talk to no one besides one another until you've reached a unanimous decision. You are now excused to commence your deliberations."

The jury filed out, and then began the pins-and-needles wait.

CHAPTER FORTY-EIGHT

DOUG ZIPES

As we collected our papers in the empty courtroom and piled them into boxes and briefcases, Papageorgio and Slaughter were doing the same at their table. Though we were no more than fifteen feet apart, neither side said anything, and we carefully avoided eye contact. I was still upset about the Hamden ambush and Papageorgio's closing remarks. Shay seemed uncertain about what lawyers did after a trial ended—were we now friends, colleagues, drinking buddies, or still enemy combatants?—so he just kept his mouth shut.

Slaughter broke the spell.

"Good job, Odinga," he said, looking across the tables. "Not bad for a bl—" He caught himself. "Young kid." I think Slaughter liked leaving racist words hanging. "Too bad you had to lie to do it though."

"Quiet, Lee," Papageorgio hissed. "Now's not the time to—"

"The hell it isn't. I was quiet throughout the trial, just like you told me. I didn't say hardly a word. Now I can do what the hell I want. And that skinny prick"—he pointed at Shay, his jowls jiggling and face flushed—"lied to the jury about everything, the testing, the warnings, our expert. Everything. If we lose this trial, it's his fault, and I'll make him pay for it."

Slaughter's threat jarred me from my funk. "Hold on, Beverly," I said, straightening up from filling my briefcase. I pronounced Beverly in three distinct syllables, Bev er ly. "Are you threatening my cocounsel? Is that what you're doing?" I moved to stand in front of Shay.

"Oh, my goodness. Will you look at that, Papa?" Slaughter said, pointing at me. "The big, bad bear aroused from hibernation. No, not a threat, big, bad Bear, just a statement. That goes for you too. Both of you will pay—and you'll pay dearly—if we lose. You think the crazy van driver or the drone was badass? Just wait."

"Jesus Christ, Lee! Are you nuts, saying those things, and here in court?" Papageorgio grabbed Slaughter by both shoulders and turned him back to his own table. "Just shut your goddamned mouth, okay? You want to spout off, do it when I'm not here. Go into your bathroom, close the door, and shout at the mirror."

He released Slaughter and pushed him toward one of the empty boxes. "Now, let's finish packing and get out of here. The court will call us when they have a verdict."

I stood with my fists clenched, staring at Slaughter, who stared right back. After the Hamden testimony, I was ready to tear into someone, and Slaughter was about to be the one. Slaughter started to walk around the table toward me, and I walked to meet him.

Shay tried to bring us back to our senses. "What are you guys doing? We pride ourselves on a system of laws to settle disagreements. As long as people are talking, they're not fighting. We've just finished exercising that principle, and now you two are going to battle physically? What the hell did we just waste a week doing?"

He jumped in front of me, and Papageorgio did the same to Slaughter.

"Not now, Bear," Shay said softly, his hands pushing against my chest, holding me back. "Calm down. The guy's an asshole. We've got this case won. Don't mess it up. You did what your sister asked. Let it go."

That hit home. My eyes moistened, and my muscles relaxed. "You're right. Let's finish packing and get out of here."

Papageorgio must've said something similar to Slaughter, who backed off. They continued to clear their table.

I gave the bailiff instructions to call the office when the jury reached a verdict, and we left the courthouse. I dropped Shay off at the office and went on to see Kat in the hospital.

CHAPTER FORTY-NINE

"**W**here's Kat? Where's my wife?" I couldn't hide my panic when I found her room empty, the second time this had happened.

"She's been moved back to intensive care," the nurse said.

"Why wasn't I called?" My voice was harsh, too harsh. After all, it wasn't the nurse's fault Kat had relapsed.

"You'll have to ask her doctor. All I know is she wasn't doing too well, and Dr. Abraham ordered her back to intensive care."

I walked quickly to the ICU, my heart thudding in my chest. Abraham was just coming out of her room. He took me by the arm and walked me to the visitor's lounge.

"What happened?" I asked, again sitting on that same Naugahyde couch. I looked around the room. I was beginning to hate coming here. The lounge always held bad news.

"She's relapsed," Abraham said with a sad expression. "Her liver deteriorated in the last several hours. I don't know why."

"How bad?" I ran a hand through my hair. I couldn't believe it. Not again. My eyes moistened.

"She slipped back into a coma, and her kidneys have slowed making urine."

"Dialysis again?" I asked, hopefully.

He shook his head. "Not this time, at least not yet. We'll give her a little spell to see if her liver can recover some function on its own. But it shows how brittle she is. A small change one way or the other—maybe too much fluid or too little—makes a big difference in her clinical status."

"Can emotional strain do it?" I knew I'd put her under intense pressure by questioning Sparafucile. I hoped Abraham's answer would be no.

"Absolutely."

So, my fault. Another cross to bear. "The trial's made her a bit tense," I said.

"She needs a new liver. A transplant. Long term, she doesn't stand a chance without that. I'll upgrade her status to semiemergency. That'll bump her up in the queue."

"What're her chances?" I asked, fingers crossed.

"I think she'll rebound from her present setback, but without a transplant, several months at best. Hopefully we'll find a donor in that time." His face was grim, and his tone didn't seem hopeful. He rose and walked to the coffee machine. "Want some?" he asked.

"No thanks." I joined him at the counter. "I get the feeling you're not telling me everything, Dr. Abraham. Is there something you're hiding?"

"Not hiding, just haven't told you yet." He took my arm, and we sat down again. "We've begun the workup for a liver transplant, and it turns out she's going to be hard to match because of her unusual blood and tissue type."

"What's that mean?" I asked. The thudding started again, faster than before.

"The ordinary wait time on the liver transplant list is six months to a year. Her immune system is complicating the match, so it may take even longer to find a donor."

"Hold on," I said, staring at him. "You're telling me she may have several months to live without a transplant, but the wait time to get a liver may be longer than a year. Do I have that right?"

"I'm afraid so." His face was drawn, and his eyes even sadder than before.

"I can't let this happen. I won't let this happen." I shook my head. I could feel my muscles tense. "Money's not an issue. I'll take her anywhere. If they can't do it here at the Medical Center, we'll go to the Cleveland Clinic, Johns Hopkins, wherever they're doing liver transplants. To Europe if we need to, but she has to get that transplant. She *will* get that transplant."

"Let's not panic just yet. I'll do my best to find a place urgently. But there're a lot of sick people waiting for a liver, Mr. Judge, and her rare immune system complicates things."

I stood. I felt an overwhelming urgency to hold her in my arms, tell her I loved her. "I need to go see her. Will she know me?"

"Doubtful," he said, "but do go talk to her. We never really know what a comatose patient perceives."

She had that yellowish tinge to her skin and eyes again and was back in cotton restraints. Her muscles twitched spasmodically like she was having a bad dream. I leaned close and stroked her hair, wrapped her in my arms, and kissed her lightly on the lips. "I love you."

I sat at the edge of her bed and watched her breathe. We'd just rebuilt our world, and it was on the verge of collapsing.

I rubbed my eyes to clear the mist. "I love you, Kat," I said, to her as well as to myself. "Fight for us, baby. Fight to live. Buy some time. We'll find you a liver somewhere. Don't give up. We're in this together. I won't let you down."

A nurse entered the room. "Mr. Judge, a man named Shay just called the nurses' station. He tried to reach you on your cell phone, but it was not working. He left a message." She checked her notes. "'Pins and needles over. Jury has reached a verdict. Meet me at the courtroom.'"

CHAPTER FIFTY

Shay and I had to push our way through a crowd of thirty or forty people standing outside the courtroom door, trying to get in. Inside, spectators were jam-packed, with an overflow lining the back wall. Police Commissioner Richard Dawson, Fisheye, Shorty, Bennett, Verity, and a group of other cops I didn't know were there. So were Dr. Dumont and his patient, Gerald Carpenter. Juror thirty sat in the last row, as he had throughout the trial. He wore a gray Salty Dog sweatshirt. CNN, MSNBC, and other networks held cell phone cameras ready to record. An artist in a front row was sketching.

"All rise for the Honorable Felix J. Maplethorpe III," intoned the bailiff. Maplethorpe entered through the back door.

"Be seated," the judge said after he sat down. He looked around the packed courtroom, surprise on his face.

"Considering this large group," he said, "I must warn you to keep silent when I read the jury's verdict. Any outbursts will not be tolerated, and spectators will be removed from the courtroom and subject to sanctions. Now, all stand for the jury."

They filed in. Shay and I studied their faces to get a hint of the decision. Several looked directly at Slaughter, then at us, but betrayed no helpful expression.

When they'd been seated, Maplethorpe said, "Ladies and gentlemen of the jury, have you reached a verdict?"

"We have, Your Honor," Demetrios said as the presiding juror.

"Please hand your verdict to the bailiff."

Maplethorpe read the paper the bailiff handed him. He turned to the courtroom and read it out loud.

"We the jury unanimously find the Electric Gun Company breached its duty by recklessly and in bad faith selling a product they knew or should have known could kill and failing to warn users about this possibility. Further, we conclude that the Electric Gun was culpable for the death of Jared Simpson. We find the Electric Gun Company did not play any direct, causal role in the deaths of Ryan Simpson or Melanie Simpson.

"We find for the plaintiff a total award of $16 million, to be distributed as follows: $3 million compensatory damages assigned to the Electric Gun Company and $3 million compensatory damages assigned to the Hopperville Police Department. We find $9 million in punitive damages assigned to the Electric Gun Company and

$1 million in punitive damages assigned to the Hopperville Police Department."

Shay and I shook hands, hugged, and pounded each other on the back. "We did it," I said. "We did it!"

Murmurs rose throughout the courtroom but no outbursts. Maplethorpe's warning had been sufficient for the spectators.

But not for Slaughter. "You fucking sons of bitches," he said in a loud whisper across the tables, raising a fist at us. "I warned you. Watch your backs, motherfuckers."

"Thank you for your service," Maplethorpe said to the jury, not hearing Slaughter's threat. "You're dismissed. This case is closed, and court is adjourned." He rose quickly and exited.

Once Maplethorpe was gone, spectators erupted with "I told you so," "They deserved it," "Maybe now they'll warn the cops not to aim at the chest," "That's a bullshit verdict," "Electric Gun should appeal," and "I think the trial was rigged."

"Great job on Hamden," I said to Shay. "You bailed me out and helped win this." I put my hand on his shoulder. "I need a partner, not just an associate but full partner."

"This a job offer? You sure you want a skinny black Kenyan with a weird hairstyle for a partner?"

"I do. I told you color wouldn't matter once we won. The world is colorblind to winners. You're a winner."

"If you're sure, I'm sure," Shay said. "You got yourself a partner."

We shook hands again and hugged.

I knew the Electric Gun Company would appeal the verdict, so it might be a while before we saw any of that money. Most likely, Papageorgio and I would enter discussions to avoid another trial neither of us wanted. I'd happily settle for half of the $12 million from Electric Gun to put all this behind us. Their liability insurance most likely covered the $3 million in compensatory damages but would not cover the punitive amount. The money from the Hopperville cops should happen quickly.

My thoughts turned to Kat, and the win became much less significant. I intended to pull out all the stops to save her. I'd have enough money to take her anywhere and pay any medical expenses her health insurance didn't cover to get her a new liver.

"How about a celebratory steak dinner at Ruth's Chris?" Shay said. "We deserve it."

"Maybe tomorrow. I'm worried about Kat." I told him about her setback. "I'm going to spend the night with her in the hospital."

Kat's condition had improved slightly, the nurse said. The coma had lightened, and the jaundice lessened. She was still nonresponsive, though the twitches had stopped. I sat next to her on the bed, stroked her hair, and kissed her lips. "Keep fighting, darling. You're going to win this battle and then the war. We're going to find you a liver somewhere, no matter how long or how much it takes. I promise."

I started the night in the chair next to her bed, just watching her sleep and holding her hand. Her twitching lessened after several hours, and I lay down on the extra bed in the room, eventually drifting into a restless sleep. I woke every several hours to check on her, but she seemed to be doing okay.

When I woke the next morning, Kat was sitting up in bed, nibbling a piece of toast.

"Well, look at you," I said, kissing her and getting a taste of bread crumbs. "Back among the living."

"Sorry to duck out on you like that," she said, giving me a hug and a smile. "I guess I fade in and out, depending on how this damn liver is doing." She poked her belly.

I pulled up a chair and sat down next to her bed. "We're going to get you a new one."

She reached for my hand. "Dr. Abraham said it might be a while. I've got some sort of weird antibody makeup."

"I've thought it all out," I said. "We're—"

"Wait, before you tell me. How did the trial go?"

I gave her a CliffsNotes summary.

"Hamden's a bastard," Kat said. "I'm so sorry I—"

I put my finger to her lips. "Past history. Back to what I was going to say. You need prolonged recovery time while we try to find a liver from someone as weird. The perfect place is my folks' farmhouse."

"Hattie's still there?"

"Yes."

Hattie'd been my parents' live-in housekeeper and cook when they got older and a bit frail. After they died, she stayed on, taking care of the house.

She was a tough lady, in her sixties. Her hands were always like sandpaper from gardening, chopping kindling for the fireplace, and doing general repairs around the house. She was the best plumber for miles around.

She piled her gray hair in a braided roll like a coiled snake on top of her head, making her five foot something six inches taller. Her ample figure belied the fact she was always trying some strange new diet to lose weight. She'd eat only radishes one week, grapefruits the next, no carbs after that, and then only carbs. Once she ate dark-meat canned tuna fish for a month. Nothing helped her slim down or dampened her enthusiasm for the next great culinary experiment.

Hattie'd be there to help Kat, along with visiting nurses from the Bloomington Hospital. The farmhouse was only a few miles from the hospital and an hour from Hopperville. I'd be able to drive to the office if I had to.

"Great plan. Have you talked to Dr. Abraham about it?"

"Yeah," I said, giving her hand a squeeze. "Right after you had the dialysis. He was all for it once you stabilized."

She brought my hand to her lips. "What would I ever do without you, my love?"

"I don't know," I said, "but the feeling's mutual."

CHAPTER FIFTY-ONE

I picked up Shay the following evening, and we drove to Ruth's Chris. This was the best I'd felt in a while. The trial was over, and Kat had stabilized without dialysis. The only anxiety I had now was to find her a liver. Somehow, somewhere, I would do that.

Sitting through the stress of Mark Hamden's testimony made me realize something about myself. Stress doesn't *change* who you are; rather, it *reveals* who you are. It unmasks your core, what you're made of. For the first time since I'd left the FBI, I felt I could forgive myself for committing that horrible mistake. Sure, I was a flawed human being, but who among us wasn't? I'd tried to make amends, to live my life as a good person, and six objective people in the jury who heard my story believed it and believed in me. That made all the difference.

"I talked to my folks last night," Shay was saying, "and of course they were thrilled. They were going to call the Hammer first thing today. He'd be proud. I told them what you said about the world being colorblind to winners."

I smiled and glanced at him, keeping my eyes on the road. "And what was their response?"

"They weren't so sure and a little disappointed I wouldn't be moving back east. For some reason, they thought I'd return home after the trial. But they were happy about me becoming a partner."

"Why don't you invite them for a visit? I bet they'd like Hopperville after they found how nice life can be in a small town."

We enjoyed a great steak dinner. We rehashed the trial, what we might've done differently, how Maplethorpe performed as a judge, and what our approach should be going into discussions with the Electric Gun Company to avoid another trial but still get a big slice of the award. Once the newspapers published the trial verdict, I predicted we'd be swamped with calls from potential plaintiffs around the US, so the future looked bright. Judge and Odinga, Attorneys at Law would specialize in police brutality cases, especially those involving use of the Electric Gun.

Shay seemed a bit wobbly as we left the restaurant. We'd been there three hours, eating and talking ... and drinking. "You okay?" I asked.

"My head's buzzing," he said with a wry smile as we walked to my car. "Feeling that last glass of wine—and the ones before that have all ganged up on me. How about you? Okay to drive?"

"I am," I said. "Well below a DUI level. You can sleep it off in the morning. No work tomorrow. We deserve a vacation day. Do something fun. Go to the zoo, play golf, or see a movie." I yawned. It'd been a long time since I'd had a good night's sleep.

We took off our jackets and laid them across the back seat of the car, climbed into my BMW, and I slowly drove out of the parking lot. I stayed under the speed limit and came to a full stop at the red light. I didn't think I was DUI vulnerable, but no sense tempting fate.

I saw a car pull out of the lot and follow close behind me, low beams not threatening but sticking a car or two in the rear. I made several stops and turns, but the car stayed glued to me. I glanced at Shay. His head was back, eyes closed, snoring softly. *That didn't take him long*, I thought with a smile.

Remembering Slaughter's threats, after several miles I started to become concerned. Would he make good on them and try another hit? I stomped on the accelerator, but the car behind sped also.

I was about to dial 911 when we hit a dark stretch of the Keystone Parkway and the trailing car flashed blue and red lights. It was a cop! I glanced at the speedometer and saw I was doing sixty in a forty-five-mile-an-hour zone. He was pulling me over for speeding.

"Shay, wake up." He didn't stir. I reached over and shook his arm. "Shay, wake up."

"Wha ... wha ... what?" he asked, finally opening his eyes and sitting up.

"We're getting stopped for speeding."

That jarred him. He became fully alert, his eyes wide as he spun around to look at the car behind us. "Oh my God," he said, panic in his voice. "A cop! That's the last thing I need."

"Easy. It's okay. This isn't New York City. I'm here with you in Hopperville."

"Maybe so, but I'm still black and you're still white."

He was right. After the trial, I couldn't be very popular with the Hopperville cops either.

I pulled to the side of the road and waited, watching in my side-view mirror as the police car pulled up behind. A cop got out of the car, closed his door, adjusted his belt, put on his hat, and slowly, deliberately walked to my car.

Sparafucile! Oh my God! And he was smiling!

I locked the car doors. I reached for my new phone, but I'd put it in the inside pocket of my jacket that I'd flung across the back seat of the car. As I turned to grab the jacket, I heard a hard rap on the window and saw a hand motion to roll it down.

Not before I get my phone.

The rap was insistent. When I didn't respond, Sparafucile tried the door, but the lock held. His face was fearsome now, with lips drawn, eyes narrowed, and brow furrowed. He took some metal object from his belt and crashed it against the window. The glass splintered into a thousand cobwebs but didn't buckle.

My heart pounded as Sparafucile raised his hand again. The glass would surely shatter this time. I turned the ignition key, hit the accelerator, and we roared away.

I glanced at Shay. He seemed paralyzed, unmoving, just staring straight ahead. "Shay, reach behind and get my jacket. My cell phone is in the inside pocket. We need to call for help."

He didn't move. "Shay! Shay! Listen to me. Get my jacket in the back seat." Still no response. He was in shock. Keeping one hand on the steering wheel, I groped behind to grab my jacket. But I couldn't reach over the back of the seat to get it and almost drove off the road trying.

The police station was in the same building as my office, and I headed there, but I figured if we reached a populated area, a gas station or an all-night grocery—any place with people—we'd be safe. The problem was at eleven thirty at night, there were no populated areas or open stores in Hopperville. There were also very few cars on the road. I passed only one.

The flashing lights reappeared in my rearview mirror, gaining on me. Even driving a BMW, I doubted I could outrun him. He kept getting closer.

Suddenly, I felt a jolt. Sparafucile crashed into my rear bumper as he tried to force me off the road. My car swerved with each hit, but I kept it on the macadam. We were reaching ninety miles an hour when Sparafucile pulled alongside me, the front of his car even with my rear wheels. Sparafucile cut to the right, collided with my left rear wheel, and spun me around. Frantically, I turned opposite to the skid and hit the brakes, but I couldn't stop the momentum. The car lifted and barrel-rolled over the side of the road. The airbags exploded, hit me in the face, and I blacked out.

I woke struggling to breathe, fighting the airbag. The windshield was shattered, the front of the car crumpled against a tree trunk. A tree limb had bayonetted through the front window in between Shay and me, narrowly missing us both.

"Shay, unbuckle your seat belt and get out. Hurry." He didn't respond. He seemed unhurt but appeared dazed.

I smelled smoke and saw a tiny flicker of flame beneath the front hood. With wobbly hands, I unbuckled my seat belt and tried to open my door. Jammed. I climbed into the back seat, grabbed my jacket for the cell phone, forced open the rear door, and jumped out.

I ran around to the passenger side, yanked open the door, and tried to pull Shay out. The flames were more intense, and I was afraid the gas tank would soon explode.

"Shay, help me. Undo your seat belt. You've got to get out now." He didn't move. I reached in and tried to free him, but the buckle was smashed and wouldn't release. I took out my pen knife, cut the seat belt, and dragged Shay from the car. We were on an embankment and rolled down about twenty feet when the gas tank exploded, and the car shot up in flames. The impact of the explosion tossed us into tall grass another ten feet from the road.

When my vision cleared, I looked up to see that Sparafucile had stopped his car a few hundred yards down the road and was running back toward us. The gun in his hand glinted in the silvery moonlight.

"You're both under arrest," he yelled as he drew near. I watched him stand next to the flaming car and peer in to see if we might be toast. Finding nothing, he scanned the area. I heard him mutter, "Where the fuck are they?"

I thought, *If I can just dial 911 and keep hidden until help arrives, we could get out of here alive.*

Shay began to stir. He sat up and looked around, a bewildered expression on his face. I tried to hold him down in the grass and keep him quiet, but he shook me off and stood. His eyes locked onto

Sparafucile standing on the road, back-illuminated by the car flames. The cop could've been the devil himself glaring at us from the fires of Hades.

"Aaaaiiiieeee!" Shay screamed and took off running out of the woods, onto the road. Helpless, I saw Sparafucile take aim and shoot. The bullet caught Shay in the right hip, and he fell, crashing onto the pavement. He tried to get up, but his leg crumpled, and he went down again, shrieking in pain.

"Don't move, you black bastard," Sparafucile yelled, coming up fast. Shay tried to stand again but collapsed. Sparafucile straddled him and pressed the gun against Shay's forehead. I heard him say, "Not such a hot-shit lawyer now, are you, motherfucker? You're done, and then comes the Bear."

Even though I was unarmed, I scrambled up the embankment and was about to charge Sparafucile when I heard someone say, "Can I help?"

I stopped at the edge of the road and watched Sparafucile whirl to see a tall, gray-haired man running toward him. He holstered his Glock. "Who the fuck are you?" he shouted.

"Retired EMT. You guys whipped past me a couple of minutes ago. I sped up to see if I could help. When I saw the crash, I dialed 911. Ambulance should be here shortly."

I could hear sirens in the distance.

"Yeah, he needs help. He just blacked out," Sparafucile said, his face a blank mask. "I'm Lieutenant Sparafucile. This guy took off when I tried to stop him for a burned-out taillight. He crashed, got out of his car, and ran. I shot him when he wouldn't stop. See if you can stop the hemorrhage. I need to go back to my car to call in."

Sparafucile ran off. He hopped into his car and drove away as the ambulance pulled up.

CHAPTER FIFTY-TWO

It was close to seven in the morning before they let me see Shay. He was still a bit groggy from the anesthesia, but the doctor said he was out of the woods after four units of blood and a new titanium hip.

"How do you feel?" I asked as he sucked on some ice chips. He blinked several times, trying to focus on me. It was a stupid question, but I didn't know what else to say.

"Like shit," he said, his words a little slurred and his face pale. "How would you feel if you almost died in a car accident, got shot, and had a gun pressed against your head by a crazy cop bent on killing you?" He pointed to his forehead where I could see the circular outline of a gun barrel. "I've never been so frightened in my life." He shivered, and tears welled up. "I must've blacked out when Sparafucile put the gun to my head—from the bleeding or maybe because I knew I was a dead man. Thanks for saving me." He stifled a moan.

"I'm so sorry." I spooned him another mouthful of ice and told him about the EMT guy. "I don't know his name, but he was the one who saved you, not me. Sparafucile must've figured he couldn't shoot you in cold blood with the EMT as a witness. He took off so fast I don't think he even saw me standing by the side of the road. The EMT controlled the bleeding until the ambulance arrived."

Shay slurped the ice. "My God, winning my first trial, and I almost get killed. I can't stay here if that's what the law's going to be like," he said, shaking his head.

I pulled up a chair alongside his bed. "No, it's not, and you know it. This has never happened to me before," I said, trying to put a smile on my face to lighten the conversation.

"Yeah, but how many police brutality cases have you done before this one?"

He was right. This was going to be a new world for me—hopefully, for us. But suing the police for brutality wasn't going to be popular with a lot of people.

"Watch your back," Shay said, pointing his finger at me. "Sparafucile said you're next."

I'd stopped packing the Glock after Melanie died and we got involved with trial preparations. I guess it was time to start carrying again. It might be a good idea for Shay as well. I'd have to teach him how to shoot.

"You know anything about guns?" I asked.

He shook his head. The sudden movement caused him to gag on an ice chip and triggered a bout of coughing. "Oh," he groaned, pressing down on his new hip. "That hurts."

"Take some time off," I said, standing. I figured he needed to rest. "Visit your folks until this dies down. Sparafucile will be captured by then, and we can—"

He frowned. "You wish. His buddies must be hiding him. That Fisheye guy. Or his mother."

"Maybe, but if he's going to come after me, he's got to come out of hiding," I said.

"Aren't you scared?" Shay asked, a concerned look on his face.

"Yes, but that just makes me hyper alert. I've dealt with his kind before."

"Not with cracked ribs."

I smiled. "Maybe not, but they won't affect my aim."

"I'm going to take you up on your offer," he said, getting comfortable in the bed and starting to close his eyes. "As soon as they release me, I'm going back to New York to stay with my folks. Call me when this is over, and we can talk about the future."

I spent the next few days in the hospital, alternating visits between Kat and Shay. I slept on the extra bed in Kat's room. Requests to accept police brutality lawsuits came rolling in, as I expected, and I kept busy fielding them.

I stopped by Shay's room the day he was discharged.

"I'm good, Bear," he said, smiling as he walked the length of the corridor with only a slight limp. "I wish my head healed as quickly as my hip."

"Nightmares?"

"Yeah, and daytime's not much better. I keep picturing that bastard standing over me pressing that gun to my head."

Goddamn Sparafucile, I thought. Two deaths, a suicide, and the mental anguish of Kat and Shay, and the sonofabitch still on the loose. His buddies had to be protecting him.

A week later, we moved to the farmhouse. Southern Indiana was beautiful this time of year, especially Brown County with its bumper crop of late-blooming wildflowers sprinkled among orange, yellow, and red foliage. Our farm bordered the southwest corner of the state park, and I was looking forward to walks among the trees.

I'd bought a wheelchair, so Kat could enjoy the park as well. She was too weak to walk unassisted but was gaining strength daily. The jaundice had disappeared, and her appetite was returning. The blood test on her last hospital day showed improved liver function. She was starting to look like my lovely again.

Hattie was in the garden as we drove up. She greeted us with hugs and laughter. "Welcome home."

"Glad to be back," I said, looking around. I hadn't been in the homestead for a year or more.

She opened the door and ushered us in.

"Same old place. Nothing's changed," I said.

"Not so. Come see the bedroom," Hattie said, leading the way.

She'd transformed the master bedroom on the first floor into a hospital room, complete with an IV stand, monitors, and an adjustable bed. She'd installed a walk-in tub for Kat. "I have visiting nurses on standby," she said. "But you're looking so good, Kat, I don't think you'll need them."

"Thanks, Hattie," Kat said, taking her hand. "I hope not."

"I've got dinner ready," Hattie said. "I can bring it to you in bed if you're tired from the drive down or we can eat in the dining room. Whatever works for you."

"Just give me a few minutes to freshen up," Kat said, "and then let's try the dining room. If I get tired, I can always lie down."

Hattie and I left Kat alone and walked room to room through the house. I tested doors, windows, and locks. All seemed solid.

"Not FBI again?" Hattie asked, concerned. "Chasing bad guys?"

"No." I told her about Slaughter and his threats, and Sparafucile. "Kat doesn't know what happened to Shay, so don't mention anything. She was scared plenty when the bastard arrested her."

"I would think so," Hattie said.

"Time enough to tell her if—when, I hope—Shay comes back to work in the firm."

Over the next four weeks, Kat's strength returned, and she was soon working by my side four or five hours a day. I called Shay several times each week. He was seeing a therapist who specialized in posttraumatic stress and seemed to be returning toward normal. He was sleeping better and spending time with his folks.

Kat and I started each day with breakfast, then a short walk through the park, and we'd work until lunch. She'd nap, help me for another hour or two, and we'd finish with a longer walk in the woods. In the beginning, I rolled the wheelchair along, but she never needed it. As our walks lengthened, the trail roughened, and I stopped bringing it. On one trip, I thought I saw Snooky but couldn't be sure. I figured she must be getting ready to hibernate for the winter. I saw her distinguishing claw marks on several birch trees near the stream she liked, so I knew she was still around. She scratched the trees to mark her territory and keep other bears away.

I was never without my Glock, day or night. At one point, I tried teaching Kat to shoot, but merely handling the gun made her hand wobble, and I soon gave up.

Papageorgio called for a meeting to talk about the court's judgment. That would mean a half day away from the farm.

"Kat, come with me. I don't want to leave you alone."

"I'm not alone. I've got Hattie, and no one's going to mess with her. She's on an all-spinach diet now and determined to grow Popeye biceps."

I laughed. "She probably will. Seriously, though, I don't want to leave you just with Hattie." The police had put out an all-points bulletin to bring in Sparafucile for attempted murder, but no results so far. I hoped he was far away by now.

"I'll be fine. Not to worry. Do your thing and bring back lots of money."

Against better judgment, I drove to Hopperville two days later. Before I left, I called the Bloomington police to let them know the ladies would be alone. I left strict instructions for Kat and Hattie to call 911 at the slightest threat. I wanted to leave my Glock, but neither would take it.

The meeting with Papageorgio went better than I'd anticipated. He'd flown in from Boston, and we met at my office, sitting in the conference room. To avoid Slaughter and Hopperville police appealing the court's judgment and setting up a retrial neither of us wanted, he offered a $6 million cash settlement from the Electric Gun Company and $3.5 million from the Hopperville Police Department. "We want to put this behind us as quickly as possible and move on," he said. He had approvals from CEO Slaughter and Police Commissioner Dawson.

"What about warnings?" I asked, hesitating. The dollar amount was fine, but I wanted to be sure they educated future users about the possibility of cardiac arrest. "I'll agree if you'll warn about potential heart problems and make sure Hopperville police receive new training documents."

"Warnings already written," Papageorgio said with a nod. He reached into his briefcase and handed me a letter. "This will be mailed to all gun buyers tomorrow—past and future—if you agree to the settlement today. We'll add it to the brochure, website, and all sales from now on."

The letter warned of "a remote possibility of cardiac arrest" following a chest shot and for users to "avoid aiming at the chest if possible, avoid trigger pulls exceeding five seconds, and be prepared to resuscitate victims unresponsive after a shooting," everything they should have said from the beginning.

"Can you put a number on 'remote'?" I asked, handing the letter back to him.

He shrugged. "I wish I could, but we have no data. I think you'd agree cardiac arrest is uncommon, but how uncommon, we don't know. You raised some good points about keeping track of chest shots. The term 'remote' is as close as we can come. Slaughter agreed to that wording."

I supposed I could object, but I had no information either. As long as they included cardiac arrest as a possibility, even remote, that was probably as good as I'd get. To insist on a wording change would slow the whole process, since Papageorgio would have to go back to Slaughter for approval.

"Deal," I said, extending my hand. I knew he hadn't written the letter for me. It was to prevent future lawsuits by transferring liability to the shooter. The warning protected the Electric Gun Company. "We told you about the heart risk," they could claim. In the future, I suspected only cops would be sued for inappropriate use of force.

"You guys played pretty rough," I said with a frown.

"I return the sentiment," he said, his brow also creased. "You pushed Sparafucile hard."

"Maybe so, but Hamden had a grudge to settle. Using him was dishonest." My heart pounded as I remembered. I guess I hadn't totally forgiven myself after all. Shay had to deal with his posttraumatic stress, and so did I.

"Dishonest? No." He swept the idea away with the back of his hand. "Deceitful? Maybe. But nothing's untouchable when I litigate, Counselor." He locked eyes with me. "You know the Gadsden flag with the coiled rattlesnake that says, 'Don't tread on me'? That's what I want anybody looking to sue Electric Gun to think about. Hamden gave me a shot at influencing how the jury saw you and how they might decide the verdict. I took it."

"Didn't work," I said, staring back at him.

"Maybe not. You're not so squeaky clean either."

"What're you getting at?" I asked, bristling. I pushed my chair back from the conference table.

"Zabriskie," he said with a thin smile. "You took a shot in the dark. You never found Slaughter's secretary, and you had no evidence she had records of the gun starting VF in humans. You planted that seed in the jury's mind with no proof. Same with the three guys who were going to bust up you and your partner."

He was right. But I ignored him and rose to let him know we were done. "When will I receive payment?"

He stood also. "Within the next thirty days. I need to hear from my insurance company. By the way, I was impressed how your sidekick stepped in. Odinga has a great future."

I told him what had happened to us.

"I'm sorry to hear that. We play rough but not that rough. Sparafucile is a bad apple. I had no choice but to defend him, but what he did has nothing to do with our gun. That's still a good product."

I was done arguing. I held out my hand. "Goodbye. I hope I never see you again."

CHAPTER FIFTY-THREE

The meeting took a little more than an hour, and I was back on the road by ten that morning.

Halfway home, my new cell phone rang.

"Bear, where are you?" Kat asked. I heard terror in her shaking voice.

"Half hour away. What's the matter?"

"Hattie and I are in the kitchen. Somebody's walking around the yard."

I tried to stifle my panic. "Did you call 911?"

"Right away. They put me on hold. When they came back, they asked if I was really sure it was a threat and not just some workman or farmhand wandering around. When I told them I didn't know, they said they'd send someone as soon as they could, but right now all the police officers were busy. I'm scared, Bear. So is Hattie."

"Lock all the doors?"

"Yes."

"Good. Now—" I heard a crash.

"Kat … Kat, what's happening? Kat, are you there?"

Nothing. I floored the accelerator. The two-lane road made it difficult to pass. I slowed for a red light but then drove through it when I saw no other cars at the intersection.

"Kat, talk to me."

No answer. My heart started racing.

"I'm back," she said at last, breathing heavily.

"Thank God. What happened?"

"Hattie saw the guy go around back and went into the bedroom to check what he was doing. He looked at her in the window, and she screamed. I dropped the phone and ran to her, but the guy had disappeared."

"Tell Hattie not to open the door. Not even if it's a cop in uniform."

"Okay."

"Here's what you do," I said. "Hit the panic button on the house alarm. That might rouse some of the neighbors and scare the guy off. Check the locks on all the doors and go into the basement with Hattie. Barricade yourselves in. Don't open the door for anyone except me. I'll be there in twenty-five minutes, sooner if I can."

"I'll lose phone reception in the basement," Kat said.

"Good point, but we'll have to take that chance. With no windows, it's the safest place for you and Hattie. Wait for me there."

Most of the traffic was light and traveling in the opposite direction. I ran several more red lights and stop signs and swerved around cars in the way, narrowly avoiding a couple of crashes. The last thing I wanted was an accident. I hoped I'd spot a cop, maybe even get one to flag me for speeding, but there were none around.

I made it to the farm in the longest twenty minutes of my life. I heard the shrill blast of the house alarm when I was still a block away. A state trooper was parked in the driveway, talking to a tall white guy.

I jumped out of my car. "I'm Bear Judge," I said, running up to them. "This is my house. My wife—"

"Mr. Judge," the cop said, holding his hand up, "slow down. I'm Indiana State Police Officer Stan Dalloway." He smiled and seemed pretty calm. "This is Jim Horner, a meter reader for the Indiana Electric Company. I think he's the guy that upset your wife."

"Oh my God," I said, first noticing that the guy was wearing a brown Indiana Electric Company jacket and cap. "I'm so sorry." I offered my hand to Horner and let out a deep breath. "We're a little hyper." I briefed them about Sparafucile.

"Not a problem, Mr. Judge," Horner said with an understanding look. "I rang the bell to let your wife know I'd be traipsing around looking for the electric meter mounted outside your house. I'm new on this job. I'm sorry I scared her."

"Not your fault. We overreacted." I ran a hand over my wet forehead.

"Forget it, Mr. Judge," the trooper said, touching a finger to the rim of his hat in a half salute. "All part of the job. I'll take false alarms over real ones any day."

"Thank you both," I said, shaking hands with the trooper. "Now, if you'll excuse me, my wife's barricaded herself in the basement. I need to let her out."

I heard them laughing and saying something about Rapunzel as I ran to the house. I was tempted to tell them Rapunzel was imprisoned in a tower, not a basement, but I let it go.

CHAPTER FIFTY-FOUR

BEAR'S PROMISE

The weather began to turn cold, foretelling winter's approach. The trees lost their vibrant leaves and stood naked in the wind; frost nipped the rainbow of wildflowers, and steel-leaden gray skies blanketed out the sun. I hated this time of year when the drab of winter and shorter days dominated the landscape until the first snows redecorated in silvery, pristine whiteness.

To my surprise, this day opened bright, sunny, and not too chilly. I suspected it would be the last nice day for many months.

"You sure you're up for a walk in the woods?" I asked Kat, still a bit jittery after the meter reader encounter a week ago. I had to invite Horner into the house to convince her he wasn't Sparafucile.

"Let's do it, a nice leisurely walk," Kat said. "The weather report predicted a lovely day."

Hattie scrambled eggs for breakfast, with bacon, oniony hash browns, and rye toast.

We sat down at the breakfast table. "Here you are, Kat," Hattie said, serving. "No nerdlings. Eggs just the way you like them."

Kat was a unique scrambled-egg eater. The eggs had to be totally and thoroughly mixed, so no egg white emerged when they were cooked. Any nerdlings—Kat's term for exposed, cooked egg white—had to be surgically extracted from the rest of the scrambled eggs. White flecks among the yellow scramble were unacceptable.

I plopped down alongside Kat. Hattie handed me my plate loaded with nerdlings.

Before I began to eat, I watched Kat's egg-eating ritual, as unique as her nerdling antipathy. She ate in bite-size sandwiches. First, she tore off a corner of the rye toast and buttered it. On this she piled a tiny mouthful of egg, a snippet of potato, and a crispy sliver of bacon, then popped it all in her mouth. A sip of coffee completed the ceremony.

I'd finished second helpings before Kat ate her first.

When we were done, Hattie handed us a knapsack. "Tuna-salad sandwiches, two plums, celery and carrots from the garden, a bag of chips, and coffee, okay?"

"You're a dear," Kat said. "Thanks. We'll bring back any late-blooming berries before the birds eat them all."

"That reminds me. Careful about drunk birds. The early frost killed a lot of the berries, and the birds get drunk eating those fermenting on the ground."

"We'll be careful," I said, laughing. I remembered as a kid watching tipsy birds fly into each other, bump into tree branches, and stagger about on the ground like drunks outside a tavern.

We set off wearing jeans, bulky knit wool sweaters, and hiking shoes. Kat wrapped herself in a woolen scarf as a safeguard against sundown when the day cooled.

I packed my Glock in a sports belt gun holster under my sweater.

The day was beautiful. The woods were alive with flashing fur as the hibernators fattened up on the last mouthfuls they could forage before the snows came. We kept an eye out for Snooky but only saw her fresh scratch marks on several trees. We walked hand in hand until we reached the small stream about a mile from the house.

"Tired?" I asked. Kat looked a little peaked with a moist forehead and pale skin. She was still pretty frail.

"A little," she said with a tiny smile.

"Let's take a rest." I was a bit fatigued also. I'd not kept up my gym routine because of the trial and had grown soft. Amazing how quickly my body deconditioned without regular exercise.

We sat on a rocky overhang and faced the sun, breathing in the warm, fresh air.

I reached for Kat's hand. "I love you," I said, overcome by the stillness of the woods and the peaceful solitude. She folded into my arms, kissed me, and we just stayed there, warming in the sun, alone together, eyes closed, deep in our own thoughts.

A twig snapped, and a shadow fell.

He stood there, in front of us, looming like a giant, blocking out the sun.

Sparafucile, in full police uniform. His face was a dark, malevolent mask with a fake smile that said I-got-you-now.

Kat screamed, but the forest absorbed her cry.

I pushed her from me to reach for my Glock, but Sparafucile was too quick. He was on me in an instant and knocked me off the rock with a hard fist to my chest. As I hit the ground, he seized the gun from my holster and tossed it into the stream. He grabbed handfuls of my sweater and yanked me to my feet. My ribs hadn't healed completely, and splinters of pain stabbed my chest.

With a sneer, he released my sweater. Eyes locked on mine, he unbuckled his duty belt and tossed it aside.

"Mano a mano, motherfucker," he said, standing in front of me with that fake smile, clenching his fists. "I want the pleasure of killing you with my bare hands, slowly and painfully. After that, I'll have the lady for dessert as my reward for a job well done."

"No!" Kat screamed again, running at him. "No! Get away from us. Leave us alone."

He backhanded her hard across the face, like a bothersome fly. She collapsed onto the forest floor, not moving.

"You and me, Counselor. We got a score to settle. Now."

"Kat," I yelled, "run. Get away. Go for help."

She didn't move. My poor wife. I'd dragged her into this.

We circled each other, wary combatants searching for a weakness, probing for an opening to launch an attack.

He made the first move, a sudden, whirling judo kick that glanced off my left shoulder. My thick sweater cushioned much of the blow, but it still rocked me.

I lashed out with a right hand that caught him in the nose and started a trickle of blood.

"Oh," he said, wiping the drip with the heel of his hand, "the lawyer fights back. Let's see how long you last."

He lunged at me and tried to wrap his arms around mine in a frontal bear hug. I fought him off, driving fists into his gut, but I tripped over the rock behind me and went down, dragging him with me. We rolled across the embankment and plunged into the ice-cold water.

Regaining our footing, we traded blow for blow, slugging at each other while standing knee-deep in the rushing stream. My sweater had absorbed a lot of water, and my arms felt like lead. I began to tire, slipped on a rock in the water, and went down on one knee. Sparafucile leaped at me, grabbed my shoulders, and tried to shove my head under the water. I bucked and kicked and finally landed a foot to his groin that made him let go.

I got up and tried to make it to dry ground, to get to Kat.

"Kat," I shouted, "go back to the house and get help. Call 911." She didn't move.

Enraged at what he'd done to Kat, I flew at Sparafucile with renewed force, fists flying. He hung on, dragged me back midstream, and bowled me over. I fell backward, ending up sitting in the water. As I pushed myself to stand, my right hand closed around a rock at the bottom of the stream bed. I hurled it at Sparafucile's head, but the heavy weight of my sweater plus the cold water had sapped my strength, and he easily caught the slow-flying missile.

He stood over me, watching me try to catch my breath while still sitting in the water.

"Now, you son of a bitch, now you die," he shouted. "How do you want me to do it? By drowning or should I just bash your head in with this?" He flipped the fist-sized rock up and down, tossing it from one hand to the other.

"Kat, get help!" I yelled. "Go, run, get help, now!" I was panicked and almost didn't recognize my own voice.

"Too late, Counselor. By the time anybody gets here, you're a dead man."

He pounced on me, raised the rock over his head, and brought it down hard. I twisted to one side, and the stone glanced off my forehead. When he tried a second time, I swung blindly and connected with his jaw. He dropped the stone.

Now he straddled me, grabbed me by the neck with both hands, and forced my head under water. I fought him with my last bit of strength, holding my breath ... holding ... holding ... until I had to breathe. My next breath would fill my lungs with water.

This is what it feels like to die, I thought. *Is this what that poor youngster felt when I shot him?*

Suddenly, his grip loosened, and he rolled off me. I heaved up, gasping and coughing. I sucked in mouthfuls of fresh air.

Sparafucile lay in the water beside me, still as death. The left side of his face was in shreds, ripped to the bone, bleeding, his left eye hanging by a strand. A gash in his neck pumped blood into the stream, and red ripples swirled around his face.

I heard the growl.

BEAR'S PROMISE

Snooky rose on her hind legs over Sparafucile, flailing her curved claws and snarling. She bent down, grabbed him by the neck in her powerful jaws, lifted, and shook him like a stuffed doll.

I rose from the stream. "Snooky, stop!" I shouted, raising my hand in our traffic cop signal. She paused and looked at me, Sparafucile dangling from her mouth.

"Snooky, stop!" I repeated. She opened her jaws, and Sparafucile dropped into the water.

"Good girl."

I lifted his head and dragged him to the riverbank. I ran to check on Kat. She was starting to move, and I helped her sit up.

Snooky lumbered toward me, tentative at first, sniffing to make sure who I was. She'd aged. Her muzzle was gray, and her huge, muscular bulk had thinned, but she was still a formidable creature, strong enough to almost tear Sparafucile's head off.

She must have been foraging nearby her favorite stream, eating berries and getting ready to hibernate for the winter when she heard my cries. She'd responded to my voice and swiped at Sparafucile when I was under water.

I greeted her, speaking in a low, soothing tone. "Hey, Snooky, it's good to see you again. How you doing, big girl? Thanks for saving my life. I owe you big-time."

She pressed her body against me. I stroked her muzzle and behind her ears, as I'd done years ago, and hugged her around the neck. She made a contented noise, a low-pitched rumble deep in her throat, and stayed at my side for several minutes until her ears perked up and she looked to the woods. Something beckoned her, perhaps a mate or maybe cubs she'd been protecting, and she ambled off without a backward glance.

I was exhausted, shivering from the fight and the icy water. I peeled off my sweater despite the cold. The wool was so waterlogged it was like shedding a hundred pounds. I bent over Sparafucile and saw he was breathing, though with bubbles and froth coming from his nose and mouth. I didn't know how long his head had been under water, but he'd certainly inhaled a lot of the stream. The bleeding in his face and neck continued but less so, and I figured Snooky hadn't ripped a major artery. She might have broken his neck, however.

Kat was still sitting on the ground, looking bewildered. She must have been knocked unconscious by Sparafucile's hit.

"Are you okay?"

She moaned. "Barely. My head hurts, and I'm dizzy. He bashed my jaw." She opened and closed her mouth in wide yawns.

"Let's get you up." I took her by the underarms and lifted her upright.

"I'm okay," she said with a wan smile.

"We need to get him back to the farm and get help. He's probably going into shock and may die."

She took off her scarf. I wrapped it around Sparafucile's head and shoulders.

I pulled out my cell phone from my pants pocket, but it was dead from the water. "Does your phone work?"

She took hers out and tried phoning. "No reception. We're too deep in the woods."

"Here's what we do. I'm going to try to carry him as far as I can. Depends on how well my ribs hold up. Doubt I'll get too far, but I'll point you in the direction of the house. Just follow the trail and keep dialing 911 until you get reception. Once you connect, tell them to send a rescue team. Can you direct them to where we are?"

"Yes, I think so."

He probably shouldn't have been moved without a neck brace, but I had no choice. I wrapped Sparafucile's arms around my neck and hoisted him onto my back, fireman style. Kat bound his head to my neck with the scarf, and we started off. I staggered under his dead weight and half dragged, half carried him. My ribs sang out, but I gritted my teeth and kept going. Kat found a broken tree limb I used as a crutch to help distribute the weight. I sank to my knees every fifty feet or so to catch my breath and ease my back and chest. Sparafucile was still bleeding, and at this rate, he'd be dead before we got help.

When we reached the path to the house, Kat bolted ahead. "Be careful not to trip," I shouted after her. I marveled at her courage and stamina after what she'd been through.

CHAPTER FIFTY-FIVE

I heard the ATV before I saw it. I hadn't made much progress and was still at least three-quarters of a mile from the farm. Two EMTs approached with a stretcher lashed to the back of the ATV. They hopped off, quickly assessed Sparafucile, started an IV, braced his neck, loaded him onto the stretcher, and sped away to the Bloomington Hospital. The transfer took less than five minutes.

They had no room for me on the ATV. I just hoped they made it in time to save Sparafucile's life. I didn't want anyone blaming Snooky for his death and hunting her down as a rogue killer.

Relieved of my heavy load, I picked up my pace and arrived at the farm about fifteen minutes later. Hattie was waiting for me.

"Kat told me what happened. Are you okay?"

"Yeah. My chest hurts like hell, and I have a headache, but I'll survive. I'm not certain about Sparafucile. EMTs took him to the hospital. Where's Kat?"

"Bedroom. She pretty much collapsed once she got here, and I put her to bed."

"Did you call the doctor?"

"Didn't know who to call. I waited for you."

I went into the bedroom. Kat was stretched out on the bed, mumbling incoherently. Her arms and legs were twitching, as they had when she lapsed into hepatic coma. I was afraid that was happening all over again.

"Kat, talk to me. Kat ..." No response.

I phoned Dr. Abraham, the liver specialist who'd treated Kat before. He told me to bring her to the University Hospital immediately. I called Bloomington Hospital emergency department to see if they'd provide an ambulance, but they said unless she was a patient, they could not. Rather than wait for a commercial ambulance, Hattie and I loaded Kat into the back seat of my BMW, and we sped to the University Hospital.

Dr. Abraham met us in the emergency room and whisked Kat to the ICU.

"It's bad this time, Bear," Abraham said, "really bad. The physical and emotional trauma have precipitated total liver shutdown."

I collapsed into a chair alongside Kat's bed in the ICU, holding her hand. Numb, I watched the IV and equipment keeping her alive.

"She's comatose, and I'm not certain she'll regain consciousness," Abraham said.

"Ever?" I tried to stifle a sob.

"It's possible but uncertain without a new liver." His expression was sad.

"Dialysis again?" I asked hopefully.

"Definitely, but I think it'll buy us days, maybe a week or two, tops. She has hepatorenal failure more severe than before," he said, checking her blood chemistries. "The only thing that'll save her is a new liver. Because she's so sick, we can jump her to the top of the transplant list, but the odds of finding a match are pretty remote, as we've discussed."

I brought her hand to my lips and kissed her fingers.

"I'm sorry to be so pessimistic, but you need to know the truth. We'll start the dialysis right away. Hopefully, that'll nudge her kidneys to start functioning again. If it doesn't, she may need renal dialysis as well. But that's a lot for any person to tolerate."

"What choice does she have?" I asked, my eyes so wet I could barely see.

"None, I'm afraid. Not if we're going to save her."

"We are going to save her, Dr. Abraham. Make no mistake about that," I said. "Have you checked other centers for a liver? Cleveland Clinic, Mayo, Hopkins, hospitals in Europe?" I needed to push him past the usual inquiries.

"The transplant list includes all member US hospitals but not Europe."

I'd promised Kat I'd find a liver for her, and by damn, I was going to do it. I'd gladly give her half of mine, but I was the wrong blood type.

"How do we search Europe for a liver?" I asked.

"Frankly, I don't know," Abraham said. "I've never had to do that. Give me a day or two to find out. I have European colleagues I can contact. Meanwhile, let's get the dialysis started."

The liver dialysis improved her more than Abraham had anticipated. She regained consciousness intermittently, her kidneys started working again, and we were cautiously optimistic. She was too sick to leave the ICU, and we waited ... and waited for a liver. None available in the US or Europe.

"What about China or India?" I asked, desperate. "Any chances there?"

"I'll inquire," Abraham said.

I called Bloomington Hospital to check on Sparafucile. They told me he'd been helicoptered to the University Hospital the same day the EMTs had brought him in. His injuries were too complex for them to handle. He'd been admitted to a room at the other end of the ICU. I had merely to walk several hundred feet to see him.

A stout elderly woman, gray hair twisted into a bun at the back of her head, sat in a chair alongside the bed, knitting. A tortoise hair comb looking like a giant bug held the bun in place. She glanced up when I knocked.

"I'm sorry to bother you," I said, "but I wanted to come by and check on Lieutenant Sparafucile. My name's Bear Judge."

She rested gnarled, arthritic hands in her lap and scowled at me, face wrinkled in concentration. "I'm Rosa Sparafucile, Vinny's mother."

I walked to the bedside. I would not have recognized Sparafucile. White bandages covered the entire left half of his face and were spotted red at several places where blood had seeped through. The right half of his face was ashen, wasted-looking, and drained of all life. His right eyelid had been taped shut to protect his eye, which was sunken in its socket. A breathing tube distorted his mouth into a lopsided sag and was connected to a respirator that breathed for him. Two IVs were running, one in his neck and the other in his arm—a clear fluid in the first, and blood in the second.

"I know who you are now that I see you up close," she said in an angry voice, pointing a crooked index finger at me. "I was at the trial when you attacked my son. I'm just sorry his Electric Gun failed." She scowled, and I might have been looking at Vincenzo. The dark, bunched eyebrows, narrowed eyes, and mean mouth had passed undiluted from mother to son.

"And I know who you are," I said. "I first saw you in a dimly lit hallway at night, wearing a pink robe and slipping a Sig Sauer handgun into the waistband of your son's pants. He used that gun to kill my nephew Ryan. Remember?"

She sat stunned, her finger-pointing hand dropped to her lap, quivering like a dying fish.

"Perhaps," I said with a shrug, "we should both give first impressions a second chance."

She looked at her son lying in the bed and shook her head. She became tearful. "No way in hell. You're responsible for this," she said, again pointing at me, "my son's ripped face. He's paralyzed and may die because of you."

"He tried to kill me."

"I'm sorry he didn't."

I returned to my bedside vigil down the hall. Kat faded in and out of consciousness, sometimes mumbling incoherently, and other times just twitching and nonresponsive. Her eyes and skin had turned a lemony yellow. Abraham said a chemical in the blood called bilirubin had built up from the liver failure. Her breath smelled like ammonia again.

Sitting at her bedside over the next several days triggered an uncomfortable consciousness. I found myself hoping, even praying, that one person would die—and not just any person, someone with Kat's specific immune system—so she could live. How could I justify the moral implications? What code did I live by, what ethics, I wondered, that hoping for one death to restore one life was acceptable? Where was it written that you could trade one life for another? I suppose not causing the death and not knowing the person who died made it morally and ethically acceptable, like an impersonal car accident leaving someone brain-dead. Society certainly felt that way and even encouraged the effort by promoting organ donor programs.

A knock on the door changed everything.

Dr. Abraham walked in.

"You're never going to believe this," he said without preamble, walking to me with his hand extended and a smile on his face. "We may have a match."

"Thank God," I said, taking his hand. "China? India?"

He laughed. "Two hundred feet away."

I looked at him, my expression blank.

"Sparafucile."

"Oh my God! How did you find out?" I felt my eyes get big.

"I just had coffee with Lucas Overby. He heads up the blood bank. Lucas told me about a patient admitted a few days ago with an unusual immune system they were having a hard time matching to give blood, even O negative blood. It sounded like your wife's problem. I pulled up the patient's lab results and saw who it was. Sparafucile's a perfect match."

"He's pretty sick," I said. "May not survive."

"Who's next of kin? I hate to sound like a vampire, but do you think we can get permission for an organ donation if he dies?"

I thought back to my conversation with Rosa Sparafucile. "If she doesn't know who'd get the liver, she might agree. If she at all suspected it would be my wife, I doubt it." I was very pessimistic.

"You two don't get along?" he asked, a querulous look on his face.

"It's complicated," I said with a snort.

"Ordinarily, the donor's family does not know where the transplant goes," Abraham said, "unless both they and the recipient agree to swap names. In this situation, I doubt it'll be possible to keep it secret. Some personnel would be exposed both to him and your wife. People talk."

"We have to try. If the mother finds out, she'll refuse."

"I'll do my best. Meantime—I hate to say it, but it's true—it's a race between who dies first."

"Who lives longer sounds better," I said.

After he closed the door, I was left to my own thoughts again. The moral implications of my brooding deliberations had changed. No longer would the donor be anonymous. And worse, I contributed to his death, even though he was the devil incarnated.

CHAPTER FIFTY-SIX

"'**N**o. Absolutely not.'" Abraham told me Rosa Sparafucile exploded when she found out who'd get her son's liver. "'No organ donations. Let him die peacefully. He's suffered enough.'"

"Suppose I talk with her?" I asked. "Maybe I could change her mind."

"You can try. It can't hurt. But it's got to be today, now. She's decided to stop life support since he's developing multiorgan failure. His lungs finally gave out from the drowning, then his kidneys, and now his heart's failing. The transplant has to be soon before his liver's affected."

"Did he ever regain consciousness?" I asked.

"No. He bled into his brain. He's also paralyzed from the neck down."

"And you're sure she's next of kin? No wife or child?"

"The hospital checked. She's the only one who can give permission, and she's unequivocally said no."

Sparafucile was about to win the race for death but not by much. Kat was on her last legs, Abraham said, and her life wouldn't last but a few days past his.

A dozen police officers had filled Sparafucile's room, and I could barely squeeze in. I recognized Fisheye, Bennett, and the police commissioner, Richard Dawson. Some others looked vaguely familiar, probably from seeing their faces at the trial. I hoped Sparafucile was the only bad cop, or I didn't stand much chance getting out of this room without a busted head.

Rosa Sparafucile sat in the same chair I'd seen her in several days before, knitting put aside and holding court like a grand dame. The cops waited in turn to offer their condolences.

She looked away from the latest supplicant when she saw me enter the room.

"There's the son of a bitch responsible for my son's death," she shouted, crooked finger pointing again. "He killed Vinny. You should arrest him for murder."

All heads turned in my direction. I froze as everyone looked at me. Most of their faces initially showed surprise that quickly turned into angry scowls.

"And now the bastard wants my son's liver for his wife. Over my dead body. No goddamned chance of that happening. Ever! You hear me, prick?" Her mouth was set in a mean line.

Fisheye stepped out of the crowd. "Whoa, Rosa. What are you saying?" he asked. "How did he kill Chilli?"

"I don't know how," Rosa said, "but I know he did. He was there when it happened. He was the one who called the EMTs to come and get Vinny. They told me that."

The cops began crowding me, looking more and more angry. I had to tell them what'd happened, and by the expressions on their faces, I'd better make it good.

"Your friend, Lieutenant Sparafucile," I said to the group, looking directly at Fisheye, "followed my wife and me as we walked in the woods. When Lieutenant Sparafucile found us, he knocked my wife unconscious, then attacked and tried to kill me. He was holding my head under water in a stream where we'd been fighting, trying to drown me, when some wild animal attacked him. It slashed his face, broke his neck, and then took off. I think it was a big male cougar, but it happened too quickly to be absolutely sure."

"Why didn't the cougar attack you?" Fisheye asked, suspicious. The cops murmured agreement.

I nodded. "Good question. I think because I was under water and it didn't see me initially. Then, when I got up, I scared it, and it ran off."

I paused and looked around. Some of the faces had softened, others not.

"The animal's attack left Lieutenant Sparafucile unconscious with his face in the water, drowning and bleeding. I dragged him to the riverbank and carried him partway to my farm. My wife ran on ahead and called the EMTs, who met us and took him to the Bloomington Hospital. They transferred him here. That's the story."

"So, you saved his life," Jim Bennett said, coming to my rescue, an encouraging look on his face.

I shrugged. "I did what I could."

"Don't believe that bullshit for a minute," Rosa yelled, standing up and pointing her shaking finger at me. "Arrest the fucker for murder. He killed my poor boy, my only child ..." She broke down in sobs, collapsed in her chair, and cradled her head in her arms.

Fisheye went to her, kneeled down at her chair, put his arms around her, and rocked her gently. "It's okay, Rosa, it's okay," he said in a soothing voice.

"I'm sorry it turned out as it did," I said, trying to be as convincing as I could. "I know he was a friend to many of you, but I did not kill him." With that, I turned and pushed my way out of the room.

Rosa Sparafucile had been my last hope. I fought back tears.

Jim Bennett followed me into the hall. "Thanks for trying to save him, Mr. Judge," he said, looking genuinely concerned. "I believe what you told us. Rosa hasn't given the final order to stop life support, so technically he's still alive."

"Thanks, Jim. You're a good cop." I shook his hand. "I can't say that about your friend."

"I try, and I think Chilli did also. He was a little rough around the edges. I'll give you that." Bennett looked me in the eye. "What's this stuff about Chilli's liver?"

I explained. "Rosa is next of kin and has the final say."

He glanced back at the room, put his arm across my shoulders, and led me away. "Let's walk a bit," he said.

CHAPTER
FIFTY-SEVEN

I downloaded and printed the attachment in the hospital's business office, called Abraham to alert him, and went running—literally—to the hospital's administrative offices.

"I need to speak with the hospital's chief legal officer immediately," I told the receptionist as I panted to catch my breath.

Jackson Riley emerged from his office. "How can I help you, Mr. Judge?" he asked. Riley looked like he was ready for court, wearing a dark blue suit, blue-and-white-striped tie, off-white shirt, and gray hair neatly combed.

I handed him the advanced health directive and living will prepared and signed by Vincenzo Sparafucile, duly witnessed by Police Commissioner Richard Dawson, by Jose Diaz (a.k.a. Fisheye), and by a notary. The document stated that, in the event of his death, it was Vincenzo Sparafucile's final wish and directive that any and all of his organs be donated to anyone in need, the recipients to be chosen at the discretion of the University Hospital medical professionals.

According to Jim Bennett, the entire Hopperville police force, in a show of unity, humanity, and humility against a reporter's claim that they were a Hopper*vile* police department, had signed identical papers. Every Hopperville cop, without exception, was an organ donor.

All six of the University Hospital lawyers, the CEO and chairman of the board, and the chairperson of the hospital's Ethics Committee met in emergency session. They agreed unanimously that Sparafucile's advanced health directive and living will took precedence over his mother's objections.

When confronted by her son's directive, Rosa Sparafucile backed down.

"If that's what he wanted, I won't stand in the way. But I still think that guy Judge should be arrested for murder and his wife should not get Vinny's liver."

Moments after receiving hospital approval, the medical personnel, at Rosa's request, stopped Sparafucile's life support and whisked him to the operating room for organ salvage.

BEAR'S PROMISE

Kat made the same trip soon after. I kissed her unconscious lips just before she left. "Goodbye, my lovely. Return to me with a healthy liver. You've got a new lease on life, and because you do, so do I. Come back pink instead of yellow."

I sat in Kat's room, now depressingly quiet with the machines turned off, waiting for her return. The surgeons had warned me to be patient; it would be a long operation. They promised to send a nurse in every several hours to let me know how things were going.

I mused about history's twists and turns, how I'd saved the life of a little bit of black fur so many years ago, who now returned as a full-grown bear to save mine. How the evils of a company, and particularly one bad cop, had taken the lives of my sister and her family, but who paid with his own life in the end, hopefully saving my wife in the process. And how the legal system, with all its flaws, helped me keep my promise to my sister.

I called my law partner. "Shay, how are you doing?"

"Hey, Bear. Getting better every day."

He sounded cheerful. I brought him up to date on the settlement.

"That's great. Well done. So, do I get a raise?" he asked.

"You coming back?" I crossed my fingers.

"You bet, and you're going to teach me how to shoot. I think a Glock 17 would be perfect. I plan to get a concealed carry license."

"Wow. What brought this change about?" I smiled at him through the phone.

"Nyundo Odinga. My folks and I paid a visit to Kenya. I had a long talk with the Hammer. He convinced me what I had to do and gave me the courage to do it."

I got so excited that I stood and started pacing in the small room. "That's wonderful. We've received lots of requests for litigation, so the sooner you come back, the better. I need you."

There was a pause, and I heard him breathing heavily through the phone. "What about Sparafucile?" he asked after a while in a quiet voice. "Since that night, he's been living rent-free in my head."

"Consider him evicted." I told him what'd happened and that Kat was in the operating room right then, receiving Sparafucile's liver.

"That makes my decision even easier," he said. "Good luck to her. We'll need a great paralegal."

Almost twelve hours later—the surgery was grueling and complex, requiring three different surgeons, each bringing a different skill set into the operating room—Kat emerged with Sparafucile's liver implanted in her abdomen.

The anesthesia wore off quickly, but Kat didn't regain consciousness.

"Not to worry, Bear," Abraham said. "The surgery went well, but it's going to take the new liver several days to process the accumulated toxins. A day from now, two days guaranteed, she'll be sitting up in bed eating breakfast."

"Promise?"

"Boy Scout's honor," he said with a mock salute.

I slept in the extra bed and spent hours watching her toss and turn, willing her to get better. On the morning of the third day, with a bright yellow sun cascading warmth through the window, I opened my eyes to find her sitting up in bed, her skin a perfect rosy color and her eyes bluer than ever.

I blinked and sat up. "Hello, my darling."

She smiled at me and said, "Who made these scrambled eggs? They're loaded with nerdlings!"

ABOUT THE AUTHOR

Doug Zipes graduated from Dartmouth College, Harvard Medical School, and Duke University Medical Center. He is a distinguished professor at Indiana University Medical Center. He has published almost nine hundred medical articles, fifteen textbooks (forty-plus including multiple editions), several nonfiction articles, three novels (*The Black Widows, Ripples in Opperman's Pond*, and *Not Just a Game*), and a memoir (*Damn the Naysayers*). He has been the founding editor in chief of five cardiology journals and editor in chief of two others. Recipient of many awards, he also writes a health column for the *Saturday Evening Post*. He has been married for fifty-eight years, has three children and five grandchildren, and lives in Carmel, Indiana, and Bonita Springs, Florida. He dedicates *Bear's Promise* to brave law enforcement men and women all over the world.

Email: dzipes@iu.edu

Printed in the United States
By Bookmasters